"She is a miser, in spite of that sudden attack of the gaming fever. Money is the only passion of her life."

"Possibly, though I doubt it. There is Monsieur Leroy, you know."

Lamberti spoke the name with contempt, but Guido said nothing, for, after all, the high and mighty lady about whom they were talking was his father's sister, and he preferred not to talk scandal about her, even with his intimate friend.

"If matters grow worse," said Lamberti, "there are at least the worthless securities in her name, to prove that you acted for her."

"You are mistaken. That is the worst of it. Everything was done in my name, for she would not let her own appear. She used to give me the money in cash, telling me exactly what to do with it, and I brought her the broker's accounts."

"I daresay she made you sign receipts for the sums she gave you," laughed Lamberti.

"Yes, she did."

Lamberti sat up suddenly and stared at his friend. Such folly was hardly to be believed.

"She is capable of saying that she lent you the money on your promise!" he cried.

"That is exactly what she threatens to do," answered Guido d'Este, dejectedly. "As I cannot possibly pay it, she can force me to do one of two things."

"What things?"

"Either to disappear from honourable society and begin life somewhere else, or else to make an end of myself. And she will do it. I have felt for more than a year that she means to ruin me."

Lamberti set his teeth, and stared at the stone-pine. If Guido had not been just the man he was, sensitive to morbidness where his honour was concerned, the situation might have seemed less desperate. If his aunt, her Serene Highness the Princess Anatolie, had not been a monster of avarice, selfishness, and vindictiveness, there would perhaps have been some hope of moving her. As it was, matters looked ill, and to make them worse there was the well-known fact that Guido had formerly played high and had lost considerable sums at cards. It would be easy to make society believe that he had paid his debts, which had always been promptly settled, with money which the Princess had intrusted to him for investment.

"What possible object can she have in ruining you?" asked Lamberti, presently.

"I cannot guess," Guido answered after another short pause. "I have little enough left as it is, except the bare chance of inheriting something, some day, from my brother, who likes me about as much as my aunt does, and is not bound to leave me a penny."

"But, after all," argued Lamberti, "you are the only heir left to either of them."

"I suppose so," assented Guido in an uncertain tone.

"What do you mean?"

"Nothing—it does not matter. Of course," he continued quietly, "this may go on for some time, but it can only end in one way, sooner or later. I shall be lucky if I am only reduced to starvation."

"You might marry an heiress," suggested Lamberti, as a last resource.

"And pay my aunt out of my wife's fortune? No. I will not do that."

"Of course not. But I should think that if ever an honest man could be tempted to do such a thing, it would be in some such case as yours."

"Perhaps to save his father from ruin, or his mother from starvation," said Guido. "I could understand it then; but not to save himself. Besides, no heiress in our world would marry me, for I have nothing to offer."

Lamberti smiled incredulously. He was not a cynic, because he believed in action; but his faith in the disinterested simplicity of mankind was not strong. He had also some experience of the world, and was quite ready to admit that a marriageable heiress might fairly expect an equivalent for the fortune she was to bring her husband. Yet he wholly rejected the statement that Guido d'Este had nothing of social value to offer, merely because he was now a poor man and had never been a very rich one. Guido had neither lands nor money, and bore no title, it was true; and could but just live like a gentleman on the small allowance that was paid him yearly according to his father's will. But there was no secret about his birth, and he was closely related to several of the reigning houses of Europe. His father had been one of the minor sovereigns dethroned in the revolutions of the nineteenth century; late in life, a widower, the ex-king had married a beautiful young girl of no great family, who had died in giving birth to Guido. The marriage had of course been morganatic, though perfectly legal, and Guido neither bore the name of his father's royal race, nor could he ever lay claim to the succession, in the utterly improbable event of a restoration. But he was half brother to the childless man, nearly forty years older than himself, whose faithful friends still called him "your Majesty" in private; he was nephew to the extremely authentic Princess Anatolie, and he was first cousin to at least one king who had held his own. In the eyes of an heiress in search of social position as an equivalent for her millions, all this would more than compensate for the fact that his visiting card bore the somewhat romantic and unlikely name, "Guido d'Este," without any title or explanation whatever.

But apart from the sordid consideration of values to be given and received, Guido was young, good-looking if not handsome, and rather better gifted than most men; he had reached the age of twenty-seven without having what society is pleased to call a past—in other words without ever having been the chief actor in a social tragedy, comedy, or farce; and finally, though he had once been fond of cards, he had now entirely given up play. If he had been a little richer, he could almost have passed for a model young man in the eyes of the exacting and prudent parent of marriageable daughters. Judging from the Princess Anatolie, it was probable that he resembled his mother's family more than his father's.

For all these reasons his friend thought that, if he chose, he might easily find an heiress who would marry him with enthusiasm; but, being his friend, Lamberti was very glad that he rejected the idea.

The two were not men who ever talked together of their principles, though they sometimes spoke of their beliefs and differed about them. Belief is usually absolute, but principle is always a matter of conscience, and the conscience is a part of the mixed self in which soul and mind and matter are all

Cecilia: A Story of Modern Rome by F. Marion Crawford

Francis Marion Crawford was born on August 2nd, 1854 at Bagni di Lucca, Italy. An only son and a nephew to Julia Ward Howe, the American poet and writer of 'The Battle Hymn of the Republic'.

His education began at St Paul's School, Concord, New Hampshire, then to Cambridge University; University of Heidelberg; and the University of Rome.

In 1879 Crawford went to India, to study Sanskrit and then edited The Indian Herald. In 1881 he returned to America to continue his Sanskrit studies at Harvard University.

At this time in Boston he lived at his Aunt Julia house and in the company of his Uncle, Sam Ward. His family was concerned about his employment prospects. After a singing career as a baritone was ruled out, he was encouraged to write.

In December 1882 his first novel, 'Mr Isaacs', was an immediate hit which was amplified by 'Dr Claudius' in 1883.

In October 1884 he married Elizabeth Berdan. They went on to have two sons and two daughters.

Encouraged by his excellent start to a literary career he returned to Italy with Elizabeth to make a permanent home, principally in Sant' Agnello, where he bought the Villa Renzi that then became Villa Crawford.

In the late 1890s, he began to write his historical works: 'Ave Roma Immortalis' (1898), 'Rulers of the South' (1900) and 'Gleanings from Venetian History' (1905). The Saracinesca series is perhaps his best work. 'Saracinesca' was followed by 'Sant' Ilario' in 1889, 'Don Orsino' in 1892 and 'Corleone' in 1897, that being the first major treatment of the Mafia in literature.

Francis Marion Crawford died at Sorrento on Good Friday 1909 at Villa Crawford of a heart attack.

Index of Contents

Chapter I
Chapter II
Chapter III
Chapter IV
Chapter V
Chapter VI
Chapter VII
Chapter VIII
Chapter IX
Chapter X
Chapter XI
Chapter XII
Chapter XIII
Chapter XIV
Chapter XV
Chapter XVI
Chapter XVII
Chapter XVIII

Chapter XIX
Chapter XX
Chapter XXI
Chapter XXII
Chapter XXIII
Chapter XXIV
Chapter XXV
Chapter XXVI
Chapter XXVII
Chapter XXVIII
F. Marion Crawford – A Short Biography
F. Marion Crawford – A Concise Bibliography

CHAPTER I

Two men were sitting side by side on a stone bench in the forgotten garden of the Arcadian Society, in Rome; and it was in early spring, not long ago. Few people, Romans or strangers, ever find their way to that lonely and beautiful spot beyond the Tiber, niched in a hollow of the Janiculum below San Pietro in Montorio, where Beatrice Cenci sleeps. The Arcadians were men and women who loved poetry in an artificial time, took names of shepherds and shepherdesses, rhymed as best they could, met in pleasant places to recite their verses, and played that the world was young, and gentle, and sweet, and unpoisoned, just when it had declined to one of its recurring periods of vicious old age. The Society did not die with its times, and it still exists, less sprightly, less ready to mask in pastorals, but rhyming, meeting, and reciting verses now and then, in the old manner, though rarely in the old haunts. Even now fresh inscriptions in honour of the Arcadians are set into the stuccoed walls of the little terraced garden under the hill.

It is very peaceful there. Above, the concave wall of the small house of meeting looks down upon circular tiers of brick seats, and beyond these there are bushes and a little fountain. To the right and left, symmetrical walks lead down in two wide curves to the lower levels, where the water falls again into a basin in a shaded grotto, and rises the third time in another fountain. An ancient stone-pine tree springs straight upwards, spreading out lovely branches. There are bushes again and a magnolia, and a Japanese medlar, and there is moss. The stone mouldings of the fountains are rich with the green tints of time. The air is softly damp, smelling of leaves and flowers; there are corners into which the sunlight never shines, little mysteries of perpetual shade that are full of sadness in winter, but in summer repeat the fanciful confidences of a delicious and imaginary past.

The Sister who had let in the two visitors had left them to themselves, and had gone back to the little convent door; for she was the portress, and therefore a small judge of character in her way, and she understood that the two gentlemen were not like the other half-dozen strangers who came every year to see the garden, and went away after ten minutes, dropping half a franc into her hand for the Sisters, and not even lifting their hats to her as she let them out. These two evidently knew the place; they spoke to each other as intimate friends do; they had come to enjoy the peace and silence for an hour, and they would neither carry off the flowers from the magnolia tree, as some did, nor scrawl their names in pencil on the stucco. Therefore they might safely be left to their own leisure and will.

The men were friends, as the portress had guessed; they were very unlike, and their unlikeness was in part the reason of their friendship. The one was squarely built, of average height, a man of action at every point, with bold blue eyes that could be piercing, a rugged Roman head, prominent at the brows, short reddish hair and pointed beard, great jaw and cheek-bones, a tanned and freckled skin. He sat leaning back, one leg crossed over the other, the knee that was upper-most pressing against the stout stick he held across it, and the big veins swelled on his hands and wrists. He was a sailor, and a born fighting man; and in ten years of service he had managed to find himself in every affair that had concerned Italy in the remotest degree, in Africa, in China, and elsewhere. He was now at home on leave, expecting immediate promotion. He bore a historical name; he was called Lamberto Lamberti.

His companion sat with folded arms and bent head, a rather dark young man with deep-set grey eyes that often looked black, a thoughtful face, a grave mouth that could smile suddenly and almost strangely, with a child's sweet frankness, and yet with a look that was tender and human—the smile of a man who understands the meaning of life and yet does not despise it. Most people would have taken him for a man of leisure, probably given to reading or the cultivation of some artistic taste. Guido d'Este was one of those Italians who are content to survive from a very beautiful past without joining the frantic rush for a very problematic future. But there was more in him than a love of books and a knowledge of pictures; for he was a dreamer, and there are dreams better worth dreaming than many deeds are worth the doing.

"I sometimes wonder what would have happened to you and me," he said, after there had been a long pause, "if we had been obliged to live each other's lives."

"We should both have been bored to extinction," answered Lamberti, without hesitating.

"I suppose so," assented Guido, and relapsed into silence.

He was very glad that he was not condemned to the life of a naval officer, to the perpetual motion of active service, to the narrow quarters of a lieutenant on a modern man-of-war, to the daily companionship of a dozen or eighteen other officers with whom he could certainly not have an idea in common. It would be a detestable thing to be sent at a moment's notice from one end of the world to the other, from heat to cold, from cold to heat, through all sorts of weather, only to be a part of an organisation, a wheel in a machine, a pawn in some one's game of chess. He had been on board a line-of-battle ship once to see his friend off, and had mentally noted the discomfort. There was nothing in the cabin but a bunk built over a chest of drawers, a narrow transom, a wash-stand that disappeared into a recess when pushed back, an exiguous table fastened to a bulkhead, and one camp-stool. There was no particular means of ventilation, and the place smelt of cold iron, paint, and soft soap. Yet his friend had been about to live at least six months in this cell, which would have been condemned as too narrow in an ordinarily well-managed prison.

Nevertheless, it would be pleasant in itself, no doubt, to be a living part of what most men only read about, to really know what fighting meant, to be one of the few who are invariably chosen first for missions of danger and difficulty. Besides, Guido d'Este was just now in a very difficult situation, which might become dangerous, and from which he saw no immediate means of escape; and, for once in his life, he almost envied his friend his simple career, in which nothing seemed to be required of a man but courage and obedience.

"I suppose I should be bored," he said again, after a short and thoughtful pause, "but I would rather be bored than live the life I am living."

The sailor looked at him sharply a moment, and instantly understood that Guido had brought him to the little garden in order to tell him something of importance without risk of interruption.

"Have you had more trouble with that horrible old woman?" he asked roughly.

"Yes. She is draining the life out of me. She will ruin me in the end."

Guido did not look up as he spoke, and he slowly tapped the hard earth with the toe of his shoe. He felt very helpless, and he shook his head over his misfortunes, which seemed great.

"That comes of being connected with royalty," said Lamberti, in the same rough tone.

"Is it my fault?" asked Guido, with a melancholy smile.

The sailor snorted discontentedly, and changed his position.

"What can I do?" he asked presently. "Tell me."

"Nothing."

"If I were only rich!"

"My dear friend," said Guido, "she demands a million of francs!"

"There are men who have fifty. Would a hundred thousand francs be of any use?"

"Not the least. Besides, that is all you have."

"What would that matter?" asked Lamberti.

Guido looked up at last, for he knew that the words were true and earnest.

"Thank you," he answered. "I know you would do that for me. But it would not be of any use. Things have gone too far."

"Shall I go to her and talk the matter over? I believe I could frighten her into justice. After all, she has no legal claim upon you."

Guido shook his head.

"That is not the question," he answered. "She never pretends that her right is legal, for it is not. On the contrary, she says it is a question of honour, that I have lost her money for her in speculations, and that I am bound to restore it to her. It is true that I only did with it exactly what she wished, and what she insisted that I should do, against my own judgment. She knows that."

"But then, I do not see—"

"She also knows that I cannot prove it," interrupted Guido, "and as she is perfectly unscrupulous, she will use everything against me to make out that I have deliberately cheated her out of the money."

"But it cannot make so much difference to her, after all," objected Lamberti. "She must have an immense fortune somewhere."

involved together. Men born in the same surroundings and brought up in the same way generally hold to the same principles as guides in life, and show the same abhorrence for the sins that are accounted dishonourable, and the same indulgence for those not condemned by the code of honour, not even admitting discussion upon such points. But the same men may have very different opinions about spiritual matters.

Eliminating the vulgar average of society, there remain always a certain number who, while possibly holding even more divergent beliefs than most people, agree more precisely, or disagree more essentially, about matters of conscience, either stretching or contracting the code of honour according to their own temper, and especially according to the traditions of their own most immediate surroundings. Other conditions being favourable, it seems as if men whose consciences are most alike should be the best fitted for each other's friendship, no matter what they may think or believe about religion.

This was certainly the case with Guido d'Este and Lamberto Lamberti, and they simultaneously dismissed, as detestable, dishonourable, and unworthy, the mere thought that Guido should try to marry an heiress, with a view to satisfying the outrageous claims of his ex-royal aunt, the Princess Anatolie.

"In simpler times," observed Lamberti, who liked to recall the middle ages, "we should have poisoned the old woman."

Guido did not smile.

"Without meaning to do her an injustice," he answered, "I think it much more probable that she would have poisoned me."

"With the help of Monsieur Leroy, she might have succeeded."

At the thought of the man whom he so cordially detested, Lamberti's blue eyes grew hard, and his upper lip tightened a little, just showing his teeth under his red moustache. Guido looked at him and smiled in his turn.

"There are your ferocious instincts again," he said; "you wish you could kill him."

"I do," answered Lamberti, simply.

He rose from his seat and stretched himself a little, as some big dogs always do after the preliminary growl at an approaching enemy.

"I think Monsieur Leroy is the most repulsive human being I ever saw," he said. "I am not exactly a sensitive person, but it makes me very uncomfortable to be near him. He once gave me his hand, and I had to take it. It felt like a live toad. How old is that man?"

"He must be forty," said Guido, "but he is wonderfully well preserved. Any one would take him for five-and-thirty."

"It is disgusting!" Lamberti kicked a pebble away, as he stood.

"He looked just as he does now, when I was seventeen," observed Guido.

"The creature paints his face. I am sure of it."

"No. I have seen him drenched in a shower, when he had no umbrella. The rain ran down his cheeks, but the colour did not change."

"It is all the more disgusting," retorted Lamberti, illogically, but with strong emphasis.

Guido rose from his seat rather wearily. As he stood up, he was much taller than his friend, who had seemed the larger man while both were seated.

"I am glad that we have talked this over," he said. "Not that talking can help matters, of course. It never does. But I wanted you to know just how things stand, in case anything should happen to me."

Lamberti turned rather sharply.

"In case what should happen to you?" he asked, his eyes hardening.

"I am very tired of it all," Guido answered, "I have nothing to live for, and I am being driven straight to disgrace and ruin without any fault of my own. I daresay that some day I may—well, you know what I mean."

"What?"

"I should not care to exile myself to South America. I am not fit for that sort of life."

"Well?"

"There is the other alternative," said Guido, with a tuneless little laugh. "When life is intolerable, what can be simpler than to part with it?"

Lamberti's strong hand was already on his friend's arm, and tightened energetically.

"Do you believe in God?" he asked abruptly.

"No. At least, I think not."

"I do," said Lamberti, with conviction, "and I shall not let you make away with yourself if I can help it."

He loosed his hold, thrust his hands into his pockets, and looked as if he wished he could fight somebody or something.

"A man who kills himself to escape his troubles is a coward," he said.

Guido made a gesture of indifference.

"You know very well that I am not a coward," he said.

"You will be, the day you are afraid to go on living," returned his friend. "If you kill yourself, I shall think you are an arrant coward, and I shall be sorry I ever knew you."

Guido looked at him incredulously.

"Are you in earnest?" he asked.

"Yes."

There was no mistaking the look in Lamberti's hard blue eyes. Guido faced him.

"Do you think that every man who commits suicide is a coward?"

"If it is to escape his own troubles, yes. A man who gives his life for his country, his mother, or his wife, is not a coward, though he may kill himself with his own hand."

"The Church would call him a suicide."

"I do not know, in all cases," said Lamberti. "I am not a theologian, and as the Church means nothing to you, it would be of no use if I were."

"Why do you say that the Church means nothing to me?" Guido asked.

"Since you are an atheist, what meaning can it possibly have?"

"It means the whole tradition of morality by which we live, and our fathers lived. Even the code of honour, which is a little out of shape nowadays, is based on Christianity, and was once the rule of a good life, the best rule in the days when it grew up."

"I daresay. Even the code of honour, degenerate as it is, and twist it how you will, cannot give you an excuse for killing yourself when you have always behaved honourably, or for running away from the enemy simply because you are tired of fighting and will not take the trouble to go on."

"Perhaps you are right," Guido answered. "But the whole question is not worth arguing. What is life, after all, that we should attach any importance to it?"

"It is all you have, and you only have it once."

"Who knows? Perhaps we may come back to it again, hundreds and hundreds of times. There are more people in the world who believe that than there are Christians."

"If that is what you believe," retorted Lamberti, "you must believe that the sooner you leave life, the sooner you will come back to it."

"Possibly. But there is a chance that it may not be true, and that everything may end here. That one chance may be worth taking."

"There is a chance that a man who deserts from his ship may not be caught. That is not an argument in favour of desertion."

Guido laughed carelessly.

"You have a most unpleasant way of naming things," he said. "Shall we go? It is growing late, and I have promised to see my aunt before dinner."

"Will there be any one else there?" asked Lamberti.

"Why? Did you think of going with me?"

"I might. It is a long time since I have called. I think I shall be a little more assiduous in future."

"It is not gay, at my aunt's," observed Guido. "Monsieur Leroy will be there. You may have to shake hands with him!"

"You do not seem anxious that I should go with you," laughed Lamberti.

Guido said nothing for a moment, and seemed to be weighing the question, as if it might be of some importance. Lamberti afterwards remembered the slight hesitation.

"By all means come," Guido said, when he had made up his mind.

He glanced once more at the place, for he liked it, and it was pleasant to carry away pictures of what one liked, even of a bit of neglected old garden with a stone-pine in the middle, clearly cut out against the sky. He wondered idly whether he should ever come again—whether, after all, it would be cowardly to go to sleep with the certainty of not waking, and whether he should find anything beyond, or not.

The world looked too familiar to him to be interesting, as if he had known it too long, and he vaguely wished that he could change it, and desire to stay in it for its own sake; and just then it occurred to him that every man carries with him the world in which he must live, the stage and the scenery for his own play. It would be absurd to pretend, he thought, that his own material world was the same as Lamberti's, even when the latter was at home. They knew the same people, heard the same talk, ate the same things, looked on the same sights, breathed the same air. There was perhaps no sacrifice worthy of honourable men which either of them would not make for the other. Yet, to Guido d'Este, life seemed miserably indifferent where it did not seem a real calamity, while to Lamberti every second of it was worth fighting for, because it was worth enjoying.

Guido looked at his friend's tanned neck and sturdy shoulders, following him to the door, and he realised more clearly than ever before that he was not of the same race. He felt the satiety bred in many generations of destiny's spoilt and flattered sons; the absence of anything like a grasping will, caused by the too easy fulfilment of every careless wish; the over-critical sense that guesses at hidden imperfection, the cruelly unerring instinct of a taste too tired to enjoy and yet too fine to be deceived.

Lamberti turned at the door and saw his face.

"What are you thinking about?"

"I was envying you," Guido murmured. "You are glad to be alive."

Lamberti made rather an impatient gesture, but said nothing. The Sister who had admitted the two opened the little iron door for them to go out. She was a small woman, with a worn face and kind brown eyes, one of the half-dozen who live in the little convent and work among the children of the very poor in that quarter. Both men had taken out money.

"For the poor children, if you please," said Guido, placing his offering in the nun's hand.

"And tell them to pray for a man who is in trouble," added Lamberti, giving her money.

She looked at him curiously, thinking, perhaps, that he meant himself. Then she gravely bent her head.

"I thank you very much," she said.

The small iron door closed with a rusty clang, and the friends began to descend the steep way that leads down from the Porta San Pancrazio to the Via Garibaldi.

"Why did you say that to the nun?" asked Guido.

"Are you past praying for?" enquired Lamberti, with a careless and good-natured laugh.

"It is not like you," said Guido.

"I do not pretend to be more consistent than other people, you know. Are you going directly to the Princess's?"

"No. I must go home first. The old lady would never forgive me if I went to see her without a silk hat in my hand."

"Then I suppose I must dress, too," said Lamberti. "I will leave you at your door, and drive home, and we can meet at your aunt's."

"Very well."

They walked down the street and found a cab, scarcely speaking again until they parted at Guido's door.

He lived alone in a quiet apartment of the Palazzo Farnese, overlooking the Via Giulia and the river beyond. The afternoon sun was still streaming through the open windows of his sitting room, and the warm breeze came with it.

"There are two notes, sir," said his servant, who had followed him. "The one from the Princess is urgent. The man wished to wait for you, but I sent him away."

"That was right," said Guido, taking the letters from the salver. "Get my things ready. I have visits to make."

The man went out and shut the door. He was a Venetian, and had been in the navy, where he had served Lamberti during the affair in China. Lamberti had recommended him to his friend.

Guido remained standing while he opened the note. The first was an engraved invitation to a garden party from a lady he scarcely knew. It was the first he had ever received from her, and he was not aware that she ever asked people to her house. The second was from his aunt, begging him to come to tea that afternoon as he had promised, for a very particular reason, and asking him to let her know beforehand if anything made it impossible. It began with "Dearest Guido" and was signed

"Your devoted aunt, Anatolie." She was evidently very anxious that he should come, for he was generally her "dear nephew," and she was his "affectionate aunt."

The handwriting was fine and hard to read, though it was regular. Some of the letters were quite unlike those of most people, and many of them were what experts call "blind."

Guido d'Este read the note through twice, with an expression of dislike, and then tore it up. He threw the invitation upon some others that lay in a chiselled copper dish on his writing table, lit a cigarette, and looked out of the window. His aunt's note was too affectionate and too anxious to bode well, and he was tempted to write that he could not go. It would be pleasant to end the afternoon with a book and a cup of tea, and then to dine alone and dream away the evening in soothing silence.

But he had promised to go; and, moreover, nothing was of any real importance at all, nothing whatsoever, from the moment of beginning life to the instant of leaving it. He therefore dressed and went out again.

CHAPTER II

Lamberto Lamberti never wasted time, whether he was at sea, doing his daily duty as an officer, or ashore in Africa, fighting savages, or on leave, amusing himself in Rome, or Paris, or London. Time was life, and life was far too good to be squandered in dawdling. In ten minutes after he had reached his room he was ready to go out again. As he took his hat and gloves, his eye fell on a note which he had not seen when he had come in.

He opened it carelessly and found the same formal invitation which Guido had received at the same time. The Countess Fortiguerra requested the pleasure of his company at the Villa Palladio between four and six, and the date was just a fortnight ahead.

Lamberti was a Roman, and though he had only seen the Countess three or four times in his life, he remembered very well that she had been twice married, and that her first husband had been a certain Count Palladio, whose name was vaguely connected in Lamberti's mind with South American railways, the Suez Canal, and a machine gun that had been tried in the Italian navy; but it was not a Roman name, and he could not remember any villa that was called by it. Palladio—it recalled something else, besides a great architect—something connected with Pallas—but Lamberti was no great scholar. Guido would know. Guido knew everything about literature, ancient and modern—or at least Lamberti thought so.

He had kept his cab while he dressed, and in a few minutes the little horse had toiled up the long hill that leads to Porta Pinciana, and Lamberti got out at the gate of one of those beautiful villas of which there are still a few within the walls of Rome. It belonged to a foreigner of infinite taste, whose love of roses was proverbial. A legend says that some of them were watered with the most carefully prepared beef tea from the princely kitchen. The rich man had gone back to his own country, and the Princess Anatolie had taken the villa and meant to spend the rest of her life there. She was only seventy years old, and had made up her mind to live to be a hundred, so that it was worth while to make permanent arrangements for her comfort.

Lamberti might have driven through the gate and up to the house, but he was not sure whether the Princess liked to see such plebeian vehicles as cabs in her grounds. He had a strong suspicion that, in spite of her royal blood, she had the soul of a snob, and thought much more about appearances than he did; and as for Monsieur Leroy, he was one of the most complete specimens of the snob species in the world. Therefore Lamberti, who now had reasons for wishing to propitiate the dwellers in the villa, left his cab outside and walked up the steep drive to the house.

He did not look particularly well in a frock coat and high hat. He was too muscular, his hair was too red, his neck was too sunburnt, and he was more accustomed to wearing a uniform or the rough clothes in which fighting is usually done. The footman looked at him and did not recognise him.

"Her Highness is not at home," said the man, coolly.

A private carriage was waiting at a little distance from the porch, and the footman who belonged to it was lounging in the vestibule within.

"Be good enough to ask whether her Highness will see me," said Lamberti.

The fellow looked at him again, and evidently made up his mind that it would be safer to obey a red-haired gentleman who had such a very unusual look in his eyes and spoke so quietly, for he disappeared without making any further objection.

When Lamberti entered the drawing-room, he was aware that the Princess was established in a high arm-chair near a tea-table, that Monsieur Leroy was coming towards him, and that an elderly lady in a hat was seated near the Princess in an attitude which may be described as one of respectful importance. He was aware of the presence of these three persons in the room, but he only saw the fourth, a young girl, standing beside the table with a cup in her hand, and just turning her face towards him with a look that was like a surprised recognition after not having seen him for a very long time. He started perceptibly as his eyes met hers, and he almost uttered an exclamation of astonishment.

He was checked by feeling Monsieur Leroy's toad-like hand in his.

"Her Highness is very glad to see you," said an oily voice in French, but with a thick and rolling pronunciation that was South American unless it was Roumanian.

For once Lamberti did not notice the sensual, pink and white face, the hanging lips, the colourless brown hair, the insolent eyes, the effeminate figure and dress of the little man he detested, and whose mere touch was disgusting to him. By a strong effort he went directly up to the Princess without looking again at the young girl whose presence had affected him so oddly.

Princess Anatolie was gracious enough to give him her hand to kiss; he bent over it, and his lips touched a few of the cold precious stones in the rings that loaded her fingers. She had not changed in the year that had passed since he had seen her, except that her eyes looked smaller than ever and nearer together. Her hair might or might not be her own, for it was carefully crimped and arranged upon her forehead; it was not certain that her excellent teeth were false; there was about her an air of youth and vitality that was really surprising, and yet it was impossible not to feel that she might be altogether a marvellous sham, on the verge of dissolution.

"This is most charming!" she said, in a voice that was not cracked, but rang false. "I expect my nephew, Guido, at any moment. He is your great friend, is he not? Yes, I never forget anything. This is my nephew Guido's great friend," she continued volubly, and turning to the elderly lady on her right, "Prince Lamberti."

"Don Lamberto Lamberti," said Monsieur Leroy in a low voice, correcting her. But even this was not quite right.

"I have the good fortune to know the Countess Fortiguerra," said Lamberti, bowing, as he suddenly recognised her, but very much surprised that she should be there. "I have just received a very kind invitation from you," he added, as she gave him her hand.

"I hope you will come," she said quietly. "I knew your mother very well. We were at the school of the Sacred Heart together."

Lamberti bent his head a little, in acknowledgment of the claim upon him possessed by one of his mother's school friends.

"I shall do my best to come," he answered.

He felt that the young girl was watching him, and he ventured to look at her, with a little movement, as if he wished to be introduced. Again he felt the absolute certainty of having met her before, somewhere, very long ago—so long ago that she could not have been born then, and he must have been a small boy. Therefore what he felt was absurd.

"Cecilia," said the Countess, speaking to the girl, "this is Signor Lamberto Lamberti." "My daughter," she explained, as he bowed, "Cecilia Palladio."

"Most charming!" cried the Princess, "the son and the daughter of two old friends."

"Touching," echoed Monsieur Leroy. "Such a picture! There is true sentiment in it."

Lamberti did not hear, but Cecilia Palladio did, and a straight shadow, fine as a hair line, appeared for an instant, perpendicular between her brows, while she looked directly at the man before her. A moment later Lamberti was seated between her and her mother, and Monsieur Leroy had resumed the position he had left to welcome the newcomer, sitting on a very low cushioned stool almost at the Princess's feet.

In formal circumstances, a man who has been long in the army or navy can usually trust himself not to show astonishment or emotion, and after the first slight start of surprise, which only Monsieur Leroy had seen, Lamberti had behaved as if nothing out of the common way had happened to him. But he had felt as if he were in a dream, while healthily sure that he was awake; and now that he was more at ease, he began to examine the cause of his inward disturbance.

It was not only out of the question to suppose that he had ever before now met Cecilia Palladio, but he was quite certain that he had never seen any one who was at all like her.

If extinct types of men could be revived now and then, of those which the world once thought admirable and tried to copy, it would be interesting to see how many persons of taste would acknowledge any beauty in them. Cecilia Palladio had been eighteen years old early in the winter, and in the usual course of things would have made her appearance in society during the carnival season. The garden party for which her mother had now sent out invitations was to take the place of the dance which should have been given in January. Afterwards, when it was over, and everybody had seen her, some people said that she was perfectly beautiful, others declared that she was a freak of nature and would soon be hideous, but, meanwhile, was an interesting study; one young gentleman, addicted to art, said that her face belonged to the type seen in the Elgin marbles; a Sicilian lady said that her head was even more archaic than that, and resembled a fragment from the temples of Selinunte, preserved in the museum at Palermo; and the Russian ambassador, who was of unknown age, said that she was the perfect Psyche of Naples, brought to life, and that he wished he were Eros.

In southern Europe what is called the Greek type of beauty is often seen, and does not surprise any one. Many people think it cold and uninteresting. It was a small something in the arch of the brows, it was a very slight upward turn of the point of the nose, it was the small irregularity of the broader and less curving upper lip that gave to Cecilia Palladio's face the force and character that are so utterly wanting in the faces of the best Greek statues. The Greeks, by the time they had gained the perfect knowledge of the human body that produced the Hermes of Olympia, had made a conventional mask of the human face, and rarely ever tried to give it a little of the daring originality that stands out in the features of many a crudely archaic statue. The artist who made the Psyche attempted something of the kind, for the right side of the face differs from the left, as it generally does in living people. The right eyebrow is higher and more curved than the left one, which lends some archness to the expression, but its effect is destroyed by the tiresome perfection of the simpering mouth.

Cecilia Palladio was not like a Greek statue, but she looked as if she had come alive from an age in which the individual ranked above the many as a model, and in which nothing accidentally unfit for life could survive and nothing degenerate had begun to be. With the same general proportion, there was less symmetry in her face than in those of modern beauties, and there was more light, more feeling, more understanding. She was very fair, but her eyes were not blue; it would have been hard to define their colour, and sometimes there seemed to be golden lights in them. While she was standing, Lamberti had seen that she was almost as tall as himself, and therefore taller than most women; and she was slender, and moved like a very perfectly proportioned young wild animal, continuously, but without haste, till each motion was completed in rest. Most men and women really move in a succession of very short movements, entirely interrupted at more or less perceptible intervals. If our sight were perfect we should see that people walk, for instance, by a series of jerks so rapid as to be like the vibrations of a humming-bird's wings. Perhaps this is due to the unconscious exercise of the human will in every voluntary motion, for a man who moves in his sleep seems to move continuously like an animal, till he has changed his position and rests again.

Lamberti made none of these reflections, and did not analyse the face he could not help watching whenever the chance of conversation allowed him to look at Cecilia without seeming to stare at her. He only tried to discover why her face was so familiar to him.

"We have been in Paris all winter," said her mother, in answer to some question of his.

"They have been in Paris all winter!" cried the Princess. "Think what that means! The cold, the rain, the solitude! What in the world did you do with yourselves?"

"Cecilia wished to continue her studies," answered the Countess Fortiguerra.

"What sort of things have you been learning, Mademoiselle?" asked Lamberti.

"I followed a course of lectures on philosophy at the Sorbonne, and I read Nietzsche with a man who had known him," answered the young lady, as naturally as if she had said that she had been taking lessons on the piano.

A momentary silence followed, and everybody stared at the girl, except her mother, who smiled pleasantly and looked from one to the other with the expression which mothers of prodigies often assume, and which clearly says: "I did it. Is it not perfectly wonderful?"

Then Monsieur Leroy laughed, in spite of himself.

"Hush, Doudou!" cried the Princess. "You are very rude!"

No one present chanced to know that she always called him Doudou when she was in a good humour. Cecilia Palladio turned her head quietly, fixed her eyes on him and laughed, deliberately, long, and very sweetly. Monsieur Leroy met her gaze for a moment, then looked away and moved uneasily on his low seat.

"What are you laughing at?" he asked, in a tone of annoyance.

"It seems so funny that you should be called Doudou—at your age," answered Cecilia.

"Really—" Monsieur Leroy looked at the Princess as if asking for protection. She laughed good-humouredly, somewhat to Lamberti's surprise.

"You are very direct with my friends, my dear," she said to Cecilia, still smiling. The Countess Fortiguerra, not knowing exactly what to do, also smiled, but rather foolishly.

"I am very sorry," said Cecilia, with contrition, and looking down. "I really beg Monsieur Leroy's pardon. I could not help it."

But she had been revenged, for she had made him ridiculous.

"Not at all, not at all," he answered, in a tone that did not promise forgiveness. Lamberti wondered what sort of man Palladio had been, since the girl did not at all resemble her mother, who had clearly been pretty and foolish in her youth, and had only lost her looks as she grew older. The obliteration of middle age had set in.

There might have been some awkwardness, but it was dispelled by the appearance of Guido, who came in unannounced at that moment, glancing quickly at each of the group as he came forward, to see who was there.

"At last!" exclaimed the Princess, with evident satisfaction. "How late you are, my dear," she said as Guido ceremoniously kissed her hand.

"I am very sorry," he said. "I was out when your note came. But I should have come in any case."

"You know the Countess Fortiguerra, of course," said the Princess.

"Certainly," answered Guido, who had not recognised the lady at all, and was glad to be told who she was, and that he knew her.

Lamberti watched him closely, for he understood every shade of his friend's expression and manner. Guido shook hands with a pleasant smile, and then glanced at Cecilia.

"My nephew, Guido d'Este," said the Princess, introducing him.

Cecilia looked at him quietly, and bent her head in acknowledgment of the introduction.

"My daughter," murmured the Countess Fortiguerra, with satisfaction.

"Mademoiselle Palladio and her mother have just come back from Paris," explained Monsieur Leroy officiously, as Guido nodded to him.

Guido caught the name, and was glad of the information it conveyed, and he sat down between the young girl and her mother. Lamberti was now almost sure that his friend was not especially struck by Cecilia's face; but she looked at him with some interest, which was not at all to be wondered at, considering his looks, his romantic name, and his half-royal birth. For the first time Lamberti envied him a little, and was ashamed of it.

Barely an hour earlier he had wished that he could make Guido more like himself, and now he wished that he were more like Guido.

"The Countess has been kind enough to ask me to her garden party," Guido said, looking at his aunt, for he instinctively connected the latter's anxiety to see him with the invitation.

So did Lamberti, and it flashed upon him that this meeting was the first step in an attempt to marry his friend to Cecilia Palladio. The girl was probably an heiress, and Guido's aunt saw a possibility of recovering through her the money she had lost in speculations.

This explanation did not occur to Guido, simply because he was bored and was already thinking of an excuse for getting away after staying as short a time as possible.

"I hope you will come," said Cecilia, rather unexpectedly.

"Of course he will," the Princess answered for him, in an encouraging tone.

"The villa is really very pretty," continued the young girl.

"Let me see," said Guido, who liked her voice as soon as she spoke, "the Villa Palladio—I do not quite remember where it is."

"It used to be the Villa Madama," explained Monsieur Leroy. "I have always wondered who the 'Madama' was, after whom it was called. It seems such a foolish name."

The Princess looked displeased, and bit her lip a little.

"I think," said Guido, as if suggesting a possibility, rather than stating a fact, "that she was a daughter of the Emperor Charles the Fifth, who was Duchess of Parma."

"Of course, of course!" cried Monsieur Leroy, eagerly assenting, "I had forgotten!"

"My daughter's guardians bought it for her not long ago," explained the Countess Fortiguerra, "with my approval, and we have of course changed the name."

"Naturally," said Guido, gravely, but looking at Lamberti, who almost smiled under his red beard. "And you approved of the change, Mademoiselle," Guido added, turning to Cecilia, and with an interrogation in his voice.

"Not at all," she answered, with sudden coldness. "It was Goldbirn—"

"Yes," said the Countess, weakly, "it was Baron Goldbirn who insisted upon it, in spite of us."

"Goldbirn—Goldbirn," repeated the Princess vaguely. "The name has a familiar sound."

"Your Highness has a current account with them in Vienna," observed Monsieur Leroy.

"Yes, yes, certainly. Doudou acts as my secretary sometimes, you know."

The information seemed necessary, as Monsieur Leroy's position had been far from clear.

"Baron Goldbirn was associated with Cecilia's father in some railways in South America," said the Countess, "and is her principal guardian. He will always continue to manage her fortune for her, I hope."

Clearly, Cecilia was an heiress, and was to marry Guido d'Este as soon as the matter could be arranged. That was the Princess's plan. Lamberti thought that it remained to be seen whether Guido would agree to the match.

"Has Baron Goldbirn made many—improvements—in the Villa Madama?" enquired Guido, hesitating a little, perhaps intentionally.

"Oh no!" Cecilia answered. "He lets me do as I please about such things."

"And what has been your pleasure?" asked Guido, with a beginning of interest, as well as for the sake of hearing her young voice, which contrasted pleasantly with her mother's satisfied purring and the Princess's disagreeable tone.

"I got the best artist I could find to restore the whole place as nearly as possible to what it was meant to be. I am satisfied with the result. So is my mother," she added, with an evident afterthought.

"My daughter is very artistic," the Countess explained.

Cecilia looked at Guido, and a faint smile illuminated her face for a moment. Guido bent his head almost imperceptibly, as if to say that he knew what she meant, and it seemed to Lamberti that the two already understood each other. He rose to go, moved by an impulse he could not resist. Guido looked at him in surprise, for he had expected his friend to wait for him.

"Must you go already?" asked the Princess, in a colourless tone that did not invite Lamberti to stay. "But I suppose you are very busy when you are in Rome. Good-bye."

As he took his leave, his eyes met Cecilia's. It might have been only his imagination, after all, but he felt sure that her whole expression changed instantly to a look of deep and sincere understanding, even of profound sympathy.

"I hope you will come to the villa," she said gravely, and she seemed to wait for his answer.

"Thank you. I shall be there."

There was a short silence, as Monsieur Leroy went with him to the door at the other end of the long room, but Cecilia did not watch him; she seemed to be interested in a large portrait that hung opposite the nearest window, and which was suddenly lighted up by the glow of the sunset. It represented a young king, standing on a step, in coronation robes, with a vast ermine mantle spreading behind him and to one side, and an uncomfortable-looking crown on his head; a sceptre lay on a highly polished table at his elbow, beside an open arch, through which the domes and spires of a city were visible. There was no particular reason why he should be standing there, apparently alone, and in a distinctly theatrical attitude, and the portrait was not a good picture; but Cecilia looked at it steadily till she heard the door shut, after Lamberti had gone out.

"Your friend is not a very gay person," observed the Princess. "Is he always so silent?"

"Yes," Guido answered. "He is not very talkative."

"Do you like silent people?" enquired Cecilia.

"I like a woman who can talk, and a man who can hold his tongue," replied Guido readily.

Cecilia looked at him and smiled carelessly. The Princess rose slowly, but she was so short, and her arm-chair was so high, that she seemed to walk away from it without being any taller than when she had been sitting, rather than really to get up.

"Shall we go into the garden?" she suggested. "It is not too cold. Doudou, my cloak!"

Monsieur Leroy brought a pretty confusion of mouse-coloured silk and lace, disentangled it skilfully, and held it up behind the Princess's shoulders. It looked like a big butterfly as he spread it in the air, and it had ribands that hung down to the floor.

When she had put it on, the Princess led the way to a long window, which Leroy opened, and leaning lightly on the Countess Fortiguerra's arm, she went out into the evening light. She evidently meant to give the young people a chance of talking together by themselves, for as soon as they were outside she sent Monsieur Leroy away.

"My dear Doudou!" she cried, as if suddenly remembering something, "we have quite forgotten those invitations for to-morrow! Should you mind writing them now, so that they can be sent before dinner?"

Monsieur Leroy disappeared with an alacrity which suggested that the plan had been arranged beforehand.

"Take Mademoiselle Palladio round the garden, Guido," said the Princess. "We will walk a little before the house till you come back. It is drier here."

Guido must have been dull indeed if he had not at last understood why he had been made to come, and what was expected of him. He was annoyed, and raised his eyebrows a little.

"Will you come, Mademoiselle?" he asked coldly.

"Yes," answered Cecilia in a constrained tone, for she understood as well as Guido himself.

Her mother was often afraid of her, and had not dared to tell her that the whole object of their visit was that she should see Guido and be seen by him. She thought that the Princess was really pushing matters too hastily, considering the time-honoured traditions of Latin etiquette, which forbid that young people should be left alone together for a moment, even when engaged to be married. But the Countess had great faith in the correctness of anything which such a very high-born person as the Princess Anatolie chose to suggest, and as the latter held her by the arm with affectionate condescension, she could not possibly run after her daughter.

The two moved away in silence towards the flower garden, and soon disappeared round the corner of the house.

"The roses are pretty," said Guido, apologetically. "My aunt likes people to see them."

"They are magnificent," answered Cecilia, without enthusiasm, and after a suitable interval.

They went on, along a narrow gravel path, and though there was really room enough for Guido to walk by her side, he pretended that there was not, and followed her. She was very graceful, and he would not have thought of denying it. He even looked at her as she went before him, and he noticed the fact; but after he had taken cognisance of it, he was quite as indifferent as before. He no longer thought her voice pleasant, in his resentment at finding that a trap had been laid for him.

"You see, there are a good many kinds of roses," he observed, because it would have been rude to say nothing at all. "They are not all in flower yet."

"It is only the beginning of May," the young girl answered, without interest.

They came to the broader walk on the other side of the plot of roses, and Guido had to walk by her side again.

"I like your friend," she said suddenly.

"I am very glad," Guido replied, unbending at once and quietly looking at her now. "People do not always like him at first sight."

"No, I understand that. He has the look in his eyes that men get who have killed."

"Has he?" Guido seemed surprised. "Yes, he killed several men in Africa, when he was alone against many, and they meant to murder him. He is brave. Make him tell you about it, if you can induce him to talk."

"Is that so very hard?" Cecilia laughed. "Is he really more silent than you?"

"Nobody ever called me silent," answered Guido, smiling. "I suppose you thought so—stopped."

"Because I did not know how to begin, and because you would not. Is that what you were going to say?"

"It is very near the truth," Guido admitted, very much amused.

"I do not blame you," said Cecilia. "How could you suppose that a mere girl like me could possibly have anything to say—a child that has not even been to her first party?"

"Perhaps I was afraid that the mere child might talk about philosophy and Nietzsche," suggested Guido.

"And that would be dreadful, of course! Why? Is there any reason why a girl should not study such things? If there is, tell me. No one ever tells me what I ought to do."

"It is quite unnecessary, I have no doubt," Guido answered promptly, and smiling again.

"You mean quite useless, because I should not do it?"

"Why should I be supposed to know that you are spoiled—if you are? Besides, you must not take up a man every time he makes you a silly compliment."

"Ah, now you are telling me what I ought to do! I like that better. Thank you!" Guido was amused.

"Are you really grateful?" he asked, laughing a little. "Do you always speak the truth?"

"Yes! Do you?" She asked the question sharply, as if she meant to surprise him.

"I never lied to a man in my life," Guido answered.

"But you have to women?"

"I suppose so," said Guido, considerably diverted. "Most of us do, in moments of enthusiasm."

"Really! And—are you often—enthusiastic?"

"No. Very rarely. Besides, I do not know whether it is worse in a man to tell fibs to please a woman, than it is in a woman to disbelieve what an honest man tells her on his word. Which is the least wrong, do you think?"

"But since you admit that most men do not tell the truth to women—"

"I said, on one's word of honour. There is a difference."

"In theory," said Cecilia.

"Are there theories about lying?" asked Guido.

"Oh yes," answered the young girl, without hesitation. "There is Puffendorf's, for instance, in his book on the Law of Nature and Nations—"

"Good heavens!" exclaimed Guido.

"Certainly. He makes out that there is a sort of unwritten agreement amongst all men that words shall be used in a definite sense which others can understand. That sounds sensible. And then, Saint Augustin, and La Placette, and Noodt—"

"My dear young lady, you have led me quite out of my depth! What do those good people say?"

"That all lying is absolutely wrong in itself, whether it harms anybody or not."

"And what do you think about it? That would be much more interesting to know."

"I told you, I always tell the truth," Cecilia answered demurely.

"Oh yes, of course! I had forgotten."

"And you do not believe it," laughed the young girl. "It is time to go back to the house."

"If you will stay a little longer, I will believe everything you tell me."

"No, it is late," answered Cecilia, her manner suddenly changing as the laugh died out of her voice.

She walked on quickly, and he kept behind her.

"I shall certainly go to your garden party," said Guido.

"Shall you?"

She spoke in a tone of such utter indifference that Guido stared at her in surprise. A moment later they had rejoined her mother and the Princess.

CHAPTER III

At the beginning of the twentieth century Rome has become even more cosmopolitan than it used to be, for the Romans themselves are turning into cosmopolitans, and the old traditional, serious, gloomy, and sometimes dramatic life of the patriarchal system has almost died out. One meets Romans of historical names everywhere, nowadays, in London, in Paris, and in Vienna, speaking English and French, and sometimes German, with extraordinary correctness, as much at home, to all appearance, in other capitals as they are in their own, and intimately familiar with the ways of many societies in many places.

Cecilia Palladio, at eighteen years of age, had probably not spent a third of her life in Rome, and had been educated in different parts of the world and in a variety of ways. Her father, Count Palladio, as has been explained, had been engaged in promoting a number of undertakings, of which several had succeeded, and at his death, which had happened when Cecilia had been eight years old, he had left her part of his considerable fortune in safe guardianship, leaving his wife a life interest in the remainder. His old ally, the banker Solomon Goldbirn of Vienna, had administered the whole inheritance with wisdom and integrity, and at her marriage Cecilia would dispose of several millions of francs, and would ultimately inherit as much more from her mother's share. From a European point of view, she was therefore a notable heiress, and even in the new world of millionnaires she would at least have been considered tolerably well off, though by no means what is there called rich.

Two years after Palladio's death her mother had married Count Fortiguerra, who had begun life in the army, then passed to diplomacy, had risen rapidly to the post of ambassador, and had died suddenly at Madrid when barely fifty years old, and when Cecilia was sixteen.

The girl had a clear recollection of her own father, though she had never been with him very much, as his occupations constantly took him to distant parts of the world. He had seemed an old man to her, and had indeed been much older than her mother, for he had been a patriot in the later days of the Italian revolutions, and when still young he had been with Garibaldi in 1860. Cecilia remembered him a tall, active, grey-haired man with a pointed beard and big moustaches, and eyes which she now knew had been like her own. She remembered his unbounded energy, his patriotic and sometimes rather boastful talk, his black cigars, the vast heap of papers that always seemed to be in hopeless confusion on his writing table when he was at home, and the numerous eccentric-looking people who used to come and see him. She had been told that he was never to be disturbed, and never to be questioned, and that he was a great man. She had loved him with all her heart when he told her stories, and at other times she had been distinctly afraid of him. These stories had been fairy tales to the child, but she had now discovered that they had been history, or what passes for it.

He had told her about King Amulius of Alba Longa, and of the twin founders of Rome, and of all the far-off times and doings, and he had described to her six wonderful maidens who lived in a palace in the Forum and kept a little fire burning day and night, which he compared to the great Roman race over whose destiny the mystic ladies were always watching. It was only quite lately that she had heard any learned men say in earnest some of the things which he had told her with a smile as if he were inventing a tale to amuse her child's fancy. But what he had said had made a deep and abiding impression, and had become a part of her thought. She sometimes dreamed very vividly that she was again a little girl, sitting on his knee and listening to his wonderful stories. In other ways she had not missed him much after his death. Possibly her mother had not missed him either; for though she spoke of him occasionally with a sort of awe, it was never with anything like emotion.

Count Fortiguerra had been kind to the child, or it might be truer to say that he had spoilt her by encouraging her without much judgment in her insatiable thirst for knowledge, and in her unnecessary ambition to excel in everything her fancy led her to attempt. Her mother, with a good deal of social foolishness and a very pliable character, possessed nevertheless a fair share of womanly intelligence, and knew by instinct that a young girl who is very different from other girls, no matter how clever she may be, rarely makes what people call a good marriage.

There is probably nothing which leads a young woman to think a man a desirable husband so much as some exceptional gift, or even some brilliant eccentricity, which distinguishes him from other people; but there is nothing which frightens away the average desirable husband so much as anything of that sort in the young lady of his affections, and every married woman knows it very well.

The excellent Countess used to wish that her daughter would grow up more like other girls, and in the sincere belief that a little womanly vanity must certainly counteract a desire for super-feminine mental cultivation, she honestly tried to interest Cecilia in such frivolities as dress, dancing, and romantic fiction. The result was only very partially successful. Cecilia was dressed to perfection, without seeming to take any trouble about it, and she danced marvellously before she had ever been to a ball; but she cared nothing for the novels she was allowed to read, and she devoured serious books with increasing intellectual voracity.

Her stepfather laughed, and said that the girl was a genius and ought not to be hampered by ordinary rules; and his wife, who had at first feared lest he should dislike the child of her first husband, was only too glad that he should, on the contrary, show something like paternal infatuation for Cecilia, since no children of his own were born to him. He was a man, too, of wide reading and experience, and having considerable political insight into his times. Before Cecilia was eleven years old he talked to her about serious matters, as if she had been grown up, and often wished that the child should be at table and in the drawing-room when men who were making history came informally to the embassy. Cecilia had listened to their talk, and had remembered a very large part of what she had heard, understanding more and more as she grew up; and by far the greatest sorrow of her life had been the death of her stepfather.

She was a modern Italian girl, and her mother was a Roman who had been brought up in something of the old strictness and narrowness, first in a convent, and afterwards in a rather gloomy home under the shadow of the most rigid parental authority. Exceptional gifts, exceptional surroundings, and exceptional opportunities had made Cecilia Palladio an exception to all types, and as unlike the average modern Italian young girl as could be imagined.

The sun had already set as the mother and daughter drove away, but it was still broad day, and a canopy of golden clouds, floating high over the city, reflected rosy lights through the blue shadows in the crowded streets. The Countess Fortiguerra was pleasantly aware that every man under seventy turned to look after her daughter, from the smart old colonel of cavalry in his perfect uniform to the ragged and haggard waifs who sold wax matches at the corners of the streets. She was not in the least jealous of her, as mothers have been before now, and perhaps she was able to enjoy vicariously what she herself had never had, but had often wished for, the gift of nature which instantly fixes the attention of the other sex.

"Why did you not tell me?" asked Cecilia, after a silence that had lasted five minutes.

The Countess pretended not to understand, coloured a little, and tried to look surprised.

"Why did you not tell me that you and the Princess wish me to marry her nephew?"

This was direct, and an answer was necessary. The Countess laughed soothingly.

"Dear child!" she cried, "it is impossible to deceive you! We only wished that you two might meet, and perhaps like each other."

"Well," answered Cecilia, "we have met."

The answer was not encouraging, and she did not seem inclined to say more of her own accord, but her mother could not restrain a natural curiosity.

"Yes," she said, in a conciliatory tone, "but how do you like him?"

Cecilia seemed to be hesitating for a moment.

"Very much," she answered, unexpectedly, after the pause.

The Countess was so much pleased that she coloured again. She had never been able to hide what she felt, and she secretly envied people who never blushed.

"I am so glad!" she said. "I was sure you would like each other."

"It does not follow that because I like him, he likes me," answered Cecilia, quietly. "And even if he does, that is not a reason why we should marry. I may never marry at all."

"How can you say such things!" cried the Countess, not at all satisfied.

Cecilia shrank a little in her corner of the deep phaeton and instinctively drew the edges of her little silk mantle together over her chest, as if to protect herself from something.

"You know," she said, almost sharply.

"I shall never understand you," her mother sighed.

"Give me time to understand myself, mother," answered the young girl, suddenly unbending. "I am only eighteen; I have never been into the world, and the mere idea of marrying—"

She stopped short, and her firm lips closed tightly.

"No, I do not understand," said the Countess. "The thought of marriage was never disagreeable to me, even when I was quite young. It is the natural object of a woman's life."

"There are exceptions, surely! There are nuns, for instance."

"Oh, if you wish to go into a convent—"

"I have no religious vocation," Cecilia answered gravely. "Or if I have, it is not of that sort."

"I am glad to hear it!" The Countess was beginning to lose her temper. "If you thought you had, you would be quite capable of taking the veil."

"Yes," the young girl replied. "If I wished to be a nun, and if I were sure that I should be a good nun, I would enter a convent at once. But I am not naturally devout, I suppose."

"In my time," said the Countess, with emphasis, "when young girls did not take the veil, they married."

As an argument, this was weak and lacked logic, and Cecilia felt rather pitiless just then.

"There are only two possible ways of living," she said; "either by religion, if you have any, and that is the easier, or by rule."

"And pray what sort of rule can there be to take the place of religion?"

"Act so that the reason for your actions may be considered a universal law."

"That is nonsense!" cried the Countess.

"No," replied Cecilia, unmoved, "it is Kant's Categorical Imperative."

"It makes no difference," retorted her mother. "It is nonsense."

Cecilia said nothing, and her expression did not change, for she knew that her mother could not understand her, and she was not at all sure that she understood herself, as she had almost confessed. Seeing that she did not answer, the excellent Countess took the opportunity of telling her that her head had been turned by too much reading, though it was all her poor, dear stepfather's fault, since he had filled her head with ideas. What she meant by "ideas" was not clear, except that they were of course dangerous in themselves and utterly subversive of social order, and that the main purpose of all education should be to discourage them in the young.

"They should be left to old people," she concluded; "they have nothing else to think of."

Cecilia had heard very little, being absorbed in her own reflections, but as her mother often spoke in the same way, the general drift of what she had said was unmistakable. The two were very unlike, but they were not unloving. In her heart the Countess took the most unbounded pride in her only child's beauty and cleverness, except when the latter opposed itself to her social inclinations and ambitions; and the young girl really loved her mother when not irritated by some speech or action that offended her taste. That her mother should not always understand her seemed quite natural.

They had almost reached their door, the great pillared porch of the mysterious Palazzo Massimo, in which they had an apartment, for they did not live in the villa where the garden party was to be given. Cecilia's gloved hand went out quietly to the Countess's and gently pressed it.

"Let me think my own thoughts, mother," she said; "they shall never hurt you."

"Yes, dear, of course," answered the elder woman meekly, her little burst of temper having already subsided.

Cecilia left her early that evening and went to her own room to be alone. It was not that she was tired, nor painfully affected by a strange sensation she had felt during the afternoon; but she realised that she had reached the end of the first stage in life, and that another was going to begin, and it was part of her nature to seek for a complete understanding of everything in her existence. It seemed to her unworthy of a thinking being to act or to feel, without clearly defining the cause of every feeling and action. Youth dreams of an impossible completeness in carrying out its self-set rules of perfection, and is swayed and stunned, and often paralysed, when they are broken to pieces by rebellious human nature.

The room was very large and dim, for Cecilia had put out the electric light, and had lit two big wax candles, of the sort that are burned in churches. The blinds and shutters of the windows were open, and the moonlight fell in two broad floods upon the pale carpet, half across the floor. The white bed with its high canopy of lace looked ghostly against the furthest wall, like a marble sepulchre under a mist. The light blue damask on the walls was dark in the gloom, and there was not much furniture to break the long surfaces. The dusky air was cool and pure, for Cecilia detested perfumes of all sorts.

She sat motionless in a high carved seat, just in the moonlight, one hand upon an arm of the chair, the other on her breast. She had gathered her hair into a knot, low at the back of her head, and the folds of a soft white robe just followed the outlines of her figure. The table on which the candles stood was a little behind her, and away from the window, and the still yellow light only touched her hair in one or two places, sending back dull golden reflections.

The strange young face was very quiet, and even the lids rarely moved as she steadily stared into the shadow. There was no look of thought, nor any visible effort of concentration in her features; there was rather an air of patient waiting, of perfect readiness to receive whatever should come to her out of the depths. So, a beautiful marble face on a tomb gazes into the shadows of a dim church, and gazes on, and waits, neither growing nor changing, neither satisfied nor disappointed, but calm and enduring, as if expecting the resurrection of the dead and the life of the world to come. But for the rare drooping of the lids, that rested her sight, the girl would have seemed to be in a trance; she was in a state of almost perfect contemplation that approached to perfect happiness, since she was hardly conscious that her strongest wishes were still unsatisfied.

She had been in the same state before now—last week, last month, last year, and again and again, as it seemed to her, very long ago; so long, that the time seemed like ages, and the intervals like centuries, until it all disappeared altogether in the immeasurable, and the past, the present, and the future were around her at once, unbroken, always ending, yet always beginning again. In the midst floated the soul, the self, the undying individuality, a light that shot out long rays, like a star, towards the ever present moments in an ever recurring life of which she had been, and was, and was to be, most keenly conscious.

So far, the truth, perhaps; the truth, guessed by the mystics of all ages, sometimes hidden in secret writings, sometimes proclaimed to the light in symbols too plain to be understood, now veiled in the reasoned propositions of philosophers, now sung in sublime verse by inspired seers; present, as truth always is, to the few, misunderstood, as all truths are, by the many.

But beside the truth, and outshining it, came the illusion, clear and bright, and appealing to the heart with the music of all the changes that are illusion's life. Sitting very still in the moonlight, Cecilia saw pictures in the shadow, and herself walking in the mazes of many dreams; and she watched them, till even her eyelids no longer drooped from time to time, and her breathing ceased to stir the folds of white upon her bosom.

Even then, she knew that she herself was not dreaming, but was calling up dreams which she saw, which could be nothing but visions after all, and would end in a darkness beyond which she could see nothing, and in which she would feel real physical pain, that would be almost unbearable, though she knew that she would gladly bear it again and again, for the sake of again seeing the phantasms of herself drawn in mystic light upon the shadow.

They came and followed one upon another, like days of life. There was the beautiful marble court with its deep portico, its pillars, and its overhanging upper story, all gleaming in the low morning sun; she could hear the water softly laughing its way through the square marble-edged basins, level with the ground, she could smell the spring violets that grew in the neatly trimmed borders, she knew the faces of the statues that stood between the columns, and smiled at her. She knew herself, young, golden-haired, all in white, a little pale from the night's vigil before the eternal fire, just entering the court as she came back from the temple, and then standing quite still for a moment, facing the morning sun and drinking in long draughts of the sweet spring air. From far above, the matin song of birds came down out of the gardens of Cæsar's palace, and high over the court the sounds of the Forum began to ring and echo, as they did all day and half the night.

It was herself, her very self, that was there, resting one hand upon a fluted column and looking upwards, her eyes, her face, her figure, real and unchanged after ages, as they were hers now; and in her look there was the infinite longing, the readiness to receive, which she felt still and must feel always, to the end of time.

Now, the dream would move on, slowly and full of details. The lithe dream figure would rest in the small white room at the upper end of the court, and resting, would dream dreams within that dream; and, looking on, she herself would know what they were. They would be full of a deep desire to be free for ever from earth and body and life, joined for all eternity with something pure and high that could not be seen, but of which her soul was a part, mingled with the changing things for a time, but to be withdrawn from them again, maiden and spotless as it had come amongst them, a true and perfect Vestal.

The precious treasures in the secret places of the little temple would pass away, the rudely carved wooden image of Pallas would crumble to dust, the shields that had come down from heaven would fall to pieces in green corrosion, the sacred vessels would be broken or come to a base use, the fire would go out and Vesta's hearth would be cold for ever.

At the mere thought, the sleeping face in the vision would tremble and grow pale for a moment, but soon would smile again, for the fire had been faithfully tended all the night long.

But it would all pass away, even the place, even Rome herself, and in the sphere of divine joy the sleeper would forget even to dream, and would be quite at rest, until the mid-hour of day, when a companion would come softly to the door and wake her with gentle words and kindly touch, to join the other Vestals at the thrice-purified table in the cool hall.

So the warm hours would pass, and later, if she chose, the holy maiden might go out into the city, whithersoever she would, borne in a high, open litter by many slaves, with a stern lictor walking before her, and the people would fall back on either side. If she chanced to meet one of the Prætors, or even the Consul himself, their guards would salute her as no sovereign would be saluted in Rome; and should she see some wretched thieving slave being led to death on the cross upon the Esquiline, her slightest word could reverse all his condemnation, and blot out all his crimes. For she was sacred to the Goddess, and above Consuls and Prætors and judges. But none of those things would touch her heart nor please her vanity, for all her pure young soul was bent on freedom from this earth, divine and eternal, as the end of a sinless life.

The eyes in the dream, the eyes of the girl who stood by the column, drinking the morning air, had never met the eyes of a man with the wish that a glance might linger to a look. But she who watched the dream knew that the time was at hand, and that the dark cloud of fear was already gathering which was to darken her sun and break by and by in an unknown fear. She knew it, she, the waking Cecilia Palladio; but the other Cecilia, the Vestal of long ago, guessed nothing of the future, and stood there breathing softly, already refreshed after the night's watching. It would all happen, as it always happened, little by little, detail after detail, till the dreaded moment.

But it did not. The dream changed. Instead of crossing the marble court, and lingering a moment by the water, the Vestal stood by the column, against the background of shade cast by the portico. She was listening now, she was expecting some one, she was glancing anxiously about as if to see whether any one were there; but she was alone.

Then it came, in the shadow behind her, the face of a man, moving nearer—a rugged Roman head, with deep-set, bold blue eye, big brows, a great jaw, reddish hair. It came nearer, and the girl knew it was coming. In an instant more, she would spring forward across the court, crying out for protection.

No, she did not move till the man was close to her, looking over her shoulder, whispering in her ear. Cecilia saw it all, and it was so real that she tried to call out, to shriek, to make any sound that could save her image from destruction, for the kiss that was coming would be death to both, and death with unutterable shame and pain. But her voice was gone, and her lips were frozen. She sat paralysed with a horror she had never known before, while the face of the phantom girl blushed softly, and turned to the strong man, and the two gazed into each other's eyes a moment, knowing that they loved.

She felt that it was her other self, and that she had the will to resist, even then, and that the will must still be supreme over the illusion. Never, it seemed to her, had she made such a supreme effort, never had she felt such power concentrated in her strong determination, never in all her life had she been so sure of the result when she had willed anything with all her might. Every fibre of her being, every nerve in her body, every throbbing cell of her brain was strained to breaking. The two faces were quite close, the longing lips had almost met—nothing could hinder, nothing could save; the phantasms did not know that she was watching them.

Suddenly something changed. She no longer saw herself in a vision, she was herself there, somewhere, in the dark, in the light—she did not know—and there was no will, nor thought, nor straining resistance any more, for Lamberto Lamberti held her in his arms, her, Cecilia Palladio, her very living self, and his lips were upon hers, and she loved him beyond death, or life, or fear, or torment. Surely she was dying then, for the darkness was whirling with her, spinning itself into myriads of circles of fiery stars, tearing her over the brink of the world to eternity beyond.

One second more and it must have ended so. Instead, she was leaning back in her chair, between the moonlight and the steadily burning candles, in her own room, alone. From head to foot she trembled, and now and then drew a short and gasping breath. Her parted lips were moist and very cold. She touched them, and they felt like flowers at night, wet with dew. She pushed the hair from her forehead, and her brow was strangely damp.

She sprang to her feet with a cry of terror, and stared at the door, for she was quite sure that she had heard it close softly. It was a heavy door, that turned noiselessly on its hinges and fitted perfectly, and she knew the soft click of the well-made French lock when the spring quietly pushed the bevelled latch-bolt into the socket. In an instant she had crossed the room and had turned the handle to draw it in. But the door was locked, beyond all doubt—she had turned the key before she had sat down in the chair. She felt intensely cold, and an icy wave seemed to lift her hair from her forehead. Her hand instinctively found the white button, close beside the door-frame, which controlled all the electric lamps, and pushed it in, and the room was flooded with light. She must have imagined that she had heard the sound that had frightened her.

Half dazed, she moved slowly to the windows, and closed the inner shutters, one by one, shutting out the cold moonlight, then stood by the chair a moment, looked at it, and glanced in the direction whence the vision had come to her out of the shadow.

She did not know how it happened, but presently she was lying on her bed, her face buried in the pillows, and she was tearing her heart out in a tearless storm of shame and self-contempt.

What right had that man whom she had so often seen in her dreams to be alive in the real world, walking among other men, recognising her, as she had felt that he did that very afternoon? What right had he to come to her again in the vision and to change it all, to take her in his violent arms and kiss her on the mouth, and burn the mark of shame into her soul, and fill her with a pleasure more horrible than any pain? Was this the end of all her girlish meditation, of the Vestal's longing for higher things, of the mystic's perfect way? A man's brutal kiss not even resisted? Was that all? It could not have been worse if on that same day she had been alone with him in the garden, instead of with Guido d'Este, and if he had suddenly put his arms round her, and if she had not even turned her face from his.

It was only a dream. Yes, to-morrow she would awake, if she slept at all, and the sunshine would be streaming in where the moonlight had shone, and it would only be a dream, past and to be forgotten. Perhaps. But what were dreams, then? She had not been asleep, she was quite sure. There was not even that poor excuse. The man's phantasm had come to her awake.

And Lamberto Lamberti was nothing to her. Beyond the startling recognition of a face long familiar, but never seen among the living, he was to her a man she had met but once, and did not wish to meet again. She had been aware of his presence near her at the Princess's, and when he had gone away she had looked at him once more with a sort of wonder; but she had felt nothing else, she had not touched his hand, the thought that he would ever dare to seize her roughly in his arms brought burning blushes to her cheek and outraged all her maiden senses. She had never seen any man whom she could suffer to touch her; her whole nature revolted at the thought. Yet, just now, there had been neither revolt nor resistance; she felt that she had been herself, awake, alive, and consenting to an unknown but frightfully real contamination, from which her soul could never again be wholly clean.

The storm subsided, and sullen waves of self-contempt swelled and sank, as if to overwhelm her drowning soul. She understood at last the ascetic's wrath against the mortal body and his irresistible craving for bodily pain.

CHAPTER IV

Very early in the morning Cecilia fell into a dreamless sleep at last, and awoke, unrefreshed, after nine o'clock. She felt very tired and listless as she opened the window a little and let in the light and air, with the sounds of the busy thoroughfare below. The weather was suddenly much warmer, and her head was heavy.

It had all been a dream, no doubt, and was gone where dreams go; but it had been like a fight, out of which she had come alive by a miracle, bruised and wounded, and offended in her whole being. Never again would she sit alone at night and look for her image in the shadow, since such things could come of playing with visions; and she trusted that she might never again set eyes upon Lamberto Lamberti. She was alone, but at the thought of meeting him she blushed and bit her lip angrily. How was it possible that he should know what she had dreamt? For years, in that dream of the Vestal, a being had played a part, a being too like him in face to be another man, but who had loved her as a goddess, and whom she had loved for his matchless bravery and his glorious strength over himself. It was a long story, that had gradually grown clear in every detail, that had gone far beyond death to a spiritual life in a place of light, though it had always ended in something vaguely fearful that brought her back to the world, and to her present living self, to begin again. She could not go over it now, but she was conscious, and to her shame, that the spell of perfect happiness had always been broken at last by the taint of earthly longing and regret that crept up stealthily from the world below, an evil mist, laden with poison and fever and mortality.

That change had been undefined, though it had been horrible and irresistible; it had been evil, but it had not been brutal, and it had thrilled her with the certainty of passion and pain to come, realising neither while dreading and loving both.

She had read the writings of men who believe that by long meditation and practised intention the real self of man or woman can be separated from all that darkens it, though not easily, because it is bound up with fragments, as it were, of the selves of others, with all the inheritances of a hundred generations of good and bad, with sleeping instincts and passions any of which may suddenly spring up and overwhelm the rest. She had also read that the real self, when found at last, might be far better and purer than the mixed self of every day, which each of us knows and counts upon; but that it might also be much worse, much coarser, much more violent, when freed from every other influence, and that coming upon it unawares and unprepared, men had lost their reason altogether beyond recovery.

She asked herself now whether this was what had happened to her, and no answer came; there was only the very weary blank of a great uncertainty, in which anything might be, or in which there might be nothing; and then, there was the vivid burning fear of meeting Lamberto Lamberti face to face. That was by far the strongest and most clearly defined of her sensations.

If the Princess Anatolie could have known what Cecilia felt that morning, she would have been exceedingly well pleased, and Cecilia's own mother would have considered that this was a case in which the powers of evil had been permitted to work for the accomplishment of a good end. Nothing could have distressed the excellent Countess more than that her daughter should accidentally fall in love with Lamberti, who was a younger son in a numerous family, with no prospects beyond those offered by his profession. Nothing could have interfered more directly with the Princess's sensible intentions for her nephew. Perhaps nothing could have caused greater surprise to Lamberti himself. On the other hand, Guido d'Este would have been glad, but not surprised. He rarely was.

In the course of the day he left a card at the Palazzo Massimo for the Countess Fortiguerra, and as he turned away he regretted that he could not ask for her, and see her, and possibly see her daughter also. That was evidently out of the question as yet, according to his social laws, but his regret was real. It was long since any woman's face had left him more than a vague impression of good looks, or dulness, but he had thought a good deal about Cecilia Palladio since he had met her, and he knew that he wished to talk with her again, however much he might resent the idea that he was meant to marry her. She was the first young girl he had ever known who had not bored him with platitudes or made conversation impossible by obstinate silence.

It was true that he had not talked with her much, and at first it had seemed hard to talk at all, but the ice had been broken suddenly, and for a few minutes he had found it easy. As for the chilling coldness of her last words, he could account for that easily enough. Like himself, she had seen that a marriage had been planned for her without her knowledge, and, like him, she had resented the trap. For a while she had forgotten, as he had done, but had remembered suddenly when they were about to part. She had meant to show him plainly that she had not had any voice in the matter, and he liked her the better for it, now that he understood her meaning.

She was like the Psyche, he thought, and it occurred to him that he could buy a cast of the statue. He had always thought it beautiful. He strolled through narrow streets in the late afternoon till he came to the shop of a dealer in casts, of whom he had once bought something, and he went in. The man had what he wanted, and he examined it carefully.

She was not like the Psyche after all, and the crude white plaster shocked his taste for the first time. If the marble original had been in Rome, instead of in Naples, he could have gone to see it. He left the shop disappointed, and walked slowly towards the Farnese palace. The day seemed endless, and there was no particular reason why all days should not seem as long. There was nothing to do; nothing amused him, and nobody asked anything of him. It would be very strange and pleasant to be of use in the world.

He went home and sat down by the open window that looked across the Tiber. The wide room was flooded with the evening light, and warm with much colour that lingered and floated about beautiful objects here and there. It was not a very luxuriously furnished room, but it was not the habitation of an ascetic or puritanical man either. Guido cared more for rare engravings and etchings than for pictures, and a few very fine framed prints stood on the big writing table; there was Dürer's Melancholia, and the Saint Jerome, and the Little White Horse, and the small Saint Anthony, and Rembrandt's Three Trees, all by itself, as the most wonderful etching in the world deserved to be; and here and there, about the room, were a few good engravings by Martin Schöngauer, and by Mantegna, and by Marcantonio Raimondi. The bold, careless, effective drawing of the Italian engravers contrasted strongly with the profoundly conscientious work of Schöngauer and Lucas van Leyden, and revealed at a glance the incomparable mastery of Dürer's dry point and Rembrandt's etching needle, the deep conviction of the German, and the inexhaustible richness of the Dutchman's imagination.

A picture hung over the fireplace, the picture of a woman, at half length and a little smaller than life, holding in exquisite hands a small covered vessel of silver encrusted with gold, and gazing out into the warm light with the gentlest hazel eyes. A veil of olive green covered her head, but the fair hair found its way out, tresses and ringlets, on each side of the face. The woman was perhaps a Magdalen, not like any other Magdalen in all the paintings of the world, and more the great lady of the castle of Magdalon, she of the Golden Legend. When Andrea del Sarto painted that face, he meant something that he never told, and it pleased Guido d'Este to try and guess the secret. As he glanced at the canvas, glowing in the rich light, it struck him that perhaps Cecilia Palladio was more like the woman in the picture than she was like the Psyche. Then he almost laughed, and turned away, for he realised that he was thinking of the girl continually, and saw her face everywhere.

He turned away impatiently, in spite of the smile. He was annoyed by the attraction he felt towards Cecilia, because the thought of marrying an heiress, in order that his aunt might recover money she had literally thrown away, was grossly repulsive; and also, no doubt, because he was not docile, though he was good-natured, and he hated to have anything in his life planned for him by others. He was still less pleased now that he found himself searching for reasons which should justify him in marrying Cecilia in spite of all this. Nothing irritates a man more than his own inborn inconsistency, whereas he enjoys diabolical satisfaction in convicting any woman of the same fault.

After all, said his Inclination, as if coolly arguing the case, if poor men were only to marry poor girls, and rich men rich ones, something unnatural would happen to the distribution of wealth, which was undesirable for the future of society. Of course, a rich man might marry a poor girl if he chose. That was done, and the men who did it got an extraordinary amount of credit for being disinterested, unless they were laughed at for falling in love with a pretty face. If anything could prove the hopeless inequality of woman with man, it would be that! No one thought much the worse of a penniless girl who married for money, whereas a starving dandy who did the same thing immediately became an object of derision.

But then, added the Inclination, with subtlety, the opinions of society were entirely manufactured by women for their own advantage, and that was an excellent reason for not caring what society thought. The all-powerful, impersonal "they," of whom we only know what "they say," what "they wear," and what "they pretend," are feminine and plural; they rule all that region of the world within which women do not work with their hands, and are therefore at full liberty to exercise those gifts of intelligence which it has pleased Providence to bestow upon them so plentifully. They do so to some purpose.

Surely, argued Inclination, it was not very dignified of Guido to care much, and to care beforehand, for the opinions of a pack of women, supposing that he should come to like Cecilia enough to wish to marry her for her own sake. And besides, though he was poor, he was not uncomfortably so. Poverty meant not having horses and carriages, nor a yacht, and living in bachelor's rooms, and not giving dinner parties, and not playing cards, and not giving every woman whatever she fancied, if it happened to be a pearl or a pigeon's blood ruby. That was poverty, of course, but it was relative.

If his aunt did not drive him to blow out his brains in a fit of impatience, there was no reason why Guido should not go on living, as he lived now, to the far end of a long and sufficiently well-fed life. And if he married Cecilia and her fortune, it would certainly not be because he wished to give other women rubies and pearls, nor for the sake of keeping a couple of hunters, two or three carriages, and a coach; still less, because he could ever wish to lose money again at baccara, or poker, or bridge. He had done all those things, and they had not amused him long. If he ever married Cecilia, it would be because he fell in love with her, which, thank goodness, had not happened yet. Inclination was quite sure of that, but was willing to admit the possibility in the future, merely for the sake of argument.

Before it was time to dress for dinner that evening, Guido received a long letter from his aunt, written with her own hand, which probably meant that Monsieur Leroy knew little or nothing of its contents. Guido glanced at the pages, one after another, and saw that the whole letter was in the writer's most affectionate manner. Then he read it carefully. It had been so kind of him to be civil to her friends on the previous day, said the Princess. He reminded her of his poor father, her dear brother, who, in all his many misfortunes, had never once lost his beautiful affability of temper and unfailing courtesy to every one about him.

This was very pretty, but Guido had heard that his father's beautiful affability had sometimes been ruffled so far as to allow a certain harmless violence, such as hurling a light chair at the head of a faithful courtier and friend who gave him advice that was too good to be taken, or summarily boxing the ears of his son and heir when the latter was already over thirty years old.

Guido sometimes wondered why he had not inherited some of that very unroyal temper, which must have been such a thoroughly satisfactory relief to the ex-king's feelings. He never felt the least desire to dance with rage and throw the furniture about the room.

His aunt's letter was evidently meant to please him and flatter his vanity, and she did not once refer to matters of business. She asked his opinion about a new novel he had not read yet, and had he thought of leaving a card on the Countess Fortiguerra? She lived in the Palazzo Massimo. What a strange girl the daughter was, to be sure! so very unlike other girls that it was almost disquieting to talk with her. Of course there was nothing real behind all that superficial talk about lectures at the Sorbonne, and Nietzsche, and all that. Everybody pretended to have read Nietzsche nowadays, and after all the girl might be quite sensible. One could not help wondering what she would make of her life, with her handsome fortune, and her odd ideas, and no one to look after her except that dear, gentle, sweet-tempered, foolish mother, who was in perpetual adoration before her! It would be a brave man who would marry such a girl, the Princess wrote, in spite of her money; but there was this to be said, he would not have any trouble with his mother-in-law.

Subtle, very subtle of the Princess, who left the subject there and ended her letter by asking a favour of Guido. It was indeed only for the sake of asking it, she explained, that she was writing to him at all. Would he allow a great friend of hers to see his Andrea del Sarto? It was the celebrated art critic, Doctor Baumgarten, of whom he had heard. Leroy would bring him the next morning about ten o'clock, if Guido had no objection. He need not answer; he must not take any trouble about the matter. If he had an engagement at ten, perhaps he would leave orders that the Doctor should be allowed to see the picture.

Guido did not think at once of any good reason for refusing such a request. He was very fond of his Andrea del Sarto; indeed, he liked it much better than a small Raphael of undoubted authenticity which was hung in another part of the room. The German critic was quite welcome to see both, and perhaps knew something about prints which might be worth learning. He was probably writing a book. Germans were always writing books. Guido wrote a line to thank his aunt for her letter, and to say that her friend would be welcome at the appointed hour.

He was sealing the note when the door opened and Lamberto Lamberti came in.

"Will you come and dine with me?" he asked, standing still before the writing table.

"Let us dine here," answered Guido, without looking up, and examining the little seal he had made on the envelope. "I daresay there is something to eat." He held out the note to his servant, who stood in the open doorway. "Send this at once," he said.

"Yes," said Lamberti, answering the invitation. "I do not care whether there is anything to eat or not, and it is always quiet here."

"What is the matter?" asked Guido, looking at him attentively for the first time since he had entered. "Yes," he added to his man, "Signor Lamberti will dine with me."

The servant disappeared and shut the door. Guido repeated his question, but Lamberti only shook his head carelessly and relit his half-smoked cigar. Guido watched him. He was less red than usual, and his eyes glittered in the light of the wax match. His voice had sounded sharp and metallic, as Guido had never heard it before.

When two men are intimate friends and really trust each other they do not overwhelm one another with questions. Each knows that each will speak when he is ready, or needs help or sympathy.

"I have just been answering a very balmy letter from my aunt," Guido said, rising from the table. "Sweeter than honey in the honeycomb! Read it. It has a distinctly literary and biographical turn. The allusion to my father's gentle disposition is touching."

Lamberti looked through the letter carelessly, dropped it on the table, and sucked hard at his cigar.

"What did you expect?" he asked, between two puffs. "For the present you are the apple of her eye. She will handle you as tenderly as a new-laid egg, until she gets what she wants!"

Lamberti's similes lacked sequence, but not character.

"The Romans," observed Guido, "began with the egg and ended with the apple. I have an idea that we are going to do the same thing at dinner, and that there will be nothing between. But we can smoke between the courses."

"Yes," answered Lamberti, who had not heard a word. "I daresay."

Guido looked at him again, rather furtively. Lamberti never drank and had iron nerves, but he was visibly disturbed. He was what people vaguely call "not quite himself."

Guido went to the door of his bedroom.

"Where are you going?" asked Lamberti, sharply.

"I am going to wash my hands before dinner," Guido answered with a smile. "Do you want to wash yours?"

"No, thank you. I have just dressed."

He turned his back and went to the open window as Guido left the room. In a few seconds his cigar had gone out again, and he was leaning on the sill with both hands, staring at the twilight sky in the west. The colours had all faded away to the almost neutral tint of straw-tempered steel.

The outline of the Janiculum stood out sharp and black in an uneven line. Below, there were the scattered lights of Trastevere, the flowing river, and the silence of the deserted Via Giulia. Lamberti looked steadily out, biting his extinguished cigar, and his features contracted as if he were in pain.

He had come to his friend instinctively, as his friend would have come to him, meaning to tell him what had happened. But he hesitated. Besides, it might all have been only his imagination; in part it could have been nothing else, and the rest was a mere coincidence. But he had never been an imaginative man, and it was strange that he should be so much affected by a mere illusion.

He started and turned suddenly, sure that some one was close behind him. But there was no one, and a moment later Guido came back. Anxious not to annoy his friend by anything like curiosity, he made a pretence of setting his writing table in order, turned one of the lamps down a little—he hated electric light—and then looked at the picture over the fireplace.

"Did you ever hear of that Baumgarten, the German art critic?" he asked, without turning round.

"Baumgarten—let me see! I fancy I have seen the name to-day." Lamberti tried to concentrate his attention.

"You just read it in my aunt's letter," Guido answered. "You remember—she asks if he may come to-morrow. I wonder why."

"To value your property, of course," replied Lamberti, roughly.

"Do you think so?" Guido did not seem at all surprised. "I daresay. She is quite capable of it. She is welcome to everything I possess if she will only leave me in peace. But just now, when she has evidently made up her mind to marry me to this new heiress, it does not seem likely that she would take trouble to find out what my pictures are worth, does it?"

"It all depends on what she thinks of the chances that you will marry or not."

"What do you think of them, yourself?" asked Guido, idly.

He was glad of anything to talk about while Lamberti was in his present mood.

"What a question!" exclaimed the latter. "How should I know whether you are going to fall in love with the girl or not?"

"I am half afraid I am," said Guido, thoughtfully.

His man announced dinner, and the two friends crossed the hall to the little dining room, and sat down under the soft light of the old-fashioned olive-oil lamp that hung from the ceiling. Everything on the table was old, worn, and spotless. The silver was all of the style of the first Empire, with an interlaced monogram surmounted by a royal crown. The same device was painted in gold in the middle of the plain white plates, which were more or less chipped at the edges. The glasses and decanters were of that heavy cut glass, ornamented with gold lines, which used to be made in Venice in the eighteenth century. Some of them were chipped, too, like the plates. It had never occurred to Guido to put the whole service away as a somewhat valuable collection, though he sometimes thought that it was growing shabby. But he liked the old things which had come to him from the ex-king, part of the furniture of a small shooting box that had been left to him, and which he had sold to an Austrian Archduke.

Lamberti took a little soup and swallowed half a glass of white wine.

"I had an odd dream last night," he said, "and I have had a little adventure to-day. I will tell you by-and-by."

"Just as you like," Guido answered. "I hope the adventure was not an accident—you look as if you had been badly shaken."

"Yes. I did not know that I could be so nervous. You see, I do not often dream. I generally go to sleep when I lay my head upon the pillow and wake when I have slept seven hours. At sea, I always have to be called when it is my watch. Yes, I have solid nerves. But last night—"

He stopped, as the man entered, bringing a dish.

"Well?" enquired Guido, who did not suppose that Lamberti could have any reason for not telling his dream in the presence of the servant.

Lamberti hesitated a moment, and helped himself before he answered.

"Do you believe in dreams?" he asked.

"What do you mean? Do I believe that dreams come true? No. When they do, it is a coincidence."

"Yes. I suppose so. But this is rather more than a coincidence. I do not understand it at all. After all, I am a perfectly healthy man. It never occurred to you that my mind might be unbalanced, did it?"

Guido looked at the rugged Roman head, the muscular throat, the broad shoulders.

"No," he answered. "It certainly never occurred to me."

"Nor to me either," said Lamberti, and he ate slowly and thoughtfully.

"My friend," observed Guido, "you are just a little enigmatical this evening."

"Not at all, not at all! I tell you that my nerves are good. You know something about archæology, do you not?"

The apparently irrelevant question came after a short pause.

"Not much," Guido answered, supposing that Lamberti wished to change the subject on account of the servant. "What do you want to know?"

"Nothing," said Lamberti. "The question is, whether what I dreamt last night was all imagination or whether it was a memory of something I once knew and had forgotten."

"What did you dream?" Guido sipped his wine and leaned back to listen, hoping that his friend was going to speak out at last.

"Was the temple of Vesta in the Forum?" enquired Lamberti.

"Certainly."

"But why did they always say that it was the round one in front of Santa Maria in Cosmedin? I have an old bronze inkstand that is a model of it. My mother used to tell me it was the temple of Vesta."

"People thought it was—thirty years ago. There is nothing left of the temple but the round mass of masonry on which it stood. It is between the Fountain of Juturna and the house of the Vestals. I have Signor Boni's plans of it. Should you like to see them?"

"Yes—presently," answered Lamberti, with more eagerness than Guido had expected. "Is there anything like a reconstruction of the temple or of the house—a picture of one, I mean?"

"I think so," said Guido. "I am sure there is Baldassare Peruzzi's sketch of the temple, as it was in his day."

"I dreamt that I saw it last night, the temple and the house, and all the Forum besides, and not in ruins either, but just as everything was in old times. Could the Vestals' house have had an upper story? Is that possible?"

"The archæologists are sure that it had," answered Guido, becoming more interested. "Do you mean to say that you dreamt you saw it with an upper story?"

"Yes. And the temple was something like the one they used to call Vesta's, only it was more ornamented, and the columns seemed very near together. The round wall, just within the columns, was decorated with curious designs in low relief—something like a wheel, and scallops, and curved lines. It is hard to describe, but I can see it all now."

Guido rose from his seat quickly.

"I will get the number that has the drawing in it," he said, explaining.

During the few moments that passed while he was out of the room Lamberti sat staring at his empty place as fixedly as he had stared at the dark line of the Janiculum a few minutes earlier. The man-servant, who had been with him at sea, watched him with a sort of grave sympathy that is peculiarly Italian. Then, as if an idea of great value had struck him, he changed Lamberti's plate, poured some red wine into the tumbler, and filled it up with water. Then he retired and watched to see whether his old master would drink. But Lamberti did not move.

"Here it is," said Guido, entering the room with a large yellow-covered pamphlet open in his hands. "Was it like this?"

As he asked the question he laid the pamphlet on the clean plate before his friend. The pages were opened at Baldassare Peruzzi's rough pen-and-ink sketch of the temple of Vesta; and as Lamberti looked at it, his lids slowly contracted, and his features took an expression of mingled curiosity and interest.

"The man who drew that had seen what I saw," he said at last. "Did he draw it from some description?"

"He drew it on the spot," answered Guido. "The temple was standing then. But as for your dream, it is quite possible that you may have seen this same drawing in a shop window at Spithoever's or Loescher's, for instance, without noticing it, and that the picture seemed quite new to you when you dreamt it. That is a simple explanation."

"Very," said Lamberti. "But I saw the whole Forum."

"There are big engravings of imaginary reconstructions of the Forum, in the booksellers' windows."

"With the people walking about? The two young priests standing in the morning sun on the steps of the temple of Castor and Pollux? The dirty market woman trudging past the corner of the Vestals' house with a basket of vegetables on her head? The door slave sweeping the threshold of the Regia with a green broom?"

"I thought you knew nothing about the Forum," said Guido, curiously. "How do you come to know of the Regia?"

"Did I say Regia? I daresay—the name came to my lips."

"Somebody has hypnotised you," said Guido. "You are repeating things you have heard in your sleep."

"No. I am describing things I saw in my sleep. Am I the sort of man who is easily hypnotised? I have let men try it once or twice. We were all interested in hypnotism on my last ship, and the surgeon made some curious experiments with a lad who went to sleep easily. But last night I was at home, alone, in my own room, in bed, and I dreamt."

Guido shrugged his shoulders a little indifferently.

"There must be some explanation," he said. "What else did you dream?"

Lamberti's lids drooped as if he were concentrating his attention on the remembered vision.

"I dreamt," he said, "that I saw a veiled woman in white come out of the temple door straight into the sunlight, and though I could not see the face, I knew who she was. She went down the steps and then up the others to the house of the Vestals, and entered in without looking back. I followed her. The door was open, and there was no one to stop me."

"That is very improbable," observed Guido. "There must have always been a slave at the door."

"I went in," continued Lamberti without heeding the interruption, "and she was standing beside one of the pillars, a little way from the door. She had one hand on the column, and she was facing the sun; her veil was thrown back and the light shone through her hair. I came nearer, very softly. She knew that I was there and was not afraid. When I was close to her she turned her face to mine. Then I took her in my arms and kissed her, and she did not resist."

Guido smiled gravely.

"And she turned out to be some one you know in real life, I suppose," he said.

"Yes," answered Lamberti. "Some one I know—slightly."

"Beautiful, of course. Fair or dark?"

"You need not try to guess," Lamberti said. "I shall not tell you. My head went round, and I woke."

"Very well. But is it this absurd dream that has made you so nervous?"

"No. Something happened to me to-day."

Lamberti ate a few mouthfuls in silence, before he went on.

"I daresay I might have invented some explanation of the dream," he said at last. "But it only made me want to see the place. I never cared for those things, you know. I had never gone down into the Forum in my life—why should I? I went there this morning."

"And you could not find anything of what you had seen, of course."

"I took one of those guides who hang about the entrance waiting for foreigners. He showed me where the temple had been, and the house, and the temple of Castor and Pollux. I did not believe him implicitly, but the ruins were in the right places. Then I walked up a bridge of boards to the house of the Vestals, and went in."

"But there was no lady."

"On the contrary," said Lamberti, and his eyes glittered oddly, "the lady was there."

"The same one whom you had seen in your dream?"

"The same. She was standing facing the sun, for it was still early, and one of her hands was resting against the brick pillar, just as it had rested against the column."

"That is certainly very extraordinary," said Guido, his tone changing. Then he seemed about to speak again, but checked himself.

Lamberti rested his elbows on the table and his chin on his folded hands, and looked into his friend's eyes in silence. His own face had grown perceptibly paler in the last few minutes.

"Guido," he said, after what seemed a long pause, "you were going to ask what happened next. I do not know what you thought, nor what stopped you, for between you and me there is no such thing as indiscretion, and, besides, you will never know who the lady was."

"I do not wish to guess. Do not say anything that could help me."

"Of course not. Any woman you know might have taken it into her head to go to the Forum this morning."

"Certainly."

"This is what happened. I stood perfectly still in surprise. She may have heard my footstep or not; she knew some one was behind her. Then she slowly turned her head till we could see each other's faces."

He paused again, and passed one hand lightly over his eyes.

"Yes," said Guido, "I suppose I can guess what is coming."

"No!" Lamberti cried, in such a tone that the other started. "You cannot guess. We looked at each other. It seemed a very long time—two or three minutes at least—as if we were both paralysed. Though we recognised each other perfectly well, we could neither of us speak. Then it seemed to me that something I could not resist was drawing me towards her, but I am sure I did not really move the hundredth part of a step. I shall never forget the look in her face."

Another pause, not long, but strangely breathless.

"I have seen men badly frightened in battle," Lamberti went on. "The cheeks get hollow all at once, the eyes are wide open, with black rings round them, the face turns a greenish grey, and the sweat runs down the forehead into the eyebrows. Men totter with fear, too, as if their joints were unstrung. But I never saw a woman really terrified before. There was a sort of awful tension of all her features, as though they were suddenly made brittle, like beautiful glass, and were going to shiver into fragments. And her eyes had no visible pupils—her lips turned violet. I remember every detail. Then, without warning, she shrieked and staggered backwards; and she turned as I moved to catch her, and she ran like a deer, straight up the court, past those basins they have excavated, and up two or three steps, to the dark rooms at the other end."

"And what did you do?" asked Guido, wondering.

"My dear fellow, I turned and went back as fast as I could, without exactly running, and I found the guide looking for me below the temple, for he had not seen me go into the Vestals' house. What else was there to be done?"

"Nothing, I suppose. You could not pursue a lady who shrieked with fear and ran away from you. What a strange story! You say you only know her slightly."

"Literally, very slightly," answered Lamberti.

He had become fluent, telling his story almost excitedly. He now relapsed into his former mood, and stared at the pamphlet before him a moment, before shutting it and putting it away from him.

"It is like all those things—perfectly unaccountable, except on a theory of coincidence," said Guido, at last. "Will you have any cheese?"

Lamberti roused himself and saw the servant at his elbow.

"No, thank you. I forgot one thing. Just as I awoke from that dream last night, I heard the door of my room softly closed."

"What has that to do with the matter?" enquired Guido, carelessly.

"Nothing, except that the door was locked. I always lock my door. I first fell into the habit when I was travelling, for I sleep so soundly that in a hotel any one might come in and steal my things. I should never wake. So I turn the key before going to bed."

"You may have forgotten to do it last night," suggested Guido.

"No. I got up at once, and the key was turned. No one could have come in."

"A mouse, then," said Guido, rather contemptuously.

CHAPTER V

Cecilia Palladio was very much ashamed of having uttered a cry of terror at the sight of Lamberti, and still more of having run away from him like a frightened child. To him it seemed as if she had really shrieked with fear, whereas she fancied that she had scarcely found voice enough to utter an incoherent exclamation. The truth lay somewhere between the two impressions, but Cecilia now felt that she could easily have accounted for being startled into crying out, but that it would always be impossible to explain her flight. She had run the whole length of the Court, which must be fifty yards long, before realising what she was doing, and had not paused for breath till she was out of his sight and within the second of the three rooms on the left. There were no gates to the rooms then, as there are now, and she could not have given any reason for her entering the second instead of the first, which was the nearest. The choice was instinctive.

She certainly had not gone there to join the elderly woman servant who had come to the Forum with her. That excellent and obedient person was waiting where Cecilia had made her sit down, not far from the entrance to the Forum, and would not move till her mistress returned. The young girl hated to be followed about and protected at every step, especially by a servant, who could have no real understanding of what she saw.

"I shall only be seen by foreigners and Cook's Tourists," she had said, "and they do not count as human beings at all!"

Therefore the middle-aged Petersen, who was a German, and therefore a species of foreigner herself, had meekly sat down upon the comparatively comfortable stone which Cecilia had selected for her, and which was one of the steps of the Julian Basilica. She was called Frau Petersen, Mrs. Petersen, or Madame Petersen, according to circumstances, by the servants of different nationalities who were successively in the employment of the Countess Fortiguerra, for she was a superior woman and the widow of a paymaster in the Bavarian army, and so eminently respectable and well educated that she had more than once been taken for Cecilia's governess.

Petersen was excessively near-sighted, but her nose was not adapted by its nature and position for wearing eyeglasses; for it was not only a flat nose without anything like a prominent bridge to it, but it was placed uncommonly low in her face, so that a pair of eyeglasses pinched upon it would have found themselves in the region of Petersen's cheek-bones. Even when she wore spectacles, they were always slipping down, which was a great nuisance; so she resigned herself to seeing less than other people, except when something interested her enough to make the discomfort of glasses worth enduring.

This sufficiently explains why she noticed nothing unusual in Cecilia's looks when the latter came back to her, pale and disturbed; and she had not heard her mistress's faint cry, the distance being too great for that, not to mention the fact that the huge ruins intercepted the sound. Cecilia was glad of that, as she drove home with Petersen.

"Signor Lamberti has called," said the Countess Fortiguerra the next day at luncheon. "I see by his card that he is in the Navy. You know he is one of the Marchese Lamberti's sons. Shall we ask him to dinner?"

"Did you like him?" enquired Cecilia, evasively.

"He is not very good-looking," observed the Countess, whose judgment of unknown people always began with their appearance, and often penetrated no farther. "But he may be intelligent, for all that," she added, as a concession.

"Yes," said Cecilia, thoughtfully, "perhaps."

"I think we might ask him to dinner, then," answered the Countess, as if she had given an excellent reason for doing so.

"Is it not rather early, considering that we have only met him once?" Cecilia ventured to ask.

"I used to know his mother very well, though she was older than I. It is pleasant to find that he is so intimate with Signor d'Este. We might ask them together."

"After the garden party," suggested Cecilia. "Of course, as you and the Marchesa were great friends, that is a reason for asking the other, but Signor d'Este—really! It would positively be throwing me at his head, mother!"

"He expects it, my dear," answered the Countess, with more precision than tact. "I mean," she added hastily, "I mean, that is, I did not mean—"

Cecilia laughed.

"Oh yes, you did, mother! You meant exactly that, you know. You and that dreadful old Princess have made up your minds that I am to marry him, and nothing else matters, does it?"

"Well," said the Countess, without any perceptible hesitation, "I cannot help hoping that you will consent, for I should like the match very much."

She knew that it was always better to be quite frank with her daughter; and even if she had thought otherwise, she could never have succeeded in being diplomatic with her. While her second husband had been alive, her position as an ambassadress had obliged her to be tactful in the world, and even occasionally to say things which she had some difficulty in believing, being a very simple soul; but with Cecilia she was quite unable to conceal her thoughts for five minutes. If the girl loved her mother, and she really did, it was largely because her mother was so perfectly truthful. Cynical people called her helplessly honest, and said that her veracity would have amounted to a disease of the mind if she had possessed any; but that since she did not, it was probably a form of degeneration, because all perfectly healthy human beings lied naturally. David had said in his heart that all men were liars, and his experience of men, and of women, too, was worth considering.

"Yes," Cecilia said, after a thoughtful pause, "I know that you wish me to marry Signor d'Este, and I have not refused to think of it. But I have not promised anything, either, and I do not like to feel that he expects me to be thrust upon him at every turn, till he is obliged to offer himself as the only way of escaping the persecution."

"I wish you would not express it in that way!"

The Countess sighed and looked at her daughter with a sort of half-comical and loving hopelessness in her eyes—as a faithful dog might look at his master who, seeming to be hungry, would refuse to steal food that was within reach. The dog would try to lead the man to the bread, the man would gently resist; each would be obeying the dictation of his own conscience—the man would know that he could never explain his moral position to the dog, and the dog would feel that he could never understand the man. Yet the affection between the two would not be in the least diminished.

On the next evening Cecilia found herself next to Guido d'Este at dinner. Though she was not supposed to make her formal appearance in society before the garden party, the Countess's many old friends, some of whom had more or less impecunious sons, were anxious to welcome her to Rome, and asked her to small dinners with her mother. Guido had arrived late, and had not been able to speak to her till he was told by their host that he was to take her in. It was quite natural that he should, for, in spite of his birth, he was only plain Signor d'Este, and was not entitled to any sort of precedence in a society which is, if anything, overcareful in such matters.

Neither spoke as they walked through the rooms, near the end of the small procession. Guido glanced at the young girl, who knew that he did, but paid no attention. He thought her rather pale, and there was no light in her eyes. Her hand lay like gossamer on his arm, so lightly that he could not feel it; but he was aware of her perfectly graceful motion as she walked.

"I suppose this was predestined," he said, as soon as the rest of the guests were talking.

She glanced at him quickly now, her head bent rather low, her eyebrows arching higher than usual. He was not sure whether the little irregularity of her upper lip was accentuated by amusement, or by a touch of scorn.

"Is it?" she asked. "Do you happen to know that it was arranged?"

It was amusement, then, and not scorn. They understood each other, and the ice was in no need of being broken again.

"No," Guido answered with a smile. Then his voice grew suddenly low and earnest. "Will you please believe that if I had been told beforehand that I was asked in order to sit next to you, I would not have come?"

Cecilia laughed lightly.

"I believe you, and I understand," she answered. "But how it sounds! If you had known that you were to sit next to me, nothing would have induced you to come!"

From her place next the master of the house, the Countess Fortiguerra looked at them, and was pleased to see that they were already on good terms.

"Thank you," Cecilia added in a quiet voice, and gravely. "Besides," she continued, "there is no reason, in the world why we should not be good friends, is there?"

She looked full at him now, without a smile, and he realised for the first time how very young she was. A married woman with an instinct for flirtation might have made the speech, but a girl older than Cecilia would have known that it might be misunderstood. Guido answered her look with one in which doubt did not keep the upper hand more than a single second.

"There is no reason whatever why we should not be the best of friends," he answered, in a tone as low as her own. "Perhaps I may be of service to you. I hope so. Besides, I am made for friendship!"

He laughed rather carelessly as he spoke the last words, and glanced round the table to see whether anybody was watching him. He met the Countess Fortiguerra's approving glance.

"Why do you laugh at friendship?" asked Cecilia, not quite pleased.

"I do not laugh at friendship at all," Guido answered. "I laugh in order that people may see me and hear me. This is the first service I can render you, to be natural and unconcerned, as I generally am. If I behaved in any unusual way—if I were too grave, or too much interested—you understand!"

"Yes. You are thoughtful. Thank you."

There was a little pause, during which a luxuriant lady in green, who sat on Guido's other side, determined to attract his attention, and spoke to him; but before he could answer, some one opposite asked her a question about dress, which was intensely interesting to her, because she dressed abominably. She promptly fell into the snare which had been set for her with the evil intention of leading her on to talk foolishly. She followed at once, and Guido was free again.

"Now that we are friends," he said to Cecilia, "may I ask you a friendly question?"

"Ask me anything you like," she answered, and her innocent eyes promised him the truth.

"Were you told anything, before we met at my aunt's the other day?"

"Not a word! And you?"

"Nothing," he replied. "I remember that on that very afternoon—" he stopped short.

"What?"

"You may not like what I was going to say."

"I shall, if it is true, and if you have a good reason for saying it."

"Lamberti and I were together, talking, and I said that nothing would ever induce me to marry an heiress, unless it were to save my father or mother from ruin. As that can never happen, all heiresses are perfectly safe from me! Do you mind my having said that?"

"No. I am sure you were in earnest."

A shadow had crossed her face at the mention of Lamberti's name.

"You do not like my friend," he said, and as he spoke, the shadow came again and deepened.

"How can I like him or dislike him? I hardly know him."

She felt very uncomfortable, for it would have been quite natural that Lamberti should have spoken to Guido of her strange behaviour in the Forum. Guido answered that one often liked or disliked people at first sight.

"I think that you and I liked each other as soon as we met," he concluded.

"Yes," Cecilia answered, after a little thought. "I am sure we did. Tell me, what makes you think that I dislike your friend? I should be very sorry if he thought I did."

"When I first spoke of him a few moments ago, your expression changed, and when I referred to him again, you frowned."

"Is that all? Are you sure that is the only reason for your opinion?"

Guido laughed a little.

"What other reason could I have?" he asked. "Do not take it so seriously!"

"He might have told you that he himself had the impression—"

"He has hardly mentioned your name since we both met you," Guido answered.

It was a relief to know that Lamberti had not spoken of having met her unexpectedly, and of her cry, and of her flight. Yet somehow she had already been sure that he had kept the matter to himself. As a matter of fact, Guido had never thought of her, even in the most passing way, as the possible heroine of the adventure in the Forum. The story had interested him, but the personality of the lady did not; and, moreover, from the way in which Lamberti had spoken, Guido had very naturally supposed her to be a married woman, for it would not have occurred to him that a young girl could be strolling among the ruins quite alone.

Cecilia felt relieved, and yet, at the same time, she felt a little girlish disappointment at the thought that Lamberti had hardly ever spoken of her to his most intimate friend, for she was quite sure that Guido told her the exact truth. She was angry with herself for being disappointed, too. The man's face had haunted her so long in half-waking dreams; or at least, a face exactly like his, which, the last time, had turned into his without doubt. Yet she had evidently made no impression upon him, until she had made a very bad one, the other day. She wondered whether he thought she was a little mad. She was afraid of meeting him wherever she went, and yet she now wished he were at the table, in order that she might prove to him that she was not only sane, but very clever. She knew that she wished it, and for a few moments she did not hear what Guido was saying, but gazed absently at the flowers on the table, unconsciously hoping that she might see them turn into the face she feared; but that did not happen.

Guido talked on, till he saw that she was not listening, and then he was silent, and only glanced at her from time to time while he heard in his ears the cackling of the vivid lady in green. There was going to be a change in the destinies of womankind, and everybody was to be perfectly frightful for ever afterwards. To be plain, the sleeves "they" were wearing now were to be altogether given up. "They" had begun to wear the new ones already in Paris. Réjane had worn them in her new piece, and of course that meant an imminent and universal change. And as for the way the skirts were to be made, it was positively indecent. Réjane was far too much of a lady to wear one, of course, but one could see what was coming. Here some one observed that coming events cast their shadows before.

"Not at all, not at all!" cried the lady in green. "I mean behind."

"How long shall you stay in Rome?" Guido asked, to see whether Cecilia would hear him now.

"Always," she answered. "For the rest of my life."

"I am glad of that. But I meant to ask how late you intended to stay this year?"

"I should like to spend the summer here."

"It is the pleasantest time," Guido said.

"Is it? Or are you only saying that in order to agree with me? You need not, you know. I like people who have their own opinions, and are full of prejudices, and try to force them upon everybody, whether they are good for every one or not!"

"I am afraid I shall not please you, then. I have no prejudices to speak of, and my opinions are worth so little that I never hesitate to change them."

"But you do not look at all feeble-minded," said Cecilia, innocently studying his face.

"Thank you!" Guido laughed. "You are adorable!" he added rather flippantly.

"Is that your opinion?" asked the young girl, smiling, too, as if she were pleased.

"Yes. That is my firm opinion. Do you object to it?"

"Oh no!" Cecilia answered, still smiling sweetly. "You have just told me that your opinions are worth so little that you never hesitate to change them. So why in the world should I object to any of them?"

"Exactly," said Guido, unmoved. "Why should you? Especially as this particular one gives me so much pleasure while it lasts."

"It will not last long, I daresay. Do you know that you are not at all dull?"

"No one could be in your company."

"That is the first dull thing you have said this evening," Cecilia answered, to see what he would say.

"Shall it be the last?" he asked.

"Yes, please."

There was a little wilful command in the tone that Guido liked. He felt her presence in a way he did not remember to have felt that of any woman, and in the atmosphere of her own in which she seemed to live he breathed as one does in some very high places, less easily, perhaps, but with conscious pleasure in drawing breath. He could not have described his sensations in those first meetings with her, and he could have analysed them less. One might as well seek the form and perfume of the flower in the first tender shoot that thrusts up its joy of living out of the mystery of the dull brown earth. Yet he knew well enough that something was beginning to grow in him which had not begun, and grown, and perished before.

Many times he had talked with women famous for their beauty, or for their charm, or for their wit, and he himself had said clever things which he had remembered with a little vanity or had forgotten with regret, and had turned compliments in many manners, guessing at the taste of her who sat beside him, wishing to please her, and wishing even more to find some general key to women's thought, some universal explanation of their ways, some logical solution of their seemingly inconsequent actions. His mind was of the sort that is satisfied by suspended judgment, that dreads the chillingly triumphant phrase of reason, "which was to be proved," as much as the despairing tone of a reduction to the impossible. He loved problems that could not be solved easily, if at all, because he could think of them continually in a hundred new and different ways. He hated equally a final affirmation past appeal, and an ultimate negation which might make his thoughts ridiculous in his own eyes. A quiet suspense was his natural state of equilibrium. Anything might be, or might not be, and decision was hateful; it was delicious to float on the calm waters of meditative indifference, between the giant rocks, hope and despair, in the straits that lead the sea of life to the ocean of eternity.

He knew that he was the end of a race that had reigned and could never reign again. It was better that the end should be a question than a hope deceived, or a cry of impotent hatred uttered against Something which might not exist after all. If he had a philosophy it was that, and nothing more; and though it was not much, it had helped him to live without much pain and almost always with a certain dreamy, intellectual, wondering pleasure in his own thoughts. Sometimes he was irritated out of that state by the demands and doings of the Princess Anatolie, as on the day when he and his friend had talked in the garden beyond the river; and then he spoke of ending all at a stroke, and almost believed that he might do it; and he envied Lamberti his love of life and action. But such moods soon passed and left him himself again, so that he marvelled how he could ever have been so much moved. It was always the same, in the end, but such as it was the world was not a bad world for him.

Here was something different from all the past, and it had begun without warning, and was growing against his will, because it fed on that with which his will had nothing to do. There is no fatalism like that of the indifferent man who believes in nothing, not even in himself, and who admits nothing to be positive except crime and dishonour. Why should he not fall in love with Cecilia Palladio, since he had previously stated to himself, to her, and to his trusted friend, that nothing could induce him to marry her? It was quite clear from the first that she, on her side, would never fall in love with him. He looked upon that as altogether out of the question, and perhaps with reason. On the other hand, he had not the slightest faith in the lasting nature of anything he might feel, and therefore he was not afraid of consequences, which rarely indeed frighten a man who is doing what he likes. It is more generally the woman that thinks of them, and points them out because "there is still time!" She also heaps her scorn upon the man if he is wise enough to agree with her; but that is a detail, and perhaps it ought not to be mentioned.

As for the fact that he was beginning to be in love, Guido no longer doubted it. The pleasure he felt in saying to Cecilia things of even less than average conversational merit was proof enough that it was not only what he said that interested him. When a man of ordinary assurance wishes to shine in the eyes of a woman, he generally succeeds at least in shining in his own.

Guido was not any more self-conscious than most people, and he was certainly not more diffident of his own gifts, which he could judge impartially because he attached little importance to what they might bring him. But the categorical command to say nothing dull made it quite impossible to say anything witty, and the conversation languished a little and then broke off.

It was past ten o'clock when Guido again found a chance of speaking to Cecilia. He had looked at her more often than he knew, after dinner, and had given rather vague answers to one or two people who had spoken to him. He had moved about the great room idly, looking at the familiar old portraits, and at objects he had known in the same places for years. He had smoked a cigarette, standing with his host, while the latter talked to him about the Etruscan tomb he had just discovered on his place, and he had nodded pleasantly to the sound of the old gentleman's voice without hearing a word. Then he had smoked another cigarette at the opposite end of the room with a group of younger men, who talked of nothing but motor cars; and when they asked his opinion about something, he had said that he had none, and preferred walking, which speech caused such a perceptible chill that he turned away and left the young men to their discussion.

All the while his eyes followed Cecilia's movements, and lingered upon her when she stood still or sat down. In the course of the evening each of the young men who talked about motor cars managed to try his luck at a conversation with her, and all, by way of being original, talked to her about the same thing. As she had just come from Paris, and was rich, it was to be supposed that she, of course, owned a motor car, had passed her examination as an engineer, and spent most of her time in a mask and broad-visored cap scouring Europe at the rate of fifty miles an hour.

"But why do you not get an automobile?" asked each of the young men, as soon as her answer had disappointed him.

"Do you play the violin?" she enquired sweetly of each.

"No," each answered.

"Then why do you not get a violin?"

In this way she confounded the young men, and their heads moved uneasily on the tops of their high collars, until they were able to get away from her.

Guido saw how they left her, with a discomfited expression, and as if they had suddenly acquired the conviction that their clothes did not fit them, for that is generally the first sensation experienced by a very well-dressed young man when he has been made to feel that he is foolish. Guido saw, and understood, and he was worldly wise enough to know that unless Cecilia would show a little more willingness to seem pleased, she would presently be sitting alone on a sofa, waiting for her mother to go home. As soon as this inevitable result followed, he sat down beside her. She turned her face slowly, when he had settled himself, and she looked at him with slightly bent head, a little upwards, from under her lids. The light that fell from a shaded lamp above her marked the sharp curve of arching brows sharply against the warm shadow over the deep-set and widely opened eyes.

For a few seconds Guido returned the steady gaze, before he spoke.

"Are you the Sphinx?" he asked suddenly. "Have you come to life again to ask men your riddle?"

"I ask it of myself," she answered softly, and then looked away. "I cannot answer it."

"Are you good or evil?" Guido asked, speaking again.

The questions came to his lips as if some one else were asking them with his voice.

"Good—I think," answered the young girl, motionless beside him. "But I might be very bad."

"What is the riddle?" Guido enquired, and now he felt that he was speaking out of his own curiosity, and not as the mouthpiece of some one in a dream. "Do you ask yourself what it all means? I suppose so. We all ask that, and we never get any answer."

"It is too vague a question. It cannot have a definite answer. No. I ask three questions which I found in a German book of philosophy when I was a little girl. I tried hard to understand what all the rest of the book was about, but I found on one page three questions, printed by themselves. I can see the page now, and the questions were numbered one, two, and three. I have asked them ever since."

"What were they?"

"They were these: 'What can I know? What ought I to do? What may I hope?'"

"There would be everything in the answers," Guido said, "for they are big questions. I think I have answered them all in the negative in my own life. I know nothing, I do nothing, and I hope nothing."

Cecilia looked at him again. "I would not be you," she said gravely. "I can do nothing, perhaps, and I am sure I know nothing worth knowing, but I hope. I have that at least. I hope everything, with all my heart and soul—everything, even things you could not dream of."

"Help me to dream of them. Perhaps I might."

"Then dream that faith is knowledge, that charity is action, and that hope is heaven itself," answered Cecilia.

Her voice was sweet and low, and far away as spirit land, and Guido wondered at the words.

"Where did you hear that?" he asked.

"Ah, where?" she asked, almost sadly, and very longingly. "If I could tell you that, I should know the great secret, the only secret ever yet worth knowing. Where have we heard the voices that come back to us, not in sleeping dreams only, but when we are waking, too, voices that come back softly like evening bells across the sea, with the touch of hands that lay in ours long ago, and faces that we know better than our own! Where was it all, before the memory of it all was here?"

"I have often wondered whether those impressions are memories," said Guido.

"What else could they be?" Cecilia asked, her tone growing colder at once.

Guido had been happy in listening to her talk, with its suggestion of fantastical extravagance, but he had not known how to answer her, nor how to lead her on. He felt that the spell was broken, because something was lacking in himself. To be a magician one must believe in magic, unless one would be a mere conjurer. Guido at least knew enough not to answer the girl's last question with a string of so-called scientific theories about atavism and transmitted recollections. If he had taken that ground he would have been surprised to find that Cecilia Palladio was quite as familiar with it as himself.

"I am afraid," he said, "that I am not fit to talk with you about such things. You start from a point which I can never hope to reach, and instead of coming down to me, you rise higher and higher, almost out of my sight. I am afraid that if our friendship is to be real, it will be a one-sided bond."

"How do you mean?" asked the young girl, who had listened.

"It will mean much more to me than it ever can to you."

"No," Cecilia answered. "I think I shall like you very much."

"I like you very much already," said Guido, smiling. "I have an amusing idea."

"Have you? What is it? Neither of us has been very amusing this evening."

"Suppose that we take advantage of the Princess's conspiracy. Shall we?"

"My mother is the other conspirator!" Cecilia laughed.

"Is there any harm in letting people see that we like each other?" Guido asked.

"None in the least. Every one hopes that we may. Besides—" she stopped short.

"What is the other consideration?" Guido enquired.

"If I am perfectly frank—brutally frank—shall you be less my friend?"

"No. Much more."

"I do not wish to marry at all," said Cecilia, and again she reminded him of the Sphinx. "But if I ever should change my mind, since you and I have been picked out to make a match, I suppose I might as well marry you as any one else."

"Oh, quite as well!"

Then Guido laughed, as he rarely did, not loudly, but with all his heart, and Cecilia did not try to check her amusement either.

"I suppose it really is very funny," she said.

"The only thing necessary is that no one should ever guess that we have made a compact. That would be fatal."

"No one!" cried the young girl, eagerly. "No one! Not even your friend!"

"Lamberti? No, least of all, Lamberti!"

"Why do you say, least of all?"

"Because you do not like him," Guido answered, with perfect sincerity.

"Oh! I see. I am not sure, of course, but I am glad you do not mean to tell him. It would make me nervous to think that he might know. I—I am not quite certain why it makes me nervous, but it does."

"Have no fear. When shall I see you?"

He had noticed that Cecilia's mother was beginning that little comedy of movements, and glances, and uneasy turnings of the head, by which mothers of marriageable daughters signify their intention of going home. The works of a clock probably act in the same way before striking.

"I will make my mother ask you to dinner. Are you free to-morrow night?"

"Any night."

"No—I mean really. Are you?"

"Yes, really. Lamberti does not count, for we generally dine together when we have no other engagement."

The shadow again flitted across Cecilia's brow, and she said nothing, only nodding quickly. Then she looked across the room at her mother. Young girls are always instantly aware that their mothers are making signs. When Nelson's commander-in-chief signalled to him at the battle of Copenhagen the order to retire, Nelson put his spy-glass to his blind eye and assured his officers that he could see nothing, went on, and won the fight. Every young girl is totally blind of one eye during periods that vary between ten minutes and three hours.

Cecilia having recovered her sight, and seen her mother, rose with obedient alacrity.

"Good night," she said to Guido. "I am glad we are friends."

Their glances met for a moment, and Guido made an imperceptible gesture to put out his hand, but she did not answer it. He thought her refusal a little old-fashioned, since young girls now shake hands in Italy more often than not; but he liked her ways, chiefly because they were hers, and, moreover, he remembered just then that at her age she was supposed to be barely out of the schoolroom or the convent.

CHAPTER VI

"Spiritualism, your Highness, is the devil, without doubt," said the learned ecclesiastical archæologist, Don Nicola Francesetti, in an apologetic tone, and looking at his knees. "If there is anything more heretical, it is a belief in a possible migration of souls from one body to another, in a series of lives."

The Princess Anatolie smiled at the excellent man and exchanged a glance of compassionate intelligence with Monsieur Leroy. She did not care a straw what the Church thought about anything except Protestants and Jews, and she did not believe that Don Nicola cared either. He chanced to be a priest, instead of a professor, and it was of course his duty to protest against heresy when it was thrust under his cogitative observation. Spiritualism was not exactly heresy, therefore he said it was the devil, and no mistake; but as she was sure that he did not believe in the devil, that only proved that he did not believe in spiritualism.

In this she was mistaken, however, as people often are in their judgment of priests. Nicola Francesetti had long ago placed his conscience in safety, so to speak, by telling himself that he was not a theologian, but an archæologist, and that as he could not afford to divide his time and his intelligence between two subjects, where one was too vast, it was therefore his plain duty to think about all questions of religion as the Church taught him to think. He admitted that if his life could begin again he would perhaps not again enter the priesthood, but he would never have conceded that he could have been anything but a believing Catholic. He had no vocation whatever for saving souls, whereas he possessed the archæological gift in a high degree; and yet, as a clergyman and a good Christian, he was convinced at heart that a man in holy orders had no right to give his whole life and strength to another profession. He had asked the advice of a wise and good man on this point, however, and the theologian had thought that he should continue to live as he was living. Had he a cure? No, he had none. Had he ever evaded a priest's work? That is, had work been offered to him where a priest was needed, and where he could have done active good, and had he refused because it was distasteful to him? No, never. Was he receiving any stipend for performing a priest's duties, with the tacit understanding that he was at liberty to pay an impecunious substitute a part of the money for taking his place, so that he himself profited by the transaction? No, certainly not. Don Nicola had a sufficient income of his own to live on. Had he ever made a solemn promise to devote his life to missionary labours among the heathen? No.

"In that case, my dear friend," concluded the theologian, "you are tormenting yourself with perfectly useless scruples. You are making a mountain of your molehill, and when you have made your mountain you will not be satisfied until you have made another beside it. In the course of time you will, in fact, oppress your innocent conscience with a whole range of mountains; you will be immobilised under the weight, and then you will become hateful to yourself, useless to others, and an object of pity to wise men. Stick to your archæology."

"Is pure study a good in itself?" asked Don Nicola.

"What is good?" retorted the theologian viciously. "I wish you would define it!"

Don Nicola was silent, for though he could think of a number of synonyms for the conception, he remembered no definition corresponding to any of them. He waited.

"Good and goodness are not the same thing," observed the theologian; "you might as well say that study and knowledge are the same thing."

"But study should lead to knowledge."

"And goodness should lead to good; and, compared with ignorance, knowledge is a form of good. Therefore study is a form of goodness. Consequently, as you have a turn for erudition, the best thing you can do is to go on with your studies."

"I see," said Don Nicola.

"I wish I did," sighed the theologian, when the priest was gone. "How very pleasant it must be, to be an archæologist!"

After that, whenever Don Nicola was troubled with uneasiness about his profession, he soothed himself with his friend's little syllogism, which was as full of holes as a sieve, as flimsy as a tissue-paper balloon, and as unstable as a pyramid upside down, but nevertheless perfectly satisfactory.

"Of course," says humanity, "I know nothing about it. But I am perfectly sure."

And so forth. And moreover, if humanity were not frequently quite sure of things concerning which it knows nothing, the world would soon come to a standstill, and never move again; like the ass in the fable, that died of hunger in its stall between two bundles of hay, unable to decide which to eat first. That also was an instance of stable equilibrium.

Don Nicola avoided all questions of religion in general conversation, and tried to make other people avoid them when he was the only clergyman present, because he did not like to be asked his opinion about them. But when the Princess Anatolie and Monsieur Leroy gravely declared their belief in the communications of departed persons by means of rappings, not to say by touch, and by strains of music, and perfumes, and even, on rare occasions, by actual apparition, then Don Nicola felt that it was his duty to protest, and he accordingly protested with considerable energy. He said that spiritualism was the devil.

"The chief object of the devil's existence," observed Monsieur Leroy, "is to bear responsibility."

The Princess laughed and nodded her approval, as she always did when Monsieur Leroy said anything which she thought clever. Don Nicola was too wise to discuss the matter, if, indeed, it admitted of discussion; for the devil was certainly responsible for a good deal.

"Your definition of spiritualism is so very liberal," Monsieur Leroy added, with a fine supercilious smile on his red lips.

"It is not mine," answered Don Nicola, modestly.

"No. I suppose it is the opinion of the Church. At all events, you do not doubt the possibility of communicating with the spirits of dead persons, do you?"

"I have never examined the matter, my dear sir."

"It seems to me," said Monsieur Leroy, with airy superiority, "that it is rather rash to attribute to Satan everything which you will not take the trouble to examine."

"Hush, Doudou!" cried the Princess. "You are very rude!"

"Not at all, not at all, your Highness!" protested Don Nicola, rising. "I should be very much surprised if Monsieur Leroy expressed himself differently."

Monsieur Leroy had no retort ready, and tried to smile.

"It will give me the greatest pleasure to be your guide to the new excavations in the Forum," added the priest, as he took his leave.

The Princess and Monsieur Leroy were left alone.

"Shall we?" he asked after a moment's silence, and waited anxiously for the answer.

"I am afraid They will not come to-night, Doudou," said the Princess. "You have excited yourself in argument. You know that always has a bad effect."

"That man irritates me," answered Monsieur Leroy, peevishly. "Why do you receive him?"

He spoke in the tone of a spoilt child—a spoilt child of forty, or thereabouts.

"I thought you liked him," replied the Princess, very meekly. "I will give orders that he is not to be received. We will not go to the Forum with him."

"No, no! How you exaggerate! You always think that I mean a great deal more than I say. I only said that he irritated me."

"Why should you be irritated for nothing? You know it is bad for you."

She looked at him with an air of concern, and there was a gentleness in her eyes which few had ever seen in them.

"It does not matter," answered Monsieur Leroy, crossly.

He had risen, and he brought a very small and light mahogany table from a corner. It was one of those which used to be made during the second Empire in sets of six and of successive sizes, so that each fitted each under the next larger one. He moved awkwardly and yet without noise; there was something very womanish in his figure and gait.

He set the little table before the Princess, very close to her, lit a single candle, which he placed on the floor behind an arm-chair, and turned out the electric light. Then he sat down on the opposite side of the table and spread out his hands upon it, side by side, the right thumb resting on the left. The Princess did the same. They glanced at each other once or twice, hardly distinguishing each other's features in the gloom. Then they looked steadily down upon the table, and neither stirred for a long time.

"I am sure They will not come," said the Princess at last, in a very low voice.

"Hush!"

Silence again, for a quarter of an hour. Somewhere in the room a small clock, or a watch, ticked quickly, with a little rhythmical, insisting accent on the fourth beat.

"It moved, then!" whispered the Princess, excitedly.

"Yes. Hush!"

The little table certainly moved, with a queerly soft rocking motion, as if its feet only just touched the carpet and supported no weight. The Princess's hands felt as if they were floating over tiny rippling waves, and between her shoulders came the almost stinging thrill she loved. She wished that the room were quite dark now, in order that she might feel more. There were tiny beads of perspiration on Monsieur Leroy's forehead, and his hands were moist. The candle behind the arm-chair flickered.

"Are You there?" asked Monsieur Leroy, in a voice unlike his own.

There was no answer. The table moved more uneasily.

"Rap once for 'yes,' twice for 'no,'" said Monsieur Leroy. "Is this the first time you have come to us?"

One rap answered the question, sharp and clear, as if the butt of a pencil had struck the table underneath it and near the middle.

"Are you the spirit of a man?"

Two raps very distinct.

"Then you are a woman. Tell us—"

Several raps came in quick succession, in pairs, as if to repeat the negative energetically. Monsieur Leroy seemed to hesitate what question to ask.

"Perhaps it is a child," suggested the Princess, in a tremulous tone.

A sharp rap. Yes, it was a child. Was it a little girl? Yes. Had it been dead long? Yes. More than ten years? Yes. More than twenty? Yes. Fifty? No. Forty? Yes.

Monsieur Leroy began to count, pausing after each number.

"Forty-one—forty-two—forty-three—forty-four—"

The sharp rap again. The Princess drew a quick breath.

"How old was it when it died?" she managed to ask.

Monsieur Leroy began to count again, beginning with one. At the word seven, the rap came. The Princess started violently, almost upsetting the table against her companion.

"Adelaide!" She cried in a broken voice.

One rap.

"Oh, my darling, my darling!"

The old woman bent down over the table, and her outspread hands tried frantically to take up the flat surface, and she kissed the polished wood passionately, again and again, not knowing what she did, nor hearing her own incoherent words of mixed joy and agony.

"My child! My little thing—my sweet—speak to me—"

Her whole being was convulsed. Little storms of rappings seemed to answer her. The perspiration trickled down Monsieur Leroy's temples. He seemed to be making an effort altogether beyond his natural strength.

"Speak to me—call me by the little name!" sobbed the Princess, and her tears wet her hands and the table.

Monsieur Leroy began to repeat the alphabet. From time to time a rap stopped him at a letter, and then he began over again. In this way the rapping spelt out the word "Mamette."

"She says 'Mamette,'" said Monsieur Leroy, in a puzzled tone. "Does that mean anything?"

But the Princess burst into passionate weeping. It was the name she had asked for, the child's own pet name for her, its mother; it was the last word the poor little dying lips had tried to form. Never since that moment had the heart-broken woman spoken it, never since the fourth year before Monsieur Leroy had been born.

He looked at her, for he seemed to have preserved his self-control, and he saw that if matters went much further the poor sobbing woman would reach a state which might be dangerous. He withdrew his hands from the table and waited.

"She is gone, but she will come again now, whenever you call her," he said gently.

"No, do not go!" cried the Princess, clutching at the smooth wood frantically. "Come back, come back and speak to me once more!"

"She is gone, for to-night," said Monsieur Leroy, in the same gentle tone. "I am very much exhausted."

He pressed his handkerchief to his forehead and to his temples, again and again, while the Princess moaned, her cheek upon the table, as she had once let it rest upon the breast of her dead child.

Monsieur Leroy rose cautiously, fearing to disturb her. He was trembling now, as men sometimes do who have escaped alive from a great danger. He steadied himself by the back of the arm-chair, behind which the candle was burning steadily. With an effort, he stooped and took up the candlestick and set it on the table. Then he looked at his watch and saw that it was past eleven o'clock.

CHAPTER VII

It was some time since Guido had seen Lamberti, but the latter had written him a line to say that he was going with a party of men to stop in an old country house near the seashore, not far from Città Vecchia. The quail were very abundant in May that year, and Lamberti was a good shot. He had left home suddenly on the morning after telling Guido the story of his adventure in the Forum. Guido had at first been mildly surprised that his friend should not have spoken of his intention on that evening; but some one had told him that the party had been made up at the club, late at night, which accounted for everything.

Guido was soon too much occupied to miss the daily companionship, and was glad to be alone, when he could not be with Cecilia. He no longer concealed from himself that he was very much in love with her, and that, compared with this fact, nothing in his previous life had been of any importance whatever. Even the circumstances of his position with regard to his aunt sank into insignificance. She might do what she pleased, she might try to ruin him, she might persecute him to the extreme limit of her ingenuity, she might invent calumnies intended to disgrace him; he was confident of victory and sure of himself.

One of the first unmistakable signs of genuine love is the certainty of doing the impossible. An hour before meeting Cecilia, Guido had been reduced to the deepest despondency, and had talked gravely of ending a life that was not worth living. A fortnight had passed, and he defied his aunt, Monsieur Leroy, the whole world, an adverse fate, and the powers of evil. They might do their worst, now, for he was full of strength, and ten times more alive than he had ever been before.

It was true that he could not see the smallest change in Cecilia's manner towards him since the memorable evening on which she had laughingly agreed to take advantage of what was thrust upon them both. Her colour did not change by the least shade of a blush when she met him; there was not the slightest quivering of the delicate eyelids, there was nothing but the most friendly frankness in the steady look of welcome. But she liked him very much, and was at no pains to conceal it. She liked him better than any one she had ever met in her short life, except her stepfather, and she told Guido so with charming unconcern. As he could not be jealous of the dead ambassador, he was not at all discouraged by the comparison. Sometimes he was rather flattered by it, and he could not but feel that he had already acquired a position from which any future suitor would find it hard to dislodge him.

The Countess Fortiguerra looked on with wondering satisfaction. Her daughter had not led her to believe that she would readily accept what must soon be looked upon by society as an engagement, and what would certainly be one before long. When Guido went to see his aunt, she received him with expansive expressions of affection.

He noticed a change in the Princess, which he could only explain by the satisfaction he supposed she felt in his conduct. There were times when her artificial face softened with a look of genuine feeling, especially when she was silent and inattentive. Guido knew her well enough, he thought, to impute these signs to her inward contentment at the prospect of his marriage, from which she was sure of extracting notable financial advantage. But in this he was not just, though he judged from long experience. Monsieur Leroy alone knew the secret, and he kept his own counsel.

An inquisitive friend asked the Countess Fortiguerra boldly whether she intended to announce the engagement of her daughter at the garden party.

"No," she answered, without hesitation, "that would be premature."

She was careful, in a way, to do nothing irrevocable—never to take Guido into her carriage, not to ask him to dinner when there were other guests, not to leave him alone with Cecilia when there was a possibility of such a thing being noticed by the servants, except by the discreet Petersen, who could be trusted, and who strongly approved of Guido from the first. But when it was quite safe, the

Countess used to go and sit in a little boudoir adjoining the drawing-room, leaving the doors open, of course, and occupying herself with her correspondence; and Guido and Cecilia talked without restraint.

The Countess had enough womanly and instinctive wisdom not to ask questions of her daughter at this stage, but on the day before the long-expected garden party she spoke to Guido alone, in a little set speech which she had prepared with more conscientiousness than diplomatic skill.

"You have seen," she said, "that I am always glad to receive you here, and that I often leave you and Cecilia together in the drawing-room. Dear Signor d'Este, I am sure you will understand me if I ask you to—to—to tell me something."

She had meant to end the sentence differently, rounding it off with "your intentions with regard to my daughter"; but that sounded like something in a letter, so she tried to make it more vague. But Guido understood, which is not surprising.

"You have been very kind to me," he said simply. "I love your daughter sincerely, and if she will consent to marry me I shall do my best to make her happy. But, so far, I have no reason to think that she will accept me. Besides, whether you know it already or not, I must tell you that I am a poor man. I have no fortune whatever, though I receive an allowance by my father's will, which is enough for a bachelor. It will cease at my death. Your daughter could make a very much more brilliant marriage."

The good Countess had listened in silence. The Princess, for reasons of her own, had explained Guido's position with considerable minuteness, if not with scrupulous accuracy.

"Cecilia is rich enough to marry whom she pleases," the Countess answered. "Even without considering her inclinations, your social position would make up for your want of fortune."

"My social position is not very exalted," Guido answered, smiling at her frankness. "I am plain 'Signor d'Este,' without any title whatsoever, or without the least prospect of one."

"But your royal blood—" protested the Countess.

"I am more proud of the fact that my mother was an honest woman," replied Guido, quietly.

"Yes—oh—of course!" The Countess was a little abashed. "But you know what I mean," she added, by way of making matters clear. "And as for your fortune—I would say, your allowance, and all that—it really does not matter. It is natural that you should have made debts, too. All young men do, I believe."

"No," said Guido. "I have not a debt in the world."

"Really?"

The single word sounded more like an exclamation of extreme surprise than like an interrogation, and the Countess, who was incapable of concealment, stared at Guido for a moment in undisguised astonishment.

"Why are you so much surprised?" he asked, with evident amusement. "My allowance is fifty thousand francs a year. That is not wealth, but it is quite enough for me."

"Yes. I should think so. That is—of course, it is not much—is it? I never know anything about money, you know! Baron Goldbirn manages everything for us."

"I suppose," Guido said, looking at her curiously, "that some one must have told you that I had made debts."

"Yes—yes! Some one did tell me so."

"Whoever said it was quite mistaken. I can easily satisfy you on that point, for I am a very orderly person. I used to play high when I was twenty-one, but I got tired of it, and I do not care for cards any longer."

"It is very strange, all the same!" The Countess was still wondering, though she believed him. "How people lie!" she exclaimed.

"Oh, admirably, and most of the time," Guido answered, with a little laugh.

There was a short pause. He also was wondering who could have maligned him. No doubt it must have been some designing mother who had a son to marry.

"Forgive me," he said at last. "I have told you exactly what my position is. Have you, on your side, any reason to think that your daughter will consent?"

"Oh, I am sure she will!" answered the Countess, promptly.

Guido repressed a movement, and for an instant the colour rose faintly in his face, then sank away.

"Quite sure?" he asked, controlling his voice.

"I mean, in the end, you know. She will marry you in the end. I am convinced of it. But I think I had better not ask her just yet."

There were matters in regard to which she was distinctly afraid of her daughter.

"May I?" Guido enquired. "Will you let me ask her to marry me, when I think that the time has come?"

"Certainly! That is—" The Countess believed that she ought to hesitate. "After all, we have only known you a fortnight. That is not long. Is it?"

"No. But, on the other hand, you had never seen me when you and my aunt agreed that your daughter and I should be married."

"How did you know that we had talked about it?"

"It was rather evident," Guido answered, with a smile.

The artlessness which is often a charm in a young girl looks terribly like foolishness if it lasts till a woman is forty. Yet in old age it may seem charming again, as if second childhood brought with it a second innocence.

Guido was an Italian only by his mother, and from his father he inherited the profoundly complicated character of races that had ruled the world for a thousand years or more, and not always either wisely or justly. Under his indifference and quiet dislike of all action, as well as of most emotions, he had always felt the conflicting instincts towards good and evil, and the contempt of consequences bordering on folly, if not upon real insanity, which had brought about the decline and fall of his father's kingdom. The perfect simplicity of the real Italian character when in a state of equilibrium always amused him, and often pleased him, and he had a genuine admiration for the splendidly violent contrasts which it develops when roused by passion. He could read it like an open book, and predict what it would do in almost any circumstances.

For the first time in his life, he felt something of its directness in himself, moving to a definite aim through the maze of useless complications, hesitations, and turns and returns of thought with which he was familiar in his own character. He smiled at the idea that he might end by resembling Lamberti, with whom to think was to feel, and to feel was to act. Were there two selves in him, of which the one was in love, and the other was not? That was an amusing theory, and a fortnight ago it would have been pleasant to sit in his room at night, among his Dürers, his Rembrandts, and his pictures, with an old book on his knee, dreaming about his two conflicting individualities. But somehow dreaming had lost its charm of late. He thought only of one question, and asked only one of the future. Was Cecilia Palladio's friendship about to turn into anything that could be called love, or not? His intention warned him that if the change had come she herself was not conscious of it. He was authorised to ask her, now that the Countess had spoken—formally authorised, but he was quite sure that if he had believed that she already loved him, he would not have waited for any such permission. His father's blood resented the restraint of all ordinary conventions, and in the most profound inaction he had always morally and inwardly reserved the right to do what he pleased, if he should ever care to do anything at all.

He was just going to dress for dinner that evening when Lamberti came in, a little more sunburned than usual, but thinner, and very restless in his manner. Guido explained that he was going to dine with the Countess Fortiguerra. He offered to telephone for permission to bring Lamberti with him.

"Do you know them well enough for that already?" Lamberti asked.

"Yes. I have seen them a great deal since you left. Shall I ask?"

"No, thank you. I shall dine at home with my people."

"Shall you go to the garden party to-morrow?"

"No."

Guido looked at him curiously, and he immediately turned away, unlike himself.

"Have you had any more strange dreams since I saw you?" Guido asked.

"Yes."

Lamberti did not turn round again, but looked attentively at an etching on the table, so that Guido could not see his face. His monosyllabic answers were nervous and sharp. It was clear that he was under some kind of strain that was becoming intolerable, but of which he did not care to speak.

"How is it going?" he asked suddenly.

"I think everything is going well," answered Guido, who knew what he meant, though neither of them had spoken to the other of Cecilia, except in the most casual way, since they had both met her.

"So you are going to marry an heiress after all," said Lamberti, with something like a laugh.

"I love her," Guido replied. "I cannot help the fact that she is rich."

"It does no harm."

"Perhaps not, but I wish she had no more than I. If she had nothing at all, I should be just as anxious to marry her."

"You do not suppose that I doubt that, do you?" Lamberti asked quickly.

"No. But you spoke at first as if you were reproaching me for changing my mind."

"Did I? I am sorry. I did not mean it in that way. I was only thinking that fate generally makes us do just what we do not intend. There is something diabolically ingenious about destiny. It lies in wait for you, it seems to leave everything to your own choice, it makes you think that you are a perfectly free agent, and then, without the least warning, it springs at you from behind a tree, knocks you down, tramples the breath out of you, and drags you off by the heels straight to the very thing you have sworn to avoid. Man a free agent? Nonsense! There is no such thing as free will."

"What in the world has happened to you?" Guido asked, by way of answer. "Is anything wrong?"

"Everything is wrong. Good night. You ought to be dressing for dinner."

"Come with me."

"To dine with people whom I hardly know, and who have not asked me? Besides, I told you that I meant to dine at home."

"At least, promise me that you will go with me to-morrow to the Villa Madama."

"No."

"Look here, Lamberti," said Guido, changing his tone, "you and I have known each other since we were boys, and I do not believe there exist two men who are better friends. I am not sure that the Contessina Palladio will marry me, but her mother wishes it, and heaven knows that I do. They are both perfectly well aware that you are my most intimate friend. If you absolutely refuse to go near them they can only suppose that you have something against them. They have already asked me if they are never to see you. Now, what will it cost you to be decently civil to a lady who may be my wife next year, and to her mother, who was your mother's friend long ago? You need not stay half an hour at the villa unless you please. But go with me. Let them see you with me. If I really marry, do you suppose I am going to have any one but you for my best man?"

Lamberti listened to this long speech without attempting to interrupt Guido. Then he was silent for a few moments.

"If you put it in that light," he said, rising to go, "I cannot refuse. What time shall you start? I will come here for you."

"Thank you," said Guido. "I should like to get there early. At four o'clock, I should say. I suppose we ought not to leave here later than half-past three."

"Very well. I shall be here in plenty of time. Good night."

When Guido pressed his hand, it was icy cold.

CHAPTER VIII

On the following morning Lamberti went out early, and before nine o'clock he was in the private study of a famous physician, who was a specialist for diseases of the nerves. Lamberti had never seen him and had not asked for an appointment, for the simple reason that his visit was spontaneous and unpremeditated. He had spent a wretched night, and it suddenly struck him that he might be ill. As he had never been ill in his life except from two or three wounds got in fight, he had been slow to admit that anything could be wrong with his physical condition. But it was possible. The strongest men sometimes fell ill unaccountably. A good doctor would see the truth at a glance.

The specialist was a young man, squarely built, with a fresh complexion, smooth brown hair, and a well-trimmed chestnut beard. At first sight, no one would have noticed anything remarkable in his appearance, except, perhaps, that he had unusually bright blue eyes, which had a fixed look when he spoke earnestly.

"I am a naval officer," said Lamberti, as he took the seat the doctor offered him. "Can you tell me whether I am ill or not? I mean, whether I have any bodily illness. Then I will explain what brings me."

The doctor looked at him keenly a few seconds, felt his pulse, pressed one ear on his waistcoat to listen to his heart, and then against his back, made him face the light and gently drew down the lower lids of his eyes, and finally stood off and made a sort of general survey of his appearance. Then he made him stretch out one hand, with the fingers spread out. There was not the least tremor. Last of all, he asked him to shut his eyes tightly and walk slowly across the room, turn round, and walk back. Lamberti did so, steadily and quietly.

"There is nothing wrong with your body," said the doctor, sitting down. "Before you tell me why you come here, I should like to know one thing more. Do you come of sound and healthy people?"

"Yes. My father is the Marchese Lamberti. My brothers and sisters are all alive and well. So far as I know, there was never any insanity in my family."

"Were your father and mother cousins?" enquired the doctor.

"No."

"Very good. That is all I need to know. I am at your service. What is the matter?"

"If we lived in the Middle Ages," said Lamberti, "I should say that I was possessed by the devil, or haunted." He stopped and laughed oddly.

"Why not say so now?" asked the doctor. "The names of things do not matter in the least. Let us say that you are haunted, if that describes what troubles you. Very good. What haunts you?"

"A young girl," Lamberti answered, after a moment's pause.

"Do you mean that you see, or think you see, the apparition of a young girl who is dead?"

"She is alive, but I have only met her once. That is the strange thing about it, or, at least, the beginning of the strange thing. Of course it is perfectly absurd, but when I first saw her, the only time we met, I had the sensation of recognising some one I had not seen for many years. As she is only just eighteen, that is impossible."

"Excuse me, my dear sir, nothing is impossible. Every one is absent-minded sometimes. You may have seen the young lady in the street, or at the theatre. You may have stared at her quite unconsciously while you were thinking of something else, and her features may have so impressed themselves upon your memory, without your knowing it, that you actually recognised her when you met her in a drawing-room."

"I daresay," admitted Lamberti, indifferently. "But that is no reason why I should dream of her every night."

"I am not sure. It might be a reason. Such things happen."

"And every night when I wake from the dream, I hear some one close the door of my room softly, as if she were just going out. I always lock my door at night."

"Perhaps it sometimes shakes a little in the frame."

"It began at home. But I have been stopping in the country nearly a fortnight, and the same thing has happened every night."

"You dream it. One may get the habit of dreaming the same dream every time one sleeps."

"It is not always the same dream, though the door is always closed softly when she goes away. But there is something else. I was wrong in saying that I only met the lady once. I should have said that I have spoken with her only once. This is how it happened."

Lamberti told the doctor the story of his meeting Cecilia at the house of the Vestals. The specialist listened attentively, for he was already convinced that Lamberti was a man of solid reason and practical good sense, probably the victim of a series of coincidences that had made a strong impression on his mind. When Lamberti paused, there was a moment's silence.

"What do you yourself think was the cause of the lady's fright?" asked the doctor at last.

"I believe that she had dreamed the same dream," Lamberti answered without hesitation.

"What makes you believe anything so improbable?"

"Well—I hardly know. It is an impression. It was all so amazingly real, you see, and when our eyes met, she looked as if she knew exactly what would happen if she did not run away—exactly what had happened in the dream."

"That was on the morning after you had first dreamt it, you say. Of course it helped very much to strengthen the impression the dream had made, and it is not at all surprising that the dream should have come again. You know as well as I, that a dream which seems to last hours really passes in a second, perhaps in no time at all. The slightest sound in your room which suggested the closing of a door would be enough to bring it all back before you were awake, and the sound might still be audible to you."

"Possibly. Whatever it is, I wish to get rid of it."

"It may be merely coincidence," the doctor said. "I think it is. But I do not exclude the theory that two people who have made a very strong impression one on another, may be the subjects of some sort of mutual thought transference. We know very little about those things. Some queer cases come under my observation, but my patients are never sound and sane men like you. What I should like to know is, why did the lady run away?"

"That is probably the one thing I can never find out," Lamberti answered.

"There is a very simple way. Ask her." The doctor smiled. "Is it so very hard?" he enquired, as Lamberti looked at him in surprise. "I take it for granted that you can find some opportunity of seeing her in a drawing-room, where she cannot fly from you, and will not do anything to attract attention. What could be more natural than that you should ask her quite frankly why she was so frightened the other day? I do not see how she could possibly be offended. Do you? When you ask her, you need not seem too serious, as if you attached a great deal of importance to what she had done."

"I certainly could try it," said Lamberti thoughtfully. "I shall see her to-day."

"She may try to avoid you, because she is ashamed of what she did. But if I were you, I would not let the chance slip. If you succeed in talking to her for a few minutes, and break the ice, I can almost promise that you will also break the habit of this dream that annoys you. Will you make the attempt? It seems to me by far the wisest and most sensible remedy, for I am nearly sure that it will turn out to be one."

"I daresay you are right. Is there any other way of curing such habits of the mind?"

"I could hypnotise you and stop your dreaming by suggestion."

"Nobody could make me sleep against my will." Lamberti laughed at the mere idea.

"No," answered the doctor, "but it would not be against your will, if you submitted to it as a cure. However, try the simpler plan first, and come and see me in a day or two. You seem to hesitate. Perhaps you have some reason for not wishing to make the nearer acquaintance of the lady. That is your affair, but one more interview of a few minutes will not make much difference, as your health is at stake. You are under a mental strain altogether out of proportion with the cause that produces it, and the longer you allow it to last the stronger the reaction will be, when it comes."

"I have no good reason for not knowing her better," Lamberti said after a moment's thought, for he was convinced against his previous determination. "I will take your advice, and then I will come and see you again."

He took his leave and went out into the bright morning air. It was a relief to feel that he had been brought to a determination at last, and he knew that it was a sensible one, from any ordinary point of view, and that his one great objection to acting upon it had no logical value.

But the objection subsisted, though he had made up his mind to override it. It was out of the question that he could really be in love with Cecilia Palladio, who was probably quite unlike what she seemed to be in his dreams. He had fallen in love with a fancy, a shadow, an unreal image that haunted him as soon as he closed his eyes; but when he was wide awake and busy with life the girl was nothing to him but a mere acquaintance. His pulse would not beat as fast when he met her that very afternoon as it had done just now, in the doctor's study, when he had been thinking of the vision.

Besides, what Guido had said was quite true. He could not possibly continue not to know Guido's future wife; and as there was no danger of his falling in love with her when his eyes were open, he really could not see why he should be so anxious to avoid her. So the matter was settled. He took a long walk, far out of Porta San Giovanni, and turned to the right by the road that leads through the fields to the tomb of Cecilia Metella.

As he passed the great round monument, swinging along steadily, its name naturally came to his mind, and it occurred to him for the first time that Cecilia had been a noble name among the old Romans, that it had come down unchanged, and that there had doubtless been more than one Vestal Virgin who had borne it. The Vestal in his dream was certainly called Cecilia. He was in the humour, now, to smile at what he called his own folly, and as he strode along he almost laughed aloud. Before the sun should set, the whole matter would be definitely at rest, and he would be wondering how he could ever have been foolish enough to attach any importance to it. He followed the Appian Way back to the city, with a light heart.

CHAPTER IX

The Villa Madama was probably never inhabited, for it was certainly never quite finished, and the grand staircase was not rebuilt after Cardinal Pompeo Colonna set fire to the house. That was in the wild days when Rome was sacked by the Constable of Bourbon's Spaniards and Franzperg's Germans, and Pope Clement the Seventh was shut up in the stronghold of Sant' Angelo; and at nightfall he looked from the windows of the fortress and saw the flames shoot up on the slope of Monte Mario, from the beautiful place which Raphael of Urbino had designed for him, and which Giovanni of Udine had decorated, and he told those who were with him that Cardinal Colonna was revenging himself for his castles sacked and burned by the Pope's orders.

That was nearly four hundred years ago, and the great exterior staircase was never rebuilt; but in order to save that part of the little palace from ruin unsightly arches were reared up against the once beautiful wing, and because of Giulio Romano's frescoes and Giovanni of Udine's marvellous stucco work, the roof has been always kept in good repair. Moreover, a good deal has been written about the building, some of which is inaccurate, to say the least; as, for instance, that one may see the dome of Saint Peter's from the windows, whereas the villa stands halfway down the slope of the hill on the side which is away from the church, and looks towards the Sabines and towards Tivoli and Frascati.

Those who have taken the trouble to visit the villa in its half-ruinous condition, and who have lingered on the grass-grown terraces and at the noble windows, on spring afternoons, when the sun is behind the hill, can easily guess what it became when it passed into the ownership of the Contessina Cecilia Palladio. Her guardian, the excellent Baron Goldbirn, had bought it for her because it was offered for sale at a low price, and was an excellent investment as well as a treasure of art; and he had purposed to coat the brown stone walls with fresh stucco, to erect a "belvedere" with nice green blinds on the roof, to hang the rooms with rich magenta damask, to carpet them with Brussels carpets, to furnish them with gilt furniture, to warm the house with steam heat, and to light it with electricity.

To his surprise, his ward rejected each of these proposals in detail and all of them generally, and declared that since the villa was hers she could deal with it according to her own taste, which, she maintained, was better than Goldbirn's. The latter answered that as he was sixty-five years old and Cecilia was only eighteen, this was impossible; but that under the circumstances he washed his hands of the matter, only warning her that the Italian law would not allow her to cut down the trees more than once in nine years.

"As if anything could induce me to cut them down at all!" Cecilia answered indignantly. "There are few enough as it is!"

"My dear," the Countess had answered with admirable relevancy, "I hope you are not ungrateful to your guardian."

Cecilia was not ungrateful, but she had her own way, for it was preordained that she generally should, and it was well for the Villa Madama that it was so. She only asked her guardian how much he would allow her to spend on the place, and then, to his amazement and satisfaction, she only spent half the sum he named. She easily persuaded a good artist, whom her stepfather had helped at the beginning of his career, to take charge of the work, and it was carried out with loving and reverent taste. The wilderness of sloping land became a garden, the beautiful "court of honour" was so skilfully restored with old stone and brick that the restoration could hardly be detected, the great exterior staircase was rebuilt, the close garden on the other side was made a carpet of flowers; the water that gushed abundantly from a deep spring in the hillside poured into an old fountain bought from the remains of a villa in the Campagna, and then, below, filled the vast square basin that already existed, and thence it was distributed through the lower grounds. There were roses everywhere, already beginning to climb, and the scent of a few young orange trees in blossom mingled delicately with the odour of the flowers. Within the house the floor of the great hall was paved with plain white tiles, and up to the cornice and between the marvellous pilasters the bare walls were hung with coarse linen woven in simple and tasteful patterns and in subdued colours.

The little gods and goddesses and the emblematic figures of the seasons in the glorious vaults overhead, smiled down upon such a scene as had not rejoiced the great hall for centuries. The Countess had asked all Rome to come, with an admirable indifference to political parties and social discords; and all Rome came, as it sometimes does, in the best of tempers with itself and with its hostess. Roman society is good to look at, when it is gathered together in such ways; for mere looks, there is perhaps nothing better in all Europe, except in England. The French are more brilliant, no doubt, for their women, and, alas, their men also, affect a greater variety of dress and ornament than any other people. German society is magnificent with military uniforms, Austrians generally have very perfect taste; and so on, to each its own advantage. But the Romans have something of their own, a beauty most distinctly theirs, a sort of distinction that is genuine and unaffected, but which nevertheless seems to belong to more splendid times than ours. When the women are beautiful, and they often are, they are like the pictures in their own galleries; among the men there are heads and faces that remind one of Lionardo da Vinci, of Cæsar Borgia, of Lorenzo de' Medici, of Guidarello Guidarelli, even of Michelangelo. Romans, at their best, have about them a grave suavity, or a suave gravity, that is a charm in itself, with a perfect self-possession which is the very opposite of arrogance; when they laugh, their mirth is real, though a little subdued; when they are grave, they do not look dull; when they are in deep earnest, they are not theatrical.

Those who went to the Fortiguerra garden party never quite forgot the impression they received. It was one of those events that are remembered as memorable social successes, and spoken of after many years. It was unlike anything that had ever been done in Rome before, unlike the solemn receptions of the chief of the clericals, when the cardinals come in state and are escorted by torch-bearers from their carriages to the entrance of the great drawing-room, and back again when they go away; unlike the supremely magnificent balls in honour of the foreign sovereigns who occasionally spend a week in Rome, and are amusingly ready to accept the hospitality of Roman princes; most of all, it was unlike an ordinary garden party, because the Villa Madama is quite unlike ordinary villas.

Moreover, every one was pleased that such very rich people should not attempt to surprise society by vulgar display. There were no state liveries, there were no ostentatious armorial bearings, there was no overpowering show of silver and gold, there was no Hungarian band brought expressly from Vienna, nor any fashionable pianist paid to play about five thousand notes at about a franc apiece, to the great annoyance of all the people who preferred conversation to music. Everything was simple, everything was good, everything was beautiful, from the entrancing view of Rome beyond the yellow river, and of the undulating Campagna beyond, with the soft hills in the far distance, to the lovely flowers in the garden; from the flowers without, to the stately halls within; from their charming frescoes and exquisite white traceries, to the lovely girl who was the centre, and the reason, and the soul of it all.

Her mother received the guests out of doors, in the close garden, and thirty or forty people were already there when Guido d'Este and Lamberti arrived; for every one came early, fearing lest the air might be chilly towards sunset. The Countess introduced the men and the young girls to her daughter, and presented her to the married women. Presently, when the garden became too full, the people would go back through the house and wander away about the grounds, lighting up the shadowed hillside with colour, and filling the air with the sound of their voices. They would stray far out, as far as the little grove on the knoll, planted in old times for the old-fashioned sport of netting birds.

Guido had told Cecilia on the previous evening that his friend had returned from the country and was coming to the villa, and he had again seen the very slight contraction of her brows at the mere mention of Lamberti's name. He wondered whether there were not some connection between what he took for her dislike of Lamberti, and the latter's strong disinclination to meet her. Perhaps Lamberti had guessed at a glance that she would not like him. He would of course keep such an opinion to himself.

Guido watched Cecilia narrowly from the moment she caught sight of him with Lamberti—so attentively indeed that he did not even glance at the latter's face. It was set like a mask, and under the tanned colour any one could see that the man turned pale.

"You know Cecilia already," said the Countess Fortiguerra, pleasantly. "I hope the rest of your family are coming?"

"I think they are all coming," Lamberti answered very mechanically.

He had resolutely looked at the Countess until now, but he felt the daughter's eyes upon him, and he was obliged to meet them, if only for a single instant. The last time he had met their gaze she had cried aloud and had fled from him in terror. He would have given much to turn from her now, without a glance, and mingle with the other guests.

He was perfectly cool and self-possessed, as he afterwards remembered, but he felt that it was the sort of coolness which always came upon him in moments of supreme danger. It was familiar to him, for he had been in many hand-to-hand engagements in wild countries, and he knew that it would not forsake him; but he missed the thrill of rare delight that made him love fighting as he loved no sport he had ever tried. This was more like walking bravely to certain death.

Cecilia was all in white, but her face was whiter than the silk she wore, and as motionless as marble; and her fixed eyes shone with an almost dazzling light. Guido saw and wondered. Then he heard Lamberti's voice, steady, precise, and metallic as the notes of a bell striking the hour.

"I hope to see something of you by-and-by, Signorina."

Cecilia's lips moved, but no sound came from them. Then Guido was sure that they smiled perceptibly, and she bent her head in assent, but so slightly that her eyes were still fixed on Lamberti's.

Other guests came up at that moment, and the two friends made way for them.

"Come back through the house," said Guido, in a low voice.

Lamberti followed him into the great hall, and to the left through the next, where there was no one, and out to a small balcony beyond. Then both stood still and faced each other, and the silence lasted a few seconds. Guido spoke first.

"What has there been between you two?" he asked, with something like sternness in his tone.

"This is the second time in my life that I have spoken to the Contessina," Lamberti answered. "The first time I ever saw her was at your aunt's house."

Guido had never doubted the word of Lamberto Lamberti, but he could not doubt the evidence of his own senses either, and he had watched Cecilia's face. It seemed utterly impossible that she should look as she had looked just now, unless there were some very grave matter between her and Lamberti. All sorts of horrible suspicions clouded Guido's brain, all sorts of reasons why Lamberti should lie to him, this once, this only time. Yet he spoke quietly enough.

"It is very strange that two people should behave as you and she do, when you meet, if you have only met twice. It is past my comprehension."

"It is very strange," Lamberti repeated.

"So strange," said Guido, "that it is very hard to believe. You are asking a great deal of me."

"I have asked nothing, my friend. You put a question to me,—a reasonable question, I admit,—and I have answered you with the truth. I have never touched that young lady's hand, I have only spoken with her twice in my life, and not alone on either occasion. I did not wish to come here to-day, but you practically forced me to."

"You did not wish to come, because you knew what would happen," Guido answered coldly.

"How could I know?"

"That is the question. But you did know, and until you are willing to explain to me how you knew it—"

He stopped short and looked hard at Lamberti, as if the latter must understand the rest. His usually gentle and thoughtful face was as hard and stern as stone. Until lately his friendship for Lamberti had been by far the strongest and most lasting affection of his life. The thought that it was to be suddenly broken and ended by an atrocious deception was hard to bear.

"You mean that if I cannot explain, as you call it, you and I are to be like strangers. Is that what you mean, Guido? Speak out, man! Let us be plain."

Guido was silent for a while, leaning over the balcony and looking down, while Lamberti stood upright and waited for his answer.

"How can I act otherwise?" asked Guido, at last, without looking up. "You would do the same in my place. So would any man of honour."

"I should try to believe you, whatever you said."

"And if you could not?" Guido enquired almost fiercely.

It was very nearly an insult, but Lamberti answered quietly and firmly.

"Before refusing to believe me, merely on apparent evidence, you can ask the Contessina herself."

"As if a woman could tell the truth when a man will not!" Guido laughed harshly.

"You forget that you love her, and that she probably loves you. That should make a difference."

"What do you wish me to do? Ask her the question you will not answer?"

"The question I have answered," said Lamberti, correcting him. "Yes. Ask her."

"Your mother was an old friend of her mother's," Guido said, with a new thought.

"Yes."

"Why is it impossible that you two should have met before now?"

"Because I tell you that we have not. If we had, I should not have any reason for hiding the fact. It would be much easier to explain, if we had. But I am not going to argue about the matter, for it is quite useless. Before you quarrel with me, go and ask the Contessina to explain, if she will, or can. If she cannot, or if she can and will not, I shall try to make you understand as much as I do, though that is very little."

Guido listened without attempting to interrupt. He was not a rash or violent man, and he valued Lamberti's friendship far too highly to forfeit it without the most convincing reasons. Unfortunately, what he had seen would have convinced an even less suspicious man that there was a secret which his friend shared with Cecilia, and which both had an object in concealing from him. Lamberti ceased speaking and a long silence followed, for he had nothing more to say.

At last Guido straightened himself with an evident effort, as if he had forced himself to decide the matter, but he did not look at Lamberti.

"Very well," he said. "I will speak to her."

Lamberti bent his head, silently acknowledging Guido's sensible conclusion. Then Guido turned and went away alone. It was long before Lamberti left the balcony, for he was glad of the solitude and the chance of quietly thinking over his extraordinary situation.

Meanwhile Guido found it no easy matter to approach Cecilia at all, and it looked as if it would be quite impossible to speak with her alone. He went back through the great hall where people were beginning to gather about the tea-table, and he stood in the vast door that opens upon the close garden. Cecilia was still standing beside her mother, but they were surrounded by a group of people who all seemed to be trying to talk to them at once. The garden was crowded, and it would be impossible for Guido to get near them without talking his way, so to say, through countless acquaintances. By this time, however, most of the guests had arrived, and those who were in the inner garden would soon begin to go out to the grounds.

Cecilia was no longer pale; on the contrary, she had more colour than usual, and delicate though the slight flush in her cheeks was, it looked a little feverish to Guido. As he began to make his way forward he tried to catch her eye, but he thought she purposely avoided an exchange of glances. At last he was beside her, and to his surprise she looked at him quite naturally, and answered him without embarrassment.

"You must be tired," he said. "Will you not sit down for a little while?"

"I should like to," she answered, smiling.

Then she looked at her mother, and seemed to hesitate.

"May I go and sit down?" she asked, in a low voice. "I am so tired!"

"Of course, child!" answered the Countess, cheerfully. "Signor d'Este will take you to the seat over there by the fountain. I hardly think that any one else will come now."

Guido and Cecilia moved away, and the Countess smiled affectionately at their backs. Some one said that they were a very well-matched pair, and another asked if it were true that Signor d'Este would inherit the Princess Anatolie's fortune at her death. A third observed that she would never die; and a fourth, who was going to dine with her that evening, said that she was a very charming woman; whereupon everybody laughed a little, and the Countess changed the subject.

Cecilia was really tired, and gave a little sigh of satisfaction as she sat down and leaned back. Guido looked at her and hesitated.

"I must have shaken hands with at least two hundred people," she said, "and I am sure I have spoken to as many more!"

"Do you like it?" Guido asked, by way of gaining time.

"What an idle question!" laughed Cecilia.

"I had another to ask you," he answered gravely. "Not an idle one."

She looked at him quickly, wondering whether he was going to ask her to be his wife, and wondering, too, what she should answer if he did. For some days past she had understood that what they called their compact of friendship was becoming a mere comedy on his side, if not on hers, and that he loved her with all his heart, though he had not told her so.

"It is rather an odd question," he continued, as she said nothing. "You have not formally given me any right to ask it, and yet I feel that I have the right, all the same."

"Friendship gives rights, and takes them," Cecilia answered thoughtfully.

"Exactly. That is what I feel about it. That is why I think I may ask you something that may seem strange. At all events, I cannot go on living in doubt about the answer."

"Is it as important as that?" asked the young girl.

"Yes."

"What is it?"

"Wait a moment. Let these people pass. How in the world did you succeed in getting so many roses to grow in such a short time?"

"You must ask the gardener," Cecilia answered, in order to say something while a young couple passed before the bench, evidently very much absorbed in each other's conversation.

Guido bent forward, resting his elbows on his knees, and not looking at her, but turning his face a little, so that he could speak in a very low tone with an outward appearance of carelessness. It was very hard to put the question, after all, now that he was so near her, and felt her thrilling presence.

"Our agreement is a failure," he began. "At all events, it is one on my side. I really did not think it would turn out as it has."

She said nothing, and he knew that she did not move, and was looking at the people in the distance. He knew, also, that she understood him and had expected something of the sort. That made it a little easier to go on.

"That is the reason why I am going to ask you this question. What has there ever been between you and Lamberti? Why do you turn deathly pale when you meet him, and why does he try to avoid you?"

He heard her move now, and he slowly turned his face till he could see hers. The colour in her cheeks had deepened a little, and there was an angry light in her eyes which he had never seen there. But she said not a word in answer.

"Do you love him?" Guido asked in a very low tone, and his voice trembled slightly.

"No!" The word came with sharp energy.

"How long have you known him?" Guido enquired.

"Since I have known you. I met him first on the same day. I have not spoken with him since. I tried to-day, I could not."

"Why not?"

"Do not ask me. I cannot tell you."

"Are you speaking the truth?" Guido asked, suddenly meeting her eyes.

She drew back with a quick movement, deeply offended and angry at the brutal question.

"How dare you doubt what I tell you!" She seemed about to rise.

"I beg your pardon," he said humbly. "I really beg your pardon. It is all so strange. I hardly knew what I was saying. Please forgive me!"

"I will try," Cecilia answered. "But I think I would rather go back now. We cannot talk here."

She rose to her feet, but Guido tried to detain her, remaining seated and looking up.

"Please, please stay a little longer!" he pleaded.

"No."

"You are still angry with me?"

"No. But I cannot talk to you yet. If you do not come with me, I shall go back alone."

There was nothing to be done. He rose and walked by her side in silence. The garden was almost empty now, and the Countess herself had gone in to get a cup of tea.

"The roses are really marvellous," Guido remarked in a set tone, as they came to the door.

Suddenly they were face to face with Lamberti, who was coming out, hat in hand. He had waited for his opportunity, watching them from a distance, and Guido knew it instinctively. He was quite cool and collected, and smiled pleasantly as he spoke to Cecilia.

"May I not have the pleasure of talking with you a little, Signorina?" he asked.

Guido could not help looking anxiously at the young girl.

"Certainly," she answered, without hesitation. "You will find my mother near the tea table, Signor d'Este," she added, to Guido. "It is really time that I should make your friend's acquaintance!"

He was as much amazed at her self-possession now as he had been at her evident disturbance before. He drew back as Cecilia turned away from him after speaking, and he stood looking after the pair a few seconds before he went in. At that moment he would have gladly strangled the man who had so long been his best friend. He had never guessed that he could wish to kill any one.

Lamberti did not make vague remarks about the roses as Guido had done, on the mere chance that some one might hear him, and indeed there was now hardly anybody to hear. As for Cecilia, her anger against Guido had sustained her at first, but she could not have talked unconcernedly now, as she walked beside Lamberti, waiting for him to speak. She felt just then that she would have walked on and on, whithersoever he chose to lead her, and until it pleased him to stop.

"D'Este asked me this afternoon how long I had known you," he said, at last. "I said that I had spoken with you twice, once at the Princess's, and once to-day. Was that right?"

"Yes. Did he believe you?"

"No."

"He did not believe me either."

"And of course he asked you what there was between us," said Lamberti.

"Yes. I said that I could not tell him. What did you say?"

"The same thing."

There was a pause, and both realised that they were talking as if they had known each other for years, and that they understood each other almost without words. At the end of the walk they turned towards one another, and their eyes met.

"Why did you run away from me?" Lamberti asked.

"I was frightened. I was frightened to-day when you spoke to me. Why did you go to the Forum that morning?"

"I had dreamt something strange about you. It happened just where I found you."

"I dreamt the same dream, the same night. That is, I think it must have been the same."

She turned her face away, blushing red.

He saw, and understood.

"Yes," he said. "What am I to tell d'Este?" he asked, after a short pause.

"Nothing!" said Cecilia quickly, and the subsiding blush rose again. "Besides," she continued, speaking rapidly in her embarrassment, "he would not believe us, whatever we told him, and it is of no use to let him know—" she stopped suddenly.

"Has he no right to know?"

"No. At least—no—I think not. I do not mean—"

They were standing still, facing each other. In another moment she would be telling Lamberti what she had never told Guido about her feelings towards him. On a sudden she turned away with a sort of desperate movement, clasping her hands and looking over the low wall.

"Oh, what is it all?" she cried, in great distress. "I am in the dream again, talking as if I had known you all my life! What must you think of me?"

Lamberti stood beside her, resting his hands upon the wall.

"It is exactly what I feel," he said quietly.

"Then you dream, too?" she asked.

"Every night—of you."

"We are both dreaming now! I am sure of it. I shall wake up in the dark and hear the door shut softly, though I always lock it now."

"The door? Do you hear that, too?" asked Lamberti. "But I am wide awake when I hear it."

"So am I! Sometimes I can manage to turn up the electric light before the sound has quite stopped. Are we both mad? What is it? In the name of Heaven, what is it all?"

"I wish I knew. Whatever it is, if you and I meet often, it is quite impossible that we should talk like ordinary acquaintances. Yes, I thought I was going mad, and this morning I went to a great doctor and told him everything. He seemed to think it was all a set of coincidences. He advised me to see you and ask you why you ran away that day, and he thought that if we talked about it, I might perhaps not dream again."

"You are not mad, you are not mad!" Cecilia repeated the words in a low voice, almost mechanically.

Then there was silence, and presently she turned from the wall and began to walk back along the wide path that passed by the central fountain. The sun, long out of sight behind the hill, was sinking now, the thin violet mist had begun to rise from the Campagna far to south and east, and the mountains had taken the first tinge of evening purple. From the ilex woods above the house, the voice of a nightingale rang out in a long and delicious trill. The garden was deserted, and now and then the sound of women's laughter rippled out through the high, open door.

"We must meet soon," Lamberti said, as they reached the fountain.

It seemed the most natural thing in the world that he should say it. She stopped and looked at him, and recognised every feature of the face she had seen in her dreams almost ever since she could remember dreaming. Her fear was all gone now, and she was sure that it would never come back.

Had she not heard him say those very words, "We must meet soon," hundreds and hundreds of times, just as he had said them long ago—ever so long ago—in a language that she could not remember when she was awake? And had they not always met soon?

"I shall see you to-night," she answered, almost unconsciously.

"Tell me," he said, looking into the clear water in the fountain, "does your dreaming make you restless and nervous? Does it wear on you?"

"Oh no! I have always dreamt a great deal all my life. I rest just as well."

"Yes—but those were ordinary dreams. I mean—"

"No, they were always the same. They were always about you. I almost screamed when I recognised you at the Princess's that afternoon."

"I had never dreamt of your face," said Lamberti, "but I was sure I had seen you before."

They looked down into the moving water, and the music of its fall made it harmonious with the distant song of the nightingale. Lamberti tried to think connectedly, and could not. It was as if he were under a spell. Questions rose to his lips, but he could not speak the words, he could not put them together in the right way. Once, at sea, on the training ship, he had fallen from the foreyard, and though the fall was broken by the gear and he had not been injured, he had been badly stunned, and for more than an hour he had lost all sense of direction, of what was forward and what was aft, so that at one moment the vessel seemed to be sailing backwards, and then forwards, and then sideways. He felt something like that now, and he knew intuitively that Cecilia felt it also. Amazingly absurd thoughts passed through his mind. Was to-morrow going to be yesterday? Would what was coming be just what was long past? Or was there no past, no future, nothing but all time present at once?

He was not moved by Cecilia's presence in the same way that Guido was. Guido was merely in love with her; very much in love, no doubt, but that was all. She was to him, first, the being of all others with whom he was most in sympathy, the only being whom he understood, and who, he was sure, understood him, the only being without whom life would be unendurable. And, secondly, she was the one and only creature in the world created to be his natural mate, and when he was near her he was aware of nature's mysterious forces, and felt the thrill of them continually.

Lamberti experienced nothing of that sort at present. He was overwhelmed and carried away out of the region of normal thought and volition towards something which he somehow knew was at hand, which he was sure he had reached before, but which he could not distinctly remember. Between it and him in the past there was a wall of darkness; between him and it in the future there was a veil not yet lifted, but on which his dreams already cast strange and beautiful shadows.

"I used to see things in the water," Cecilia said softly, "things that were going to happen. That was long, long ago."

"I remember," said Lamberti, quite naturally. "You told me once—"

He stopped. It was gone back behind the wall of darkness. When he had begun to speak, quite unconsciously, he had known what it was that Cecilia had told him, but he had forgotten it all now.

He passed his hand over his forehead, and suddenly everything changed, and he came back out of an immeasurable distance to real life.

"I shall be going away in a few days," he said. "May I see you before I go?"

"Certainly. Come and see us about three o'clock. We are always at home then."

"Thank you."

They turned from the fountain while they spoke, and walked slowly towards the house.

"Does your mother know about your dreaming?" Lamberti asked.

"No. No one knows. And you?"

"I have told that doctor. No one else. I wonder whether it will go on when I am far away."

"I wonder, too. Where are you going?"

"I do not know yet. Perhaps to China again. I shall get my orders in a few days."

They reached the threshold of the door. Lamberti had been looking for Guido's face amongst the people he could see as he came up, but Guido was gone.

"Good-bye," said Cecilia, softly.

"Good night," Lamberti answered, almost in a whisper. "God bless you."

He afterwards thought it strange that he should have said that, but at the time it seemed quite natural, and Cecilia was not at all surprised. She smiled and bent her graceful head. Then she joined her mother, and Lamberti disappeared.

"My dear," said the Countess, "you remember Monsieur Leroy? You met him at Princess Anatolie's," she added, in a stage whisper.

Monsieur Leroy bowed, and Cecilia nodded. She had forgotten his existence, and now remembered that she had not liked him, and that she had said something sharp to him. He spoke first.

"The Princess wished me to tell you how very sorry she is that she cannot be here this afternoon. She has one of her attacks."

"I am very sorry," Cecilia answered. "Pray tell her how sorry I am."

"Thank you. But I daresay Guido brought you the same message."

"Who is Guido?" asked Cecilia, raising her eyebrows a little.

"Guido d'Este. I thought you knew. You are surprised that I should call him by his Christian name? You see, I have known him ever since he was quite a boy. To all intents and purposes, he was brought up by the Princess."

"And you are often at the house, I suppose."

"I live there," explained Monsieur Leroy. "To change the subject, my dear young lady, I have an apology to make, which I hope you will accept."

Cecilia did not like to be called any one's "dear young lady," and her manner froze instantly.

"I cannot imagine why you should apologise to me," she said coldly.

"I was rude to you the other day, about your courses of philosophy, or something of that sort. Was not that it?"

"Indeed, I had quite forgotten," Cecilia answered, with truth. "It did not matter in the least what you thought of my reading Nietzsche, I assure you."

Monsieur Leroy reddened and laughed awkwardly, for he was particularly anxious to win her good grace.

"I am not very clever, you know," he said humbly. "You must forgive me."

"Oh certainly," replied Cecilia. "Your explanation is more than adequate. In my mind, the matter had already explained itself. Will you have some tea?"

"No, thank you. My nerves are rather troublesome. If I take tea in the afternoon I cannot sleep at night. I met Guido going away as I came. He was enthusiastic!"

"In what way?"

"About the villa, and the house, and the flowers, and about you." He lowered his voice to a confidential tone as he spoke the last words.

"About me?" Cecilia was somewhat surprised.

"Oh yes! He was overcome by your perfection—like every one else. How could it be otherwise? It is true that Guido has always been very impressionable."

"I should not have thought it," Cecilia said, wishing that the man would go away.

But he would not, and, to make matters worse, nobody would come and oblige him to move. It was plain to the meanest mind that since Cecilia was to marry Princess Anatolie's nephew, the extraordinary person whom the Princess called her secretary must not be disturbed when he was talking to Cecilia, since he might be the bearer of some important message. Besides, a good many people were afraid of him, in a vague way, as a rather spiteful gossip who had more influence than he should have had.

"Yes," he continued, in an apologetic tone, "Guido is always falling in love, poor boy. Of course, it is not to be wondered at. A king's son, and handsome as he is, and so very clever, too—all the pretty ladies fall in love with him at once, and he naturally falls in love with them. You see how simple it is. He has more opportunities than are good for him!"

The disagreeable little man giggled, and his loose pink and white cheeks shook unpleasantly. Cecilia thought him horribly vulgar and familiar, and she inwardly wondered how the Princess Anatolie could even tolerate him, not to speak of treating him affectionately and calling him "Doudou."

"I supposed that you counted yourself among Signor d'Este's friends," said the young girl, frigidly.

"I do, I do! Have I said anything unfriendly? I merely said that all the women fell in love with him."

"You said a good deal more than that."

"At all events, I wish I were he," said Monsieur Leroy. "And if that is not paying him a compliment I do not know what you would call it. He is handsome, clever, generous, everything!"

"And faithless, according to you."

"No, no! Not faithless; only fickle, very fickle."

"It is the same thing," said the young girl, scornfully.

She did not believe Monsieur Leroy in the least, but she wondered what his object could be in speaking against Guido, and whether he were really silly, as he often seemed, or malicious, as she suspected, or possibly both at the same time, since the combination is not uncommon. What he was telling her, if she believed it, was certainly not of a nature to hasten her marriage with Guido; and yet it was the Princess who had first suggested the match, and it could hardly be supposed that Monsieur Leroy would attempt to oppose his protectress.

Just then there was a general move to go away, and the conversation was interrupted, much to Cecilia's satisfaction. There was a great stir in the wide hall, for though many people had slipped away without disturbing the Countess by taking leave, there were many of her nearer friends who wished to say a word to her before going, just to tell her that they had enjoyed themselves vastly, that Cecilia was a model of beauty and good behaviour, and of everything charming, and that the villa was the most delightful place they had ever seen. By these means they conveyed the impression that they would all accept any future invitation which the Countess might send them, and they audibly congratulated one another upon her having at last established herself in Rome, adding that Cecilia was a great acquisition to society. More than that it was manifestly impossible to say in a few well-chosen words. Even in a language as rich as Italian, the number of approving adjectives is limited, and each can only have one superlative. The Countess Fortiguerra's guests distributed these useful words amongst them and exhausted the supply.

"It has been a great success, my dear," said the Countess, when she and her daughter were left alone in the hall. "Did you see the Duchess of Pallacorda's hat?"

"No, mother. At least, I did not notice it." Cecilia was nibbling a cake, thoughtfully.

"My dear!" cried the Countess. "It was the most wonderful thing you ever saw. She was in terror lest it should come too late. Monsieur Leroy knew all about it."

"I cannot bear that man," Cecilia said, still nibbling, for she was hungry.

"I cannot say that I like him, either. But the Duchess's new hat—"

Cecilia heard her voice, but was too much occupied with her own thoughts to listen attentively, while the good Countess criticised the hat in question, admired its beauties, corrected its defects, put it a little further back on the Duchess's pretty head, and, indeed, did everything with it which every woman can do, in imagination, with every imaginary hat. Finally, she asked Cecilia if she should not like to have one exactly like it.

"No, thank you. Not now, at all events. Mother dear," and she looked affectionately at the Countess, "what a deal of trouble you have taken to make it all beautiful for me to-day. I am so grateful!"

She kissed her mother on both cheeks just as she had always done when she was pleased, ever since she had been a child, and suddenly the elder woman's eyes glistened.

"It is a pleasure to do anything for you, darling," she said. "I have only you in the world," she added quietly, after a little pause, "but I sometimes think I have more than all the other women."

Then Cecilia laid her head on her mother's shoulder for a moment, and gently patted her cheek, and they both felt very happy.

They drove home in the warm dusk, and when they reached the high road down by the Tiber they looked up and saw moving lights through the great open windows of the villa, and on the terrace, and in the gardens, like fireflies. For the servants were bringing in the chairs and putting things in order. The nightingale was singing again, far up in the woods, but Cecilia could hear the song distinctly as the carriage swept along.

Now the Countess was kind and true, and loved her daughter devotedly, but she would not have been a woman if she had not wished to know what Guido had said to Cecilia that afternoon; and before they had entered Porta Angelica she asked what she considered a leading question, in her own peculiar contradictory way.

"Of course, I am not going to ask you anything, my dear," she began, "but did Signor d'Este say anything especial to you when you went off together?"

Cecilia remembered how they had driven home from the Princess's a fortnight earlier, almost at the same hour, and how her mother had then first spoken of Guido d'Este. The young girl asked herself in the moment she took before answering, whether she were any nearer to the thought of marrying him than she had been after that first short meeting.

"He loves me, mother," she answered softly. "He has made me understand that he does, without quite saying so. I like him very much. That is our position now. I would rather not talk about it much, but you have a right to know."

"Yes, dear. But what I mean is—I mean, what I meant was—he has not asked you to marry him, has he?"

"No. I am not sure that he will, now."

"Yes, he will. He asked me yesterday evening if he might, and of course I gave him my permission."

It was a relief to have told Cecilia this, for concealment was intolerable to the Countess.

"I see," Cecilia answered.

"Yes, of course you do. But when he does ask you, what shall you say, dear? He is sure to ask you to-morrow, and I really want to know what I am to expect. Surely, by this time you must have made up your mind."

"I have only known him a fortnight, mother. That is not a long time when one is to decide about one's whole life, is it?"

"No. Well—it seems to me that a fortnight—you see, it is so important!"

"Precisely," Cecilia answered. "It is very important. That is why I do not mean to do anything in a hurry. Either you must tell Signor d'Este to wait a little while before he asks me, or else, when he does, I must beg him to wait some time for his answer."

"But it seems to me, if you like him so much, that is quite enough."

"Why are you in such a hurry, mother?" asked Cecilia, with a smile.

"Because I am sure you will be perfectly happy if you marry him," answered the Countess, with much conviction.

CHAPTER X

Guido d'Este walked home from the Villa Madama in a very bad temper with everything. He was not of a dramatic disposition, nor easily inclined to sudden resolutions, and when placed in new and unexpected circumstances his instinct was rather to let them develop as they would than to direct them or oppose them actively. For the first time in his life he now felt that he must do one or the other.

To treat Lamberti as if nothing had happened was impossible, and it was equally out of the question to behave towards Cecilia as though she had not done or said anything to check the growth of intimacy and friendship on her side and of genuine love on his. He took the facts as he knew them and tried to state them justly, but he could make nothing of them that did not plainly accuse both Cecilia and Lamberti of deceiving him. Again and again, he recalled the words and behaviour of both, and he could reach no other conclusion. They had a joint secret which they had agreed to keep from him, and rather than reveal it his best friend was ready to break with him, and the woman he loved preferred never to see him again. He reflected that he was not the first man who had been checked by a girl and forsaken by a friend, but that did not make it any easier to bear.

It was quite clear that he could not submit to be so treated by them. Lamberti had asked him to speak to Cecilia before quarrelling definitely. He had done so, and he was more fully convinced than before that both were deceiving him. There was no way out of that conviction, there was not the smallest argument on the other side, and nothing that either could ever say could shake his belief. It was plainly his duty to tell them so, and it would be wisest to write to them, for he felt that he might lose his temper if he tried to say what he meant, instead of writing it.

He wrote to Lamberti first, because it was easier, though it was quite the hardest thing he had ever done. He began by proving to himself, and therefore to his friend, that he was writing after mature reflection and without the least hastiness, or temper, or unwillingness to be convinced, if Lamberti had anything to say in self-defence. He expressed no suspicion as to the probable nature of the secret that was withheld from him; he even wrote that he no longer wished to know what it was. His argument was that by refusing to reveal it, Lamberti had convicted himself of some unknown deed which he was ashamed to acknowledge, and Guido did not hesitate to add that such unjustifiable reticence might easily be construed in such a way as to cast a slur upon the character of an innocent young girl.

Having got so far, Guido immediately tore the whole letter to shreds and rose from his writing table, convinced that it was impossible to write what he meant without saying things which he did not mean. After all, he could simply avoid his old friend in future. The idea of quarrelling with him aggressively had never entered his mind, and it was therefore of no use to write anything at all. Lamberti must have guessed already that all friendship was at an end, and it would consequently be quite useless to tell him so.

He must write to Cecilia, however. He could not allow her to think, because he had apologised for rudely doubting her word, that he therefore believed what she had told him. He would write.

Here he was confronted by much greater difficulties than he had found in composing his unsuccessful letter to Lamberti. In the first place, he was in love with her, and it seemed to him that he should love her just as much, whatever she did. He wondered what it was that he felt, for at first he hardly thought it was jealousy, and it was assuredly not a mere passing fit of ill-tempered resentment.

It must be jealousy, after all. He fancied that she had known Lamberti before, and that she had been girlishly in love with him, and that when she had met him again she had been startled and annoyed. It was not so hard to imagine that this might be possible, though he could not see why they should both make such a secret of having known each other. But perhaps, by some accident, they had become intimate without the knowledge of the Countess, so that Cecilia was now very much afraid lest her mother should find it out.

Guido's reflections stopped there. At any other time he would have laughed at their absurdity, and now he resented it. The plain fact stared him in the face, the fact he had known all along and had forgotten—Lamberti could not possibly have met Cecilia since she had been a mere child, because Guido could account for all his friend's movements during the last five years. Five years ago, Cecilia had been thirteen.

He was glad that he had torn up his letter to Lamberti, and that he had not even begun the one to Cecilia, after sitting half an hour with his pen in his hand. Yes, he went over those five years, and then took from a drawer the last five of the little pocket diaries he always carried. There was a small space for each day of the year, and he never failed to note at least the name of the place in which he was, while travelling. He also recorded Lamberti's coming and going, the names of the ships to which he was ordered, and the dates of any notable facts in his life. It is tolerably easy to record the exact movements of a sailor in active service who is only at home on very short leave once in a year or two. Guido turned over the pages carefully and set down on a slip of paper what he found. In five years Lamberti's leave had not amounted to eight months in all, and Guido could account for every day of it, for they had spent all of it either in Rome or in travelling together. He laid the little diaries in the drawer again, and leaned back in his chair with a deep sigh of satisfaction.

He was too generous not to wish to find his friend at once and acknowledge frankly that he had been wrong. He telephoned to ask whether Lamberti had come back from the Villa Madama. Yes, he had come back, but he had gone out again. No one knew where he was. He had said that he should not dine at home. That was all. If he returned before half-past ten o'clock d'Este should be informed.

Guido dined alone and waited, but no message came during the evening. At half-past ten he wrote a few words on a correspondence card, told his man to send the note to Lamberti early in the morning, and went to bed, convinced that everything would explain itself satisfactorily before long. As soon as he was positively sure that Lamberti and Cecilia could not possibly have known each other more than a fortnight, his natural indolence returned. Of course it was very extraordinary that Cecilia should have felt such a strong dislike for Lamberti at first sight, for it could be nothing else, since she seemed displeased whenever his name was mentioned; and it was equally strange that Lamberti should feel the same antipathy for her. But since it was so, she would naturally draw back from telling Guido that his best friend was repulsive to her, and Lamberti would not like to acknowledge that the young girl Guido wished to marry produced a disagreeable impression on him. It was quite natural, too, that after what Guido had said to each of them, each should have been anxious to show him that he was mistaken, and that they should have taken the first opportunity of talking together just when he should most notice it.

Everything was accounted for by this ingenious theory. Guido knew a man who turned pale when a cat came near him, though he was a manly man, good at sports and undeniably courageous. Those things could not be explained, but it was much easier to understand that a sensitive young girl might be violently affected by an instinctive antipathy for a man, than that a strong man's teeth should chatter if a cat got under his chair at dinner. That was undoubtedly what happened. How could either of them tell him so, since he was so fond of both? Lamberti had said that as a last resource, he would try to explain what the trouble was. Guido would spare him that. He knew what he had felt almost daily in the presence of Monsieur Leroy, ever since he had been a boy. Lamberti and Cecilia probably acted on each other in the same way. It was a misfortune, of course, that his best friend and his future wife should hate the sight and presence of one another, but it was not their fault, and they would probably get over it.

It was wonderful to see how everything that had happened exactly fitted into Guido's simple explanation, the passing shadow on Cecilia's face, the evident embarrassment of both when Guido asked each the same question, the agreement of their answers, the readiness both had shown to try and overcome their mutual dislike—it was simply wonderful! By the time Guido laid his head on his pillow, he was serenely calm and certain of the future. With the words of sincere regret he had written to Lamberti, and with the decision to say much the same thing to Cecilia on the following day, his conscience was at rest; and he went to sleep in the pleasant assurance that after having done something very hasty he had just avoided doing something quite irreparable.

Lamberti had spent a less pleasant evening, and was not prepared for the agreeable surprise that awaited him on the following morning in Guido's note. He was neither indolent nor at all given to self-examination, and he had generally found it a good plan to act upon impulse, and do what he wished to do before it occurred to any one else to do the same thing; and when he could not see what he ought to do, and was nevertheless sure that he ought to act at once, he lost his temper with himself and sometimes with other people.

He was afraid to go to bed that night, and he went to the club and watched some of his friends playing cards until he could not keep his eyes open; for gambling bored him to extinction. Then he walked the whole length of the Corso and back, in the hope that the exercise might prevent him from dreaming. But it only roused him again; and when he was in his own room he stood nearly two hours at the open window, smoking one cigar after another. At last he lay down without putting out the light and read a French novel till it dropped from his hand, and he fell asleep at four o'clock in the morning.

He was not visited by the dream that had disturbed his rest nightly for a full fortnight. Possibly the doctor had been right after all, and the habit was broken. At all events, what he remembered having felt when he awoke was something quite new and not altogether unpleasant after the first beginning, yet so strangely undefined that he would have found it hard to describe it in any words.

He had no consciousness of any sort of shape or body belonging to him, nor of motion, nor of sight, after the darkness had closed in upon him. That moment, indeed, was terrible. It reminded him of the approach of a cyclone in the West Indies, which he remembered well—the dreadful stillness in the air; the long, sullen, greenish brown swell of the oily sea; the appalling bank of solid darkness that moved upon the ship over the noiseless waves; the shreds of black cloud torn forwards by an unseen and unheard force, and the vast flashes of lightning that shot upwards like columns of flame. He remembered the awful waiting.

Not a storm, then, but an instant change from something to nothing, with consciousness preserved; complete, far-reaching consciousness, that was more perfect than sight, yet was not sight, but a being everywhere at once, a universal understanding, a part of something all pervading, a unification with all things past, present, and to come, with no desire for them, nor vision of them, but perfect knowledge of them all.

At the same time, there was the presence of another immeasurable identity in the same space, so that his own being and that other were coexistent and alike, each in the other, everywhere at once, and inseparable from the other, and also, in some unaccountable way, each dear to the other beyond and above all description. And there was perfect peace and a state very far beyond any possible waking happiness, without any conception of time or of motion, but only of infinite space with infinite understanding.

Another phase began. There was time again, there were minutes, hours, months, years, ages; and there was a longing for something that could change, a stirring of human memories in the boundless immaterial consciousness, a desire for sight and hearing, a gradual, growing wish to see a face remembered before the wall of darkness had closed in, to hear a voice that had once sounded in ears that had once understood, to touch a hand that had felt his long ago. And the longing became intolerable, for lack of these things, like a burning thirst where there is no water; and the perfect peace was all consumed in that raging wish, and the quiet was disquiet, and the two consciousnesses felt that each was learning to suffer again for want of the other, till what had been heaven was hell, and earth would be better, or total destruction and the extinguishing of all identity, or anything that was not, rather than the least prolonging of what was.

The last change now; back to the world, and to a human body. Lamberti was waked by a vigorous knocking at his door, which was locked as usual. It was nine o'clock, and a servant had brought him Guido's note.

"My dear friend," it said, "I was altogether in the wrong yesterday. Please forgive me. I quite understand your position with regard to the Contessina, and hers towards you, but I sincerely hope that in the end you may be good friends. I appreciate very much the effort you both made this afternoon to overcome your mutual antipathy. Thank you. G. d'E."

Lamberti read the note three times before the truth dawned upon him, and he at last understood what Guido meant. At first the note seemed to have been written in irony, if not in anger, but that would have been very unlike Guido; the second reading convinced Lamberti that his friend was in earnest, whatever his meaning might be, and at the third perusal, Lamberti saw the true state of the case. Guido supposed that he and Cecilia were violently repelled by each other.

He did not smile at the absurdity of the idea, for he felt at once that the results of such a misunderstanding must before long place Cecilia and himself in a false position, from which it would be hard to escape. Yet he was well aware that Guido would not believe the truth—that the coincidences were too extraordinary to be readily admitted, while no other rational theory could be found to explain what had happened. If Lamberti saw Cecilia often, Guido would soon perceive that instead of mutual dislike and repulsion the strongest sympathy existed between them, and that they would always understand each other without words. It would be impossible to conceal that very long.

Besides, they would love each other, if they met frequently; about that Lamberti had not the smallest doubt. His instincts were direct and unhesitating, and he knew that he had never felt for any living woman what he felt for the fair young girl whose unreal presence visited his dreams, and who, in those long visions, loved him dearly in return, with a spiritual passion that rose far above perishable things and yet was not wholly immaterial. There was that one moment when they stood near together in the early morning, and their lips met as if body, heart, and soul were all meeting at once, and only for once.

After that, in his dreams, there was much that Lamberti could not understand in himself, and which seemed very unlike the self he knew, very much higher, very much purer, very much more inclined to sacrifice, constantly in a sort of spiritual tension and always striving towards a perfect life, which was as far as anything could be, he supposed, from his own personality, as he thought he knew it. The story he dreamed was simple enough. He was a Christian, the girl a Vestal Virgin, the youngest of those last six who still guarded the sacred hearth when the Christian Emperor dissolved all that was left of the worship of the old gods. He bade the noble maidens close the doors of the temple and depart in peace to their parents' homes, freed from their vows and service, and from all obligations to the state, but deprived also of all their old honours and lands and privileges. And sadly they buried the things that had been holy, where no man knew, and watched the fire together, one last night, till it burned out to white ashes in the spring dawn; and they embraced one another with tears and went away. Some became Christians, and some afterwards married; but there was one who would not, though she loved as none of them loved, and she withdrew from the world and lived a pure life for the sake of the old faith and of her solemn vows.

So, at last, the Christian believed what she told him, that it was better to love in that way, because when he and she were freed at last from all earthly longings, they would be united for ever and ever; and she became a Christian, too, and after the other five Vestals were dead, she also passed away; and the man who had loved her so long, in her own way, died peacefully on the next day, loving her and hoping to join her, and having led a good life. After that there was peace, and they seemed to be together.

That was their story as it gradually took shape out of fragments and broken visions, and though the man who dreamt these things could not conceive, when he remembered them, that he could ever become at all a saintly character, yet in the vision he knew that he was always himself, and all that he thought and did seemed natural, though it often seemed hard, and he suffered much in some ways, but in others he found great happiness.

It was a simple story and a most improbable one. He was quite sure that no matter in what age he might have lived, instead of in the twentieth century, he would have felt and acted as he now did when he was wide awake. But that did not matter. The important point was that his imagination was making for him a sort of secondary existence in sleep, in which he was desperately in love with some one who exactly resembled Cecilia Palladio and who bore her first name; and this dreaming created such a strong and lasting impression in his mind that, in real life, he could not separate Cecilia Palladio from Cecilia the Vestal, and found himself on the point of saying to her in reality the very things which he had said to her in imagination while sleeping. The worst of it was this identity of the real and the unreal, for he was persuaded that with very small opportunity the two would turn into one.

He hated thinking, under all circumstances, as compared with action. It was easier to follow his impulses, and fortunately for him they were brave and honourable. He never analysed his feelings, never troubled himself about his motives, never examined his conscience. It told him well enough whether he was doing right or wrong, and on general principles he always meant to do right. It was not his fault if his imagination made him fall in love in a dream with the young girl who was probably to be his friend's wife. But it would be distinctly his fault if he gave himself the chance of falling in love with her in reality.

Moreover, though he did not know how much further Cecilia's dream coincided with his own, and believed it impossible that the coincidence should be nearly as complete as it seemed, he felt that she would love him if he chose that she should. The intuitions of very masculine men about women are far keener and more trustworthy than women guess; and when such a man is not devoured by fatuous vanity he is rarely mistaken if he feels sure that a woman he meets will love him, provided that circumstances favour him ever so little. There is not necessarily the least particle of conceit in that certainty, which depends on the direct attraction between any two beings who are natural complements to each other.

Lamberti was a man who had the most profound respect for every woman who deserved to be respected ever so little, and a good-natured contempt for all the rest, together with a careless willingness to be amused by them. And of all the women in the world, next to his own mother, the one whom he would treat with something approaching to veneration would be Guido's wife, if Guido married.

Without any reasoning, it was plain that he must see as little as possible of Cecilia Palladio. But as this would not please Guido, the best plan was to go away while there was time. In all probability, when he next returned, say in two years, he would no longer feel the dangerous attraction that was almost driving him out of his senses at present.

He had been in Rome some time, expecting his promotion to the rank of lieutenant-commander, which would certainly be accompanied by orders to join another ship, possibly very far away. If he showed himself very anxious to go at once, before his leave expired, the Admiralty would probably oblige him, especially as he just now cared much less for the promised step in the service than for getting away at short notice. The best thing to be done was to go and see the Minister, who had of late been very friendly to him; everything might be settled in half an hour, and next week he would be on his way to China, or South America, or East Africa, which would be perfectly satisfactory to everybody concerned.

It was a wise and honourable resolution, and he determined to act on it at once. His hand was on the door to go out, when he stopped suddenly and stood quite still for a few seconds. It was as if something unseen surrounded him on all sides, in the air, invisible but solid as lead, making it impossible for him to move. It did not last long, and he went out, wondering at his nervousness.

In half an hour he was in the presence of the Minister, who was speaking to him.

"You are promoted to the rank of lieutenant-commander. You are temporarily attached to the ministerial commission which is to study the Somali question, which you understand so well from experience on the spot. His Majesty specially desires it."

"How long may this last, sir?" enquired Lamberti, with a look of blank disappointment.

"Oh, a year or two, I should say," laughed the Minister. "They do not hurry themselves. You can enjoy a long holiday at home."

CHAPTER XI

Though it was late in the season, everybody wished to do something to welcome the appearance of Cecilia Palladio in society. It was too warm to give balls, but it did not follow that it was at all too hot to dance informally, with the windows open. We do not know why a ball is hotter than a dance; but it is so. There are things that men do not understand.

So dinners were given, to which young people were asked, and afterwards an artistic-looking man appeared from somewhere and played waltzes, and twenty or thirty couples amused themselves to their hearts' delight till one o'clock in the morning. Moreover, people who had villas gave afternoon teas, without any pretence of giving garden parties, and there also the young ones danced, sometimes on marble pavements in great old rooms that smelt slightly of musty furniture, but were cool and pleasant. Besides these things, there were picnic dinners at Frascati and Castel Gandolfo, and everybody drove home across the Campagna by moonlight. Altogether, and chiefly in Cecilia Palladio's honour, there was a very pretty little revival of winter gaiety, which is not always very gay in Rome, nowadays.

The young girl accepted it all much more graciously than her mother had expected, and was ready to enjoy everything that people offered her, which is a great secret of social success. The Countess had always feared that Cecilia was too fond of books and of serious talk to care much for what amuses most people. But, instead, she suddenly seemed to have been made for society; she delighted in dancing, she liked to be well dressed, she smiled at well-meaning young men who made compliments to her, and she chatted with young girls about the myriad important nothings that grow like wild flowers just outside life's gate.

Every one liked her, and she let almost every one think that she liked them. She never said disagreeable things about them, and she never attracted to herself the young gentleman who was looked upon as the property of another. Every one said that she was going to marry d'Este in the autumn, though the engagement was not yet announced. Wherever she was, he was there also, generally accompanied by his inseparable friend, Lamberto Lamberti.

The latter had grown thinner during the last few weeks. When any one spoke of it, he explained that life ashore did not suit him, and that he was obliged to work a good deal over papers and maps for the ministerial commission. But he was evidently not much inclined to talk of himself, and he changed the subject immediately. His life was not easy, for he was not only in serious trouble himself, but he was also becoming anxious about Guido.

The one matter about which a man is instinctively reticent with his most intimate man friend is his love affair, if he has one. He would rather tell a woman all about it, though he does not know her nearly so well, than talk about it, even vaguely, with the one man in the world whom he trusts. Where women are concerned, all men are more or less one another's natural enemies, in spite of civilisation and civilised morals; and each knows this of the other, and respects the other's silence as both inevitable and decent.

Guido had told Lamberti that he should be the first to know of the engagement as soon as there was any, and Lamberti waited. He did not know whether Guido had spoken yet, nor whether there was any sort of agreement between him and Cecilia by which the latter was to give her answer after a certain time. He could not guess what they talked of during the hour they spent together nearly every day. People made inquiries of him, some openly and some by roundabout means, and he always answered that if his friend were engaged to be married he would assuredly announce the fact at once. Those who received this answer were obliged to be satisfied with it, because Lamberti was not the kind of man to submit to cross-questioning.

He wondered whether Cecilia knew that he loved her, since what he had foreseen had happened, and he did not even try to deny the fact to himself. He would not let his thoughts dwell on what she might feel for him, for that would have seemed like the beginning of a betrayal.

She never asked him questions nor did anything to make him spend more time near her than was inevitable, and neither had ever gone back to the subject of their dreams. She had asked Lamberti to come to the house at an hour when there would not be other visitors, but he had not come, and neither had ever referred to the matter since. He sometimes felt that she was watching him earnestly, but at those times he would not meet her eyes lest his own should say too much.

It was hard, it was quite the hardest thing he had ever done in his life, and he was never quite sure that he could go on with it to the end. But it was the only honourable course he could follow, and it would surely grow easier when he knew definitely that Cecilia meant to marry Guido. It was bitter to feel that if the man had been any one but his friend, there would have been no reason for making any such sacrifice. He inwardly prayed that Cecilia would come to a decision soon, and he was deeply grateful to her for not making his position harder by referring to their first conversation at the Villa Madama.

Guido had not the slightest suspicion of the true state of things, but he himself was growing impatient, and daily resolved to put the final question. Every day, however, he put it off again, not from lack of courage, nor even because he was naturally so very indolent, but because he felt sure that the answer would not be the one hoped for. Though Cecilia's manner with him had never changed from the first, it was perfectly clear that, however much she might enjoy his conversation, she was calmly indifferent to his personality. She never blushed with pleasure when he came, nor did her eyes grow sad when he left her; and when she talked with him she spoke exactly as when she was speaking with her mother. He listened in vain for an added earnestness of tone, meant for him only; it never came. She liked him, beyond doubt, from the first, and liking had changed to friendship very fast, but Guido knew how very rarely the friendship a woman feels for a man can ever turn to love. Starting from the same point, it grows steadily in another direction, and its calm intellectual sympathy makes the mere suggestion of any unreasoning impulse of the heart seem almost absurd.

But where the man and woman do not feel alike, this state of things cannot last for ever, and when it comes to an end there is generally trouble and often bitterness. Guido knew that very well and hesitated in consequence.

Princess Anatolie could not understand the reason for this delay, and was not at all pleased. She said it would be positively not decent if the girl refused to marry Guido after acting in public as if she were engaged to him, and Monsieur Leroy agreed with her. She asked him if he could not do anything to hasten matters, and he said he would try. The old lady had felt quite sure of the marriage, and in imagination she had already extracted from Guido's wife all the money she had made Guido lose for her. It is now hardly necessary to say that she had received spirit messages through Monsieur Leroy, bidding her to invest money in the most improbable schemes, and that she had followed his advice in making her nephew act as her agent in the matter. Monsieur Leroy had pleaded his total ignorance of business as a reason for keeping out of the transaction, by which, however, it may be supposed that he profited indirectly for a time. He never hesitated to say that the unfortunate result was due to Guido's negligence and failure to carry out the instructions given him.

But the Princess knew that at least a part of the fault belonged to Monsieur Leroy, though she never had the courage to tell him so; and though it looked as if nothing could sever the mysterious tie that linked their lives together, he had forfeited some of his influence over her with the loss of the money, and had only recently regained it by convincing her that she was in communication with her dead child. So long as he could keep her in this belief he was in no danger of losing his power again. On the contrary, it increased from day to day.

"Guido is so very quixotic," he said. "He hesitates because the girl is so rich. But we may be able to bring a little pressure to bear on him. After all, you have his receipts for all the money that passed through his hands."

"Unless he marries this girl, they are not worth the paper they are written on."

"I am not sure. He is very sensitive about matters of honour. Now a receipt for money given to a lady looks to me very much like a debt of honour. What happened in the eyes of the world? You lent him money which he lost in speculation."

"No doubt," answered the Princess, willing to be convinced of any absurdity that could help her to get back her money. "But when a man has no means of paying a debt of honour—"

"He shoots himself," said Monsieur Leroy, completing the sentence.

"That would not help us. Besides, I should be very sorry if anything happened to Guido."

"Of course!" cried Monsieur Leroy. "Not for worlds! But nothing need happen to him. You have only to persuade him that the sole way to save his honour is to marry an heiress, and he will marry at once, as a matter of conscience. Unless something is done to move him, he will not."

"But he is in love with the girl!"

"Enough to occupy him and amuse him. That is all. By-the-bye, where are those receipts?"

"In the small strong-box, in the lower drawer of the writing table."

Monsieur Leroy found the papers, and transferred them to his pocket-book, not yet sure how he could best turn them to account, but quite certain that their proper use would reveal itself to him before long.

"And besides," he concluded, "we can always make him sell the Andrea del Sarto and the Raphael. Baumgarten thinks they are worth a good sum. You know that he buys for the Berlin gallery, and the British Museum people think everything of his opinion."

In this way the Princess and her favourite disposed of Guido and his property; but he would not have been much surprised if he could have heard their conversation. They were only saying what he had expected of them as far back as the day when he had talked with Lamberti in the garden of the Arcadians.

CHAPTER XII

It is not strange that Cecilia should have been much less disturbed than Lamberti by what he had described to the doctor as a possession of the devil, or a haunting. Men who have never been ailing in their lives sometimes behave like frightened children if they fall ill, though the ailment may not be very serious, whereas a hardened old invalid, determined to make the best of life in spite of his ills, often laughs himself into the belief that he can recover from the two or three mortal diseases that have hold of him. Bearing bodily pain is a mere matter of habit, as every one knows who has had to bear much, or who has tried it as an experiment. In barbarous countries conspirators have practised suffering the tortures likely to be inflicted on them to extract confession.

Lamberti had never before been troubled by anything at all resembling what people call the supernatural, nor even by anything unaccountable. It was natural that he should be made nervous and almost ill by the persistence of the dreams that had visited him since he had met Cecilia, and by what he believed to be the closing of a door each time he awoke from them.

Cecilia, on the contrary, had practised dreaming all her life and was not permanently disturbed by any vision that presented itself, nor by anything like a "phenomenon" which might accompany it. She felt that her dreams brought her nearer to a truth of some sort, hidden from most of the world, but of vital value, and after which she was groping continually without much sense of direction. The specialist whom Lamberti had consulted would have told her plainly that she had learned to hypnotise herself, and a Japanese Buddhist monk would have told her the same thing, adding that she was doing one of the most dangerous things possible. The western man of science would have assured her that a certain resemblance of the face in the dream to Lamberti was a mere coincidence, and that since she had met him the likeness had perfected itself, so that she now really dreamed of Lamberti; and the doctor would have gone on to say that the rest of her vision was the result of auto-suggestion, because the story of the Vestal Virgins had always had a very great attraction for her. She had read a great deal about them, she had followed Giacomo Boni's astonishing discoveries with breathless interest, she knew more of Roman history than most girls, and probably more than most men, and it was not at all astonishing that she should be able to construct a whole imaginary past life with all its details and even its end, and to dream it all at will, as if she were reading a novel.

She would have admitted that the pictured history of Cecilia, the last Vestal, had been at first fragmentary, and had gradually completed itself in her visions, and that even now it was constantly growing, and that it might continue to grow, and even to change, for a long time.

Further, if the specialist had known positively that similar fragments of dreams were little by little putting themselves together in Lamberti's imagination, though the latter had only once spoken with Cecilia of one or two coincidences, he would have said, provided that he chose to be frank with a mere girl, that no one knows much about telepathy, and that modern science does not deny what it cannot explain, as the science of the nineteenth century did, but collects and examines facts, only requiring to be persuaded that they are really facts and not fictions. No one, he would have said, would build a theory on one instance; he would write down the best account of the case which he could find, and would then proceed to look for another. Since wireless telegraphy was possible, the specialist would not care to seek a reason why telepathy should not be a possibility, too. If it were, it explained thoroughly what was going on between Cecilia and Lamberti; if it were not, there must be some other equally satisfactory explanation, still to be found. The attitude of science used to be extremely aggressive, but she has advanced to a higher stage; in these days she is serene. Men of science still occasionally come into conflict with the official representatives of different beliefs, but science herself no longer assails religion. Lamberti's specialist professed no form of faith, wherefore he would rather not have been called upon to answer all three of Kant's questions: What can I know? What is it my duty to do? What may I hope? But it by no means followed that his answers, if he gave any, would have been shocking to people who knew less and hoped more than he did.

Cecilia thought much, but she followed no such form of reasoning to convince herself that her experiences were all scientifically possible; on the contrary, the illusion she loved best was the one which science and religion alike would have altogether condemned as contrary to faith and revolting to reason, namely, her cherished belief that she had really once lived as a Vestal in old days, and had died, and had come back to earth after a long time, irresistibly drawn towards life after having almost attained to perfect detachment from material things.

Her meeting with Lamberti, and, most of all, her one short conversation with him, had greatly strengthened her illusion. He had come back, too, and they understood each other. But that should be all.

Then she took up Nietzsche again, not because every one read Thus spake Zarathushthra, or was supposed to read the book, and talked about it in a manner that discredited the supposition, but because she wanted to decide once for all whether his theory of the endless return to life at all suited her own case.

She turned over the pages, but she knew the main thought by heart. Time is infinite. In space there is matter consisting of elements which, however numerous, are limited in number, and can therefore only combine in a finite number of ways. When those possible combinations are exhausted, they must repeat themselves. And because time is infinite, they must repeat themselves an infinite number of times. Therefore precisely the same combinations have returned always and will return again and again for ever. Therefore in the past, every one of us has lived precisely the same life, in a precisely similar world, an infinite number of times, and will live the same life over again, to the minutest detail, an infinite number of times in the future. In the fewest words, this is Nietzsche's argument to prove what he calls the "Eternal Return."

No. That was not at all what she wished to believe, nor could believe, though it was very plausible as a theory. If men lived over again, they did not live the same lives but other lives, worse or better than the first. Nietzsche in this was speaking only of matter which combined and combined again. If it did, each combination might have a new soul of its own. It was conceivable that different souls should be made to suffer and enjoy in precisely the same way. And as for the rest, as for a good deal of Thus spake Zarathushthra, including the Over-Man, and the overcoming of Pity, and the Man who had killed God, she thought it merely fantastic, though much of it was very beautiful and some of it was terrible, and she thought she had understood what Nietzsche meant.

Tired of reading, she lay back in her deep chair and let the open book fall upon her knees. She was in her own room, late in the morning, and the blinds were drawn together to keep out the glare of the wide street, for it was June and the summer was at hand. Outside, the air was all alive with the coming heat, as it is in Italy at the end of spring, and perhaps nowhere else. The sunshine seems to grow in it, like a living thing, that also fills everything with life. It gets into the people, too, and into their voices, and even the grave Romans unbend a little, and laugh more gaily, and their step is more elastic. By-and-by, when the full warmth of summer fills the city, the white streets will be almost deserted in the middle of the day, and men who have to be abroad will drag themselves along where the walls cast a narrow shade, and everything will grow lazy and sleepy and silently hot. But the first good sunshine in June is to the southern people the elixir of life, the magic gold-mist that floats before the coming gods, the breath of the gods themselves breathed into mortals.

Within the girl's room the light was very soft on the pale blue damask hangings, and a gentle air blew now and then from window to window, as if a sweet spirit passed by, bringing a message and taking one away. It stirred Cecilia's golden hair, and fanned her forehead, and somehow, just then, it brought intuitions of beautiful unknown things with it, and inspiration with peace, and clear sight.

Maidenhood is blessed with such moments, beyond all other states. In all times and in all countries it has been half divine, and ever mysteriously linked with divine things. The maid was ever the priestess, the prophetess, and the seer, whose eyes looked beyond the veil and whose ears heard the voices of the immortals; and she of Orleans was not the only maiden, though she was the last, that lifted her fallen country up out of despair and led men to fight and victory who would follow no man-leader where all had failed.

Maidenhood meets evil, and passes by on the other side, not seeing; maidenhood is whole and perfect in itself and sweetly careless of what it need not know; maidenhood dreams of a world that is not, nor was, nor shall be, hitherwards of heaven; maidenhood is angelhood. In its unconsciousness of evil lies its strength, in its ignorance of itself lies its danger.

Cecilia was not trying to call up visions now; she was thinking of her life, and wondering what was to happen, and now and then she was asking herself what she ought to do. Should she marry Guido d'Este, or not? That was the sum of her thoughts and her wonderings and her questions.

She knew she was perfectly free, and that her mother would never try to make her marry against her will. But if she married Guido, would she be acting against her will?

In her own mind she was well aware that he would speak whenever she chose to let him do so. The most maidenly girl of eighteen knows when a man is waiting for an opportunity to ask her to be his wife, whereas most young men who are much in love do not know exactly when they are going to put the question, and are often surprised when it rises to their lips. Cecilia considered that issue a foregone conclusion. The vital matter was to find out her own answer.

She had never known any man, since her stepfather died, whom she liked nearly as much as Guido, and she had met more interesting and gifted men before she was really in society than most women ever know in a lifetime. She liked him so much that if he had any faults she could not see them, and she did not believe that he had any which deserved the name. But that was not the question. No woman likes a man because he has no faults; on the contrary, if he has a few, she thinks it will be her mission to eradicate them, and reform him according to her ideal. She believes that it will be easy, and she knows that it will be delightful to succeed, because no other woman has succeeded before. That is one reason why the wildest rakes are often loved by the best of women.

Cecilia liked Guido for his own sake, and felt an intellectual sympathy for him which took the place of what she had sorely missed since her stepfather died; she liked him also, because he was always ready to do whatever she wished; and because, with the exception of that one day at the Villa Madama, his moral attitude before her was one of respectful and chivalrous devotion; and also because he and she were fond of the same things, and because he took her seriously and never told her that she was wasting time in trying to understand Kant and Fichte and Hegel, though he possibly thought so; and she liked the little ways he had, and his modesty, though he knew so much, and his simple manner of dressing, and the colour of his hair, and a sort of very faint atmosphere of Russian leather, good cigarettes, and Cologne water that was always about him. There were a great many reasons why she was fond of him. For instance, she had found that he never repeated to any one, not even to Lamberti, a word of any conversation they had together; and if any one at a dinner party or at a picnic attacked any favourite idea or theory of hers, he defended it, using all her arguments as well as his own; and when he knew she could say something clever in the general talk, he always said something else which made it possible for her to bring out her own speech, and he was always apparently just as much pleased with it as if he had not heard it already, when they had been alone. It would be impossible to enumerate all the reasons why she was sure that there was nobody like him.

She knew that what she felt for him was affection, and she was quite willing to believe that it was love. He certainly had no rival with her at that time, and if she hesitated, it was because the thought of marriage itself was repugnant to her.

In the secondary life of her imagination she was bound by the most solemn vows, and under the most terrible penalties, to preserve herself intact from the touch of man. In the dream, it was sacrilege for a man to love her, and meant death to love him in return. She knew that it was a dream, but she loved to believe that all the dream was true, and she was too much accustomed to the thought not to be influenced by it.

There are great actors who become so used to a favourite part that they go on acting it in real life, and have sometimes gone mad in the end, it is said, believing themselves really to be the heroes or tyrants they have represented. Only great second-rate actors "learn" their parts and attain to a sort of perfection in them by mechanical means. The really great first-rate artists make themselves a secondary existence by self-suggestion, and really have two selves, one that thinks and acts like Othello, or Hamlet, or Louis the Eleventh, the other that goes through life with the opinions, convictions, and principles of Sir Henry Irving, of Tommaso Salvini, or of Madame Sarah Bernhardt.

In a higher degree, because she had never learned but one part, and that one proceeded in some way out of her own intelligence, Cecilia was in the same state of dual consciousness, and if her waking life was influenced by her imaginary existence in dreams, her dreams were probably affected also by her waking life.

"Thou shalt so act, as to be worthy of happiness," said her favourite philosopher. She could undoubtedly marry Guido, in spite of her imaginary vows, if she chose to shake off the shadowy bond by an act of everyday will. Would that be acting so as to deserve to be happy? What is happiness? The belief that one is happy; nothing else. As Guido's wife, should she believe that she was happy? Yes, if there were happiness to be found in marriage. But she was happy already without it, and would always be so, she was sure. Therefore she would be risking a certainty for a possibility. "Who leaves the old and takes new, knows what he leaves, not what he may find"; so says the old Italian proverb. And again, she had heard a friend of her stepfather's say with a laugh that hope seems cheap food, but is always paid for by those who live on it.

To act so as to be worthy of happiness, meant to act in such a way that the reason for each action might be a law for the happiness of all. That was the Categorical Imperative, and Cecilia believed in it.

Then, if she married Guido, she ought to be sure that all young girls in her position would marry under the circumstances, and that the majority of them would be happy. With a return of practical sense from the regions of philosophy, she asked herself how she should feel if Guido married some one else, one of the many young girls who were among her friends. Should she be jealous?

At the mere thought she felt a little dull sinking that was anticipated disappointment. Yes, she liked him enough, she was fond enough of him to miss him terribly if he were taken away from her. This was undoubtedly love, she thought. She could not be happy without that companionship, though she wished that it might continue all her life, without the necessity of being married to him.

Of all the other men she had met during the last month, the only one whom she instinctively understood was Lamberti, but that was different. It was the understanding of a fear that was sometimes almost abject; it was the certainty that if he only would, he could lead her anywhere, make her do anything, direct her as he directed his own hand. When she had met him in the house of the Vestals, she had been sure that if she stood a moment longer where he had come upon her, he would take her in his arms and kiss her, and she would not resist. It was of no use to argue about it, to tell herself that she would have been safe on a desert island with Guido's trusted friend; the conviction was strong. At the Villa Madama, he had made her say what he pleased, go with him where he chose, tell him her secret. It was too horrible for words. She had asked him to come to see her at an hour when there would be no visitors, and she knew that she had meant to see him alone, in spite of her mother, and even by stealth if need were. When he was out of her sight, his influence was gone with him, and she thanked heaven that he had not come, and that he apparently took care never to be alone with her for a moment now. He had only to look at her in a certain way, and she must obey him; if he ever touched her hand she would be his slave, powerless to resist him.

Sometimes she could not help looking at him, but then he never turned his eyes towards her, and she was thankful when she could turn hers away. When he was not present, she hoped that she might never see his face again, except in dreams, for there he was not the same. There, but for that one passionate kiss that told all, he was tender, and gentle, and true, and he listened to her, and in the end he lived as she wished him to live. But he had come back to life with the same face, another man—one whom she feared as she feared nothing in the world, and few things beyond it, for he was born her master, and was strong, and had ruthless eyes. Even Guido could not save her from him, she was sure.

Yet in spite of all this, she could meet him with outward indifference in the world, before other people. She felt that there was no danger so long as she was not alone with him, because he would not dare to use his power, and the world protected her by its cheerful, careless presence. She did not hate him, she only feared him, with every part of her, body and soul.

She was sure that he knew it, but she was not grateful to him for avoiding her. She could not be grateful to any one of whom she was in terror. It was merely his will to avoid her, or perhaps, as Guido seemed to think, he did not like her; or possibly it was for Guido's sake, because Guido trusted him, and he was a man of honour.

He was that beyond doubt, for every one said so, and she knew that he was brave; but though he might possess every quality and virtue under the sun, she could never be less afraid of him. Her fear had nothing to do with his character; it was bodily and spiritual, not reasonable. She had found out that he was perfectly truthful, for nothing he said escaped her, and Guido told her that he was kind, but that was hard to believe of any one with those eyes. Yet the man in the dream was gentleness itself, and his eyes never glittered when they looked at her.

To think that she could ever love Lamberti was utterly absurd. When she was married to Guido she would tell him that she feared his friend. Now, it was impossible. He would smile quietly and tell her there was nothing to be afraid of; he would smile, too, if she told him that she had a dual existence, and dreamed herself into the other every day.

And now she was smiling, too, as she thought of him, for she had thought too long about Lamberti, and it was soothing to go back to Guido's companionship and to all that her real affection for him meant to her. It was like coming home after a dangerous journey. There he was, always the same, his hands stretched out to welcome her back. She would have just that sensation presently when he came to luncheon, and he would have just that look. She and he were made to spend endless days together, sometimes talking, sometimes thoughtful and silent, always happy, and calm, and utterly peaceful.

After all, she thought, what more could a woman ask? With each other's society and her fortune, they would have all the world held that was pleasant and beautiful around them, and they would enjoy it together, as long as it lasted, and it would never make the least difference to them that they should grow old, and older, until the end came; and at eighteen it was of no use to think of that.

Surely this was love, at its best, and of the kind that must last; and if, after all, in order to get such happiness as that seemed, there was no way except to marry, why then, she must do as others did and be Guido d'Este's wife.

What could she know? That she loved him, in a way not at all like what she had supposed to be the way of love, but sincerely and truly. What should she do? She should marry him, since that was necessary. What might she hope? She could hope for a lifetime of happiness. Should she then have acted so as to deserve it? Yes. Why not? Might the reason for her marriage be a rule for others? Yes, for others in exactly the same case.

So she smilingly answered the mightiest questions of transcendental philosophy as if they all referred to the pleasant world in which she lived, instead of to the lofty regions of Pure Reason. In that, indeed, she knew that she was playing with them, or applying them empirically, if any one chose to define in those terms what she was doing. After all, why should she not? Of the three questions, the first only was "speculative," and the other two were "practical." The philosopher himself said so.

Besides, it did not matter, for Guido d'Este was coming to luncheon, and afterwards her mother would go and write notes, unless she dozed a little in her boudoir, as she sometimes did while the two talked; and then Cecilia would say something quite natural, but quite new, and she would let her look linger in Guido's a little longer than ever before, and then he would ask her to marry him. It was all decided beforehand in her small head.

She was glad that it was, and she felt much happier at the prospect of what was coming than she had expected. That must be a sign that she really loved Guido in the right way, and the pleasant little thrill of excitement she felt now and again could only be due to that; it would be outrageous to suppose that it was caused merely by the certainty that for the first time in her life she was going to receive an offer of marriage. Why should any young girl care for such a thing, unless she meant to marry the man, and why in the world should it give her any pleasure to hear a man stammer something that would be unintelligible if it were not expected, and then see him wait with painful anxiety for the answer which every woman likes to hesitate a little in giving, in order that it may have its full value? Such doings are manifestly wicked, unless they are sheer nonsense!

Cecilia rose and rang for her maid; for it was twelve o'clock, and Romans lunch at half-past twelve, because they do not begin the day between eight and nine in the morning with ham and eggs, omelets and bacon, beefsteak and onions, fried liver, cold joints, tongue, cold ham and pickles, hot cakes, cold cakes, hot bread, cold bread, butter, jam, honey, fruit of all kinds in season, tea, coffee, chocolate, and a tendency to complain that they have not had enough, which is the unchangeable custom of the conquering races, as everybody knows. It is true that the conquerors do not lunch to any great extent; they go on conquering from breakfast till dinner time without much intermission, because that is their business; but it is believed that their women, who stay at home, have a little something at twelve, luncheon at half-past two, tea between five and six, dinner at eight, and supper about midnight, when they can get it.

Cecilia rang for the excellent Petersen, and said that she would wear the new costume which had arrived from Doucet's two days ago.

There was certainly no reason why she should not wish to look well on this day of all others, and as she turned and saw herself in the glass, she had not the least thought of making a better impression than usual on Guido. She was far too sure of herself for that. If she chose, he would ask her to marry him though she might be dressed in an old waterproof and overshoes. It was merely because she was happy and was sure that she was going to do the right thing. When a normal woman is very happy, she puts on a perfectly new frock, if she has one, in real life or on the stage, even when she is not going to be seen by any one in particular. In this, therefore, Cecilia only followed the instinct of her kind, and if the pretty new costume had not chanced to have come from Paris, she would not have missed it at all, but would have worn something else. As it happened to be ready, however, it would have been a pity not to put it on, since she expected to remember that particular day all the rest of her life.

Petersen said it was perfection, and Cecilia was not far from thinking so, too.

CHAPTER XIII

Guido d'Este was already in the drawing-room with the Countess when Cecilia entered, but she knew by their faces and voices that they had not been talking of her, and was glad of it; for sometimes, when she was quite sure that they had, she felt a little embarrassment at first, and found Guido a trifle absent-minded for some time afterwards.

She took his hand, and perhaps she held it a second longer than usual, and she looked into his eyes as she spoke to her mother. Yesterday she would have very likely looked at her mother while speaking to him.

"I hope I am not late," she said, "Have I kept you waiting?"

"It was worth while, if you did," Guido said, looking at her with undisguised admiration.

"It really is a success, is it not?" Cecilia asked, turning to her mother now, for approval.

Then she turned slowly round, raised herself on tiptoe a moment, came back to her original position, and smiled happily. Guido waited for the Countess to speak.

"Yes—yes," the latter answered critically, but almost satisfied. "When one has a figure like yours, my dear, one should always have things quite perfect. A woman who has a good figure and is really well dressed, hardly ever needs a pin. Let me see. Does it not draw under the right arm, just the slightest bit? Put your arm down, child, let it hang naturally! So. No, I was mistaken, there is nothing. You really ought to keep your arm in the right position, darling. It makes so much difference! You are not going to play tennis, or ride a bicycle in that costume. No, of course not! Well, then—you understand. Do be careful!"

Cecilia looked at Guido and smiled again, and her lips parted just enough to show her two front teeth a little, and then, still parted, grew grave, which gave her an expression Guido had never seen. For a moment there was something between a question and an appeal in her face.

"It is very becoming," he said gravely. "It is a pleasure to see anything so faultless."

"I am glad you really like it," she answered. "I always want you to like my things."

Everything happened exactly as she had expected and wished, and the Countess, when she had sipped her cup of coffee after luncheon, went to the writing table in the boudoir, and though the door was open into the great drawing-room, she was out of sight, and out of hearing too.

Cecilia did not sit down again at once, but moved slowly about, went to one of the windows and looked down at the white street through the slats of the closed blinds, turned and met Guido's eyes, for he was watching her, and at last stood still not far from him, but a little further from the open door of the boudoir than he was. At the end of the room a short sofa was placed across the corner; before it stood a low table on which lay a few large books, of the sort that are supposed to amuse people who are waiting for the lady of the house, or who are stranded alone in the evening when every one else is talking. They are always books of the type described as magnificent and not dear; if they were really valuable, they would not be left there.

"How you watch me!" Cecilia smiled, as if she did not object to being watched. "Come and sit down," she added, without waiting for an answer.

She established herself in one corner of the short sofa behind the table, Guido took his place in the other, and there would not have been room for a third person between them. The two had never sat together in that particular place, and there was a small sensation of novelty about it which was delightful to them both. There was not the least calculation of such a thing in Cecilia's choice of the sofa, but only the unerring instinct of woman which outwits man's deepest schemes at every turn in life.

"Yes," Guido said, "I was watching you. I often do, for it is good to look at you. Why should one not get as much aesthetic pleasure as possible out of life?"

The speech was far from brilliant, for Guido was beginning to feel the spell, and was not thinking so much of what he was saying as of what he longed to say. Most clever men are dull enough to suppose that they bore women when they suddenly lose their cleverness and say rather foolish things with an air of conviction, instead of very witty things with a studied look of indifference. The hundred and fifty generations of men, more or less, that separate us moderns from the days of Eden, never found out that those are the very moments at which a woman first feels her power, and that it is much less dangerous to bore her just then than before or afterwards. It is a rare delight to her to feel that her mere look can turn careless wit to earnest foolishness. For nothing is ever more in earnest than real folly, except real love.

"You always say nice things," Cecilia answered, and Guido was pleasantly surprised, for he had been quite sure that the silly compliment was hardly worth answering.

"And you are always kind," he said gratefully. "Always the same," he added after a moment, with a little accent of regret.

"Am I? You say it as if you wished I might sometimes change. Is that what you mean?"

She looked down at her hands, that lay in her lap motionless and white, one upon the other, on the delicate dove-coloured stuff of her frock; and her voice was rather low.

"No," Guido answered. "That is not what I mean."

"Then I do not understand," she said, neither moving nor looking up.

Guido said nothing. He leaned forwards, his elbows on his knees, and stared down at the Persian rug that lay before the sofa on the smooth matting. It was warm and still in the great room.

"Try and make me understand."

Still he was silent. Without changing his position he glanced at the open door of the boudoir. The Countess was invisible and inaudible. Guido could hear the young girl's soft and regular breathing, and he felt the pulse in his own throat. He knew that he must say something, and yet the only thing he could think of to say was that he loved her.

"Try and make me understand," she repeated. "I think you could."

He started and changed his position a little. He had been accustomed so long to the belief that if he spoke out frankly the thread of his intercourse with her would be broken, that he made a strong effort to get back to the ordinary tone of their conversation.

"Do you never say absurd things that have no meaning?" he asked, and tried to laugh.

"It was not what you said," Cecilia answered quietly. "It was the way you said it, as if you rather regretted saying that I am always the same. I should be sorry if you thought that an absurd speech."

"You know that I do not!" cried Guido, with a little indignation. "We understand each other so well, as a rule, but there is something you will never understand, I am afraid."

"That is just what I wish you would explain," replied the young girl, unmoved.

"Are you in earnest?" Guido asked, suddenly turning his face to her.

"Of course. We are such good friends that it is a pity there should ever be the least little bit of misunderstanding between us."

"You talk about it very philosophically!"

"About what?" She had felt that she must make him lose patience, and she succeeded.

"After all, I am a man," he said rather hoarsely. "Do you suppose it is possible for me to see you day after day, to talk with you day after day, to be alone with you day after day, as I am, to hear your voice, to touch your hand—and to be satisfied with friendship?"

"How should I know?" Cecilia asked thoughtfully. "I have never known any one as well as I know you. I never liked anyone else well enough," she added after an instant.

A very faint colour rose in her cheeks, for she was afraid that she had been too forward.

"Yes. I am sure of that," he said. "But you never feel that mere liking is turning into something stronger, and that friendship is changing into love. You never will!"

She said nothing, but looked at him steadily while he looked away from her, absorbed in his own thought and expecting no answer. When at last he felt her eyes on him, he turned quickly with a start of surprise, catching his breath, and speaking incoherently.

"You do not mean to tell me—you are not—"

Again her lips parted and she smiled at his wonder.

"Why not?" she asked, at last.

"You love me? You?" He could not believe his ears.

"Why not?" she asked again, but so low that he could hardly hear the words.

He turned half round, as he sat, and covered her crossed hands with his, and for a while neither spoke. He was supremely happy; she was convinced that she ought to be, and that she therefore believed that she was, and that her happiness was consequently real.

But when she heard his voice, she knew, in spite of all, that she did not feel what he felt, even in the smallest degree, and there was a doubt which she had not anticipated, and which she at once faced in her heart with every argument she could use. She must have done right, it was absolutely necessary that what she had done should be right, now that it was too late to undo it. The mere suggestion that it might turn out to be a mistake was awful. It would all be her fault if she had deceived him, though ever so unwittingly.

His hands shook a little as they lay on hers. Then they took one of hers and held it, drawing it slowly away from the other.

"Do you really love me?" Guido asked, still wondering, and not quite convinced.

"Yes," she answered faintly, and not trying to withdraw her hand.

She had been really happy before she had first answered him. A minute had not passed, and her martyrdom had begun, the martyrdom by the doubt which made that one "yes" possibly a lie. Guido raised her hand to his lips, and she felt that they were cold. Then he began to speak, and she heard his voice far off and as if it came to her through a dense mist.

"I have loved you almost since we first met," he said, "but I was sure from the beginning that you would never feel anything but friendship for me."

A voice that was neither his nor hers, cried out in her heart:

"Nor ever can!"

She almost believed that he could hear the words. She would have given all she had to have the strength to speak them, to disappoint him bravely, to tell him that she had meant to do right, but had done wrong. But she could not. He did not pause as he spoke, and his soft, deep voice poured into her ear unceasingly the pent-up thoughts of love that had been gathering in his heart for weeks. She knew that he was looking in her face for some response, and now and then, as her head lay back against the sofa cushion, she turned her eyes to his and smiled, and twice she felt that her fingers pressed his hand a little.

It was not out of mere weakness that she did not interrupt him, for she was not weak, nor cowardly. She had been so sure that she loved him, until he had made her say so, that even now, whenever she could think at all, she went back to her reasoning, and could all but persuade herself again. It was when she was obliged to speak that her lips almost refused the word.

For she was very fond of him. It would have been pleasant to sit there, and even to press his hand affectionately, and to listen to his words, if only they had been words of friendship and not of love, and spoken in another tone—in his voice of every day. But she had waked in him something she could not understand, and to which nothing in herself responded, nothing thrilled, nothing consented; and the inner voice in her heart cried out perpetually, warning her against something unknown.

He was eloquent now, and spoke without doubt or fear, as men do when they have been told at last that they are loved; and her occasional glance and the pressure of her hand were all he wanted in return. He said everything for her, which he wished to hear her say, and it seemed to him that she spoke the words by his lips. They would be happy together always, happy beyond volumes of words to say, beyond thought to think, beyond imagination to imagine. Quick plans for the future, near and far, flashed into words that were pictures, and the pictures showed him a visible earthly paradise, in which they two should live always, in which he should always be speaking as he was speaking now, and she listening, as she now listened.

He forgot the time, and forgot to glance at the open door of the boudoir, but at last Cecilia started, and drew back her hand from his, and blushed as she raised her head from the back of the sofa. Her mother was standing in the doorway watching, and hearing, an expression of rapt delight on her face, not daring to move forwards or backwards, lest she should interrupt the scene.

Cecilia started, and Guido, following the direction of her eyes, saw the Countess, and felt that small touch of disappointment which a man feels when the woman he is addressing in passionate language is less absent-minded than he is. He rose to his feet instantly, and went forwards, as the Countess came towards him.

"My dear lady," he said, "Cecilia has consented to be my wife."

Cecilia did not afterwards remember precisely what happened next, for the room swam with her as she left her seat, and she steadied herself against a chair, and saw nothing for a moment; but presently she found herself in her mother's arms, which pressed her very hard, and her mother was kissing her again and again, and was saying incoherent things, and was on the point of crying. Guido stood a few steps away, apparently seeing nothing, but looking the picture of happiness, and very busy with his cigarette case, of which he seemed to think the fastening must be out of order, for he opened it and shut it again several times and tried it in every way.

Then Cecilia was quite aware of outward things again, and she kissed her mother once or twice.

"Let me go, mother dear," she whispered desperately. "I want to be alone—do let me go!"

She slipped away, pale and trembling, and had disappeared almost before Guido was aware that she was going towards the door. She heard her mother's voice just as she reached the threshold.

"We will announce it this evening," the Countess said to Guido.

Cecilia sped through the long suite of rooms that led to her own. She met no one, not even Petersen, for the servants were all at dinner. She locked the door, stood still a moment, and then went to the tall glass between the windows, and looked at herself as if trying to read the truth in the reflection of her eyes. It seemed to her that her beauty was suddenly gone from her, and that she was utterly changed. She saw a pale, drawn face, eyes that looked weak and frightened, lips that trembled, a figure that had lost all its elasticity and half its grace.

She did not throw herself upon her bed and burst into tears. Old Fortiguerra had taught her that it was not really more natural for a woman to cry than it is for a man; and she had overcome even the very slight tendency she had ever had towards such outward weakness. But like other people who train themselves to keep down emotion, she suffered much more than if she had given way to what she felt. She turned from the reflection of herself with a sort of dumb horror, and sat down in the place where she had come to her great decision less than two hours ago.

The room looked very differently now; the air was not the same, the June sunshine was still beating on the blinds, but it was cruel now, and pitiless, as all light is that shines on grief.

She tried to collect her thoughts, and asked herself whether it was a crime that she had committed against her will, and many other such questions that had no answer. Little by little reason began to assert itself again, as emotion subsided.

CHAPTER XIV

The news of Cecilia Palladio's engagement to Guido d'Este surprised no one, and was generally received with that satisfaction which society feels when those things happen which are appropriate in themselves and have been long expected. A few mothers of marriageable sons were disappointed, but no mothers of marriageable daughters, because Guido had no fortune and was so much liked as to have been looked upon rather as a danger than a prize.

Though it was late in the season, and she was about to leave Rome, the Princess Anatolie gave a dinner party in honour of the betrothed pair, and by way of producing an impression on Cecilia and her mother, invited all the most imposing people who happened to be in Rome at that time; and they were chiefly related to her in some way or other, as all semi-royal personages, and German dukes and grand-dukes and mediatised princes, and princes of the Holy Empire, seemed to be. Now all these great people seemed to know Cecilia's future husband intimately and liked him, and called him "Guido"; and he called some of them by their first names, and was evidently not the least in awe of any of them. They were his relations, as the Princess was, and they acknowledged him; and they were inclined to be affectionate relatives, because he had never asked any of them for anything, and differed from most of them in never having done anything too scandalous to be mentioned. They were his family, for his mother had been an only child; and Princess Anatolie, who was distinctly a snob in soul, in spite of her royal blood, took care that the good Countess Fortiguerra should know exactly how matters stood, and that her daughter ought to be thankful that she was to marry among the exalted ones of the earth—at any price.

Now, when she had been an ambassadress, the Countess had met two or three of those people, and had been accustomed to look upon them as personages whom the Embassy entertained in state, one at a time, when they condescended to accept an invitation, but who lived in a region of their own, which was often, and perhaps fortunately so, beyond the experience of ordinary society. She was therefore really pleased and flattered to find herself in their intimacy and to hear what they had to say when they talked without restraint. Her position was certainly very good already, but there was no denying that her daughter's marriage would make it a privileged one.

In the first place, Guido and Cecilia were clearly expected to visit some of his relations during their wedding trip and afterwards, and at some future time the Countess would go with them and see wonderful castles and palaces she had heard of from her childhood. That would be delightful, she thought, and the excellent Baron Goldbirn of Vienna would die of envy. Not that she wished him to die of envy, nor of anything else; she merely thought of his feelings.

Then—and perhaps that was what gave her the most real satisfaction—Cecilia was to take the place for which her beauty and her talents had destined her, but which her birth had not given her. The mother's heart was filled with affectionate pride when she realised that the marvel she had brought into the world, the most wonderful girl that ever lived, her only child, was to be the mother of kings' and queens' second cousins. It was quite indifferent that she should be called plain Signora d'Este, and not princess, or duchess, or marchioness. The Countess did not care a straw for titles, for she had lived in a world where they are as plentiful as figs in August; but to be the mother of a king's second cousin was something worth living for, and she herself would be the mother-in-law of an ex-King's son, which would have made her the something-in-law of the ex-King himself, if he had been alive. Yet she cared very little for herself in comparison with Cecilia. She was only a vicarious snob, after all, and a very motherly and loving one, with harmless faults and weaknesses which every one forgave.

The Princess Anatolie saw that the impression was made, and was satisfied for the present. She meant to have a little serious conversation with the Countess before they parted for the summer, and before the first impression had worn off, but it would have been a great mistake to talk business on such an occasion as the present. The fish was netted, that was the main thing; the next was to hasten the marriage as much as possible, for the Princess saw at once that Cecilia was not really in love with Guido, and as the fortune was hers, the girl had the power to draw back at the last moment; that is to say, that all the mothers of marriageable sons would declare that she was quite right in doing what Italian society never quite pardons in ordinary cases. An Italian girl who has broken off an engagement after it is announced does not easily find a husband at any price.

Cecilia noticed that Monsieur Leroy was not present at the dinner, and as she sat next to Guido she asked him the reason in an undertone.

"I do not know," he answered. "He is probably dining out. My aunt's relations do not like him much, I believe."

The Countess was affectionately intent on everything her daughter said and did, and was possessed of very good hearing; she caught the exchange of question and answer, and it occurred to her that an absent person might always be made a subject of conversation. She was not far from the Princess at table.

"By-the-bye," she asked, agreeably, "where is Monsieur Leroy?"

Every one heard her speak, and to her amazement and confusion her words produced one of those appalling silences which are remembered through life by those who have accidentally caused them. Cecilia looked at Guido, and he was gravely occupied in digging the little bits of truffle out of some pâté de foie gras on his plate, for he did not like truffles. Not a muscle of his face moved.

"I suppose he is at home," the Princess answered after a few seconds, in her most disagreeable and metallic tone.

As Monsieur Leroy had told Cecilia that he lived in the house, she opened her eyes. Nobody spoke for several moments, and the Countess got very red, and fanned herself. A stout old gentleman of an apoplectic complexion and a merry turn of mind struggled a moment with an evident desire to laugh, then grasped his glass desperately, tried to drink, choked himself, and coughed and sputtered, just as if he had not been a member of an imperial family, but just a common mortal.

"You are a good shot, Guido," said a man who was very much like him, but was older and had iron-grey hair, "you must be sure to come to us for the opening of the season."

"I should like to," Guido answered, "but it is always a state function at your place."

"The Emperor is not coming this year," explained the first speaker.

"Why not?" asked the Princess Anatolie. "I thought he always did."

The man with the iron-grey hair proceeded to explain why the Emperor was not coming, and the conversation began again, much to the relief of every one. The Countess listened attentively, for she was not quite sure which Emperor they meant.

"Please ask your mother not to talk about Monsieur Leroy," Guido said, almost in a whisper.

Cecilia thought that the advice would scarcely be needed after what had just happened, but she promised to convey it, and begged Guido to tell her the reason for what he said when he should have a chance.

"I am sorry to say that I cannot," he answered, and at once began to talk about an indifferent subject.

Cecilia answered him rather indolently, but not absently. She was at least glad that he did not speak of their future plans, where any one might hear what he said.

She was growing used to the idea that she had promised to marry him, and that everybody expected the wedding to take place in a few weeks, though it looked utterly impossible to her.

It was as if she had exchanged characters with him. He had become hopeful, enthusiastic, in love with life, actively exerting himself in every way. In a few days she had grown indolent and vacillating, and was willing to let every question decide itself rather than to force her decision upon circumstances. She felt that she was not what she had believed herself to be, and that it therefore mattered little what became of her. If she married Guido she should not live long, but it would be the same if she married any one else, since there was no one whom she liked half as much.

On the day after the engagement was announced Lamberti came, with Guido, to offer his congratulations. Cecilia saw that he was thin and looked as if he were living under a strain of some sort, but she did not think that his manner changed in the least when he spoke to her. His words were what she might have expected, few, concise, and well chosen, but his face was expressionless, and his eyes were dull and impenetrable. He stayed twenty minutes, talking most of the time with her mother, and then took his leave. As soon as he had turned to go, Cecilia unconsciously watched him. He went out and shut the door very softly after him, and she started and caught her breath. It was only the shutting of a door, of course, and the door was like any other door, and made the same noise when one shut it—the click of a well-made lock when the spring pushes the bevelled latch-bolt into the socket. But it was exactly the sound she thought she heard each time her dream ended.

The impression had passed in a flash, and no one had noticed her nervous movement. Since then, she had not met Lamberti, for after the engagement was made known she went out less, and Guido spent much more of his time at the Palazzo Massimo. Many people were leaving Rome, too, and those who remained were no longer inclined to congregate together, but stayed at home in the evening and only went out in the daytime when it was cool. Some had boys who had to pass their public examinations before the family could go into the country. Others were senators of the Kingdom, obliged to stay in town till the end of the session; some were connected with the ministry and had work to do; and some stayed because they liked it, for though the weather was warm it was not yet what could be called hot.

The Countess wished the wedding to take place in July, and Guido agreed to anything that could hasten it. Cecilia said nothing, for she could not believe that she was really to be married. Something must happen to prevent it, even at the last minute, something natural but unexpected, something, above all, by which she should be spared the humiliation of explaining to Guido what she felt, and why she had honestly believed that she loved him.

And after all, if she were obliged to marry him, she supposed that she would never be more unhappy than she was already. It was her fate, that was all that could be said, and she must bear it, and perhaps it would not be so hard as it seemed. A character weaker than hers might perhaps have turned against Guido; she might have found her friendly affection suddenly changed into a capricious dislike that would soon lead to positive hatred. But there was no fear of that. She only wished that he would not talk perpetually about the future, with so much absolute confidence, when it seemed to her so terribly problematic.

Such conversations were made all the more difficult to sustain by the fact that if they were married, she, as the possessor of the fortune, would be obliged to decide many questions with regard to their manner of life.

"For my part," Guido said, "I do not care where we live, so long as you like the place, but you will naturally wish to be near your mother."

"Oh yes!" cried Cecilia, with more conviction than she had shown about anything of late. "I could not bear to be separated from her!"

Lamberti had once observed to Guido that she was an indulgent daughter; and Guido had smiled and reminded his friend of the younger Dumas, who once said that his father always seemed to him a favourite child that had been born to him before he came into the world. Cecilia was certainly fond of her mother, but it had never occurred to Guido that she could not live without her. He was in a state of mind, however, in which a man in love accepts everything as a matter of course, and he merely answered that in that case they would naturally live in Rome.

"We could just live here, for the present," she said. "There is the Palazzo Massimo. I am sure it is big enough. Should you dislike it?"

She was thinking that if she could keep her own room, and have Petersen with her, and her mother, the change would not be so great after all. Guido said nothing, and his expression was a blank.

"Why not?" Cecilia insisted, and all sorts of practical reasons suggested themselves at once. "It is a very comfortable house, though it is a little ghostly at night. There are dreadful stories about it, you know. But what does that matter? It is big, and in a good part of the city, and we have just furnished it; so of what use in the world is it to go and do the same thing over again, in the next street?"

"That is very sensible," Guido was obliged to admit.

"But you do not like the idea, I am sure," Cecilia said, in a tone of disappointment.

"I had not meant that we should live in the same house with your mother," Guido said, with a smile. "Of course, she is a very charming woman, and I like her very much, but I think that when people marry they had much better go and live by themselves."

"Nobody ever used to," objected Cecilia. "It is only of late years that they do it in Rome. Oh, I see!" she cried suddenly. "How dull of me! Yes. I understand. It is quite natural."

"What?" asked Guido with some curiosity.

"You would feel that you had simply come to live in our house, because you have no house of your own for us to live in. I ought to have thought of that."

She seemed distressed, fancying that she had hurt him, but he had no false pride.

"Every one knows my position," he answered. "Every one knows that if we live in a palace, in the way you are used to live, it will be with your money."

There was a little pause, for Cecilia did not know what to say. Guido continued, following his own thoughts:

"If I did not love you as much as I do, I could not possibly live on your fortune," he said. "I used to say that nothing could ever make me marry an heiress, and I meant it. One generally ends by doing what one says one will never do. A cousin of mine detested Germans and had the most extraordinary aversion for people who had any physical defect. She married a German who had lost the use of one leg by a wound in battle, and was extremely lame."

"Did she love him?" asked Cecilia.

"Devotedly, to his dying day. They were the most perfectly loving couple I ever knew."

"Would you rather I were lame than rich?" Cecilia asked, with a little laugh.

Guido laughed too.

"That is one of those questions that have no answers. How could I wish anything so perfect as you are to have any defect? But I will tell you a story. An Englishman was very much in love with a lady who was lame, and she loved him but would not marry him. She said that he should not be tied to a cripple all his life. He was one of those magnificent Englishmen you see sometimes, bigger and better looking than other men. When he saw that she was in earnest he went away and scoured Europe till he found what he wanted—a starving young surgeon who was willing to cut off one of his legs for a large sum of money. That was before the days of chloroform. When the Englishman had recovered, he went home with his wooden leg, and asked the lady if she would marry him, then. She did, and they were happy."

"Is that true?" Cecilia asked.

"I have always believed it. That was the real thing."

"Yes. That was the real thing."

Cecilia's voice trembled a very little, and her eyes glistened.

"The truth is," said Guido, "that it is easier to have one's leg cut off than to make a fortune."

He was amused at his thought, but Cecilia was wondering what she would be willing to suffer, and able to bear, if any suffering could buy her freedom. At the same time, she knew that she would do a great deal to help him if he were in need or distress. She wondered, too, whether there could be any fixed relation between a sacrifice made for love and one made for friendship's sake.

"There must never be any question of money between us," she said, after a pause. "What is mine must be ours, and what is ours must be as much yours as mine."

"No," Guido answered gently. "That is not possible. I have quite enough for anything I shall ever need, but you must live in the way you like, and where you like, with your own fortune."

"And you will be a sort of perpetual guest in my house!"

For the first time there was a little bitterness in her laugh, and he looked at her quickly, for after the way she had spoken he had not thought that what he had said could have offended her. Of the two, he fancied that his own position was the harder to accept, the position of the "perpetual guest" in his wife's palace, just able to pay for his gloves, his cigarettes, and his small luxuries. He did not quite understand why she was hurt, as she seemed to be.

On her part she felt as if she had done all she could, and was angry with herself, and not with him, because all her fortune was not worth a tenth of what he was giving her, nor a hundredth part. For an instant she was on the point of speaking out frankly, to tell him that she had made a great mistake. Then she thought of what he would suffer, and once more she resolved to think it all over before finally deciding.

So nothing was decided. For when she was alone, all the old reasons came and arrayed themselves before her, with their hopeless little faces, like poor children standing in a row to be inspected, and trying to look their best though their clothes were ragged and their little shoes were out at the toes.

But they were the only reasons she had, and she coaxed them into a sort of unreal activity till they brought her back to the listless state in which she had lived of late, and in which it did not matter what became of her, since she must marry Guido in the end.

Her mother paid no attention to her moods. Cecilia had always been subject to moods, she said to herself, and it was not at all strange that she should not behave like other girls. Guido seemed satisfied, and that was the main thing, after all. He was not, but he was careful not to say so.

The preparations for the wedding went on, and the Countess made up her mind that it should take place at the end of July. It would be so much more convenient to get it over at once, and the sooner Cecilia returned from her honeymoon, the sooner her mother could see her again. The good lady knew that she should be very unhappy when she was separated from the child she had idolised all her life; but she had always looked upon marriage as an absolute necessity, and after being married twice herself, she was inclined to consider it as an absolute good. She would no more have thought of delaying the wedding from selfish considerations than she would have thought of cutting off Cecilia's beautiful hair in order to have it made up into a false braid and wear it herself. So she busied herself with the dressmakers, and only regretted that both Cecilia and Guido flatly refused to go to Paris. It did not matter quite so much, because only three months had elapsed since the last interview with Doucet, and all the new summer things had come; and after all one could write, and some things were very good in Rome, as for instance all the fine needle-work done by the nuns. It would have been easier if Cecilia had shown some little interest in her wedding outfit.

The girl tried hard to care about what was being made for her, and was patient in having gowns tried on, and in listening to her mother's advice. The days passed slowly and it grew hotter.

After she had become engaged to Guido, she had broken with her dream life by an effort which had cost her more than she cared to remember.

She had felt that it was not the part of a faithful woman to go on loving an imaginary man in her dreams, when she was the promised wife of another, even though she loved that other less or not at all.

It was a maidenly and an honest conviction, but at the root of it lay also an unacknowledged fear which made it even stronger. The man in the dream might grow more and more like Lamberti, the dream itself might change, the man might have power over her, instead of submitting to her will, and he might begin to lead her whither he would. The mere idea was horrible. It was better to break off, if she could, and to remember the exquisite Vestal, faithful to her vows, living her life of saintly purity to the very end, in a love altogether beyond material things. To let that vision be marred, to suffer that life to be polluted by mortality, to see the Vestal break the old promises and fall to the level of an ordinary woman, would be to lose a part of herself and all that portion of her own existence which had been dearest to her. That would happen if the man's eyes changed ever so little from what they were in the dream to the likeness of those living ones that glittered and were ruthless. For the dream had really changed on the very night after she had met Lamberti; the loving look had been followed by the one fierce kiss she could never forget, and though afterwards the rest of the dream had all come back and had gone on to its end as before, that one kiss came with it again and again, and in that moment the eyes were Lamberti's own. It was no wonder that she dared not look into them when she met him.

And worse still, she had begun to long for it in the dream. She blushed at the thought. If by any unheard-of outrage Lamberti should ever touch her lips with his in real life, she knew that she would scream and struggle and escape, unless his eyes forced her to yield. Then she should die. She was sure of it. But she would kill herself rather than be touched by him.

She did not understand exactly, that is to say, scientifically, how she put herself into the dream state, for it was not a natural sleep, if it were sleep at all. She did not put out the light and lay her head on the pillow and lose consciousness, as Lamberti did, and then at once see the vision. In real sleep, she rarely dreamed at all, and never of what she always thought of as her other life. To reach that, she had to use her will, being wide awake, with her eyes open, concentrating her thoughts at first, as it seemed to her, to a single point, and then abandoning that point altogether, so that she thought of nothing while she waited.

It was in her power not to begin the process, in other words not to hypnotise herself, though she never thought of it by that name; and when she had answered Guido's question, rightly or wrongly, she knew that it must be right to break the old habit. But she did not know what she had resolved to forego till the temptation came, that very night, after she had shut the door, and when she was about to light the candles, by force of habit. She checked herself. There was the high chair she loved to sit in, with the candles behind her, waiting for her in the same place. If she sat in it, the light would cast her shadow before her and the vision would presently rise in it.

She had taken the lid off the little Wedgwood match box and the candles were before her. It seemed as if some physical power were going to force her to strike the wax match in spite of herself. If she did, five minutes would not pass before she should see the marble court of the Vestals' house, and then the rest—the kiss, and then the rest. She stiffened her arm, as if to resist the force that tried to move it against her will, and she held her breath and then breathed hard again. She felt her throat growing slowly dry and the blood rising with a strange pressure to the back of her head. If she let her hand move to take the match, she was lost. As the temptation increased she tried to say a prayer.

Then, she did not know how, it grew less, as if a sort of crisis were past, and she drew a long breath of relief as her arm relaxed, and she replaced the lid on the box. She turned from the table and took the big chair away from its usual place. It was a heavy thing for a woman to carry, but she did not notice the weight till she had set it against the wall at the further end of the room.

She slept little that night, but she slept naturally, and when she awoke there was no sound of the door being softly closed. But she missed something, and felt a dull, inexplicable want all the next day.

A habit is not broken by a single interruption. It is hard for a man whose nerves are accustomed to a stimulant or a narcotic to go without it for one day, but that is as nothing compared with giving it up altogether. Specialists can decide whether there is any resemblance between the condition of a person under the influence of morphia or alcohol, and the state of a person hypnotised, whether by himself or by another, when that state is regularly accompanied by the illusion of some strong and agreeable emotion. Probably all means which produce an unnatural condition of the nerves at more or less regular hours may be classed together, and there is not much difference between the kind of craving they produce in those who use them. Moreover it is often said that it is harder for a woman to break a habit of that sort, than for a man.

Cecilia was young, fairly strong and very elastic, but she suffered intensely when night came and she had to face the struggle. Bodily pain would have been a relief then, and she knew it, but there was none to bear. The chair looked at her from its distant place against the wall, and seemed to draw her to it, till she had it taken away, pretending that it did not suit the room. But when it was gone, she knew perfectly well that it really made no difference, and that she could dream in any other chair as easily.

And then came a wild desire to see the man's face again, and to be sure that it had not changed. She was certain that she only wished to see it; she would have been overwhelmed with shame, all alone in her room, if she had acknowledged that it was the kiss that she craved and the one moment of indescribable intoxication that came with it.

Are there not hundreds of men who earn their living by risking their lives every night in feats of danger, and who miss that recurring moment when they cannot have it? They will never admit that what they crave is really the chance of a painful death, yet it is perfectly true.

Cecilia could not have been induced to think that she desired no longer the lovely vision of a perfect life; that she could have parted with that easily enough, though with much calm regret; and that, instead, she had a nervous, material, most earthly longing for the single moment in that life which was the contrary of perfect, which she despised, or tried to despise, and which she believed she feared.

She struggled hard, and succeeded, and at last she could go to bed quietly, without even glancing at the place where the chair had stood, or at the candles on the table.

Then, when it all seemed over, a terrible thing happened. She dreamed of the real Lamberti in her natural sleep, in a dream about real life.

CHAPTER XV

Cecilia knelt in the church of Santa Croce, near one of the ancient pillars. At a little distance behind her, Petersen sat in a chair reading a queer little German book that told her the stories of the principal Roman churches with the legends of the saints to which they are dedicated. A thin, smooth-shaven lay brother in black and white frock was slowly sweeping the choir behind the high altar. There was no one else in the church.

Cecilia was kneeling on the marble floor, resting her folded hands upon the back of a rough chair, and there was no sound in the dim building, but the regular, soft brushing of the monk's broom. The girl's face was still and pale, her eyes were half closed, and her lips did not move; she did not hear the broom.

That was the first time she had ever tried to spend an hour in meditation in a church, for her religion had never seemed very real to her. It was compounded of habit and the natural respect of a girl for what her mother practises and has taught her to practise, and it had continued to hold a place in her life because she had quietly exempted it from her own criticism; perhaps, too, because her reading had not really tended to disturb it, since by nature she was strongly inclined to believe in something much higher than the visible world.

The Countess Fortiguerra believed with the simplicity of a child. Her first husband, freethinker, Garibaldian, Mazzinian, had at first tried to laugh her out of all belief, and had said that he would baptize her in the name of reason, as Garibaldi is said to have once baptized a new-born infant. But to his surprise his jests had not the slightest effect on the rather foolish, very pretty, perfectly frank young woman with whom he had fallen in love in his older years, and who, in all other matters, thought him a great man. She laughed at his atheism much more good-naturedly than he at her beliefs, and she went to church regularly in spite of anything he could say; so that at last he shrugged his shoulders and said in his heart that all women were half-witted creatures, where priests were concerned, but that fortunately the weakness did not detract from their charm. On her side, she prayed for his conversion every day, with clock-like regularity, but without the slightest result.

Fortiguerra had been a man of remarkable gifts, extremely tolerant of other people's opinions. He never laughed at any sort of belief, though his wife never succeeded in finding out what he really thought about spiritual matters. He evidently believed in something, so she did not pray for his conversion, but interceded steadily for his enlightenment. Before he died he made no objection to seeing a priest, but his wife never knew whether he consented because it would have given her pain if he had refused, or whether he really desired spiritual comfort in his last moments. He was always most considerate of others and especially of her; but he was very reticent. So she mourned him and prayed that everything might be well with both her departed husbands, though she doubted whether they were in the same place. She supposed that Fortiguerra had sometimes discussed religion with his step-daughter, but he always seemed to take it for granted that the latter should do what her mother desired of her.

It could hardly be expected that the girl should be what is called very devout, and as Petersen turned over the pages of her little book she wondered what had happened that Cecilia should kneel motionless on the marble pavement for more than half an hour in a church to which they had never come before, and on a week-day which was not a saint's day either.

It was something like despair that had brought her to Santa Croce, and she had chosen the place because she could think of no other in which she could be quite sure of being alone, and out of the way of all acquaintances. She wanted something which her books could not give her, and which she could not find in herself; she wanted peace and good advice, and she felt that she was dealt with unjustly.

Indeed, it was of little profit that she should have forced herself to give up what was dearest to her, unreal though it might be, since she was to be haunted by Lamberti's face and voice whenever she fell asleep. It was more like a possession of the evil one now than anything else. She would have used his own words to describe it, if she had dared to speak of it to any one, but that seemed impossible. She had thought of going to some confessor who did not know her by sight, to tell him the whole story, but her common sense assured her that she had done no wrong. It was advice she needed, and perhaps it was protection too, but it was certainly not forgiveness, so far as she knew.

Lamberti pursued her, in her imagination, and she lived in terror of him. If she had been already married to Guido, she would have told her husband everything, and he would have helped her. By a revulsion that was not unnatural, it began to seem much easier to marry him now, and she turned to him in her thoughts, asking him to shield her from a man she feared. Guido loved her, and she was at least a devoted friend to him; there was no one but him to help her.

As she knelt by the pillar she went over the past weeks of her life in a concentrated self-examination of which she would never have believed herself capable.

"I am a grown woman," she said to herself, "and I have a right to think what grown women think. I know perfectly well which thoughts are good and which are bad, just as I know right from wrong in other ways. It was wrong to put myself into that dream state, because I wanted him to come to me. Yes, I confess it, I wanted him to come and kiss me that once, in the vision every night. It would not have been wrong if I had not said that I would marry Guido, but that made the difference. Therefore I gave it up. I will not do anything wrong with my eyes open. I will not. I would not, if I did not believe in God, because the thing would be wrong just the same. Religion makes it more wrong, that is all. If I were not engaged to Guido, and if I loved the other instead, then I should have a right to wish and dream that the other kissed me."

She thought some time about this point, and there was something that disturbed her, in spite of her reasoning.

"It would have been unmaidenly," she decided, at last. "I should be ashamed to tell my mother that I had done it. But it would not have been wrong, distinctly not. It would be wrong and abominable to think of two men in that way.

"That is what is happening now, against my will. I go to sleep saying my prayers, and yet he comes to me in my dreams, and looks at me, and I cannot help letting him kiss me, and it is only afterwards that I feel how revolting it was. And in the daytime I am engaged to Guido, and I cannot help knowing that when we are married he will want to kiss me like that. It was different before, since I was able to give up seeing the marble court and being the Vestal, and did give it up. This is another thing, and it is bad, but it is not a wrong thing I am doing. Therefore it is something outside of my soul that is trying to do me harm, and may succeed in the end. It is a power of evil. How can I fight against it, since it comes when I am asleep and have no will? What ought I to do?

"I am afraid to meet Signor Lamberti now, much more afraid than I was a week ago, before this other trouble began. But when I am dreaming, I am not afraid of him. I do what he makes me do without any resistance, and I am glad to do it. I want to be his slave, then. He makes me sit down and listen to him, and I believe all he says. We always sit on that bench near the fountain in my villa. He tells me that he loves me much better than Guido does, and that he is much better able to protect me than Guido. He says that his heart is breaking because he loves me and is Guido's friend, and he looks thin and worn, just as he does in real life. When I dream of him, I do not mind the glittering in his eyes, but when I meet him it frightens me. Of course, it is quite impossible that he should know how I dream of him now. Yet, I am sure he knew all about the other vision. He said very little, but I am sure of it, though I cannot explain it. This is much worse than the other. But if I go back to the other, I shall be doing wrong, because I shall be consenting; and now I am not doing wrong, because it happens against my will, and I go to sleep praying that it may never happen again, and I am in earnest. God help me! I know that when I sit beside him on the bench I love him! And yet he is the only man in all the world whom I wish never to meet again. God help me!"

Her head sank upon her folded hands at last, and her eyes were closely shut. She threw her whole soul into the appeal to heaven for help and strength, till she believed that it must come to her at once in some real shape, with inspired wisdom and the comfort of the Holy Spirit. She had never before in her life prayed as she was praying now, with heart and soul and mind, though not with any form of words.

Then came a moment in which she thought of nothing and waited. She knew it well, that blank between one state and the other, that total suspension of all her faculties just before she began to see an unreal world, that breathless stillness of anticipation before the supreme moment of change. She was quite powerless now, for her waking will was already asleep.

The instant was over, and the vision had come, but it was not what she had always seen before. It was something strangely familiar, yet beautiful and high and clear. Her consciousness was in the midst of a world of light, at peace; and then, all round her, a brightness stole upwards as out of a clear and soft horizon, more radiant than the light itself that was already in the air. And as when evening creeps up to the sky the stars begin to shine faintly, more guessed at than really seen, so she began to see heavenly beings, growing more and more distinct, and she was lifted up among them, and all her heart cried out in joy and praise. And suddenly the cross shone out in a rosy radiance brighter than all, and from head to foot and from arm to arm of it the light flowed and flashed, and joined and passed and parted, in the holy sign. From itself came forth a melody, in which she was rapt and swept upwards as though she were herself a wave of the glorious sound. But of the words, three only came to her, and they were these: Arise and conquer![1]

[1: A free translation of some passages in the fourteenth canto of Dante's Paradiso.]

Then all was still and calm again, and she was kneeling at her chair, the sight still in her inward eyes, the words still ringing in her heart, but herself awake again.

She knew the vision now that it was past; for often, reading the matchless verses of the "Paradise," she had intensely longed to see as the dead poet must have seen before he could write as he wrote. It did not seem strange that her hope should have been fulfilled at last in the church of the Holy Cross. Her lips formed the words, and she spoke them, consciously in her own voice, sweet and low:

"Arise and conquer!"

It was what she had prayed for—the peace, the strength, the knowledge; it was all in that little sentence. She rose to her feet, and stood still a moment, and her face was calm and radiant, like the faces of the heavenly beings she had looked upon. There was a world before her of which she had not dreamt before, better than that ancient one that had vanished and in which she had been a Vestal Virgin, more real than that mysterious one in which she had floated between two existences, and whence the miserable longing for an earthly body had brought her back to be Cecilia Palladio, and to fight again her battle for freedom and immortality.

It mattered little that her prayer should have been answered by the imagined sight of something described by another, and long familiar to her in his lofty verse. The prayer was answered, and she had strength to go on, and she should find wisdom and light to choose the right path. Henceforth, when she was weak and weary, and filled with loathing of what she dreaded most, she could shut her eyes as she had done just now, and pray, and wait, and the transcendent glory of paradise would rise within her, and give her strength to live, and drive away that power of evil that hurt her, and made night frightful, and day but a long waiting for the night.

She came out into the summer glare with the patient Petersen, and breathed the summer heat as if she were drawing in new life with every breath; and they drove home, down the long and lonely road that leads to the new quarter, between dust-whitened trees, and then down into the city and through the cooler streets, till at last the cab stopped before the columns of the Palazzo Massimo.

Celia ran up the stairs, as if her light feet did not need to touch them to carry her upwards, while Petersen solemnly panted after her, and she went to her own room.

She had a vague desire to change everything in it, to get rid of all the objects that reminded her of the miserable nights, and the sad hours of day, which she had spent there; she wanted to move the bed to the other end of the room, the writing table to the other window, the long glass to a different place, to hang the walls with another colour, and to banish the two tall candlesticks for ever. It would be like beginning her life over again.

CHAPTER XVI

After this Cecilia no longer avoided Lamberti; on the contrary, she sought opportunities of seeing him and of talking with him, for she was sure that she had gained some sort of new strength which could protect her against her imagination, till all her old illusions should vanish in the clear light of daily familiarity. For some time she did not dream of Lamberti, she believed that the spell was broken, and her fear of meeting him diminished quickly.

She made her mother ask him to dinner, but he wrote an excuse and did not come. Then she complained to Guido, and Guido reproached his friend.

"They really wish to know you better," he said. "If the Contessina ever felt for you quite the same antipathy which you felt for her, she has got over it. I think you ought to try to do as much. Will you?"

The invitation was renewed for another day, and Lamberti accepted it. In the evening, in order to give his friend a chance of talking with Cecilia, Guido sat down by the Countess, and began to discuss matters connected with the wedding. It would have been contrary to all established custom that the marriage should take place without a contract, and that alone was a subject about which much could be said. Guido insisted that Cecilia should remain sole mistress of her fortune, and the Countess would naturally have made no objection, but the Princess had told her, and had repeated more than once, that she expected Cecilia to bring her husband a dowry of at least a million of francs. Baron Goldbirn thought this too much, but the Countess was willing to consent, because she feared that the Princess would make trouble at the last minute if she did not. Cecilia had of course never discussed the matter with the Princess, but she was altogether of the latter's opinion, and told her mother so. The obstacle lay in Guido's refusal to accept a penny of his future wife's fortune, and on this point the whole obstinacy of his father's race was roused. The Countess could manifestly not threaten to break off the engagement because Guido would not accept the dowry, but on the other hand she greatly feared Guido's aunt. So there was ample matter for discussion whenever the subject was broached.

It was a hot evening, and all the curtains were drawn back before the open windows, only the blinds being closed. Cecilia and Lamberti gravitated, as it were, to the farther end of the room. A piano stood near the window there.

"Do you play?" Lamberti asked, looking at the instrument.

He thought that she did. All young girls are supposed to have talent for music.

"No," Cecilia answered. "I have no accomplishments. Do you play the piano?"

"Only by ear. I do not know a note of music."

"Play me something. Will you? But I suppose the piano is out of tune, for nobody ever uses it since we stopped dancing."

Lamberti touched the keys, standing, and struck a few soft chords.

"No," he said. "It is not badly out of tune. But if I play, it will be the end of our acquaintance."

"Perhaps it may be the beginning," Cecilia answered, and their eyes met for a moment.

"If it amuses you, I will try," said Lamberti, looking away, and sitting down before the keys. "You must be easily pleased if you can listen to me," he added, laughing, as he struck a few chords again.

Cecilia sat down in a low chair between him and the window, at the left of the key-board. Her mother glanced at Lamberti with a little surprise, and then went on talking with Guido.

Lamberti began to play a favourite waltz, not loud, but with a good deal of spirit and a perfect sense of time. Cecilia had often danced to the tune in the spring, and liked it. He broke off suddenly, and made slow chords again.

"Have you forgotten the rest?" Cecilia asked.

"No. I was thinking of something else. Did you ever hear this?"

He played an old Sicilian melody with one hand, and then took it up in a second part, and then a third, that made strange minor harmonies.

"I never heard that," Cecilia said, as he looked at her. "I like it. It must be very ancient. Play it again."

By way of answer, he began to sing the old song, accompanying himself with the same old harmonies. He had no particular voice, and it was more like humming than singing, so far as the tone was concerned, but he pronounced every word distinctly, and imitated the peculiar intonation of the southern people to perfection.

"Do you understand?" he asked, when he came to the end.

"Not a word." Cecilia asked, "Is it Arabic? It sounds like it."

"No. It is our own beloved Italian," laughed Lamberti, "only it is the Sicilian dialect. If that sort of thing amuses you, I can go on for hours."

Many Italians have the facility he possessed, and the good memory for both words and music, and he had unconsciously developed what talent he had, in places where time was long and there was nothing to do. He changed the key and hummed a little Arab melody from the desert.

Cecilia sat quite still and watched the outline of his head against the light. It was an energetic head, but the face was not a cruel one, and this evening she had not seen what she called the ruthless look in his eyes. She was not at all afraid of him now, nor would she have been even if they had been quite alone in the room. She almost wished to tell him so, and then smiled at the thought.

So this was the reality of the vision that had haunted her dreams and had caused her such unutterable suffering until she had found strength to break the habit of her imagination. The reality was not at all terrible. She could imagine the man roused to action, fighting for his life, single-handed against many, as she had been told that he had fought. He looked both brave and strong.

But she could not imagine that she should ever have cause to be afraid of him again. There he sat, beside her, humming snatches of songs he remembered from his many voyages, his hands moving not at all gracefully over the keys; he was evidently a very simple and good-natured man, willing to do anything that could amuse her, without the slightest affectation. He was just the kind of friend for Guido, and it was her duty to like Guido's friend. It would not be hard, now that she had got out of the labyrinth of absurd illusions that had made it impossible. She resolutely put aside the recollection of that afternoon at the Villa Madama. It belonged to the class of things about which she was determined never to think again. "Arise and conquer!" She had come back to her real self, and had overcome.

He stopped singing, but his hands still lay on the keys and he struck occasional chords; and he turned his face half towards her, and spoke in an undertone.

"I am very sorry if I offended you by not coming more often to your house," he said. "Guido told me. I thought perhaps you would understand why I did not come."

Cecilia looked at him and was silent for a moment, but she felt very strong and sure of herself.

"Signor Lamberti," she said presently, "I want to ask you to do something—for me."

There was a little emphasis on the last word. He turned quite towards her now, but he still made chords on the instrument, for he knew that the Countess had extraordinary ears. His impulse was to tell her that he would do anything she asked of him, no matter how hard it might be; but he controlled it.

"Certainly," he answered. "What is it?"

"Forget that we met in the Forum, and forget what we said to each other at the garden party. Will you? It was all a coincidence, of course, but I behaved very foolishly, and I do not like to think that you remember it. Will you try and forget it all?"

"I will try," Lamberti answered, looking down at the keys. "At all events, I can promise never to remind you of it, as I did just now."

"That is what I meant," Cecilia said. "Let us never remind each other of it. Of course we cannot really forget, in our own selves, but we can begin again from the beginning, this evening, as if it had never happened. We can be real friends, as we ought to be."

"Can we?" Lamberti asked the question in a doubtful tone, and glanced uneasily at her.

"I can, if you can," she answered courageously, "and I mean to be."

"Then I can, too," Lamberti said, but his lips shut tightly as if he regretted the words as soon as they were spoken.

"It will be easy, now," Cecilia went on. "It will be much easier because—" She stopped.

"Why will it be so much easier?" Lamberti asked, looking down again.

"We were not going to speak of those things again," Cecilia said. "We had better not begin."

"I only ask that one question. Tell me why it will be easier now. It may help me to forget."

"It will be easier—because I do not dream of you any more—I mean of the man who is like you." She was blushing faintly, but she knew that he would not look at her, and she was sitting in the shadow.

"On what day did you stop dreaming?" he asked, between two chords.

"It was last week. Let me see. It was a Wednesday. On Wednesday night I did not dream." He nodded gravely over the keys, as if he had expected the answer.

"Did you ever read anything about telepathy?" he asked. "I did not dream of you on Wednesday night either. It seemed to me that I tried to find you and could not."

"Were you trying to find me before?" Cecilia asked, as if it were the most natural question in the world.

"Yes. In my dreams I almost always found you. There was a break—I forget when. The old dream about the house of the Vestals stopped suddenly. Then I missed you and tried to find you. You were always sitting on that bench by the fountain in the villa. Last Wednesday I dreamt I was there, but you did not come."

Cecilia shuddered, as if the night air from the open window chilled her.

"Are you cold?" he asked. "Shall I shut the window?"

"No, I was frightened," she answered. "We must never talk about all that again. Do you know, I think it is wrong to talk about them. There is some power of evil—"

"I do not deny the existence of the devil at all," Lamberti answered, with a faint smile. "But I think this is only a strange case of telepathy. I will do as you wish; though my own belief is, after this evening, that it is better to talk about it all quite fearlessly, and grow used to it. We shall be much less afraid of it if we look upon it as something not at all supernatural, which could easily be explained if we knew enough about those things."

"Perhaps," Cecilia answered doubtfully. "You may be right. I do not know."

"You are going to marry my most intimate friend," Lamberti continued, "and I am unfortunately condemned to stay in Rome for some time, for a year, I fancy, and perhaps even longer."

"Why do you say that you are 'unfortunately condemned' to stay?"

"Because I did my best to get away. You look surprised. I begged the Minister to shorten my leave and send me to sea at once, with or without promotion. Instead, I was named a member of a commission which will sit a long time. Since we are talking frankly, I wanted to get away from you, and not to see you again for years. But now that I must stay here, or leave the service, we cannot help meeting; so I think it is more sensible not to take any solemn oaths never to allude to these strange coincidences, or whatever they are, but to talk them out of existence; all the more so, as they seem to have suddenly come to an end. I only tell you what would be easier for me; but I will do whatever makes it most easy for you."

"I prayed that they might stop," said Cecilia, in a very low voice. "I want you to be my friend, and as long as I dreamt of you—in that way—I felt that it was impossible."

"Of course," Lamberti answered, without hesitation. Then, with an attempt at a laugh, he corrected himself. "I apologise for all the things I said to you in my dreams."

"Please do not laugh about it." Her voice was a little unsteady, and she was looking down, so that he could not see her face.

"It is better not to take it too seriously," he replied gravely. "Could anything be more absurd than that two people who were mere acquaintances then should fall in love with each other in their dreams? It is utterly ridiculous. Any sane person would laugh at the idea."

"Yes; no doubt. But there is more than that. Call it telepathy, or whatever you please, it cannot be a mere coincidence. Do you know that, until last Wednesday, I met you in my dream, just where you dreamed of meeting me, at the bench in the villa?"

He did not seem surprised, but listened attentively while she continued.

"I am sure that we really met," she went on gravely. "It may be in some natural way or not. It does not matter. We must never meet again like that—never. Do you understand? We must promise never to try and find each other in our dreams. Will you promise?"

"Yes; I promise." Lamberti spoke gravely.

"I promise, too," Cecilia said.

Then they were both silent for a time. It was like a real parting, and they felt it, and for a few moments each was thinking of the bench by the fountain in the Villa Madama.

"We owe it to Guido," Lamberti said at last, almost unconsciously.

"Yes," the girl answered; "and to ourselves. Thank you."

With an impulse she did not suspect, she held out her hand to him, and waited for him to take it. Neither her mother nor Guido could see the gesture, for Lamberti's seated figure screened her from them; but he could not have taken her hand in his right without changing his position, since she was seated low on his other side; so he took it quietly in his left, and the two met and pressed each the other for a second.

In that touch Cecilia felt that all her fear of him ended for ever, and that of all men she could trust him the most, and that he would protect her, if ever he might, even more effectually than Guido. His hand was cool, and steady, and strong, and enfolding—the hand of a brave man. But if she had looked she would have seen that his face was paler than usual, and that his eyes seemed veiled.

She rose, and he followed her as she moved slowly forward.

"What a charming talent you have!" cried the Countess in an encouraging tone, when Lamberti was near her.

"Have you made acquaintance at last?" Guido was asking of Cecilia, in an undertone.

"Yes," she answered gravely. "I think we shall be good friends."

CHAPTER XVII

People said that Guido had ceased to be interesting since he had been engaged to be married. Until that time, there had been an element of romance about him, which many women thought attractive; and most men had been willing to look upon him as a being slightly superior to themselves, who cared only for books and engravings, though he never thrust his tastes upon other people, nor made any show of knowing more than others, and whose opinion on points of honour was the very best that could be had. It was so good, indeed, that he was not often asked to give it.

Now, however, they said that he was changed; that he was complacent and pleased with himself; that this was no wonder, because he was marrying a handsome fortune with a pretty and charming wife; that he had done uncommonly well for himself; and much more to the same purpose. Also, the mothers of impecunious marriageable sons of noble lineage said in their maternal hearts that if they had only guessed that Countess Fortiguerra would give her daughter to the first man who asked for her, they would not have let Guido be the one.

The judgments of society are rarely quite at fault, but they are almost always relative and liable to change. They are, indeed, appreciations of an existing state of things, rather than verdicts from which there is no appeal. The verdict comes after the state of things has ceased to exist.

Guido was happy, and nothing looks duller than the happiness of quiet people. Nobody will go far to look at the sea when it is calm, if he is used to seeing it at all; but those who live near it will walk a mile or two to watch the breakers in a storm.

In the first place, Guido was in love, and more in love with Cecilia's face and figure than he guessed. In the early days of their acquaintance he had enjoyed talking with her about the subjects in which she was interested. Such conversation generally brought him to that condition of intellectual suspense which was peculiarly delightful to him, for though she did not persuade him to accept her own points of view, she made him feel more doubtful about his own, so far as any of them were fixed, and doubt meant revery, musing, imaginative argument about questions that might never be answered. But he and she had now advanced to another stage. Unconsciously, all that side of his nature had fallen into abeyance, and he thought only of positive things in the immediate future. When he was with Cecilia, no matter how the conversation began, it soon turned upon their plans for their married life; and he found it so infinitely pleasant to talk of such matters that it did not occur to him to ask whether she regarded them as equally interesting.

She did not; she saw the change in him, and regretted it. A woman who is not really in love, generally likes a man less after he has fallen hopelessly in love with her. It is true that she sometimes likes herself the better for her new conquest, and there may be some compensation in that; but there is something tiresome, if not repugnant to her, in the placid, possessive complacency of a future husband, who seems to forget that a woman has any intelligence except in matters concerning furniture and the decoration of a house.

Cecilia was not capricious; she really liked Guido as much as ever, and she would not even admit that he bored her when he came back again and again to the same topics. She tried hard to look forward to the time when all the former charm of their intercourse should return, and when, besides being the best of friends, he would again be the most agreeable of companions. It seemed very far off; and yet, in her heart, she hoped that something might happen to hinder her marriage, or at least to put it off another year.

Her life seemed very blank after the great struggle was ended, and in the long summer mornings before Guido came to luncheon, she was conscious of longing for something that should take the place of the old dreams, something she could not understand, that awoke under the listlessness which had come upon her. It was a sort of sadness, like a regret for a loss that had not really been suffered, and yet was present; it was a craving for sympathy where she had deserved none, and it made her inclined to pity herself without reason. She sometimes felt it after Guido had come, and it stayed with her, a strange yearning after an unknown happiness that was never to be hers, a half-comforting and infinitely sad conviction that she was to die young and that people would mourn for her, but not those, or not that one, who ought to be most sorry that she was gone. All her books were empty of what she wanted, and for hours she sat still, doing nothing, or stood leaning on the window-sill, gazing down through the slats of the blinds at the glaring street, unconscious of the heat and the strong light, and of the moving figures that passed.

Occasionally she drove out to the Villa Madama in the afternoon with her mother, and Guido joined them. Lamberti did not come there, though he often came to the house in the evening, sometimes with his friend, and sometimes later. The two always went away together. At the villa, Cecilia never sat down on the bench by the fountain, but from a distance she looked at it, and it was like looking at a grave. In dreams she had sat there too often with another to go there alone now; she had heard words there that touched her heart too deeply to be so easily forgotten, and there had been silences too happy to forget. She had buried all that by the garden seat, but it was better not to go near the place again. What she had laid out of sight there might not be quite dead yet, and if she sat in the old place she might hear some piteous cry from beneath her feet; or its ghost might rise and stare at her, the ghost of a dream. Then, the yearning and the longing grew stronger and hurt her sharply, and she turned under the great door, into the hall, and was very glad when her mother began to chatter about dress and people.

But one day the very thing happened which she had always tried to avert. Guido insisted on walking up and down the path with her, and they passed and repassed the bench, till she was sure that he would make her sit down upon it. She tried to linger at the opposite end, but he was interested in what he was saying and did not notice her reluctance to turn back.

Then it came. He stood still by the fountain, and then he sat down quite naturally, and evidently expecting her readiness to do the same. She started slightly and looked about, as if to find some means of escape, but a moment later she had gathered her courage and was sitting beside him.

The scene came back with excessive vividness. There was the evening light, the first tinge of violet on the Samnite mountains, the base of Monte Cavo already purple, the glow on Frascati, and nearer, on Marino; Rome was at her feet, in a rising mist beyond the flowing river. Guido talked on, but she did not hear him. She heard another voice and other words, less gentle and less calm. She felt other eyes upon her, waiting for hers to answer them, she felt a hand stealing near to hers as her own lay on the bench at her side.

Still Guido talked, needing no reply, perfectly confident and happy. She did not hear what he said, but when he paused she mechanically nodded her head, as if agreeing with him, and instantly lost herself again. She could not help it. She expected the touch, and the look, and then the blinding rush that used to come after it, lifting her from her feet and carrying her whole nature away as the south wind whirls dry leaves up with it and far away.

That did not come, and presently she was covering her face with both hands, shaking a little, and Guido was anxiously asking what had happened.

"Nothing," she answered rather faintly. "It is nothing. It will be over in a moment."

He thought that she had felt the sudden chill of the evening which is sometimes dangerous in Rome in midsummer, and he rose at once.

"We had better go in before you catch cold," he said.

"Yes. Let us go in."

For the first time, his words really jarred on her. For the rest of her life, he would tell her when to go indoors before catching cold. He was possessive, complacent; he already looked upon her as a person in his charge, if not as a part of his property. Unreasoningly, she said to herself it was no concern of his whether she caught cold or not, and besides, there was no question of such a thing. She had covered her eyes with her hands for a very different reason, and was ashamed of having done it, which made matters worse. In anger she told herself boldly that she wished that he were not himself, only that once, but that he were Lamberti, who at least took the trouble to amuse her and never put on paternal airs to enquire about her health.

It was the beginning of revolt. Guido dined with them that evening, and she was silent and absent-minded. Before the hour at which he usually went away, she rose and bade him good night, saying that she was a little tired.

"I am sure you caught cold to-day," he said, with real anxiety.

"We will not go to the villa again," she answered. "Good night."

It was late before she really went to bed, for when she was at last rid of the conscientious Petersen, she sat long in her chair at the writing table with a blank sheet of letter paper before her and a pen in her hand. She dipped it into the ink often, and her fingers moved as if she were going to write, but the point never touched the paper. At last the pen lay on the table, and she was resting her chin upon her folded hands, her eyes half closed, her breath drawn in short sighs that came and went between her parted lips. Then, though she was all alone, the blood rose suddenly in her face and she sprang to her feet, angry with herself and frowning, and ashamed of her thoughts.

She felt hot, and then cold, and then almost sick with disgust. The vision that had delighted her was far away now; she had forced herself not to see it, but the man in it had come back to her in dreams; she had driven him out of them, and for a time she had found peace, but now he came to her in her waking thoughts and she longed to see his living face and to hear his real voice. With utter self-contempt and scorn of her own heart, she guessed that this was love, or love's beginning, and that nothing could save her now.

Her first impulse was to write to him, to beg him to go away at any price, never to see her again as long as she lived. As that was out of the question, she next thought of writing to Guido, to tell him that she could not marry him, and that she had made up her mind to retire from the world and spend her life in a convent. But that was impossible, too.

There was no time to be lost. Either she must make one supreme effort to drive Lamberti from her thoughts and to get back to the state in which she had felt that she could marry Guido and be a good wife to him, or else she must tell him frankly that the engagement must end. He would ask why, and she would refuse to tell him, and after that she did not dare to think of what would happen. It might ruin his life, for she knew that he loved her very much. She was honestly and truly much more concerned for him than for herself. It did not matter what became of her, if only she could speak the truth to him without bringing harm to him in the future. The world might say what it pleased.

It was right to break off her engagement, beyond question, and she had done very wrong in ever agreeing to it; it was the greatest sin she had ever committed, and with a despairing impulse she sank upon her knees and poured out her heart in full confession of her fault.

Never in her life had she confessed as she did now, with such a whole-hearted hatred of her own weakness, such willingness to bear all blame, such earnest desire for forgiveness, such hope for divine guidance in making reparation. She would not plead ignorance, nor even any omission to examine herself, as an excuse for what she had done. It was all her fault, and her eyes had been open from the first, and she was about to see the whole life of a good friend ruined through her miserable weakness.

As she went over it all, burying her face in her hands, the conviction that she loved Lamberti grew with amazing quickness to the certainty of a fact long known. This was her crime, that she had been too proud to own that she had loved him at first sight; her punishment should be never to see him again. She would abase herself before Guido and confess everything to him in the very words she was whispering now, and she would implore his forgiveness. Then, since Lamberti could not leave Rome, she and her mother would go away on a long journey, to Russia, perhaps, or to America, or China, and they would never come back. It must be easy enough to avoid one particular person in the whole world.

This she would do, but she would not deny that she loved him. All her fault had lain in trying to deny it in spite of what she felt when he was near her, and it must be still more wrong to force the fact out of sight now that it had brought her into such great trouble. There was nothing to be done but to acknowledge it, though it was shame and humiliation to do so. It stared her in the face, now that she had courage to own the truth, and a voice called out that she had lied to herself, to her mother, and to Guido for many weeks, and persistently, rather than admit that she could fall so low. But even then, in the midst of her self-abasement, another voice answered that it was no shame to love a good and true man, and that Lamberto Lamberti was both.

CHAPTER XVIII

That night seemed the longest in all Cecilia's young life. She was worn out with fatigue, and could have slept ten hours, yet she dreaded to fall asleep lest she should dream of Lamberti, and speak to him in her dream as she meant never to speak to any man now. Just when she was losing consciousness, she roused herself as one does who fears a horrible nightmare that comes back again and again. She was afraid to be alone in the dark with her fear, and she had left one light burning where it could not shine into her eyes. If she did not sleep before daylight, she might not dream after that. When she shut her eyes she saw Lamberti looking at her.

She rose and bathed her face and temples. The water was not very cold in July, after standing in the room half the night, but it cooled her brows a little and she lay down again, and tried to repeat things she knew by heart. She knew all the fourteenth canto of the "Paradise," for instance, and said it over, and tried to see what it described as she had seen it all in the church of Santa Croce. While she whispered the words she looked forward to those she loved best, the ones that bade her rise and get the victory, and she went on with intense anticipation. Before she reached them she lost herself, and they formed themselves on her lips unnoticed as she saw Lamberti's face again.

It was unbearable. She sat up on the edge of the bed and stared into the shadow, and presently she grasped her left arm above the elbow and tried to force her nails into the flesh, with the instinctive idea that pain must bring peace after it. But she could hardly hurt herself at all in that way. Again she rose, and she went and looked at her reflection in the tall glass.

There was not much light in the room, but she could see that she was very pale, and that her eyes had a strange look in them, more like Lamberti's than her own. It was a possession; she found him everywhere. Behind her image in the glass she saw the door of the room, the only one there was, which she had so often heard closed softly just as her dream ended. She shivered, for the Palazzo Massimo is a ghostly place at night, and her nerves were unstrung by what she had suffered. She knew that she was dizzy for a moment, and the glass grew misty and then clear, and reflected nothing to her sight, nothing but the whole door, as if she herself were not standing there, all in white, between it and the mirror.

It was going to open, she felt sure. It was going to open softly, though she knew it was locked, and then some one would enter. She shivered again, and felt her loose hair rising on her head, as if lifted by a cool breeze. It was a moment of agony, and her teeth chattered. He was coming, and she was paralysed, helpless to move, rooted to the spot. In one second more she must hear the slipping of the latch bolt, and he would be behind her.

No, nothing came. Gradually she began to see herself in the glass again, a faint ashy outline, then a transparent image, like the wraith of her dead self, with staring eyes and dishevelled colourless hair. Her terror was gone; she vaguely wondered where she had been, and looked curiously at her reflected face.

"I think I am going mad," she said aloud, but quite quietly, as she turned away from the mirror.

She lay down again on her back, her arms straightened by her sides, and she looked at the ceiling. Since she must think of something, she would try to think out what she was to say and do on the morrow. She would telephone to Guido in the morning to come and see her, of course, and in twenty minutes he would be sitting beside her on the little sofa in the drawing-room. Then she would tell him everything, just as she had confessed it all to herself that evening. She would throw herself upon his mercy, she would say that she was irresistibly drawn to his friend; but she would promise never to see Lamberti again, since that was to be the punishment of her fault. There was clearly nothing else to do, if she had any self-respect left, any modesty, any sense of decency. It would be hard in the beginning, but afterwards it would grow easier.

Poor Guido! he would not understand at first, and he would look at her as if he were dazed. She would give anything to save him the pain of it all, but he must bear it, and in the end it would be much better. Of course, the cowardly way would be to make her mother tell him.

She had not thought of her mother till then, but she had grown used to directing her, and to feeling that she herself was the ruling spirit of the two. Her mother would accept the decision, though she would protest a good deal, and cry a little. That was to be regretted, but it did not really matter since this was a question of absolute right or absolute wrong, in which there was no choice.

She would not see Lamberti again, not even to say good-bye. It would be wicked to see him, now that she knew the truth. But it was right to own bravely that she loved him. If she hesitated in that, there would be no sense in what she meant to do. She loved him with all her heart, with everything in her, with every thought and every instinct, as she had loved long ago in her vision. And as she had overcome then, for the sake of a vow from which she was really freed, so she would conquer again for the sake of the promise she had given to Guido d'Este, and was going to revoke to-morrow.

A far cry echoed through the silent street, and there was a faint grey light between the slats of the blinds. The darkness was ended at last, and perhaps she might allow herself to sleep now. She tried, but she could not, and she watched the dawn growing to cold daylight in the room, till the single lamp hardly glimmered in the corner. She closed her lids and rested as well as she could till it was time to get up.

She was very pale, and there were deep violet shadows under her eyes and below the sharp arches of her brows, but Petersen was very near-sighted, and noticed nothing unusual. Cecilia told her to telephone to Guido, asking him to come at ten o'clock. When the maid returned, Cecilia bade her arrange her hair very low at the back and to make it as smooth as possible. There was not the slightest conscious desire for effect in the order; when a woman has made up her mind to humiliate herself she always makes her hair look as unobtrusive as possible, just as a conscience-stricken dog drops his tail between his legs and hangs down his ears to avert wrath. We men are often very unjust to women about such things, which depend on instincts as old as humanity. Eastern mourners do not strew ashes on their heads because it is becoming to their appearance, and a woman's equivalents for ashes and sackcloth are to do her hair low and wear grey, if she chances to dislike that colour.

"Are you going to confession, my dear?" asked the Countess in some surprise when they met.

"No," Cecilia answered. "I could not sleep last night. I have telephoned to Guido to come at ten." The Countess looked at her and instantly understood that there was trouble.

"You are as white as a sheet," she said, with caution. "You had better let him come after luncheon to-day."

"No. I must see him at once."

"Something has happened," the Countess said nervously. "I know something has happened."

"I will tell you by-and-by. Please do not ask me now."

Her mother's look of anxiety turned slowly to an expression of real fear, her eyes opened wide, she grew pale, and her jaw fell as her lips parted. She looked suddenly old and grey.

"You are not going to marry him after all," she said, after a breathless little silence.

Some seconds passed before Cecilia answered, and then her voice was sad and low.

"How can I? I do not love him."

The Countess was horror-struck now, for she knew her daughter well. She began to speak rather incoherently, but with real earnestness, imploring Cecilia to think of what she was doing before it was too late, to consider Guido's feelings, her own, everybody's, to reflect upon the view the world would take of such bad faith, and, finally, to give some reason for her sudden decision.

It was in vain that she pleaded. Cecilia, grave and suffering, answered that she had taken everything into consideration and knew that she was doing right. The world might call it bad faith to break an engagement, but it would be nothing short of a betrayal to marry Guido since she had become sure that she could never love him. That was reason enough, and she would give no other. It was better that Guido should suffer for a few days than be made to suffer for a lifetime. She had not consulted any one, she said, when her mother questioned her; she would have done so if this had been a matter needing judgment and wisdom, but it was merely one of right and wrong, and she knew what was right, and meant to do it.

The Countess began to cry, and when Cecilia tried to soothe her, she pushed the girl aside and left the room in tears. A few minutes later Petersen telephoned for the carriage, and in less than half an hour the Countess was on her way to see Princess Anatolie, entirely forgetful of the fact that Cecilia would be quite alone when Guido came at ten o'clock.

Cecilia sat quite still in the drawing-room waiting for him. She was very tired and pale, and her eyes smarted for want of sleep, but her courage was not likely to fail her. She only wished that all might be over soon, as condemned men do when they are waiting for execution.

She sat still a long time and she heard the little French clock on her mother's writing table in the boudoir strike its soft chimes at the third quarter, and then ring ten strokes at the full hour. She listened anxiously for the servant's step beyond the door, and now and then she caught her breath a little when she thought she heard a sound. It was twenty minutes past ten when the door opened. She expected the man to stand still, and announce Guido, and she looked away; but the footsteps came nearer and nearer and stopped beside her. The man held out a small salver on which lay a note addressed in Guido's hand. It was like a reprieve after the long tension, for something must have happened to prevent him from coming, something unexpected, but welcome, though she would not own it.

In answer to her question, the man said that the messenger had gone away, and he left the room. She tore the envelope with trembling fingers.

Guido was ill. That was the substance of the note. He had felt ill when he awoke early in the morning, but had thought it nothing serious, though he was very uncomfortable. Unknown to him, his man had sent for a doctor, who had come half an hour ago, after Cecilia's message had been received and answered. The doctor had found him with high fever, and thought it was a sharp attack of influenza; at all events he had ordered Guido to stay in bed, and gave him little hope of going out for several days.

The note dropped on Cecilia's knees before she had read the words of loving regret with which it closed, and she found herself wondering whether Lamberti would have been hindered from coming by a mere touch of fever, under the same circumstances. But she would not allow herself to dwell on that long, for it gave her pleasure to think of Lamberti, and all such pleasure she intended to deny herself. It was quite bad enough to know that she loved him with all her heart. She went back to her own room.

There was nothing to be done but to write to Guido at once, for she would not allow the day to pass without telling him what she meant to do. She sat down and wrote as well as she could, weighing each sentence, not out of caution, but in fear lest she should not make it clear that she was altogether to blame for the mistake she had made, and meant to bear all the consequences in the eyes of the world. She was truly and sincerely penitent, and asked his forgiveness with touching humility. She did not mention Lamberti, but she confessed frankly that since she had been in Rome she had begun to love another man, as she ought to have loved Guido, a man whom she rarely saw, and who had never shown the least inclination to make love to her.

That was the substance of what she wrote. She read the words over, to be sure that they said what she meant, and she told Petersen to send a man at once with the letter. There was no answer, he was not to wait. She gave the order rather hurriedly, for she wished her decision to become irrevocable as soon as possible. It was a physical relief, but not a mental one, to feel that it was done and that she could never recall the fatal words. After reading such a letter there could be nothing for Guido to do but to accept the situation and tell his friends that she had broken the engagement. As for the immediate effect it might have on him, she did not even take his slight illness into consideration. The fact that he could not come and see her might even make it easier for him to bear the blow. Of course, if he came, she should be obliged to receive him, but she hoped that he would not. It would hurt her to see how much he was hurt, and she was suffering enough already. In time she trusted that he and she might be good friends, as young girls have an unreasonable inclination to hope in such cases.

When the Countess came back from her visit to the Princess Anatolie she was a little flushed, and there was a hard look in her face which Cecilia had never seen before, and which made her expect trouble. To her surprise, her mother kissed her affectionately on both cheeks.

"That old woman is a harpy," she said, as she left the room.

CHAPTER XIX

Guido took Cecilia's letter with a smile of pleasure when his man brought it to him, and, as he felt its thickness between his fingers, the delightful anticipation of reading it alone was already a real happiness. She was distressed and anxious for him, he was sure, and perhaps in saying so she had found some expression less formal than those she generally used when she talked with him and assured him that she really liked him very much.

"You may go," he said to his servant. "I need nothing more, thank you."

He was in bed, propped up by three or four pillows, and his face was unnaturally flushed and already looked thin. A new book of memoirs, half cut, and with the paper-knife between the leaves, lay on the arras counterpane, in the middle of which royal armorial bearings with crown and sceptre were represented in the fat arms of smiling cherubs. The head of the carved bed was towards the windows of the wide room, so that the light fell from behind; for Guido was an indolent man, and often lay reading for an hour before he got up. On the small table beside him stood a heavy Venetian tumbler of the eighteenth century, ornamented with gold designs. A cigarette-case lay beside it. The carpet of the room had been taken up for the summer, and the floor was of dark red tiles, waxed and immaculate. In a modest way, and though he was comparatively a poor man, Guido had always managed to have what he wanted in the way of surroundings.

He looked at the address on the note, prolonging his anticipation as much as possible. He recognised the neat French envelope as one of those the Countess always had on her table in a stamped leather paper-rack. He felt it again, and was sure that it contained at least four sheets. It was good of her to write so much, and he had not really expected anything. He forgot that his head was aching, that he had a tiresome pain in his bones, and could feel the fever pulse beating in his temples.

He glanced at the door, and then raised the letter to his dry lips, with a look of boyish pleasure. Five minutes later the crumpled pages were crushed in his straining fingers, and he lay twisted to one side, his face to the wall and half buried in the pillow. The grief of his life had come upon him unawares, and he was not able to bear it. Even if he had not been alone, he could not have hidden what he felt then.

After a long time he got up and softly locked the door. He felt very dizzy as he came and lay down again. One of the crumpled sheets of Cecilia's letter had fallen to the floor, the rest lay on the bed beside him and under him.

He lay still, and when he shut his eyes he saw red waves coming and going, for the fever was high, and the blood beat up under his ears as if the arteries must burst.

In an hour his man knocked at the door, and almost at the same instant turned the handle, for he was accustomed to be admitted at once.

"Go away!" cried Guido, in a hoarse voice that stuck in his throat.

The servant's footsteps echoed in the corridor, and there was silence again, and time passed. Then the knock was repeated, very discreetly and with no attempt to turn the handle. Guido answered with an oath.

But his man was not satisfied this time, and he stood still outside, with a puzzled expression. He had never heard Guido swear at any one, in all the years of his service, much less at himself. His master was either in a delirium, or something very grave had happened which he had learned by the letter. The doctor had said that he was not dangerously ill, so it was not likely that he should be already raving with the fever. The man went softly away to his pantry, where the telephone was, shutting each door carefully behind him. There was nothing to be done but to inform Lamberti at once, if he could be found.

It was late in the afternoon before he got the message, on coming home from a long day's work at the Ministry of War. He had not breakfasted that day, for he had been unexpectedly sent for in the morning and had been kept at the Ministry without a moment's respite. Without going to his room he ran down the stairs again and hailed the first cab he met as he hurried towards the Palazzo Farnese.

The bedroom door was still locked, but he spoke to Guido through it, in answer to the rough order to go away which followed his first knock. There was no reply.

"Please let me in," Lamberti said quietly. "I want very much to see you."

Something like a growl came from the room, and presently there was a sound of slippers on the smooth tiles, coming nearer. The key turned and the door was opened a little.

"What is it?" Guido asked, in a voice unlike his own.

"I heard you were ill, and I have come to see you."

Lamberti spoke gently and steadily, but he was shocked by Guido's appearance, as the latter stood before him in his loose silk garments, looking gaunt and wild. There were great rings round his eyes, his face was haggard and drawn, and his cheek-bones were flushed with the fever. He looked much more ill than he really was, so far as his body was concerned.

"Well, come in," he said, after a moment's hesitation.

As soon as Lamberti had entered Guido locked the door again to keep his servant out.

"I suppose you had better be the first to know," he said hoarsely, as he recrossed the room with unsteady steps.

He sat down upon the edge of his bed, supporting himself with his hands on each side, his head a little bent.

"What has happened?" Lamberti asked, sitting on the nearest chair and watching him. "Has your aunt been troubling you again?"

"No. It is worse than that." Guido paused, and his head sank lower. "The Contessina has changed her mind," he managed to say clearly enough to be understood.

Lamberti started and leaned forward.

"Do you mean to say that she has thrown you over?"

"Yes."

A dead silence followed. Then Guido threw himself on the bed again and turned his face away.

"Say something, man," he cried, almost angrily.

The afternoon light streamed through the closed blinds and fell on the crumpled sheet of the letter that lay at Lamberti's feet. He did not know what he saw as he stared down at it, and he would have cut off his hand rather than pry into any one's letters, but four words had photographed themselves upon his brain before he had realised their meaning, or even that he had seen them.

"I love another man."

Those were the words, and he had never seen the handwriting, but he knew that Cecilia had written them. Guido's cry for some sort of consolation was still ringing in his ears.

"It is impossible," he said, in a dull voice. "She cannot break off such an engagement."

"She has," Guido answered, still looking away. "It is done. She has written to say that she will never marry me."

"Why?" Lamberti asked mechanically.

"Because—" Guido stopped short. "That is her secret. Unless she chooses to tell you herself."

Lamberti knew the secret already, but he would not pain Guido by saying so. The four words he had read had explained enough, though he had not the slightest clew to the name of the man concerned, and his anger was rising quietly, as it did when he was going to be dangerous. He loved Cecilia much and unreasoningly, yet so long as his friend had stood between her and himself he had been strong enough not to be jealous of him; but he was under no obligation to that other man, and now he wished that he had him in his hands. Moreover, his anger was against the girl, too.

"It is outrageous," he said, at last, with a conviction that comforted Guido a little. "It is perfectly abominable! What shall you do?"

"I can do nothing, of course."

Guido tossed on his pillows, turned his head, and stared at Lamberti, hoping to be contradicted.

"It is of no use to go to bed because a woman is faithless," answered Lamberti rather savagely. Guido almost laughed.

"I am ill," he said. "I can hardly stand. She telephoned to me to go and see her, but I could not, and so she wrote what she had to say. It is just as well. I am glad she cannot see me just now."

"I wish she could," answered Lamberti, closing his teeth on the words sharply. "But you will see her, will you not?" he asked, after a pause. "You will not accept such a dismissal without telling her what you think of her?"

"Why should I tell her anything? If I have not succeeded in making her love me yet, I shall never succeed at all! It is better to bear it as if I had never expected anything else."

"Is there any reason why a woman should be allowed to do with impunity what one man would shoot another for doing?" asked Lamberti, roughly. "She has changed her mind once, she can be made to change it again."

The more he thought of what had happened the angrier he grew, and his jealousy against the unknown man who had caused the trouble was boiling up.

Guido caught at the straw like a drowning man, and raised himself on his elbow.

"Do you really think that she may change her mind? That this is only a caprice?"

"I should not wonder. All women have caprices now and then. It is a fit of conscience. She is not quite sure that she likes you enough to marry you, and you have said something that jarred on her, perhaps. If you had been able to go and see her this morning, she would have begun by being very brave, but in five minutes she would have been as ready to marry you as ever. I will wager anything that when she had written that letter she sent it off as soon as possible for fear that she should not send it at all!"

"What do you advise me to do?" asked Guido, his hopes rising. "I believe you understand women better than I do, after all!"

"They are only human animals, like ourselves," Lamberti answered carelessly. "The chief difference is that they do all the things that we are sometimes inclined to do, but should be ashamed of doing."

"I daresay. But I want your advice."

"Go and tell her that she has made a mistake, that she cannot possibly be in earnest, but that if she does not feel that she can marry you in a fortnight, she can put off the wedding till the autumn. It is quite simple. It has all been rather sudden, from the first, and it is much better that the engagement should go on a little longer."

"That is reasonable," Guido answered, growing calmer every moment. "I wish I could go to her at once."

"I suppose you cannot," said Lamberti, looking at him rather curiously.

He remembered that he had once dragged himself five miles with a bad spear-wound in his leg, to take news to a handful of men in danger, but he supposed that Guido was differently organised. He did not like him the less.

"No!" Guido answered. "The fever makes me so giddy that I can hardly stand."

He put out his hand for the tumbler on the table, but it was empty.

"Lamberti!" he said.

"Yes, I will get you some water at once," the other answered, rising to his feet.

"No," Guido said. "Never mind that, I will ring presently. Will you do something for me?"

"Of course."

"Will you speak to her for me?"

Lamberti was standing by the bedside, and he saw the serious and almost timid look in his friend's eyes. But he had not expected the request, and he hesitated a moment.

"You would rather not," said Guido, disappointed. "I suppose I must wait till I am well. Only it may be too late then. She will tell every one that she has broken off the engagement."

"You misunderstood me," Lamberti said calmly, for he had found time to think while Guido was speaking. "I will see her at once."

It had not been easy to say, for he knew what it meant.

"Thank you," Guido murmured. "Thank you, thank you!" he repeated with a profound sense of relief, as his head sank back on the pillow.

"Will it do you any harm if I smoke?" asked Lamberti, looking at a cigar he had taken from his pocket.

"No. I wish you would. I cannot even smoke a cigarette to-day. It tastes like bad hay."

There is a hideous triviality about the things people say at important moments in their lives. But Lamberti was not listening, and he lit his cigar thoughtfully, without answering. Then he went to the window and looked down through the blinds in silence, pondering on what was before him.

It was certainly the place of a friend in such a case to accept the position Guido was thrusting upon him, and from the first Lamberti had not meant to refuse. He had a strong sense of man's individual right to get what he wanted for himself without great regard for the feelings of others, and he was quite sure that he would not have done for his own brother what he was about to do for Guido. It is even possible that he would not have been so ready to do it for Guido himself if he had not accidentally seen those four words of Cecilia's letter. The knowledge of her secret had at once determined the direction of his impulses. For himself he hoped nothing, but he had made up his mind that if Cecilia would not marry Guido she should by no means marry any other man living, and he was fully determined to make her confess her passing fancy for the unknown one, in order that he might have the right to reproach her with it. He even hoped that he could find out the man's name, and, as he was of a violent disposition, he at once planned vengeance to be wreaked upon him. He turned from the window at last, and blew a cloud of grey smoke into the quiet room.

"I will send a message now," he said, "and I will go myself this evening. They can hardly be dining out."

"No. They are at home. I was to have dined with them."

Guido's voice was faint, but he was calm now. Lamberti unlocked the door and opened it. The man servant was just coming towards it followed by the doctor.

The latter found Guido worse than when he had seen him in the morning. He said it was what he had expected, a sharp attack of influenza, and that Guido must not think of leaving his bed till the fever had disappeared. He dilated a little upon the probable consequences of any exposure to the outer air, even in summer. No one could ever tell what the influenza might leave behind it, and it was much safer to be patient.

"You see," said Guido to Lamberti, when the physician was gone. "It will be quite impossible for me to go out to-morrow, or for several days."

"Quite," Lamberti answered, looking for his straw hat.

CHAPTER XX

Lamberti dined at home that evening, and soon after nine o'clock he was on his way to the Palazzo Massimo. Though the evening was hot and close he walked there, for it was easier to think on his feet than leaning back in a cab. His normal condition was one of action and not of reflection.

His thoughts also took an active dramatic shape. He did not try to bind future events together in a connected sequence leading to a result; on the contrary, he seemed to hear the very words he would soon be speaking, and Cecilia Palladio's answers to them; he saw her face and noted her expression, and the interview grew violent by degrees till he felt the inward coolness stealing through him which he had often known in fight.

He had written a note to Countess Fortiguerra which he had left at her door on his way home. He had explained that Guido, being too ill to move, had begged him to speak to the Contessina, and he expressed the hope that he might be allowed to see the young lady for a few minutes alone that evening, in the capacity of the sick man's representative and trusted friend.

Such a request could hardly be refused, and the Countess had always felt that Lamberti was one of those exceptional men in whom one may safely believe, even without knowing them well. She said that Cecilia had better see him when he came. She herself had letters to write and would sit in the boudoir.

It was the last thing Cecilia had expected, and the mere thought was like breaking the promise she had made to herself, never to see Lamberti again; yet she realised that it was impossible to avoid the meeting. The course she had taken was so extraordinary that she felt bound to give Guido a chance to answer her letter in any way he could. In the afternoon her mother had exhausted every argument in trying to make her revoke her decision. She did not love Guido; that was her only reply; but she felt that it ought to be sufficient, and she bowed her head meekly when the Countess grew angry and told her that she should have found that out long ago. Yes, she answered, it was all her fault, she ought to have known, she would bear all the blame, she would tell her friends that she had broken off the engagement, she would do everything that could be required of her. But she would not marry Guido d'Este.

The Countess could say nothing more. On her side she was reticent for once in her life, and told nothing of her own interview with Princess Anatolie. Whether something had been said which the mother thought unfit for her daughter's ears, or whether the Princess's words had been of a nature to hurt Cecilia's pride, the young girl could not guess; and though her maidenly instinct told her to accept her mother's silence without question, if it proceeded from the first cause, she could not help fearing that the Countess had done or said something hopelessly tactless which might produce disagreeable consequences, or might even do some harm to Guido.

Her heart was beating so fast when Lamberti entered the drawing-room that she wondered how she should find breath to speak to him, and she did not raise her eyes again after she had seen his face at the door, till he was close to her, and had bowed without holding out his hand.

"I hope you got my note," he said to her mother. "D'Este is ill, and has given me a verbal message for your daughter."

"Yes," said the Countess. "I will go into the next room and write my letters."

She was gone and the two stood opposite each other in momentary silence. Lamberti's voice had been formal, and his face was almost expressionless.

"Where will you sit?" he asked. "It will take some time to tell you all that he wishes me to say."

Cecilia led the way to the little sofa in the corner farthest from the boudoir. It was there that Guido had asked her to be his wife, and it was there that she had waited for him a few hours ago to tell him that she could not marry him. She took her accustomed place, but Lamberti drew forward a light chair and sat down facing her. He felt that he got an advantage by the position, and that to a small extent it placed him outside of her personal atmosphere. At such a moment he could not afford to neglect the least circumstance which might help him. As for what he should say, he had thought of many speeches while he was in the street, but he did not remember any of them now, nor even that he had seemed to hear himself speaking them.

"Why did you write that letter?" he asked, after a moment's pause.

Cecilia looked up quickly, surprised by the direct question, and then gazed into his face in silence. She had confessed to herself that she loved him, but she had not known how much, nor what it would mean to sit so near him and hear him asking the question that had only one answer. His eyes were steady and brave, when she looked at them, but not so hard as she had expected. In earlier days she had always felt that they could command her and even send her to sleep if he chose, but she did not feel that now. The question had been asked suddenly and directly, but not harshly. She did not answer it.

"Did Guido show you my letter?" she asked in a low voice.

But she was sure of the reply before it came.

"No. He told me that you broke off your engagement with him very suddenly. I suppose you have done so because you think you do not care for him enough to marry him, but he did not tell me so. Is that it?"

Cecilia nodded quickly, folded her hands nervously upon her knees, and looked across the room.

"Yes," she said. "That is it. I do not love him."

"Yet you like him very much," Lamberti answered. "I have often seen you together, and I am sure you do."

"I am very fond of him. If I had not been foolish, he might always have been my best friend."

"I do not think you were foolish. You could hardly do better than marry your best friend, I think. He is mine, and I know what his friendship is worth. You will find out, as I have, that if he is sometimes indolent and slow to make up his mind, he never changes afterwards. You may be separated from him for a year or two, but you will find him always the same when you meet him again, always gentle, always true, always the most honourable of men."

"He is that, and more," Cecilia said softly. "I like everything about him."

"And he loves you," Lamberti continued. "He loves you as men do not often love the women they marry, and as you, with your fortune, may never be loved again."

"I know it. I feel it. It makes it all the harder."

"But you thought you loved him, I am sure. You would not have accepted him otherwise."

"Yes. Thank you for believing that much of me," Cecilia answered humbly. "I thought I loved him."

"You sent for him this morning, because you had suddenly persuaded yourself that you had made a great mistake. When you heard that he could not come, you wrote the letter, and when it was written you sent it off as fast as you could, for fear that you would not send it at all. Is that true?"

"Yes. That is just what happened. How did you know?"

"Listen to me, please, for d'Este's sake. If you had not felt that you were perhaps making another mistake, should you have been in such a hurry to send the letter?"

Cecilia hesitated an instant.

"It was a hard thing to do. That is why I made haste to get it over. I knew it would hurt him, but I thought it was wrong to deceive him for even a few hours, after I had understood myself."

"It would have been kinder to wait until you could see him, and break it gently to him. He was ill when he got your letter, and it made him worse."

"How is he?" Cecilia asked quietly, a little ashamed of not having enquired already. "It is nothing very serious, is it? Only a little influenza, he said."

"He is not dangerously ill, but he had a good deal of fever this afternoon. You will not see him for a week, I fancy. That is the reason why I am here. I want you to postpone your decision, at least until he is well and you have talked with him."

"But I have decided already. I shall take all the blame. I will tell my friends that it is all my fault."

"Is that the only answer you can give me for him?"

"Yes. What can I say? I do not love him. I never shall."

"What if something happens?"

"What?"

"Suppose that I go to him to-morrow morning, and tell him what you say, and that when I have left him there alone with his servant, as I must in the course of the day, he locks the door, and in a fit of despair puts a bullet through his head? What then?"

Cecilia leaned forward, wide-eyed and frightened.

"You do not really believe that he would kill himself?" she cried in a low voice.

"I think it is more than likely," Lamberti answered quietly enough. "D'Este is the most good-hearted, charitable, honourable fellow in the world, but he believes in nothing beyond death. We differ about those questions, and never talk about them; but he has often spoken of killing himself when he has been depressed. I remember that we had an argument about it on the very afternoon when we both first met you."

"Was he so unhappy then?" Cecilia asked with nervous interest.

"Perhaps. At all events I know that he has a bad habit of keeping a loaded revolver in the drawer of the table by his bed, in case he should have a fancy to go out of the world, and it is very well known that people who talk of suicide, and think of it a great deal, often end in that way. When I left him this afternoon I gave him some hope that you might at least prolong the engagement for a few months, and give yourself a chance to grow more fond of him. If I have to tell him that you flatly refuse, I am really afraid that it may be the end of him."

Cecilia leaned back in the sofa and closed her eyes, confronted by the awful doubt that Lamberti might be right. He was certainly in earnest, for he was not the man to say such a thing merely for the sake of frightening her. She could not reason any more.

"Please, please do not say that!" she said piteously, but scarcely above her breath.

"What else can I say? It is quite true. You must have some very strong reason for refusing to reconsider your decision, since your refusal may cost as much as that."

"But men do not kill themselves for love in real life!"

"I am sorry to say they do," Lamberti answered. "A fellow-officer of mine shot himself on board the ship I was last with for exactly the same reason. He left a letter so that there should be no suspicion that he had done it to escape from any dishonour."

"How awful!"

"I repeat that you must have a very strong reason indeed for not waiting a couple of months. In that time you may learn to like Guido better—or he may learn to love you less."

"He may change," Cecilia said, not resenting the rather rough speech; "I never shall."

Lamberti fixed his eyes on her.

"There is only one reason that could make you so sure about yourself," he said. "If I thought you were like most women, I would tell you that you were heartless, faithless, and cruel, as well as capricious, and that you were risking a man's life and soul for a scruple of conscience, or, worse than that, for a passing fancy."

"Oh, please do not say such things of me!" She spoke in great distress.

"I do not. I know that you are honest and true, and are trying to do right, but that you have made a mistake which you can mend if you will. Take my advice. There is only one possible reason to account for what you have done. You think that you love some other man better than d'Este."

Cecilia started and stared at him.

"You said that Guido did not show you my letter!" She was offended as well as distressed now.

"No; he did not. But I will not pretend that I have guessed your secret. As Guido lay on his bed talking to me, I was staring at a crumpled sheet of a letter that lay on the floor. Before I knew what I was looking at I had read four words: 'I love another man.' When I realised that I ought not to have seen even that much, I knew, of course, that it was your writing. You see how much I know. All the same, if you were not what I know you are, I would call you a heartless flirt to your face."

Again he looked at her steadily, but she said nothing.

"If you are not that," he continued, "you never loved Guido at all, but really believed you did, because you did not know what love was, and you are sure that you love this other man with all your heart."

Cecilia was still silent, but a delicate colour was rising in her pale face.

"Has the other ever made love to you?" Lamberti asked.

"No, no—never!"

She could not help answering him and forgetting that she might have been offended. She loved him beyond words, he did not know it, and he was unconsciously asking her questions about himself.

"Is he younger than Guido? Handsomer? Has he a great name? A great fortune?"

"Are those reasons for loving a man?"

Cecilia asked the question reproachfully, and as she looked at him and thought of what he was, and how little she cared for the things he had spoken of, but how wholly for the man himself, her love for him rose in her face, against her will.

"There must be something about him which makes you prefer him to Guido," he said obstinately.

"Yes. But I do not know what it is. Do not ask me about him."

"Considering that you are endangering the life of my dearest friend for him, I think I have some right to speak of him."

She was silent, and they faced each other for several seconds with very different expressions. She was pale again, now, but her eyes were full of light and softness, and there was a very faint shadow of a smile flickering about her slightly parted lips, as if she saw a wonderful and absorbing sight. Lamberti's gaze, on the contrary, was cold and hard, for he was jealous of the unknown man and angry at not being able to find out who he was. She did not guess his jealousy, indeed, for she did not suspect what he felt; but she knew that his righteous anger on Guido's behalf was unconsciously directed against himself.

"You will never know who he is," she said at last, very gently.

"We shall all know, when you marry him," Lamberti answered with unnecessary roughness.

"No, I shall never marry him," she said. "I mean never to see him again. I would not marry him, even if he should ever love me."

"Why not?"

"For Guido's sake. I have treated Guido very badly, though I did not mean to do it. If I cannot marry Guido, I will never marry at all."

"That is like you," Lamberti answered, and his voice softened. "I believe you are in earnest."

"With all my heart. But promise me one thing, please, on your word."

"Not till I know whether I may."

"For his sake, not for mine. Stay with him. Do not leave him alone for a moment till you are sure that he is safe and will not try to kill himself. Will you promise?"

"Not unless you will promise something, too."

"Do not ask me to pretend that I love him. I cannot do it."

"Very well. You need not pretend anything. Let me tell him that you will let your engagement continue to all appearance, and that you will see him, but that you put off the wedding for the reasons you gave in your letter. Let me tell him that you hope you may yet care for him enough to marry him. You do, do you not?"

"No!"

"At least let me say that you are willing to wait a few months, in order to be sure of yourself. It is the only thing you can do for him. Perhaps you can accustom him by slow degrees to the idea that you will never marry him."

"Perhaps."

"In any case, you ought to do your best, and that is the best you can do. See him a few times when he is well enough, and then leave Rome. Tell him that it will be a good thing to be parted for a month or two, and that you will write to him. Do not destroy what hope he may have, but let it die out by degrees, if it will."

Cecilia hesitated. After what had passed between them she could hardly refuse to follow such good advice, though it was hard to go back to anything approaching the state of things with which she had broken by her letter. But that was only obstinacy and pride.

"Let it be distinctly understood that I do not take back my letter at all," she said. "If I consent to what you ask, it is only for Guido's sake, and I will only admit that I may be more sure of myself in a few months than I am now, though I cannot see how that is possible."

"It shall be understood most distinctly," Lamberti answered. "You say, too, that you mean never to see this other man again."

"I cannot help seeing him if I stay longer in Rome," Cecilia said.

Lamberti wondered who he might be, with growing hatred of him.

"If he is an honourable man, and if he had the slightest idea that he had unconsciously come between you and Guido, he would go away at once."

"Perhaps he could not," Cecilia suggested.

"That is absurd."

"No. Take your own case. You told me not long ago that you were unfortunately condemned to stay in Rome, unless you gave up your career. He might be in a very similar position. In fact, he is."

There was something so unexpected in the bitter little laugh that followed the last words that Lamberti started. She had kept her secret well, so far, but she had now given him the beginning of a clew. He wished, for once, that he possessed the detective instinct, and could follow the scent. There could not be many men in society who were in a position very similar to his own.

"I wish I knew his name," he said, only half aloud.

But she heard him, and again she laughed a little harshly.

"If I told you who he is, what would you do to him? Go and quarrel with him? Call him out and kill him in a duel? I suppose that is what you would do if you could, for Guido's sake."

"I should like to know his name," Lamberti answered.

"You never shall. You can never find it out, no matter how ingenious you are."

"If I ever see you together, I shall."

"How can you be so sure of that?"

"You forget something," Lamberti said. "You forget the odd coincidences of our dreams, and that I have seen you in them when you were in earnest—not as you have been with Guido, but as you seem to be about this other man. I know every look in your eyes, every movement of your lips, every tone of your voice. Do you think I should not recognise anything of all that in real life?"

"These were only dreams," Cecilia tried to say, avoiding his look. "I asked you not to speak of them."

"Do you dream of him now?" Lamberti asked the question suddenly.

"Not now—no—that is—please do not ask me such questions. You have no right to."

"I beg your pardon. Perhaps I have not."

He was not in the least sorry for having spoken, but his anger increased against the unknown man. She had evidently dreamt of him at one time or another, as she used to dream of himself.

"You have such an extraordinary talent for dreaming," he said, "that the question seemed quite natural. I daresay you have seen Guido in your visions, too, when you believed that you cared for him!"

"Never!" Cecilia could hardly speak just then.

"Poor Guido! that was a natural question too. Since you used to see a mere acquaintance, like myself, and fancy that you were—"

"Stop!"

"—that you were talking familiarly with him," continued Lamberti unmoved, "it would hardly be strange that you should often have seen Guido d'Este in the same way, while you thought you loved him, and it is stranger that you should not now dream about a man you really love—if you do!"

"I say that you have no right to talk in this way," said Cecilia.

"I have the right to say a great many things," Lamberti answered. "I have the right to reproach you—"

"You said that you believed me honest and true."

The words checked his angry mood suddenly. He passed his hand over his eyes and changed his position.

"I do," he said. "There is no woman alive of whom I believe more good than I do of you."

"Then trust me a little, and believe, too, that I am suffering quite as much as Guido. I have agreed to take your advice, to obey you, since it is that and nothing else—"

"I have no power to give you orders. I wish I had!"

"You have right on your side. That is power, and I obey you. You have told me what to do, and I shall do it, and be glad to do it. But even after what I have done, I have some privileges left. I have a secret, and I am ashamed of it, and it can do no good to Guido to know it, much less to you. Please let me keep it in my own way."

"Yes. But if you are afraid that I should hurt the man, if I knew his name, you are mistaken."

"I am not in the least afraid of that," Cecilia answered, and the light filled her eyes again as she looked at him. "You are too just to hate an innocent man. It is not his fault that I love him, and he will never know it. He will never guess that I think him the best, and truest, and bravest man alive, and that he is all this world to me, now and for ever!"

She spoke quietly enough, but there was a radiant joy in her face which Lamberti never forgot. While keeping her secret, she was telling him at last to his face that she loved him, and it was the first time she had ever spoken such words out of her dreams. In them indeed they had been familiar to her lips, as words like them had been to his.

He leaned forward, resting one elbow on his knee, and his chin upon his closed hand, and he looked at her long in silence. He envied her for having been able to say aloud what she felt, under cover of her secret, and he longed to answer her, to tell her that he loved her even better than she loved that unknown man, to hear himself say it to her only once, come what might. But for Guido he would have spoken, for as he gazed at her the instinctive masculine conviction returned stronger than ever, that if he chose he could make her love him. For a moment he was absolutely sure of it, but he only sat still, looking at her.

"You believe me now," she said at last, leaning back and turning her eyes away.

"Poor Guido!" he exclaimed.

He knew indeed that there was no longer any hope for his friend.

"Yes," he added thoughtfully. "It was in your eyes just then, when you were speaking, just as if that man had been there before you. I shall know who he is if I ever see you together. It is understood, then," he went on, changing his tone, "I am to tell him that you wish to put off the marriage till you are more sure of yourself—that you wrote that letter under an impulse."

"Yes, that is true. And you wish me to try to make him understand by degrees that it is all over, and to go away from Rome in a few days, asking him not to follow me at once."

"I think that is the kindest thing you can do. On my part I will give him what hope I can that you may change your mind again."

"You know that I never shall."

"I may hope what I please. There is always a possibility. We are human, after all. One may hope against conviction. May I see you again to-morrow to tell you how he takes your message?"

To his surprise Cecilia hesitated several seconds before she answered.

"Of course," she said at last. "Or you can write to me or to my mother, which will save you the trouble of coming here."

"It is no trouble," Lamberti answered mechanically. "But of course it is painful for you to talk about it all, so unless something unexpected happens I will write a line to your mother to say that Guido accepts your decision, and to let you know how he is. If there is anything wrong, I will come in the evening."

"Thank you. That is the best way."

"Good night." He rose as he spoke.

"Good night. Thank you." She held out her hand rather timidly.

He took it, and she withdrew it precipitately, after the merest touch. She rose quickly and went towards the door of the boudoir, calling to her mother as she walked.

"Signor Lamberti is going," she said.

There was a little rustle of thin silk in the distance, and the Countess appeared at the door and came forward.

"Well?" she asked, as she met Lamberti in the middle of the room.

"Your daughter has decided to do what seems best for everybody," Lamberti said. "She will tell you all about it. Let me thank you for having allowed me to talk it over with her. Good night."

"Do stay and have some tea!" urged the Countess, and she wondered why Cecilia, standing behind Lamberti, frowned and shook her head. "Of course, if you will not stay," she added hastily, "I will not try to keep you. Pray give my best messages to Signor d'Este, and tell him how distressed I am, and say—but you will know just what to say, I am sure. Good night."

Lamberti bowed and shook hands. As he turned, he met Cecilia face to face and bade her good night again. She nodded rather coldly, and then went quickly to ring the bell for the footman.

CHAPTER XXI

Princess Anatolie was very angry when she learned that Cecilia was breaking her engagement, and she said things to the poor Countess which she did not regret, and which hurt very much, because they were said with such perfect skill and knowledge of the world that it was impossible to answer them and it did not even seem proper to show any outward resentment, considering that Cecilia's conduct was apparently indefensible. As it is needless to say, the Princess appeared to regret the circumstance much more for Cecilia's sake than for Guido's. She said that Guido, of course, would soon get over it, for all men were perfectly heartless in reality, and could turn from one woman to another as carelessly as if women were pictures in a gallery. She really did not think that Guido had much more heart than the rest of his kind, and he would soon be consoled. After all, he could marry whom he pleased, and Cecilia's fortune had never been any object to him. She, his thoughtful and affectionate aunt, would naturally leave him her property, or a large part of it. Guido was not at all to be pitied.

But Cecilia, poor Cecilia! What a life she had before her, sighed the Princess, after treating a man in such a way! Of course, she could never live in Rome after this, and as for Paris, she would be no better off there. Guido's friends and relations were everywhere, and none of them would ever forgive her for having jilted him. Perhaps England was the only place for her now. The English were a sordid people, consisting chiefly of shopkeepers, jockeys, tyrants, and professional beauties, and as they thought of nothing but money and their own advantage, Cecilia's fortune would insure her a good reception among them, even though it was not a very large one. Not that the girl was lacking in the most charming qualities and the most exceptional gifts, which would have made her a desirable wife for any man, if only she had not made this fatal mistake. Such things stuck to a woman through life, like a disgrace, though that was a great injustice, because Cecilia was acting under conviction, poor girl, and believed she was doing right! It was most unfortunate. The Princess pitied her very much and would always treat her just as if nothing had happened, if they ever met. Guido would certainly behave in the same way and would always be kind, though he would naturally not seek her society.

The Princess was very angry, and it was not strange that the Countess should have come home a little flushed after the interview and very unexpectedly inclined to be glad, after all, that the engagement was at an end. The Princess had not said one rude word to her, but it was quite clear that she was furious at seeing Cecilia's fortune slip from the grasp of her nephew. It almost looked as if she had expected to get a part of it herself, though the Countess supposed that should be out of the question. Nevertheless the past question of the million which was to have constituted Cecilia's dowry began to rankle, and the Countess's instinct told her that the old lady had probably had some interest in the matter. Indeed, the Princess had told her that Guido had considerable debts, and had vaguely hinted that she had herself sometimes helped him in his difficulties. Of the two, Guido was more to be believed than his aunt, but there was a mysterious element in the whole matter.

The Princess and Monsieur Leroy consulted the spirits now, and she found some consolation when she was told that she should yet get back most of the money she had lost, if she would only trust herself to her truest friend, who was none other than Monsieur Leroy himself. The forlorn little ghost of the only being she had ever really loved in the world was made to assume the character of a financial adviser, and she herself was led like a lamb by the thread of affection that bound her to her dead child.

Monsieur Leroy had not foreseen what was to happen, but he was not altogether at a loss, and the first step was to insure the Princess's obedience to his will. He did not understand the nature of the phenomena he caused, but he knew that in some way certain things that passed in her mind were instantly present in his, and that he could generally produce by rappings the answers he desired her to receive. He at least knew beforehand, in almost every case, what those answers would be, if he did not consciously make the sounds that signified them. If he had ever examined his conscience, supposing that he had any left, he would have found that he himself did not know just where deception ended, and where something else began which he could not explain, which frightened him when he was alone, and which, when he had submitted wholly to it, left him in a state of real physical exhaustion. He was inclined to believe that the mysterious powers were really the spirits of dead persons which possessed him for a short time, and spoke through him. Yet when one of these spirits represented itself as being that of some one whom neither he nor the Princess had ever met in life, he was dimly conscious that it never said anything which had not been already known to her or to him at some time, or which, if unknown, was the spontaneous creation of his own clouded brain.

To her, he always gravely asserted his sure belief in the authenticity of the spirits that came, and since he had unexpectedly succeeded in producing messages from her little girl, any doubt she had ever entertained had completely disappeared. She was wholly at his mercy so long as this state of things could be made to last, and he was correspondingly careful in the use he made of his new power.

The Princess was therefore told that she must trust him altogether, and that he could get back the most of her money for her. She was consoled, indeed, but she was naturally curious as to the means he meant to use, and she questioned him when the rappings ceased and the lights were turned up. He seemed less tired than usual.

"I shall trust to the inspiration of the spirits," he said evasively. "In any case we have the law on our side. Guido cannot deny his signature to those receipts for your money, and he will find it hard to show what became of such large sums. They are a gentleman's promise to pay a lady, but they are also legal documents."

"But they are not stamped," objected the Princess, who knew more about such things than she sometimes admitted.

"You are mistaken. They are all stamped for their respective values, and the stamps are cancelled by Guido's signature."

"That is very strange! I could almost have sworn that there was not a stamp on any of them! How could that be? He used to write them on half sheets of very thick note paper, and I never gave him any stamps."

"He probably had some in his pocket-book," said Monsieur Leroy. "At all events, they are there."

"So much the better. But it is very strange that I should never have noticed them."

Like many of those singular beings whom we commonly call "mediums," Monsieur Leroy was a degenerate in mind and body, and his character was a compound of malign astuteness, blundering vanity, and hysterical sensitiveness, all directed by impulses which he did not try to understand. Without the Princess's protection through life, he must have come to unutterable grief more than once. But she had always excused his mistakes, made apologies for him, and taken infinite pains to make him appear in the best light to her friends. He naturally attributed her solicitude to the value she set upon his devotion to herself, since there could be no other reason for it. Doubtless a charitable impulse had at first impelled her to take in the starving baby that had been found on the doorstep of an inn in the south of France. That was all he knew of his origin. But he knew enough of her character to be sure that if he had not shown some exceptional gifts at an early age, he would soon have been handed over to servants or peasants to be taken care of, and would have been altogether forgotten before long. Instead, he had been spoiled, sent to the best schools, educated as a gentleman, treated as an equal, and protected like a son. The Princess had given him money to spend though she was miserly, and had not checked his fancies in his early youth. She had even tried to marry him to the daughter of a rich manufacturer, but had discovered that it is not easy to marry a young gentleman who has no certificate of birth at all, and whose certificate of baptism describes him as of unknown parents. On one point only she had been inexorable. When she did not wish him to dine with her or to appear in the evening, she insisted that he should stay away. Once or twice he had attempted to disobey these formal orders, but he had regretted it, for he had found himself face to face with one of the most merciless human beings in existence, and his own character was far from strong. He had therefore submitted altogether to the rule, well satisfied with the power he had over her in most other respects, but he felt that he must not lose it. The Princess was old and was growing daily more capricious. She had left him a handsome competence in her will, as much, indeed, as most bachelors would consider a fortune, but she was not dead yet, and she might change her mind at the last moment. He trembled to think what his end must be if she should die and leave him penniless to face the world alone at his age, without a profession and without real friends. For no one liked him, though some people feared his tongue, and he knew it. Perhaps Guido would take pity on him and give him shelter, for Guido was charitable, but the thought was not pleasant. Never having been hungry since he could remember, Monsieur Leroy thought starvation would be preferable to eating Guido d'Este's bread. There was certainly no one else who would throw him a crust, and though he had received a good deal of money from the Princess, and had managed to take a good deal more from her, he had never succeeded in keeping any of it.

It was necessary to form some plan at once for extracting money by means of Guido's receipts, since the marriage was not to take place, and as Monsieur Leroy altogether failed to hit upon any satisfactory scheme he consulted a lawyer in confidence, and asked what could be done to recover the value. The lawyer was a man of doubtful reputation but of incontestable skill, and after considering the matter in all its bearings he gave his client some slight hope of success, proportionate to the amount of money Guido could raise by the sale of his effects and by borrowing from his many friends. He was glad to learn that Guido had never borrowed, except, as Monsieur Leroy explained, from his aunt. A man in such a position could raise a round sum if suddenly driven to extremities to save his honour.

The lawyer also asked Monsieur Leroy for details concerning Guido's life during the last four or five years, inquiring very particularly about his social relations and as to his having ever been in love with a woman of his own rank, or with one of inferior station. Monsieur Leroy answered all these questions with a conscientious desire to speak the truth, which was new to him, for he realised that only the truth could be of use in such a case, and that the slightest unfounded invention of his own against Guido's character must mislead the man he was consulting. In this he showed himself wiser than he often was.

"Above all," the lawyer concluded, "never mention my name to any one, and try to appear surprised at anything unexpected which you may hear about Signor d'Este."

Monsieur Leroy promised readily enough, though reticence was not his strong point, and he went away well pleased with himself, after signing a little paper by which it was agreed that the lawyer should receive twenty per cent of any sums obtained from Guido through him. He had not omitted to inform his adviser of the celebrated Doctor Baumgarten's favourable opinion on the Andrea del Sarto and the small Raphael. The lawyer told him not to be impatient, as affairs of this sort required the utmost discretion.

But the man saw that he had a good chance of being engaged in one of those cases that make an unnecessary amount of noise and are therefore excellent advertisements for a comparatively unknown practitioner who has more wit than scruples. He did not believe that all of Guido's many high and mighty relations would take the side of Princess Anatolie, and if any of them took the trouble to defend her nephew against her, the newspapers would be full of the case and his own name would be famous in a day.

CHAPTER XXII

Cecilia told her mother what Lamberti had advised her to do for Guido's sake, and that she had sent her message by him. The Countess was surprised and did not quite like the plan.

"Either you love him, or you do not, my dear," she said. "You were sure that you did not, and you told him so. That was sensible, at least, though I think you might have found out earlier what you felt. It is much better to let him understand at once that you will not marry him. Men would always rather know the truth at once and get over it than be kept dangling at a capricious woman's beck and call."

Cecilia did not explain that Lamberti feared for his friend's life. In broad daylight that looked dramatic, and her mother would not believe it. She only said that she was sure she was acting for the best and that the engagement was to stand a little longer, adding that she wished to leave Rome, as it was very hot. In her heart she was hurt at being called capricious, but was too penitent to deny the charge.

The Countess at once wrote a formal note to Princess Anatolie in which she said that she had been hasty and spoken too soon, that her daughter seemed undecided, and that nothing was to be said at present about breaking the engagement. The marriage, she added, would be put off until the autumn.

The Princess showed this communication to Monsieur Leroy when he came in. He did not mean to tell her about his visit to the lawyer, for he had made up his mind to play on her credulity as much as he could and to attribute any advantage she might gain by his manoeuvres to supernatural intervention. The Countess's letter surprised him very much, and as he did not know what to do, it seemed easy to do nothing. He expressed his disgust at Cecilia's vacillation.

"She is a flirt and her mother is a fool," he said, and the speech seemed to him pithy and concise.

The old Princess raised her aristocratic eyebrows a little. She would have expressed the same idea more delicately. There was a vulgar streak in his character that often jarred on her, but she said nothing, for she was inexplicably fond of him. For her own part, she was glad that Cecilia had apparently changed her mind again.

Later in the day she received a few words from Guido, written in an unsteady hand, to say that he was sorry he could not come and see her as he had a bad attack of influenza. At the word she dropped the note as if it burnt her fingers, and called Monsieur Leroy, for she believed that influenza could be communicated in almost any way, and it was the only disease she really feared: she had a presentiment that she was to die of it.

"Take that thing away, Doudou!" she cried nervously. "Pick it up with the tongs and burn it. He has the influenza! I am sure I have caught it!"

Monsieur Leroy obeyed, while she retired to her own room to spend half an hour in those various measures of disinfection which prophylactic medicine has recently taught timid people. She had caused her maid to telephone to Guido not to send any more notes until he was quite well.

"You must not go near him for a week, Doudou," she said when she came back at last, feeling herself comparatively safe. "But you may ask how he is by telephone every morning. I do not believe there can be any danger in that."

Electricity was a mysterious power after all, and seemed infinitely harder to understand than the ways of the supernatural beings with whom Monsieur Leroy placed her in daily communication. She had heard a celebrated man of science say that he himself was not quite sure what electricity might or might not do since the discovery of the X-rays.

Her precautions had the effect of cutting off communication between her and her nephew until her departure from Rome, which took place in the course of a few days, considerably to the relief of the Countess, who did not wish to meet her after what had passed.

Monsieur Leroy could not make up his mind to go and see the lawyer again in order to stop any proceedings which the latter might be already taking. Below his wish to serve the Princess and his hope of profiting by his success, there lay his deep-rooted and unreasoning jealousy of Guido d'Este, which he had never before seen any safe chance of gratifying. It would be a profound satisfaction to see this man, who was the mirror of honour, driven to extremities to escape disgrace. Another element in his decision, if it could be called that, was the hopeless disorder of his degenerate intelligence, which made it far easier for him to allow anything he had done to bear fruit, to the last consequence, than to make a second effort in order to arrest the growth of evil.

The lawyer was at work, silently and skilfully, and in a few days Princess Anatolie and Monsieur Leroy were comfortably established in her place in Styria, where the air was delightfully cool.

What was left of society in Rome learned with a little surprise, but without much regret, that the wedding was put off, and those who had country places not far from the city, and had already gone out to them for the summer, were delighted to know that they would not be expected to come into town for the marriage during the great heat. No date had ever been really fixed for it, and there was therefore no matter for gossip or discussion. The only persons who knew that Cecilia had made an attempt to break it off altogether were those most nearly concerned.

The Countess and Cecilia made preparations for going away, and the dressmakers and other tradespeople breathed more freely when they were told that they need not hurry themselves any longer.

But Cecilia had no intention of leaving without having seen Guido more than once again, hard as it might be for her to face him. Lamberti had written to her mother that he accepted Cecilia's decision gladly, and hoped to be out of his room in a few days, but that he did not appear to be recovering fast. He did not seem to be so strong as his friend had thought, and the short illness, together with the mental shock of Cecilia's letter, had made him very weak. The news of him was much the same for three days, and the young girl grew anxious. She knew that Lamberti spent most of his time with Guido, but he had not been to the Palazzo Massimo since his interview with her. She wished she could see him and ask questions, if only he could temporarily be turned into some one else; but since that was impossible, she was glad that he did not come to the house. She spent long hours in reading, while Petersen and the servants made preparations for the journey, and she wrote a line to

Guido every day, to tell him how sorry she was for him. She received grateful notes from him, so badly written that she could hardly read them.

On the fourth day, no answer came, but Lamberti sent her mother a line an hour later to say that Guido had more fever than usual and could not write that morning, but was in no danger, as far as the doctor could say.

"I should like to go and see him," Cecilia said. "He is very ill, and it is my fault."

The Countess was horrified at the suggestion.

"My dear child," she cried, "you are quite mad! Why, the poor man is in bed, of course!"

"I hope so," Cecilia answered unmoved. "But Signor Lamberti could carry him to his sitting room."

"Who ever heard of such a thing!"

"We could go in a cab, with thick veils," Cecilia continued. "No one would ever know."

"Think of Petersen, my dear! Women of our class do not wear thick veils in the street. For heaven's sake put this absurd idea out of your head."

"It does not seem absurd to me."

"Then you ought to be ashamed of yourself," retorted the Countess, losing her temper. "You do not even mean to marry him, and yet you talk of going to see him when he is ill, as if he were already your husband!"

"What if he dies?" Cecilia asked suddenly.

"There will be time enough to think about it then," answered the Countess, with insufficient reflection. "Besides he is not going to die of a touch of influenza."

"Signor Lamberti says he is very ill. Several people died of it last winter, you know. I suppose you mean that I need not think of trying to see him until we hear that there is no hope for him."

"Well?"

"That might be too late. He might not know me. It seems to me that it would be better to try and save his life, or if he is not in real danger, to help him to get well."

"If you insist upon it," said the Countess, "I will go and see him myself and take a message from you. I suppose that nobody could find anything serious to say against me for it, though, really—I am not so old as that, am I?"

"I think every one would think it was very kind of you to go and see him."

"Do you? Well—perhaps—I am not sure. I never did such a thing in my life. I am sure I should feel most uncomfortable when I found myself in a young man's rooms. We had better send him some jelly and beef-tea. A bachelor can never get those things."

"It would not be the same as if I could see him," said Cecilia, mildly.

Her mother did not like to admit this proposition, and disappeared soon afterward. Without telling her daughter, she wrote an urgent note to Lamberti begging him to come and dine and tell them all about Guido's illness, as she and Cecilia were very anxious about him.

Cecilia went out alone with Petersen late in the hot afternoon. She wished she could have walked the length of Rome and back, but her companion was not equal to any such effort in the heat, so the two got into a cab. She did not like to drive with her maid in her own carriage, simply because she had never done it. For the first time in her life she wished she were a man, free to go alone where she pleased, and when she pleased. She could be alone in the house, but nowhere out of doors, unless she went to the villa, and she was determined not to go there again before leaving Rome. It had disagreeable associations, since she had been obliged to sit on the bench by the fountain with Guido a few days ago. She remembered, too, that at the very moment when his paternal warning not to catch cold had annoyed her, he had probably caught cold himself, and she did not know why this lowered him a little in her estimation, but it did. She was ashamed to think that such a trifle might have helped to make her write the letter which had hurt him so much.

She went to the Forum, for there she could make Petersen sit down, and could walk about a little, and nobody would care, because she should meet no one she knew.

As they went down the broad way inside the wicket at which the tickets are sold, she saw a party of tourists on their way to the House of the Vestals. Of late years both Germans and Americans have discovered that Rome is not so hot in summer as the English all say it is, and that fever does not lurk behind every wall to spring upon the defenceless foreigner.

The tourists were of the usual class, and Cecilia was annoyed to find them where she had hoped to be alone; but they would soon go away, and she sat down with Petersen to wait for their going, under the shadow of the temple of Castor and Pollux. Petersen began to read her guide-book, and the young girl fell to thinking while she pushed a little stone from side to side with the point of her parasol, trying to bring it each time to the exact spot on which it had lain before.

She was thinking of all that had happened to her since she left Petersen in that same place on the May morning that seemed left behind in another existence, and she was wondering whether she would go back to that point, if she could, and live the months over again; or whether, if the return were possible, she would have made the rest different from what it had been.

It would have been so much easier to go on loving the man in the dream to the end of her life, meeting him again and again in the old surroundings that were more familiar to her than those in which she lived. It would have been so much better to be always her fancied self, to be the faithful Vestal, leading the man she loved by sure degrees to heights of immaterial blessedness in that cool outer firmament where sight and hearing and feeling, and thinking and loving, were all merged in a universal consciousness. It would have been so much easier not to love a real man, above all not to love one who never could love her, come what might. And besides, if all that had gone on, she would never have brought disappointment and suffering upon Guido d'Este.

She decided that it would have been preferable, by far, to have gone on with her life of dreams, and when awake to have been as she had always known herself, in love with everything that made her think and with nothing that made her feel.

But in the very moment when the matter seemed decided, she remembered how she had looked into Lamberti's eyes three nights ago, and had felt something more delicious than all thinking while she told him how she loved that other man, who was himself. That one moment had seemed worth an age of dreams and a lifetime of visions, and for it she knew that she would give them all, again and again.

The point of the parasol did not move now, but lay against the little stone, just where she was looking, for she was no longer weighing anything in her mind nor answering reasons with reasons. With the realisation of fact, came quickly the infinite regret and longing she knew so well, yet which always consoled her a little. She had a right to love as she did, since she was to suffer by it all her life. If she had thrown over Guido d'Este to marry Lamberti, there would have been something guilty in loving him. But there was not. She was perfectly disinterested, absolutely without one thought for her own happiness, and if she had done wrong she had done it unconsciously and was going to pay the penalty with the fullest consciousness of its keenness.

The tourists trooped back, grinding the path with their heavy shoes, hot, dusty, tired, and persevering, as all good tourists are. They stared at her when they thought she was not watching them, for they were simple and discreet souls, bent on improving themselves, and though they despised her a little for not toiling like themselves, they saw that she was beautiful and cool and quiet, sitting there in the shade, in her light summer frock, and her white gloves, and her Paris hat, and the men admired her as a superior being, who might be an angel or a demon, while all the women envied her to the verge of hatred; and because she was accompanied by such an evidently respectable person as Peterson was, they could not even say that she was probably an actress. This distressed them very much.

Kant says somewhere that when a man turns from argument and appeals to mankind's common sense, it is a sure sign that his reasoning is worthless. Similarly, when women can find nothing reasonable to say against a fellow-woman who is pretty and well dressed, they generally say that she looks like an actress; and this means according to the customs of a hundred years ago, which women seem to remember though most men have forgotten them, that she is an excommunicated person not fit to be buried like a Christian. Really, they could hardly say more in a single word.

When the tourists were at a safe distance Cecilia rose, bidding Petersen sit still, and she went slowly on towards the House of the Vestals, and up the little inclined wooden bridge which at that time led up to it, till she stood within the court, her hand resting almost on the very spot where it had been when Lamberti had come upon her in the spring morning.

Her memories rose and her thoughts flashed back with them through ages, giving the ruined house its early beauty again, out of her own youth. She was not dreaming now, but she knew instinctively how it had been in those last days of the Vestals' existence, and wished every pillar, and angle, and cornice, and ornament back, each into its own place and unchanged, and herself, where she was, in full consciousness of life and thought, at the very moment when she had first seen the man's face and had understood that one may vow away the dying body but not the deathless soul. That had been the beginning of her being alive. Before that, she had been as a flower, growing by the universal will, one of those things that are created pure and beautiful and fragrant from the first without thought or merit of their own; and then, as a young bird in the nest, high in air, in a deep forest, in early summer, looking out and wondering, but not knowing yet, its little heart beating fast with only one instinct, to be out and alone on the wing. But afterwards all had changed instantly and knowledge had come without learning, because what was to make it was already present in subtle elements that needed only the first breath of understanding to unite themselves in an ordered and perfect meaning; as the electric spark, striking through invisible mingled gases, makes perfect union of them in crystal drops of water.

That had been the beginning, since conscious life begins in the very instant when the soul is first knowingly answerable for the whole being's actions, in the light of good and evil, and first asks the only three questions which human reason has never wholly answered, which are as to knowledge, and duty, and hope.

Who shall say that life, in that sense, may not begin in a dream, as well as in what we call reality? What is a dream? Sometimes a wandering through a maze of absurdities, in which we feel as madmen must, believing ourselves to be other beings than ourselves, conceiving the laws of nature to be reversed for our advantage or our ruin, seeing right as wrong and wrong as right, in the pathetic innocence of the idiot or the senseless rage of the maniac, convinced beyond all argument that the absolutely impossible is happening before our eyes, yet never in the least astonished by any wonders, though subject to terrors we never feel when we are awake. Has no one ever understood that confused dreaming must be exactly like the mental state of the insane, and that if we dreamed such dreams with open eyes, we should be raving mad, or hopelessly idiotic? It is true, whether any one has ever said so or not. Inanimate things turn into living creatures, the chair we sit on becomes a horse, the arm-chair is turned into a wild beast; and we ride a-hunting through endless drawing-rooms which are full of trees and undergrowth, till the trees are suddenly people and are all dancing and laughing at us, because we have come to the ball in attire so exceedingly scanty that we wonder how the servants could have let us in. And in the midst of all this, when we are frantically searching for our clothes, and for a railway ticket, which we are sure is in the right-hand pocket of the waistcoat, if only we could find it, and if some one would tell us from which side of the station the train starts, and we wish we had not forgotten to eat something, and had not unpacked all our luggage and scattered everything about the railway refreshment room, and that some kind person would tell us where our money is, and that another would take a few of the fifty things we are trying to hold in our hands without dropping any of them; in the midst of all this, I say, a dead man we knew comes from his grave and stares at us, and asks why we cruelly let him die, long ago, without saying that one word which would have meant joy or despair to him at the last moment. Then our hair stands up and our teeth chatter, because the secret of the soul has risen against us where we least expected it; and we wake alone in the dark with the memory of the dead.

Is not that madness? What else can madness be but that disjointing of ordered facts into dim and disorderly fiction, pierced here and there by lingering lights of memory and reason? All of us sometimes go mad in our sleep. But it does not follow that in dreaming we are not sometimes sane, rational, responsible, our own selves, good or bad, doing and saying things which we might say and do in real life, but which we have never said nor done, incurring the consequences of our words and deeds as if they were actual, keeping good faith or breaking it, according to our own natures, accomplishing by effort, or failing through indolence, as the case may be, blushing with genuine shame, laughing with genuine mirth, and burning with genuine anger; and all this may go on from the beginning to the end of the dream, without a single moment of impossibility, without one incident which would surprise us in the waking state. With most people dreams of this kind are rare, but every one who dreams at all must have had them once or twice in life.

If we are therefore sometimes sane in dreams we can remember, and act in them as we really should, according to our individual consciences and possessed of our usual intelligence and knowledge, it cannot be denied that a series of such imaginary actions constitutes a real experience, during which we have risen or fallen, according as we have thought or acted. Some dreams of this kind leave impressions as lasting as that made by any reality. The merit or fault is wholly fictitious, no doubt, because although we have fancied that we could exercise our free will, we were powerless to use it; but the experience gained is not imaginary, where the dream has been strictly sane, any more than thought, in the abstract, is fictitious because it is not action. People of some imagination can easily, while wide awake, imagine a series of actions and decide rationally what course they would pursue in each, and such decisions constitute undoubted experience, which may materially affect the conduct of the individual if cases similar to the fancied ones present themselves in life. When there is no time to be lost, the instantaneous recollection of a train of reasoning may often mean instant decision, followed by immediate action, upon which the most important consequences may follow.

Will any one venture to maintain that the vivid impressions left by rational dreams do not act in the same way upon the mind, and through the mind upon the will, and by the will upon our actions? And if we could direct our dreams as we pleased, so that they should be always rational, as some persons believe that we can, should we not be continually gaining experience of ourselves while sleeping, as well as when awake? Moreover, it is certain that there are men and women who are particularly endowed with the faculty of dreaming, and who can very often dream of any subject they please.

Since this digression is already so long, let one more thing be said, which has not been said before, so far as the writer can find out. Our waking memory is defective; with most men it is so to a lamentable degree. It often happens that people forget that they have read a story, for instance, and begin to read it again, and do not discover that they have already done so till they have turned over many pages. It happens constantly that the taste of something we eat, or the odour of something we smell, recalls a scene we cannot remember at first, but which sometimes comes back after a little while. Almost every one has felt now and then that a fragment of present conversation is not new to him, and that he has performed certain actions already, though he cannot remember when. With some people these broken recollections are so frequent and vivid as to lead to all sorts of theories to explain them, such as the possibility of former existences on earth, or the more materialistic probability that memories are transmitted from parents and ancestors from the direct ascending lines.

One theory has been neglected. At such times we may be remembering vaguely, or even with some distinctness, parts of dreams of which we had no recollection on waking, but which, nevertheless, made their impressions on the brain that produced them, while we were asleep. Unconscious ratiocination is certainly not a myth; and if, by it, we can produce our own forgotten actions, and even find objects we have lost, by doing over again exactly what we were doing when the thing we seek was last in our hands, sure that the rest of the action will repeat itself spontaneously, we should not be going much farther if we repeated both actions and words unconsciously remembered out of dreams. Much that seems very mysterious in our sensations may be explained in that way, and the explanation has the advantage of being simpler than that afforded by the theory of atavism, and more orthodox than that offered by the believers in the transmigration of souls.

Cecilia Palladio had no need of it, for she did not forget the one dream that pleased her best, and she was never puzzled by uncertain recollections of any other. Her life had begun in it, and had turned upon it always, and after she had parted with it by an act of will, she had retained the fullest remembrance of its details.

She left the place where she had paused near the entrance, and slowly walked up the long court, by the dry excavated basins; she ascended the low steps to the raised floor beyond, and stood still before the door of her own room, the second on the left. She had meant to go in and look at it quietly, but since she had taken refuge there when she ran away from Lamberti, iron gates had been placed at the entrances of all the six rooms, and they were locked. In hers a quantity of fragments of sculptured marble and broken earthen vessels were laid side by side on the floor, or were standing against the walls and in the corners.

She felt as if she had been shut out by an act of tyranny, just as when she and her five companions had sadly left the House, obedient to the Christian Emperor's decree, long ago. It had always been her room ever since she had first dreamt. The beautiful narrow bronze bedstead used to stand on the left, the carved oak wardrobe inlaid with ivory was on the right, the marble table was just under the window, covered with objects she needed for her toilet, exquisite things of chiselled silver and of polished ivory. The chair, rounded at the back and with cushioned seat, like Agrippina's, was near it. In winter, the large bronze brazier of coals, changed twice daily, was always placed in the middle of the room. The walls were wainscoted with Asian marble, and painted above that with portraits in fresco of great and ancient Vestals who had been holier than the rest, each in her snowy robes, with the white veil drawn up and backwards over her head, and brought forward again over the shoulder, and each holding some sacred vessel or instrument in her one uncovered hand. There were stories about each which the Virgo Maxima used to read to the younger ones from a great rolled manuscript, that was kept in an ancient bronze box, or which she sometimes told in the moonlight on summer nights when the maidens sat together in the court.

She closed her eyes, her forehead resting against the iron bars, and she saw it all as it had been; she looked again and the desolation hurt her and shocked her as when in a wilderness an explorer comes suddenly upon the bleached bones of one who had gone before him and had been his friend. She sighed and turned away.

The dream was better than the reality, in that and in many other ways. She was overcome by the sense of utter failure, as she sat down on the steps below the raised floor, lonely and forlorn.

It was all a comedy now, a miserable petty play to hide a great truth from herself and others. She had begun her part already, writing her wretched little notes to poor Guido. She knew that, ill as he was, the words that seemed lies to her were ten times true to him, and that he exaggerated every enquiry after his condition and each expression of hope for his recovery into signs of loving solicitude, that he had already forgiven what he thought her caprice, and was looking forward to his marriage as more certain than ever, in spite of her message. It was all a vile trick meant to save his feelings and help him to get well, and she hated and despised it.

She was playing a part with Lamberti, too, and that was no better. She had fallen low enough to love a man who did not care a straw for her, and it needed all the energy of character she had left to keep him from finding it out. Nothing could be more contemptible. If any one but he had told her that she ought to go back to the appearance of an engagement with Guido, she would have refused to do it. But Lamberti dominated her; he had only to say, "Do this," and she did it, "Say this," and she said it, whether it were true or not. She complained bitterly in her heart that if he had bidden her lie to her mother, she would have lied, because she had no will of her own when she was with him.

And this was the end of her inspired visions, of her lofty ideals, of her magnificent rules of life, of her studies of philosophy, her meditations upon religion, and her dream of the last Vestal. She was nothing but a weak girl, under the orders of a man she loved against her will, and ready to do things she despised whenever he chose to give his orders. He cared for no human being except his one friend. He was not to be blamed for that, of course, but he was utterly indifferent to every one else where his friend was concerned; every one must lie, or steal, or do murder, if that could help Guido to get well. She was only one of his instruments, and he probably had others. She was sure that half the women in Rome loved Lamberto Lamberti without daring to say so. It was a satisfaction to have heard from every one that he cared for none of them. People spoke of him as a woman-hater, and one woman had said that he had married a negress in Africa, and was the father of black savages with red hair. That accounted for his going to Somali Land, she said, and for his knowing so much about the habits of the people there. Cecilia would have gladly killed the lady with a hat pin.

She was very unhappy, sitting alone on the steps after the sun had sunk out of sight. The comedy was all to begin over again in an hour, for she must go home and defend her conduct when her mother reproached her with not acting fairly, and laughed at the idea that Guido was in danger of his life. To-morrow she would have to write the daily note to him, she would be obliged to compose affectionate phrases which would have come quite naturally if she could have treated him merely as her best friend; and he would translate affection to mean love, and another lie would have been told. There was this, at least, about Guido, that he could not order her about as Lamberti could. There was no authority in his eyes, not even when he told her not to catch cold. Perhaps in all the time she had known him, she had liked him best when he had been angry, at the garden party, and had demanded to know her secret. But she would not acknowledge that. If the situation had been reversed and Lamberti, instead of Guido, had insisted on knowing what she meant to hide, she could not have helped telling him. It was an abominable state of things, but there was nothing to be done, and that was the worst part of it. Lamberti knew Guido much better than she did, and if Lamberti told her gravely that Guido might do something desperate if she broke with him, she was obliged to believe it and to act accordingly. There might not be one chance in a thousand, but the one-thousandth chance was just the one that might have its turn. One might disregard it for oneself, but one had no right to overlook it where another's life was concerned. At all events she must wait till Guido was quite well again, for a man in a fever really might do anything rash. Why did Lamberti not take away the revolver that always lay ready in the drawer? It would be much safer, though Guido probably had plenty of other weapons that would serve the purpose. Guido was just the kind of pacific man who would have a whole armoury of guns and pistols, as if he were always expecting to kill something or somebody. She was sure that Lamberti, who had killed men with his own hand, did not keep any sort of weapon in his room. If he had a revolver of his own, it was probably carefully cleaned, greased, wrapped up and put away with the things he used when he was sent on expeditions. It was a thousand pities that Guido was not exactly like Lamberti!

Cecilia rose at last, weary of thinking about it all, disgusted with her own weakness, and decidedly ill-disposed towards her fellow-creatures. The slightly flattened upper lip was compressed rather tightly against the fuller lower one as she went back to find Petersen, and as she held her head very high, her lids drooped somewhat scornfully over her eyes. No one can ever be as supercilious as some people look when they are angry with themselves and are thinking what miserable creatures they really are.

It was late when Cecilia reached the Palazzo Massimo and went in on foot under the dark carriageway after Petersen had paid the cab under the watchful gaze of the big liveried porter. The Countess was already dressing for dinner, and Cecilia went to her own room at once. The consequence was that she did not know of her mother's invitation to Lamberti, until she came into the drawing-room and saw the two together, waiting for her.

"Did I forget to tell you that Signor Lamberti was coming to dinner?" asked her mother.

"There was no particular reason why you should have told me," she answered indifferently, as she held out her hand to Lamberti. "It is not exactly a dinner party! How is he?" she asked, speaking to him.

"He is better this evening, thank you."

Why should he say "thank you," as if Guido were his brother or his father? She resented it. Surely there was no need for continually accentuating the fact that Guido was the only person living for whom he had the slightest natural affection! This was perhaps exaggerated, but she was glad of it, just then.

She, who would have given all for him, wished savagely that some woman would make him fall in love and treat him with merciless barbarity.

CHAPTER XXIII

Cecilia felt that evening as if she could resist Lamberti's influence at last, for she was out of humour with herself and with every one else. When they had dined, and had said a multitude of uninteresting things about Guido, for they were all under a certain constraint while the meal lasted, they came back to the drawing-room. Lamberti had the inscrutable look Cecilia had lately seen in his face, and which she took for the outward sign of his indifference to anything that did not concern his friend. When he spoke to her, he looked at her as if she were a chair or a table, and when he was not speaking to her he did not look at her at all.

In the drawing-room, she waited her opportunity until her mother had sat down. The butler had set the little tray with the coffee and three cups on a small three-legged table. On pretence that the latter was unsteady, Cecilia carried the tray to another place at some distance from her mother. Lamberti followed her to take the Countess's cup, and then came back for his own. Cecilia spoke to him in a low voice while she was putting in the sugar and pouring out the coffee, a duty which in many parts of Italy and France is still assigned to the daughter of the house, and recalls a time when servants did not know how to prepare the beverage.

"Come and talk to me presently," she said. "I am sure you have more to tell me about him."

"No," said Lamberti, not taking the trouble to lower his voice much, "there is nothing more to tell. I do not think I have forgotten anything."

He stirred his coffee slowly, but with evident reluctance to stay near her. She would not have been a human woman if she had not been annoyed by his cool manner, and a shade of displeasure passed over her face.

"I have something to say to you," she answered. "I thought you would understand."

"That is different."

In his turn he showed a little annoyance. They went back together to the Countess's side, carrying their cups. In due time the good lady went to write letters, feeling that it was quite safe to leave her daughter with Lamberti, who seemed to be as cold as ice, and not at all bent on making himself agreeable. Besides, the Countess was tired of the situation, and could hardly conceal the fact that she reproached Guido for not getting well sooner, in order that she might speak to him herself.

There was silence for a time after she had gone into the next room, while Cecilia and Lamberti sat side by side on the sofa she had left. Neither seemed inclined to speak first, for both felt that some danger was at hand, which could not be avoided, but which must be approached with caution. She wished that he would say something, for she was not at all sure what she meant to tell him; but he was silent, which was natural enough, as she had asked for the interview.

She would have given anything to have seen him somewhere else, in new surroundings, anywhere except in her own drawing-room, where every familiar object oppressed her and reminded her of her mistakes and illusions. She felt that she must say something, but the blood rose in her brain and confused her. He saw her embarrassment, or guessed it.

"So far things have gone better than I expected," he said at last, "but that only makes the end more doubtful."

She turned to him slowly and with an involuntary look of gratitude for having broken the silence.

"I mean," he went on, "that since Guido is so ready to grasp at any straw you throw him, it will be hard to make him understand you, when things have gone a little further."

"Is that all you mean?" She asked the question almost sharply.

"Yes."

"You do not mean that you still wish I would marry him after—after what I told you the other evening?"

The interrogation was in her voice, and that was hard, and demanded an answer. Lamberti looked away, and did not reply at once, for he meant to tell the exact truth, and was not quite sure where it lay. He felt, too, that her manner had changed notably since they had last talked, and though he had no intention of taking the upper hand, it was not in his nature to submit to any dictation, even from the woman he loved.

"Answer me, please," said Cecilia, rather imperiously.

"Yes, I will. I wish it were possible for you to marry him, that is all."

"And you know that it is not."

"I am almost sure that it is not."

"How cautious you are!"

"The matter is serious. But you said that you had something to say to me. What is it?"

"I wanted to tell you that I am sick of all this deception, of writing notes that are meant to deceive a man for whom I have the most sincere friendship, of letting the whole world think that I will do what I would not do, if I were to die for it."

He looked at her, then clasped his hands upon his knees and shook his head.

"I must see him," she said, after a pause, "I must see him at once, and you must help me. If I could only speak to him I could make him understand, and he would be glad I had spoken, and we should always be good friends. But I must see him alone, and talk to him. Make it possible, for I know you can. I am not afraid of the consequences. Take me to him. It is the only true and honest thing to do!"

Lamberti believed that this was true; he was a man of action and had no respect for society's prejudices, when society was not present to enforce its laws. It would have seemed incredible to Romans that an Italian girl could think of doing what Cecilia proposed, and if it were ever known, her reputation would be gravely damaged. But Cecilia was not like other young girls; society should never know what she had done, and she was quite right in saying that her plan was really the best and most honourable.

"I can take you to him," Lamberti said. "I suppose you know what you are risking."

"Nothing, if I go with you. You would not let me run any risk."

She did not raise her voice, she hardly changed her tone, but nothing she had ever said had given him such a thrilling sensation of pleasure.

"Do you trust me as much as that?" he asked.

"Yes, as much as that."

She smiled, and looked down at her hand, and then glanced at him quickly, and almost happily. If she had studied men for ten years she could not have found word or look more certain to touch him and win him to her way.

"Thank you," he said, rather curtly, for he was thinking of another answer. "If I take you to Guido, what shall you say to him?"

She drew herself up against the back of the sofa, but the smile still lingered on her lips.

"You must trust me, too," she answered. "Do you think I can compose set speeches beforehand? When shall we go? How is it to be managed?"

"You often go out with your maid, do you not? What sort of woman is she? A dragon?"

"No!" Cecilia laughed. "She is very respectable and nice, and thinks I am perfection. But then, she is terribly near-sighted, and cannot wear spectacles because they fall off her nose."

"Then she loses her way easily, I suppose?" said Lamberti, too much intent on his plans to be amused at trifles.

"Yes. She is always losing her way."

"That might easily happen to her in the Palazzo Farnese. It is a huge place, and you could manage to go up one way while she went up the other. Besides, there is a lift at the back, not to mention the servants' staircases, in which she might be hopelessly lost. Can you trust her not to lose her head and make the porters search the palace for you, if you are separated from her?"

"I am not sure. But she will stay wherever I tell her to wait for me. That might be better. You see, my only excuse for going to the Palazzo Farnese would be to see the ambassador's daughter, and she is in the country."

"I think she must have come to town for a day or two, for I met her this afternoon. That is a good reason for going to see her. At the door of the embassy send your maid on an errand that will take an hour, and tell her to wait for you in the cab at the gate. If the girl is at home you need not stay ten minutes. Then you can see Guido during the rest of the time. It will be long enough, and besides, the maid will wait."

"For ever, if I tell her to! But you, where shall you be?"

"You will meet me on the stairs as you come down from the embassy. Wear something simple and dark that people have not seen you wear before, and carry a black parasol and a guide-book. Have one of those brown veils that tourists wear against the sun. Fold it up neatly and put it into the pocket of the guide-book instead of the map, or pin it to the inside of your parasol. You can put it on as soon as you have turned the corner of the stairs, out of sight of the embassy door, for the footman will not go in till you are as far as that. If you cannot put it on yourself, I will do it for you."

"Do you know how to put on a woman's veil?" Cecilia asked, with a little laugh.

"Of course! It is easy enough. I have often fastened my sister's for her at picnics."

"What time shall I come?"

"A little before eleven. Guido cannot be ready before that."

"But he has a servant," said Cecilia, suddenly remembering the detail. "What will he think?"

"He has two, but they shall both be out, and I shall have the key to his door in my pocket. We will manage that."

"Shall you be sure to know just when I come?"

"I shall see you, but you will not see me till we meet on the landing."

"I knew you could manage it, if you only would."

"It is simple enough. There is not the slightest risk, if you will do exactly what I have told you."

It seemed easy indeed, and Cecilia was almost happy at the thought that she was soon to be freed from the intolerable situation into which she allowed herself to be forced. She was very grateful, too, and beyond her gratitude was the unspeakable satisfaction in the man she loved. Instead of making difficulties, he smoothed them; instead of prating of what society might think, he would help her to defy it, because he knew that she was right.

"I should like to thank you," she said simply. "I do not know how."

He seemed to say something in answer, in a rather discontented way, but so low that she could not catch the words.

"What did you say?" she asked unwisely.

"Nothing. I am glad to be of service to you. Say the right things to Guido; for you are going to do rather an eccentric thing in order to say them, and a mistake would be fatal."

He spoke almost roughly, but she was not offended. He had a right to be rough, since he was ready to do whatever she asked of him; yet not understanding him, while loving him, her instinct made her wish him really to know how pleased she was. She put out her hand a little timidly and touched his, as a much older woman might have done. To her surprise, he grasped it instantly, and held it so tightly that he hurt her for a moment. He dropped it then, pushing it from him as his hold relaxed, almost throwing it off.

"What is the matter?" Cecilia asked, surprised.

But at that moment her mother entered the room from the boudoir.

CHAPTER XXIV

In agreeing to the dangerous scheme, Lamberti had yielded to an impulse founded upon his intuitive knowledge of women, and not at all upon his inborn love of anything in which there was risk. The danger was for Cecilia, not for himself, in any case; and it was real, for, if it should ever be known that she had gone to Guido's rooms, nothing but her marriage with him would silence the gossips. Society cannot be blamed for drawing a line somewhere, considering how very far back it sets the limit.

Lamberti, without reasoning about it, knew that no woman ever does well what she does not like doing. If he persisted in making Cecilia attempt to break gradually with Guido, she would soon make mistakes and spoil everything. That was his conviction. She felt, at present, that if she could see Guido face to face, she could persuade him to give her up; and the probability was that she would succeed, or else that she would be moved by real pity for him and thus become genuinely ready to follow Lamberti's original advice. The sensible course to follow was, therefore, to help her in the direction she had chosen.

Early in the morning Lamberti was at his friend's bedside. Guido was much better now, and there was no risk in taking him to his sitting room. Lamberti suggested this before saying anything else, and the doctor came soon afterwards and approved of it. By ten o'clock Guido was comfortably installed in a long cane chair, amongst his engravings and pictures, very pale and thin, but cheerful and expectant. As he had no fever, and was quite calm, Lamberti told him frankly that Cecilia had something to say to him which no one could say for her, and was coming herself. He was amazed and delighted at first, and then was angry with Lamberti for allowing her to come; but, as the latter explained in detail how her visit was to be managed, his fears subsided, and he looked at his watch with growing impatience. His man had been sitting up with him at night since his illness had begun, and was easily persuaded to go to bed for the day. The other servant, who cooked what Guido needed, had prepared everything for the day, and had gone out. He always came back a little after twelve o'clock. At twenty minutes to eleven Lamberti took the key of the door and went to watch for Cecilia's coming, and half an hour later he admitted her to the sitting room, shut the door after her, and left the two together. He went and sat down in the outer hall, in case any one should ring the bell, which had been muffled with a bit of soft leather while Guido was ill.

Cecilia stood still a moment, after the door was closed; behind her, and she lifted her veil to see her way, for there was not much light in the room. As she caught sight of Guido, a frank smile lighted up her face for an instant, and then died away in a look of genuine concern and anxiety. She had not realised how much he could change in so short a time, in not more than four or five days. She came forward quickly, took his hand, and bent over him, looking into his face. His eyes widened with pleasure and his thin fingers lifted hers to his lips.

"You have been very ill," she said, "very, very ill! I had no idea that it was so bad as this!"

"I am better," he answered gently. "How good of you! How endlessly good of you to come!"

"Nobody saw me," she said, by way of answer.

She smoothed the old pink damask cushion under his head, and instinctively looked to see if he had all he needed within reach, before she thought of sitting down in the chair Lamberti had placed ready for her.

"Tell me," he said, in a low and somewhat anxious voice, "you did not mean it? You were out of temper, or you were annoyed by something, or—I do not know! Something happened that made you write, and you had sent the letter before you knew what you were doing—"

He broke off, quite sure of her answer. He thought she turned pale, though the light was not strong and brought the green colour of the closed blinds into the room.

"Hush!" she exclaimed soothingly, and she sat down beside him, still holding his hand. "I have come expressly to talk to you about it all, because letters only make misunderstandings, and there must not be any more misunderstandings between us two."

"No, never again!" He looked up with love in his hollow eyes, not suspecting what she meant. "I have forgotten all that was in that letter, and I wish to forget it. You never wrote that you did not love me, nor that you loved another man. It is all gone, quite gone, and I shall never remember it again."

Cecilia sighed and gazed into his face sadly. He looked so ill and weak that she wondered how she could be cruel enough to tell him the truth, though she had risked her good name to get a chance of speaking plainly. It seemed like bringing a cup of cold water to the lips of a man dying of thirst, only to take it away again untasted and leave him to his fate. She pitied him with all her heart, but there was nothing in her compassion that at all resembled love. It was the purest and most friendly affection, of the sort that lasts a lifetime and can devote itself in almost any sacrifice; but it was all quite clear and comprehensible, without the smallest element of the inexplicable attraction that is deaf, and dumb, and, above all, blind, and which proceeds from the deep prime cause and mover of nature, and mates lions in the wilderness and birds in the air, and men and women among their fellows, two and two, from generation to generation.

"Guido," said Cecilia, after a long silence, "do you not think that two people can be very, very fond of each other all their lives, and trust each other, and like to be together as much as possible, without being married?"

She spoke quietly and steadily, trying to make her voice sound more gentle than ever before; but there was no possibility of mistaking her meaning. His thin hand started and shook under her soothing touch, and then drew itself away. The light went out of his eyes and the rings of shadow round them grew visibly darker as he turned his head painfully on the damask cushion.

"Is that what you have come to say?" he asked, in a groan.

Cecilia leaned back in her chair and folded her hands. She felt as if she had killed an unresisting, loving creature, as a sacrifice for her fault.

"God forgive me if I have done wrong," she said, speaking to herself. "I only mean to do right."

Guido moved his head on his cushion again, as if suffering unbearable pain, and a sort of harsh laugh answered her words.

"Your God will forgive you," he said bitterly, after a moment. "Man made God in his own image, and God must needs obey his creator. When you cannot forgive yourself, you set up an image and ask it to pardon you. I do not wonder."

The cruel words hurt her in more ways than one, and she drew her breath between her teeth as if she had struck unawares against something sharp and was repressing a cry of pain. Then there was silence for a long time.

"Why do you stay here?" Guido asked, in a low tone, not looking at her. "You cannot have anything more to say. You have done what you came to do. Let me be alone."

"Guido!"

She touched his shoulder gently as he lay turned from her, but he moved and pushed her away.

"It cannot give you pleasure to see me suffer," he said. "Please go away."

"How can I leave you like this?"

There was despair in her voice, and the sound of tears that would never come to her eyes. He did not answer. She would not go away without trying to appease him, and she made a strong effort to collect her thoughts.

"You are angry with me, of course," she began. "You despise me for not having known my own mind, but you cannot say anything that I have not said to myself. I ought to have known long ago. All I can say in self-defence now is that it is better to have told you the truth before we were married than to have been obliged to confess it afterwards, or else to have lied to you all my life if I could not find courage to speak. It is better, is it not? Oh, say that it is better!"

"It would have been much better if neither of us had ever been born," Guido answered.

"I only ask you to say that you would rather be suffering now than have had me tell you in a year that I was an unfaithful wife at heart. That is all. Will you not say it? It is all I ask."

"Why should you ask anything of me, even that? The only kindness you can show me now is to go away."

He would not look at her. His throat was parched, and he put out his hand to take the tumbler from the little table on the other side of his long chair. Instantly she rose and tried to help him, but he would not let her.

"I am not so weak as that," he said coldly. "My hand is steady enough, thank you."

She sighed and drew back. Perhaps it would be better to leave him, as he wished that she should, but his words recalled Lamberti's warning; his hand was steady, he said, and that meant that it was steady enough to take the pistol from the drawer in the little table and use it. He believed in nothing, in no future, in no retribution, in no God, and he was ill, lonely, and in despair through her fault. His friend knew him, and the danger was real. The conviction flashed through her brain that if she left him alone he would probably kill himself, and she fancied him lying there dead, on the red tiles. She fancied, too, Lamberti's face, when he should come to tell her what had happened, for he would surely come, and to the end of her life and his he would never forgive her.

She stood still, wavering and unstrung by her thoughts, looking steadily down at Guido's head.

"Since you will not go away," he said at last, "answer me one question. Tell me the name of the man who has come between us."

Cecilia bit her lip and turned her face from the light.

"Then it is true," Guido said, after a silence. "There is a man whom you really love, a man whom you would really marry and to whom you could really be faithful."

"Yes. It is true. Everything I wrote you is true."

"Who is he?"

She was silent again.

"Do you hope that I shall ever forgive you for what you have done to me?"

"Yes. I pray heaven that you may!"

"Leave heaven out of the question. You have turned my life into something like what you call hell. Do I know the man you love?"

"Yes," Cecilia answered, after a moment's hesitation.

"Do I often meet him? Have I met him often since you have loved him?"

She said nothing, but stood still with bent head and clasped hands.

"Why do you not answer me?" he asked sternly.

"You must never know his name," she said, in a low voice.

"Have I no right to know who has ruined my life?"

"I have. Blame me. Visit it on me."

He laughed, not harshly now, but gently and sarcastically.

"You women are fond of offering yourselves as expiatory victims for your own sins, for you know very well that we shall not hurt you! After all, you cannot help yourself if you have fallen in love with some one else. I suppose I ought to be sorry for you. I probably shall be, when I know who he is!"

He laughed again, already despising the man she had preferred in his stead. His words had cut her, but she said nothing, for she was in dread lest the slightest word should betray the truth.

"You say that I know him," Guido continued, his cheeks beginning to flush feverishly, "and you would not answer me when I asked you if I had often met him since you have loved him. That means that I have, of course. You were too honest to lie, and too much frightened to tell the truth. I meet him often. Then he is one of a score of men whom I know better than all the others. There are not many men whom I meet often. It cannot be very hard to find out which of them it is."

Cecilia turned her face away, resting one hand on the back of the chair, and a deep blush rose in her cheeks. But she spoke steadily.

"You can never find out," she said. "He does not love me. He does not guess that I love him. But I will not answer any more questions, for you must not know who he is."

"Why not? Do you think I shall quarrel with him and make him fight a duel with me?"

"Perhaps."

"That is absurd," Guido answered quietly. "I do not value my life much, I believe, but I have not the least inclination to risk it in such a ridiculous way. The man has injured me without knowing it. You have taken from me the one thing I treasured and you are keeping it for him; but he does not want it, he does not even know that it is his, he is not responsible for your caprices."

"Not caprice, Guido! Do not call it that!"

"I do. Forgive me for being frank. Say that I am ill, if you please, as an excuse for me. I call such things by their right name, caprices. If you are going to be subject to them all your life, you had better go into a convent before you throw away your good name."

"I have not deserved that!"

She turned upon him now, with flashing eyes. He had raised himself upon one elbow and was looking at her with cool contempt.

"You have deserved that and more," he answered, "and if you insist upon staying here you must hear what I choose to say. I advised you to go away, but you would not. I have no apology to make for telling you the truth, but you are free to go. Lamberti is in the hall and will see you to your carriage."

There was something royal in his anger and in his look now, which she could not help respecting, in spite of his words. She had thought that he would behave very differently; she had looked for some passionate outburst, perhaps for some unmanly weakness, excusable since he was so ill, and more in accordance with his outwardly gentle character. She had thought that because he had made his friend speak to her for him he lacked energy to speak for himself. But now that the moment had come, he showed himself as manly and determined as ever Lamberti could be, and she could not help respecting him for it. Doubtless Lamberti had always known what was in his friend's nature, below the indolent surface. Perhaps he was like his father, the old king. But Cecilia was proud, too.

"If I have stayed too long," she said, facing him, "it was because I came here at some risk to confess my fault, and hoped for your forgiveness. I shall always hope for it, as long as we both live, but I shall not ask for it again. I had thought that you would accept my devoted friendship instead of what I cannot give you and never gave you, though I believed that I did. But you will not take what I offer. We had better part on that rather than risk being enemies. You have already said one thing which you will regret and which I shall always remember. Good-bye."

She held out her hand frankly, and he took it and kept it a moment, while their eyes met, and he spoke more gently.

"I said too much. I am sorry. I shall forgive you when I do not love you any more. Good-bye."

He let her hand fall and looked away.

"Thank you," she said.

She left his side and went towards the door, her head a little bent. As she laid her hand upon the handle, and looked back at Guido once again, it turned in her fingers and was drawn quickly away from them. She started and turned her head to see who was there.

Lamberti stood before her, and immediately pushed her back into the room and shut the door, visibly disturbed.

"This way!" he said quickly, in an undertone.

He led her swiftly to another door, which he opened for her and closed as soon as she had passed.

"Wait for me there!" he said, as she went in.

"What is the matter?" asked Guido rather faintly, when he realised what his friend had done.

"Her mother is in the hall," Lamberti said. "Do not be startled, she knows nothing. She insists on seeing for herself how you are. She says her daughter begged her to come."

"Tell her I am too ill to see her, please, and thank her very much. It is all over, Lamberti, we have parted."

A dark flush rose in Lamberti's face.

"You must see the Countess," he said hurriedly. "I am sorry, but unless she comes here, her daughter cannot get out without being seen. We cannot leave her in your room. I will not do it, for your man may wake up and go there. There is no time to be lost either!"

"Bring the Countess in," said Guido, with an effort, and moving uneasily on his couch.

He felt that nothing was spared him. In the few seconds that elapsed, he tried to decide what he should say to the Countess, and how he could account for knowing that Cecilia had now definitely broken off the engagement. Before he had come to any conclusion the Countess was ushered in, rosy and smiling, but a little timid at finding herself in a young bachelor's quarters.

Meanwhile, Cecilia was in Guido's bedroom. An older woman might have suspected some ignoble treachery, but her perfect innocence protected her from all fear. Lamberti would not have brought her there in such a hurry unless there had been some absolute necessity for getting her out of sight at once. Undoubtedly some visitor had come who could not be turned away. Perhaps it was the doctor. Moreover, she was too much disturbed by what had taken place to pay much attention to what was, after all, a detail.

She looked about her and saw that there was another door by which Lamberti would presently enter to let her out. There was the great bed with the coverlet of old arras displaying the royal arms, and beside it stood a small table of mahogany inlaid with brass. It had tall and slender legs that ended below in little brass lions' paws, and it had a single drawer.

Without hesitation she went and opened it. Lamberti had been right. There was the revolver, a silver-mounted weapon with an ivory handle, much more for ornament than use, but quite effective enough for the purpose to which Guido might put it. Beside it lay a little pile of notes in their envelopes, and she involuntarily recognised her own handwriting. He had kept all she had written to him within his reach while he had been ill, and the thought pained her. The revolver was a very light one, made with only five chambers. She took it and examined it when she had shut the drawer again, and she saw that it was fully loaded. Old Fortiguerra had taught her to use firearms a little, and she knew how to load and unload them. She slipped the cartridges out quickly and tied them together in her handkerchief, and then dropped them into her parasol and the revolver after them.

She went to the tall mirror in the door of the wardrobe and began to arrange her veil, expecting Lamberti every moment. She had hardly finished when he entered and beckoned to her. She caught up her parasol by the middle so as to hold its contents safely, and in a few seconds she was outside the front door of the apartment. Lamberti drew a breath of relief.

"Take those!" she said quickly, producing the pistol and the cartridges. "He must not have them."

Lamberti took the weapon and put it into his pocket, and held the parasol, while she untied the handkerchief and gave him the contents. Both began to go downstairs.

"I had better tell you who came," Lamberti said, as they went. "You will be surprised. It was your mother."

"My mother!" Cecilia stopped short on the step she had reached. "I did not think she meant to come!"

She went on, and Lamberti kept by her side.

"You can seem surprised when she tells you," he said. "You have definitely broken your engagement, then? Guido had time to tell me so."

"Yes, I could not lie to him. It was very hard, but I am glad it is all over, though he is very angry now."

They reached the last landing before the court without meeting any one, and she paused again. He wondered what expression was on her face while she spoke, for he could scarcely see the outline of her features through the veil.

"Thank you again," she said. "We may not meet for a long time, for my mother and I shall go away at once, and I suppose we shall not come back next winter." She spoke rather bitterly now. "My reputation is damaged, I fancy, because I have refused to marry a man I do not love!"

"I will take care of your reputation," Lamberti answered, as if he were saying the most natural thing in the world.

"It is hardly your place to do that," Cecilia answered, much surprised.

"It may not be my right," Lamberti said, "as people consider those things. But it is my place, as Guido's friend and yours, as the only man alive who is devoted to you both."

"I am more grateful than I can tell you. But please let people say what they like of me, and do not take my defence. You, of all the men I know, must not."

"Why not I, of all men? I, of all men, will."

She was standing with her back to the wall on the landing, and he was facing her now. His face looked a little more set and determined than usual, and he was rather pale, and he stood sturdily still before her. She could see his face through her veil, though he could hardly distinguish hers. He felt for a moment as if he were talking to a sort of lay figure that represented her and could not answer him.

"I, of all men, will take care that no one says a word against you," he said, as she was silent.

"But why? Why you?"

"You have definitely given up all idea of marrying Guido? Absolutely? For ever? You are sure, in your own conscience, that he has no sort of claim on you left, and that he knows it?"

"Yes, yes! But—"

"Then," he said, not heeding her, "as you and I may not meet again for a long time, and as it cannot do you the least harm to know it, and as you will have no right to feel that I shall be lacking in respect to you, if I say it, I am going to give myself the satisfaction of telling you something I have taken great pains to hide since we first met."

"What is it?" asked Cecilia, nervously.

"It is a very simple matter, and one that will not interest you much."

He paused one moment, and fixed his eyes on the brown veil, where he knew that hers were.

"I love you."

Cecilia started violently, and put out one hand against the wall behind her.

"Do not be frightened, Contessina," he said gently. "Many men will say that to you before you are old. But none of them will mean it more truly than I. Shall we go? Your mother may not stay long with Guido."

He moved, expecting her to go on, but she leaned against the wall where she stood, and she stared at his face through her veil. For an instant she thought she was going to faint, for her heart stopped beating and the blood left her head. She did not know whether it was happiness, or surprise, or fear that paralysed her, when his simple words revealed the vastness of the mistake in which she had lived, and the immensity of joy she had missed by so little. She pressed her hand flat against the wall beside her, sure that if she moved it she must fall.

"Have I offended you, Signorina?" Lamberti asked, and the low tones shook a little.

She could not speak yet, but his voice seemed to steady her, and her heart beat again. As if she were making a great effort her hand slowly left the wall, and she stretched it out towards him, silently asking for his. He did not understand, but he took it and held it quietly, coming a little nearer to her.

"You have forgiven me," he said. "Thank you. You are kind. Good-bye."

But then her fingers closed on his with almost frantic pressure.

"No, no!" she cried. "Not yet! One moment more!"

Still he did not understand, but he felt the blood rising and singing in his heart like the tide when it is almost high. A strange expectation filled him, as of a great change in his whole being that must come in the most fearful pain, or else in a happiness almost unbearable, something swelling, bursting, overwhelming, and enormous beyond imagination.

She did not know that she was drawing him nearer to her, she would have blushed scarlet at the thought; he did not know that his feet moved, that he was quite close to her, that she was clutching his hand and pressing it upon her own heart. They did not see what they were doing. They were standing together by a marble pillar in the Vestals' House. They were out in the firmament beyond worlds, not seeing, not hearing, not touching, but knowing and one in knowledge.

The veil touched his cheek and lightly pressed against it. It was the Vestal's veil. He had felt it in dreams, between his face and hers. Then the world broke into visible light, and he heard her whisper in his ear.

"That was my secret. You know it now."

A distant footfall echoed from far up the stone staircase. Once more as she heard it she pressed his hand to her heart with all her might, and he, with his left round her neck, drew her veiled face against his and held it there an instant in simple pressure, not trying to kiss her.

Then those two separated and went down the remaining steps in silence, side by side, and very demurely, as if nothing had happened. The Countess's brougham was in the courtyard, and the porter, just going into his lodge under the archway, touched his big-visored cap to Lamberti and glanced at Cecilia carelessly as they went out. Petersen was sitting in an open cab in the blazing sun, under a large white parasol lined with green cotton, and her mistress was seated beside her before she had time to rise. Cecilia had quickly turned up her veil over the brim of her hat as soon as she had passed the porter's lodge, for he knew her face and she did not wish him to see her go out with Lamberti.

"Thank you," she said in a matter-of-fact tone as Lamberti stood hat in hand in the sun by the step of the cab. "Palazzo Massimo," she called out to the coach-man.

She nodded to Lamberti indifferently, and the cab drove quickly away to the right, rattling over the white paving-stones of the Piazza Farnese in the direction of San Carlo a Catinari.

"Did you see your mother?" Petersen asked. "She stopped the carriage and called me when she saw me, and she said she was going to ask after Signor d'Este. I said you had gone up to the embassy."

"No," Cecilia answered, "I did not see her. We shall be at home before she is."

She did not speak again on the way. Petersen was too near-sighted and unsuspicious to see that she surreptitiously loosened the brown veil from her hat, got it down beside her on the other side, and rolled it up into a ball with one hand. Somehow, when she reached her own door, it was inside the parasol, just where the revolver had been half an hour earlier.

Lamberti put on his straw hat and glanced indifferently at the departing cab as he turned away, quite sure that Cecilia would not look round. He went back into the palace, feeling for a cigar in his outer breast pocket. His hands felt numb with cold under the scorching sun, and he knew that he was taking pains to look indifferent and to move as if nothing extraordinary had happened to him; for in a few minutes he would be face to face with Guido d'Este and the Countess Fortiguerra. He lit his cigar under the archway, and blew a cloud of smoke before him as he turned into the staircase; but on the first landing he stopped, just where he had stood with Cecilia. He paused, his cigar between his teeth, his legs a little apart as if he were on deck in a sea-way, and his hands behind him. He looked curiously at the wall where she had leaned against it, and he smoked vigorously. At last he took out a small pocket knife and with the point of the blade scratched a little cross on the hard surface, looked at it, touched it again and was satisfied, returned the knife to his pocket, and went quietly upstairs. Most seafaring men do absurdly sentimental things sometimes. Lamberti's expression had neither softened nor changed while he was scratching the mark, and when he went on his way he looked precisely as he did when he was going up the steps of the Ministry to attend a meeting of the Commission. He had good nerves, as he had told the specialist whom he had consulted in the spring.

But he would have given much not to meet Guido for a day or two, though he did not in the least mind meeting the Countess. Cecilia could keep a secret as well as he himself, almost too well, and there was not the slightest danger that her mother should guess the truth from the behaviour of either of them, even when together. Nor would Guido guess it for that matter; that was not what Lamberti was thinking of just then.

He felt that chance, or fate, had made him the instrument of a sort of betrayal for which he was not responsible, and as he had never been in such a position in his life, even by accident, it was almost as bad at first as if he had intentionally taken Cecilia from his friend. He had always been instinctively sure that she would love him some day, but when he had at last spoken he had really not had the least idea that she already loved him. He had acted on an impulse as soon as he was quite sure that she would never marry Guido; perhaps, if he could have analysed his feelings, as Guido could have done, he would have found that he really meant to shock her a little, or frighten her by the point-blank statement that he loved her, in the hope of widening the distance which he supposed to exist between them, and thereby making it much more improbable that she should ever care for him.

Even now he did not see how he could ever marry her and remain Guido's friend. He was far too sensible to tell Guido the truth and appeal to his generosity, for the best man living is not inclined to be generous when he has just been jilted, least of all to the man to whom he owes his discomfiture. In the course of time Guido might grow more indifferent. That was the most that could be hoped.

Nevertheless, from the instant in which Lamberti had realised the truth, coming back to his senses out of a whirlwind of delight, he had known that he meant to have the woman he loved for himself, since she loved him already, and that he would count nothing that chanced to stand in his way, neither his friend, nor his career, nor his own family, nor neck nor life, either, if any such improbable risk should present itself. He was very glad that he had waited till he was quite sure that she was free, for he knew very well that if the moment had come too soon he should have felt the same reckless desire to win her, though he would have exiled himself to a desert island in the Pacific Ocean rather than yield to it.

And more than that. He, who had a rough and strong belief in God, in an ever living soul within him, and in everlasting happiness and suffering hereafter, he, who called suicide the most dastardly and execrable crime against self that it lies in the power of a believing man to commit, would have shot himself without hesitation rather than steal the love of his only friend's wedded wife, content to give his body to instant destruction, and his soul to eternal hell—if that were the only way not to be a traitor. God might forgive him or not; salvation or damnation would matter little compared with escaping such a monstrous evil.

He did not think these things. They were instinctive with him and sure as fate, like all the impulses of violent temperaments; just as certain as that if a man should give him the lie he would have struck him in the face before he had realised that he had even raised his hand. Guido d'Este, as brave in a different way, but hating any violent action, would never strike a man at all if he could possibly help it, though he would probably not miss him at the first shot the next morning.

A quarter of an hour had not elapsed since Lamberti had left the Countess and Guido together when he let himself in again with his latch-key. He went at once to the bedroom, walking slowly and scrutinising the floor as he went along. He had heard of tragedies brought about by a hairpin, a glove, or a pocket handkerchief, dropped or forgotten in places where they ought not to be. He looked everywhere in the passage and in Guido's room, but Cecilia had not dropped anything. Then he examined his beard in the glass, with an absurd exaggeration of caution. Her loose brown veil had touched his cheek, a single silk thread of it clinging to his beard might tell a tale. He was a man who had more than once lived among savages and knew how slight a trace might lead to a broad trail. Then he got a chair and set it against the side of the tall wardrobe. Standing on it he got hold of the cornice with his hands, drew himself up till he could see over it, remained suspended by one hand and, with the other, laid the revolver and the cartridges on the top. Guido would never find them there.

The Countess's unnecessary shyness had disappeared as soon as she saw how ill Guido looked. His head was aching terribly now, and he had a little fever again, but he raised himself as well as he could to greet her, and smiled courteously as she held out her hand.

"This is very kind of you, my dear lady," he managed to say, but his own voice sounded far off.

"I was really so anxious about you!" the Countess said, with a little laugh. "And—and about it all, you know. Now tell me how you really are!"

Guido said that he had felt better in the morning, but now had a bad headache. She sympathised with him and suggested bathing his temples with Eau de Cologne, which seemed simple. She always did it herself when she had a headache, she said. The best was the Forty-Seven Eleven kind. But of course he knew that.

He felt that he should probably go mad if she stayed five minutes longer, but his courteous manner did not change, though her face seemed to be jumping up and down at every throb he felt in his head. She was very kind, he repeated. He had some Eau de Cologne of that very sort. He never used any other. This sounded in his own ears so absurdly like the advertisements of patent soap that he smiled in his pain.

Yes, she repeated, it was quite the best; and she seemed a little embarrassed, as if she wanted to say something else but could not make up her mind to speak. Could she do anything to make him more comfortable? She could go away, but he could not tell her so. He thanked her. Lamberti and his man had taken most excellent care of him. Why did he not have a nurse? There were the Sisters of Charity, and the French sisters who wore dark blue and were very good; she could not remember the name of the order, but she knew where they lived. Should she send him one? He thanked her again, and the room turned itself upside down before his eyes and then whirled back again at the next throb. Still he tried to smile.

She coughed a little and looked at her perfectly fitting gloves, wishing that he would ask after Cecilia. If he had been suffering less he would have known that he was expected to do so, but it was all he could do just then to keep his face from twitching.

Then she suddenly said that she had something on her mind to say to him, but that, of course, as he was so very ill, she would not say it now, but as soon as he was quite well they would have a long talk together.

Guido was a man more nervous than sanguine, and probably more phlegmatic than either, and his nervous strength asserted itself now, just when he began to believe that he was on the verge of delirium. He felt suddenly much quieter and the pain in his head diminished, or he noticed it less. He said that he was quite able to talk now, and wished to know at once what she had to say to him.

She needed no second invitation to pour out her heart about Cecilia, and in a long string of involved and often disjointed sentences she told him just what she felt. Cecilia had done her best to love him, after having really believed that she did love him, but it was of no use, and it was much better that Guido should know the truth now, than find it out by degrees. Cecilia was dreadfully sorry to have made such a mistake, and both Cecilia and she herself would always be the best friends he had in the world; but the engagement had better be broken off at once, and of course, as it would injure Cecilia if everything were known, it would be very generous of him to let it be thought that it had been broken by mutual agreement, and without any quarrel. She stopped at last, rather frightened at having said so much, but quite sure that she had done right, and believing that she knew the whole truth and had told it all. She waited for his answer in some trepidation.

"My dear lady," he said at last, "I am very glad you have been so frank. Ever since your daughter wrote me that letter I have felt that it must end in this way. As she does not wish to marry me, I quite agree that our engagement should end at once, so that the agreement is really mutual and friendly, and I shall say so."

"How good you are!" cried the Countess, delighted.

"There is only one thing I ask of you," Guido said, after pressing his right hand upon his forehead in an attempt to stop the throbbing that now began again. "I do not think I am asking too much, considering what has happened, and I promise not to make any use of what you tell me."

"You have a right to ask us anything," the Countess answered, contritely.

"Who is the man that has taken my place?"

The Countess stared at him blankly a moment, and her mouth opened a little.

"What man?" she asked, evidently not understanding him.

"I naturally supposed that your daughter felt a strong inclination for some one else," Guido said.

"Oh dear, no!" cried the Countess. "You are quite mistaken!"

"I beg your pardon, then. Pray forget what I said."

He saw that she was speaking the truth, as far as she knew it, and he had long ago discovered that she was quite unable to conceal anything not of the most vital importance. She repeated her assurance several times, and then began to review the whole situation, till Guido was in torment again.

At last the door opened and Lamberti entered. He saw at a glance how Guido was suffering, and came to his side.

"I am afraid he is not so well to-day," he said. "He looks very tired. If he could sleep more, he would get well sooner."

The Countess rose at once, and became repentant for having stayed too long.

"I could not help telling him everything," she explained, looking at Lamberti. "And as for Cecilia being in love with some one else," she added, looking down into Guido's face and taking his hand, "you must put that out of your head at once! As if I should not know it! It is perfectly absurd!"

Lamberti stared fixedly at the top of her hat while she bent down.

"Of course," Guido said, summoning his strength to bid her good-bye courteously, and to show some gratitude for her visit. "I am sorry I spoke of it. Thank you very much for coming to see me, and for being so frank."

In a sense he was glad she had come, for her coming had solved the difficulty in which he had been placed. He sank back exhausted and suffering as she left the room, and was hardly aware that Lamberti came back soon afterwards and sat down beside him. Before long his friend carried him back to his bed, for he seemed unable to walk.

Lamberti stayed with him till he fell asleep under the influence of a soporific medicine, and then called the man-servant. He told him he had taken the revolver from the drawer, because his master was not to be married after all, and might do something foolish, and ought to be watched continually, and he said that he would come back and stay through the night. The man had been in his own service, and could be trusted now that he had slept.

Lamberti left the Palazzo Farnese and walked slowly homeward in the white glare, smoking steadily all the way, and looking straight before him.

CHAPTER XXV

The Countess wrote that afternoon to Baron Goldbirn, of Vienna, and to the Princess Anatolie, now in Styria, that the engagement between her daughter and Signor Guido d'Este was broken off by mutual agreement. She had told Cecilia that she had been to see Guido and had confessed the plain truth, and that there need be no more comedies, because men never died of that sort of thing after all, and it was much better for them to be told everything outright. Cecilia seemed perfectly satisfied and thanked her. Then the Countess said she would like to go to Brittany, or perhaps to Norway, where she had never been, but that if Cecilia preferred Scotland, she would make no objection. She would go anywhere, provided the place were cool, and on the top of a mountain, or by the sea, but she wished to leave at once. Everything had been ready for their departure several days ago.

"You do not really mean to leave Rome till Guido—I mean, till Signor d'Este is out of all danger, do you?" asked the young girl.

"My dear, since you are not going to marry him, what difference can it make?" asked the Countess, unconsciously heartless. "The sooner we go, the better. You are as pale as a sheet and as thin as a skeleton. You will lose all your looks if you stay here!"

Cecilia was in a loose white silk garment with open sleeves. She looked at the perfect curve of her arm, from the slender wrist to the delicately rounded elbow, and smiled.

"I am not a skeleton yet," she said.

"You will be in a few days," her mother answered cheerfully. "There is a telegraph to everywhere nowadays, and Signor Lamberti will be here and can send us news all the time. You cannot possibly go and see the poor man, you know. If you could only guess how I felt, my dear, when I found myself there this morning alone with him! I confess, I half expected that the walls would be covered with the most dreadful pictures, those things I do not like you to look at in the Paris Salon, you know. Women apparently waiting for tea on the lawn—before dressing—that sort of thing." The good Countess blushed at the thought.

"They are only women!" said Cecilia. "Why should I not look at them?"

"Because they are horrid," answered the Countess. "But I must say I saw nothing of the sort in Guido's rooms. Nevertheless, I felt like the wicked ladies in the French novels, who always go out in thick veils and have little gold keys hidden somewhere inside their clothes. It must be very uncomfortable."

She prattled on and her daughter scarcely heard her. All sorts of hard questions were presenting themselves to Cecilia's mind together. Had she done wrong, or right? And then, though it might have been quite right to let Lamberti know that she loved him, had her behaviour been modest and maidenly, or over bold? After all, could she have helped putting out her hand to find his just then? And when she had found it, could she possibly have checked herself from drawing him nearer to her? Had she any will of her own left at that moment, or had she been taken unawares and made to do something which she would never have done, if she had been quite calm? Calm! She almost laughed at the word as it came into her thought.

Her mother was reading the Figaro now, having given up talking when she saw that Cecilia did not listen. Ever since Cecilia could remember her mother had read the Figaro. When it did not come by the usual post she read the number of the preceding day over again.

Cecilia was trying to decide where to spend the rest of the summer, tolerably sure that she could make her mother accept any reasonable plan she offered. By a reasonable plan she meant one that should not take her too far from Rome. For her own part she would have been glad not to go away at all. There was Vallombrosa, which was high up and very cool, and there was Viareggio, which was by the sea, but much warmer, and there was Sorrento, which had become fashionable in the summer, and was never very hot and was the prettiest place of all. Something must be decided at once, for she knew her mother well. When the Countess grew restless to leave town, it was impossible to live with her. A startled exclamation interrupted Cecilia's reflections.

"My dear! How awful!"

"What is it?" asked Cecilia, placidly, expecting her mother to read out some blood-curdling tale of runaway motor cars and mangled nursery maids.

"This is too dreadful!" cried the Countess, still buried in the article she had found, and reading on to herself, too much interested to stop a moment.

"Is anybody amusing dead?" enquired Cecilia, with calm.

"What did you say?" asked the Countess, reaching the end. "This is the most frightful thing I ever heard of! A million of francs—in small sums—extracted on all sorts of pretexts—probably as blackmail—it is perfectly horrible."

"Who has extracted a million of francs from whom?" asked Cecilia, quite indifferent.

"Guido d'Este, of course! I told you—from the Princess Anatolie—"

"Guido?" Cecilia started from her seat. "It is a lie!" she cried, leaning over her mother's shoulder and reading quickly. "It is an infamous lie!"

"My dear?" protested the Countess. "They would not dare to print such a thing if it were not true! Poor Guido! Of course, I suppose they take an exaggerated view, but the Princess always gave me to understand that he had large debts. It was a million, you see, just that million they wished us to give for your dowry! Yes, that would have set him straight. But they did not get it! My child, what an escape you have made! Just fancy if you had been already married!"

"I do not believe a word of it," said Cecilia, indignantly throwing down the paper she had taken from her mother's hand. "Besides, there is only an initial. It only speaks of a certain Monsieur d'E."

"Oh, there is no doubt about it, I am afraid. His aunt, 'a certain Princess,' his father 'one of the great of the earth.' It could not be any one else."

"I should like to kill the people who write such things!" Cecilia was righteously angry.

The seed sown by Monsieur Leroy was bearing fruit already, and in a much more public place than he had expected, or even wished. The young lawyer cared much less for the money he might make out of the affair than for the advantage of having his name connected with a famous scandal, and he had not found it hard to make the story public. The article appeared in the shape of a letter from an occasional correspondent, and said it was rumoured that since her nephew was to make a rich marriage the Princess would bring suit to recover the sums she had been induced to lend him on divers pretences. Her legal representative in Rome, it was stated, had been interviewed, but had positively refused to give any information, and his name was given in full, whereas all the others were indicated by initials followed by dots. The lawyer flattered himself that this was a remarkably neat way of letting the world know who he was and with what great discretion he was endowed.

As Cecilia thought of Guido's face as she had seen it that morning, her heart beat with anger and she clenched her hand and turned away. Her mother believed the story, or a part of it, and others would believe as much. The Figaro had come in the morning, and the article would certainly appear in the Roman papers that very evening. Guido would not hear of it at present, because Lamberti would keep it from him, but he must know it in the end.

The girl was powerless, and realised it. If she had been mistress of her own fortune she would readily have satisfied the Princess's demands on Guido, for she suspected that in some way the abominable article had been authorised by his aunt. But she was still Baron Goldbirn's ward, and the sensible financier would have laughed to scorn the idea of ransoming Guido d'Este's reputation. So would her mother, though she was generous; and besides, the Countess could not touch her capital, which was held in trust for Cecilia.

"What a mercy that you are not married to him!" she said, reading the article again, while her daughter walked up and down the small boudoir.

"You should not say such things!" Cecilia answered hotly. "Why do you read that disgusting paper? You know the story is a vile falsehood, from beginning to end. You know that as well as I do! Signor Lamberti will go to Paris to-night and kill the man who wrote it."

Her eyes flashed, and she had visions of the man she loved shaking a miserable creature to death, as a terrier kills a rat. Oddly enough the miserable creature took the shape of Monsieur Leroy in her vivid imagination.

"Monsieur Leroy is at the bottom of this," she said with instant conviction. "He hates Guido."

"I daresay," answered the Countess. "I never liked Monsieur Leroy. Do you remember, when I asked about him at the Princess's dinner, what an awful silence there was? That was one of the most dreadful moments of my life! I am sure her relations never mention him."

"He does what he likes with her. He is a spiritualist."

"Who told you that, child?"

"That dear old Don Nicola Francesetti, the archæologist who showed us the discoveries in Saint Cecilia's church."

"I remember. I had quite forgotten him."

"Yes. He told me that Monsieur Leroy makes tables turn and rap, and all that, and persuades the Princess that he is in communication with spirits. Don Nicola said quite gravely that the devil was in all spiritualism."

"Of course he is," assented the Countess. "I have heard of dreadful things happening to people who made tables turn. They go mad, and all sorts of things."

"All sorts of things," in the Countess's mind represented everything she could not remember or would not take the trouble to say. The expression did not always stand grammatically in the sentence, but that was of no importance whatever compared with the convenience of using it in any language she chanced to be speaking. She belonged to a generation in which a woman was considered to have finished her education when she had learned to play the piano and had forgotten arithmetic, and she had now forgotten both, which did not prevent her from being generally liked, while some people thought her amusing.

Just at that moment she seemed hopelessly frivolous to Cecilia, who was in the greatest distress for Guido, and left her to take refuge in solitude. She could remember no day in her life on which so much had happened to change it, and she felt that she must be alone at last.

In her old way she sat down to let herself dream with open eyes in the darkened room. There could be no harm in it now, and the old longing came upon her as if she had never tried to resist it. She sat facing the shadows and concentrated all her thoughts on one point with a steady effort, sure that presently she should be thinking of nothing and waiting for the vision to appear, and for the dream-man she had loved so long. He might take her into his arms now, and she would not resist him; she would let his lips meet hers, and for one endless instant she would be lifted up in strong and strange delight, as when to-day her veiled cheek had pressed against his for a second—or an hour—she did not know. He might kiss her in dreams now, for in real life he loved her as she loved him, and some day, far off no doubt, when poor Guido was well and strong again, and Lamberti had silenced all the calumnies invented against him, then it would all surely come true indeed.

But now she waited long, patiently, in the certainty that she could go back to the marble court and stand by the pillar in the morning light till she felt him coming up behind her. Yet she saw nothing, and her eyes grew weary of watching the shadows, and closed themselves, for it was afternoon, and very hot, and she was tired. She fell into a sweet sleep in her chair, and presently the refreshing breeze that springs up in Rome towards five o'clock in summer blew through the drawn blinds to fan her delicate cheek, and stir the little golden ringlets at her temples. While she slept her face grew sad by slow degrees, and on her lap her hands moved and lay with their palms turned upwards as if she were appealing piteously to some higher power for mercy and help.

Shadows darkened softly under her eyes, as she lay thus, and the young lids swelled and trembled; and she, who never shed tears waking, wept silently in her sleep. The bright drops hung by the lashes and broke, trickling down her cheeks, one by one, till they fell sideways upon her bare white neck. Many they were and long they fell, and when they ceased at last, her face was very white and still, as if she were quite dead, and dead of a sorrow that could be consoled only in heaven.

She had dreamed that the Vestal's vow was broken at last, and that she was sitting alone at night on the steps of the closed Temple, leaning back against the base of a pillar, watching the stars that slowly ascended out of the east; and she was thinking of what she had been, and that she should never again stand within the holy place to feed the sacred fire with the consecrated wood, and sweep the precious ashes into the mysterious pit beneath the altar. Never again was she to write down the records of the lordly Roman unions that had kept the stock great and pure and the free blood clean from that of slaves for a thousand years. Never might she sit at the feet of the Chief Virgin in the moonlit court, listening to tales of holy Vestals in old time, while the slow water murmured in the channels between one fountain and another.

It was all over, all ended, all behind her in the past for ever. Her vow was broken, because her veiled cheek had touched the cheek of a living, breathing man who had laid a strong hand upon her neck and had pressed her close to him, she consenting, and always to consent. She was not to die for it, since it was no mortal sin, but she was no longer a Vestal now, and the Temple and the house of the pure in heart were shut against her henceforth and would not be opened again. She knew that she had passed the threshold for the last time, and that the man she loved would soon come and take her away to another life. After that there would be no fear in the world, since she would always be with him, and he would make her forget all. But he had not come yet, and while she waited her tears flowed quietly and sadly for all that was no more to be hers, but most of all because she had broken a high and solemn promise which had been the foundation of her life. In the old dream, when the Vestals were dismissed from their office each to her own home, she was the most faithful of them all, to the very end. But now she had been the very first to yield, and they had put her out of their midst, sadly and silently, to wait alone in the night for him she loved. So she waited and wept, and the night wind seemed to freeze the salt tears on her face and neck; yet he did not come.

Then she heard his step; but she was wakened by the soft sound of the latch bolt of her door in its socket, and she sprang to her feet, straight and white, with a little sharp cry, for the fancied sound had always frightened her as nothing else could. This time she had not turned the key, and the door opened.

"Did I startle you, child?" asked her mother's voice, kindly. "I am sorry. Signor Lamberti is in the drawing-room. I think you had better come. He has heard of the article in the Figaro, and is reading it now."

"I will come in a minute, mother," Cecilia answered, turning her face away. "Let me slip on my frock."

"It is only Signor Lamberti," the Countess observed, rather thoughtlessly. "But I will send you Petersen."

The door was shut again, and Cecilia heard her mother's tripping footsteps on the glazed tiles in the corridor. She knew that she had blushed quickly, for she had been taken unawares, but the room was darkened and her mother had noticed nothing. She was suddenly aware that her cheeks and her neck were wet, and she remembered what she had dreamt and wondered that her tears should have been real. She had let in more light now and she looked at herself in the glass with curiosity, for she did not remember to have cried since she had been a little girl. The dried tears gave her face a stained and spotted look she did not like, and she made haste to bathe it in cold water. Even the near-sighted Petersen might see something unusual, and she would not let Lamberti guess that she had been crying on that day of all days.

It was all very strange, and while she dressed she wondered still why the real tears had come, and why she had dreamt she had broken her vow. She had never dreamt that before, not even when she used to meet Lamberti in her dreams by the fountain in the Villa Madama. It was stranger still that she should not have been able to call up the waking vision in the old way. It was as if some power she had once possessed had left her very suddenly, a power, or a faculty, or a gift; she could not tell what it was, but it was gone and something told her that it would not return. She made haste, and almost ran along the broad passage.

When she went into the drawing-room Lamberti was standing with the Figaro in his hand, before her mother who was sitting down. He bowed rather stiffly, though he smiled a little, and she saw that his blue eyes glittered and his face had the ruthless look she used to dread. She knew what it meant now, and was pleased. She wished she could see him shake the wretch who had written the article; she was glad that he was just what he was, not too tall, strong, active, red-haired and angry, a fighting man from head to foot, roused and ready for a violent deed. She had waited for him so long, outside the closed Temple of Vesta in the cold night wind!

"It is not the article that matters," he said, taking it for granted that she knew the contents. "It is what Guido would feel if he read it."

"Especially just now," observed the Countess, looking at Cecilia.

"What are you going to do?" Cecilia asked as quietly as she could. "Shall you go to Paris?"

"No! this was written in Rome. I will wager my life that the lawyer who is mentioned here wrote it all and got some clever Frenchman to translate it for him. I know the fellow by name."

"I thought Monsieur Leroy was at the bottom of it," said Cecilia.

Lamberti looked at her a moment.

"I daresay," he said. "I am sure that the Princess never meant that anything of this sort should be printed. Did Guido ever tell you about her money dealings with him?"

Guido had never mentioned them, of course, and Lamberti explained in a few words exactly what had happened, and the nature of the receipts Guido had given to his aunt.

"I daresay you are right about Monsieur Leroy," he concluded, "for the old lady is far too clever to have done such an absurd thing as this, and it is just like his blundering hatred of Guido."

"I wish he were here," said Cecilia, looking at Lamberti's hands. "I wonder what you would do to him."

"The lawyer is here, which is more to the purpose," Lamberti answered.

"You cannot fight a lawyer, can you?" asked the young girl. "You cannot shoot him."

"One can without doubt," returned Lamberti, smiling. "But it will not be necessary."

"My dear child," cried the Countess in a reproachful tone, "I had no idea you could be so bloodthirsty! Your father fought with Garibaldi, but I am sure he never talked like that."

"Men have no need of talking, mother. They can fight themselves."

"May I take the Figaro with me?" asked Lamberti. "I may not be able to buy a copy. By the bye, Baron Goldbirn is your guardian, is he not? He must have important relations with the financiers in Paris."

Cecilia looked at her mother, meaning her to answer the question.

"He is always in Paris himself," said the Countess. "I mean when he is not in Vienna."

"Can you telegraph to him to use his influence in Paris, so that the Figaro shall correct the article? Newspapers never take back what they say, but it will be enough if a paragraph appears in a prominent part of the paper stating that some ill-disposed people having supposed that the person referred to in a recent letter from a Roman correspondent was Guido d'Este, the editors take the opportunity of stating positively that no reference to him was intended. Will you telegraph that?"

"But will it be of any use?" asked the Countess, who was slightly in awe of Baron Goldbirn.

"Please write the telegram yourself," Cecilia said. "Then there cannot be any mistake. The address is Kärnthner Ring, Vienna."

"You will find writing paper in my boudoir," said the Countess. "Cecilia will show you."

The young girl led the way to her mother's table in the next room, and Lamberti sat down before it, while she pulled out a sheet of paper and gave him a pen. Neither looked at the other, and Lamberti wrote slowly in a laboured round hand unlike his own, intended for the telegraph clerk to read easily.

"How shall I sign it?" he asked when he had finished.

"'Countess Fortiguerra.'"

He wrote, blotted the page, and rose. For one moment he stood close beside her.

"Shall I tell your mother?" he asked, in a low voice.

"Not yet."

He bent his head and looked at her, and his face softened wonderfully in that instant. But there was not a touch of their hands, though they were alone in the room, nor a tender word spoken in a whisper to have told any one that they loved each other so well. They were alike, and they understood without speech or touch.

Lamberti read the telegram to the Countess, who seemed satisfied, but not very hopeful about the result.

"I never could understand what financiers and newspapers have to do with each other," she observed. "They seem to me so different."

"There is not often any resemblance between a horse and his rider," said Lamberti, enigmatically.

"Will you come this evening and tell us what the lawyer says?" Cecilia asked.

"Yes, if I may."

"Pray do," said the Countess. "We should so much like to know. Poor Guido! Good-bye!" Lamberti left the room.

CHAPTER XXVI

When Lamberti reached the Palazzo Farnese at eight o'clock he had all Guido's receipts for the Princess's money in his pocket. He had difficulty in getting the lawyer to see him on business so late in the afternoon, and when he succeeded at last he did not find it easy to carry matters with a high hand; but he had come prepared to go to any length, for he was in no gentle humour, and if he could not get the papers by persuasion, he fully intended to take them by force, though that might be the end of his career as an officer, and might even bring him into court for something very like robbery.

The lawyer was obdurate at first. He of course denied all knowledge of the article in the Figaro, but he said that he was the Princess's legal representative, that the case had been formally placed in his hands, and that he should use all his professional energy in her interests.

"After all," said Lamberti at last, "you have nothing but a few informal bits of writing to base your case upon. They have no legal value."

"They are stamped receipts," answered the lawyer.

"They are not stamped," Lamberti replied.

"They are!"

"They are not!"

"You are giving me the lie, sir," said the lawyer, angrily.

"I say that they are not stamped," retorted Lamberti. "You dare not show them to me."

The lawyer was human, after all. He opened his safe, in a rage, found the receipts, and showed one of them to Lamberti triumphantly.

"There!" he cried. "Are they stamped or not? Is the signature written across the stamp or not?"

Lamberti had the advantage of knowing positively that when Guido had given the acknowledgments to his aunt, there had been no stamps on them. He did not know how they had got them now, but he was sure that some fraud had been committed. It was broad daylight still, and he examined the signature carefully while the lawyer held the half sheet of note paper before his eyes. The paper was certainly the Princess's, and the writing was Guido's beyond doubt. The Princess always used violet ink, and Guido had written with it. It struck Lamberti suddenly that it had turned black where the signature crossed the stamp, but had remained violet everywhere else. Now violet ink sometimes turns black altogether, but it does not change colour in parts. As he looked nearer, he saw that the letters formed on the stamp were a little tremulous. Though he had never heard of such a thing, it now occurred to him that the stamp had been simply stuck upon the middle of the signature, and that the part of the latter that had been covered by it had been cleverly forged over it.

"The stamp makes very much less difference in law than you seem to suppose," said the lawyer, enjoying his triumph.

"It will make a considerable difference in law," answered Lamberti, "if I prove to you that the stamp was put on over the first writing, and part of the signature forged upon it. It has not even been done with the same ink! The one is black and the other is violet. Do you know that this is forgery, and that you may lose your reputation if you try to found an action at law upon a forged document?"

The lawyer was now scrutinising the signatures of the notes one by one in the strong evening light. His anger had disappeared and there were drops of perspiration on his forehead.

"There is only one way of proving it to you," Lamberti said quietly. "Moisten one of the stamps and raise it. If the signature runs underneath it in violet ink, I am right, and the wisest thing you can do is to hand me those pieces of paper and say nothing more about them. You can write to Monsieur Leroy that you have done so. I even believe that he would pay a considerable sum for them."

It was as he said, and the lawyer was soon convinced that he had been imposed upon, and had narrowly escaped being laughed at as a dupe, or prosecuted as a party accessory to a fraud. He was glad to be out of the whole affair so easily. Therefore, when Lamberti reached his friend's door, he had the receipts in his pocket and he now meant to tell Guido what had happened, after first giving them back to him. Guido would laugh at Monsieur Leroy's stupid attempt to hurt him. But some one had been before Lamberti.

"He is very ill," said the servant, gravely, as he admitted him. "The doctor is there and has sent for a nurse. I telephoned for him."

Lamberti asked him what had happened, fearing the truth. Guido had felt a little better in the afternoon and had asked for his letters and papers. Half an hour later his servant had gone in with his tea and had found him raving in delirium. That was all, but Lamberti knew what it meant. Guido did not take the Figaro, but some one had sent the article to him and he had read it. He had brain fever, and Lamberti was not surprised, for he had suffered as much on that day as would have killed some men, and might have driven some men mad.

Lamberti did not wish to frighten Cecilia or her mother, but he sent them word that he would not leave Guido that night, nor till he was better, and that he had seen the lawyer and had recovered a number of forged papers.

After that there was nothing to be done but to watch and wait, and hear the broken phrases that fell from the sick man's lips, now high, now low, now laughing, now despairing, as if a host of mad spirits were sporting with his helpless brain and body and mocking each other with his voice.

So it went on, hour after hour, and all the next day, till his strength seemed almost spent. Lamberti listened, because he could not help it when he was in the room, and again and again Cecilia's name rang out, and the first passionate words of speeches that ran into incoherent sounds and were drowned in a groan.

Lamberti had nursed men who were ill and had seen them die in several ways, but he had never taken care of one who was very near to him. It was bad enough, but it was worse to know that he had an unwilling share in causing his friend's suffering, and to feel that if Guido lived he must some day be told that Lamberti had taken his place. It was strangest of all to hear the name of the woman he loved so constantly on another's lips. When the two men talked of her she had always been "the Contessina," while she had been "Cecilia" in the hearts of both.

There was something in the thought of not having told Guido all before the delirium seized him, that still offended Lamberti's scrupulous loyalty. It would be almost horrible if Guido should die without knowing the truth. Somehow, his consent still seemed needful to Lamberti's love, and it seemed so to Cecilia, too, and there was no denying that he was now in danger of his life. If he was to die, there would probably be a lucid hour before death, but what right would his best friend have to embitter those final moments for one who would certainly go out of this world with no hope of the next? Yet, when he was gone at last, would it be no slur on the memory of such true friendship to do what would have hurt him, if he could have known of it? Lamberti was not sure. Like some strong men of rough temperament, he had hidden delicacies of feeling that many a girl would have thought foolish and exaggerated, and they were the more sensitive because they were so secret, and he never suffered outward things to come in contact with them, nor spoke of them, even to Guido.

Some people said that Guido was Quixotic, and he was certainly the personification of honour. If the papers Lamberti had safe in his pocket had come into Guido's possession as they had come into Lamberti's own, Guido would have sent them back to Princess Anatolie, quite sure that she had a right to them, whether they were partly forged or not, because he had originally given them to her and nothing could induce him to take them back. The reason why Guido's illness had turned into brain fever was simply that he believed his honourable reputation among men to have been gravely damaged by an article in a newspaper. Honour was his god, his religion, and his rule of life; it was all he had beyond the material world, and it was sacred. He had not that something else, simple but undefinable, and as sensitive as an uncovered nerve, that lay under his friend's rougher character and sturdier heart. Nature would never have chosen him to be one instrument in that mysterious harmony of two sleeping beings which had linked Cecilia and Lamberti in their dreams. It was not the melancholy and intellectual Cassius who trembled before Cæsar's ghost at Philippi; it was rough Brutus, the believer in himself and the man of action.

The illness ran its course. While it continued Lamberti went every other day to the Palazzo Massimo and told the two ladies of Guido's state. He and Cecilia looked at each other silently, but she never showed that she wished to be alone with him, and he made no attempt to see her except in her mother's presence. Both felt that Guido was dying, and knew that they had some share in his sufferings. As soon as the Countess learned that the danger was real she gave up all thought of leaving Rome, and there was no discussion about it between her and her daughter. She was worldly and often foolish, but she was not unkind, and she had grown really fond of Guido since the spring. So they waited for the turn of the illness, or for its sudden end, and the days dragged on painfully. Lamberti was as lean as a man trained for a race, and the cords stood out on his throat when he spoke, but nothing seemed to tire him. The good Countess lost her fresh colour and grew listless, but she complained only of the heat and the solitude of Rome in summer, and if she felt any impatience she never showed it. Cecilia was as slender and pale as one of the lilies of the Annunciation, but her eyes were full of light. In the early morning she often used to go with her maid to the distant church of Santa Croce, and late in the afternoons she went for long drives with her mother in the Campagna. Twice Lamberti came to luncheon, and the three were silent and subdued when they were together.

Then the news came that Princess Anatolie had died suddenly at her place in Styria, and one of the secretaries of the Austrian embassy, who was obliged to stay in town, came to the Palazzo Massimo the same afternoon and told the Countess some details of the old lady's death. There was certainly something mysterious about it, but no one regretted her translation to a better world, though it put a number of high and mighty persons into mourning for a little while.

She died in the drawing-room after dinner, almost with her coffee cup in her hand. It was the heart, of course, said the young secretary. Two or three of her relations were staying in the house, and one of them was the man who had been at her dinner-party given for the engaged couple, and who resembled Guido but was older. The Countess remembered his name very well. It had leaked out that he was exceedingly angry at the article in the Figaro and had said one or two sharp things to the Princess, when Monsieur Leroy had come in unexpectedly, though the Princess had sent him away for a few days. No one knew exactly what followed, but Monsieur Leroy was an insolent person and the Princess's cousin was not patient of impertinence nor of anything like an attack on Guido d'Este. It was said that Monsieur Leroy had left the room hastily and that the other had followed him at once, in a very bad temper, and that the Princess, who thought Monsieur Leroy was going to be badly hurt, if not killed, had died of fright, without uttering a word or a cry. She had always been unaccountably attached to Monsieur Leroy. The secretary glanced at Cecilia, asked for another cup of tea, and discreetly changed the subject, fearing that he had already said a little too much.

"I believe Guido may recover, now that she is dead," Lamberti said, when he heard the story.

The change in Guido's state came one night about eleven o'clock, when Lamberti and the French nun were standing beside the bed, looking into his face and wondering whether he would open his eyes before he died. He had been lying motionless for many hours, turned a little on one side, and his breathing was very faint. There seemed to be hardly any life left in the wasted body.

"I think he will die about midnight," Lamberti whispered to the nurse.

The good nun, who thought so too, bent down and spoke gently close to the sick man's ear. She could not bear to let him go out of life without a Christian word, though Lamberti had told her again and again that his friend believed in nothing beyond death.

"You are dying," she said, softly and clearly. "Think of God! Try to think of God, Signor d'Este!"

That was all she could find to say, for she was a simple soul and not eloquent; but perhaps it might do some good. She knelt down then, by the bedside.

"Look!" cried Lamberti in a low voice, bending forwards.

Guido had opened his eyes, and they were wide and grave.

"Thank you," he said, after a few seconds, faintly but distinctly. "You are very kind. But I am not going to die."

The quiet eyes closed, and the mystery of life went on in silence. That was all he had to say. The nun knelt down again and folded her hands, but in less than a minute she rose and busied herself noiselessly, preparing something in a glass. It would be the last time that anything would pass his lips, she thought, and it might be quite useless to give it to him, but it must be ready. Many and many a time she had heard the dying declare quietly that they were out of danger. Lamberti stood motionless by the bedside, thinking much the same things and feeling as if his own heart were slowly turning into lead.

He stood there a long time, convinced that it was useless to send for the doctor, who always came about midnight, for Guido would probably be dead before he came. He would stop breathing presently, and that would be the end. The lids would open a little, but the eyes would not see, there would be a little white froth on the parted lips, and that would be the end. Guido would know the great secret then.

But the breathing did not cease, and the eyes did not open again; on the contrary, at the end of half an hour Lamberti was almost sure that the lids were more tightly closed than before, and that the breath came and went with a fuller sound. In ten minutes more he was sure that the sick man was peacefully sleeping, and not likely to die that night. He turned away with a deep sigh of relief.

The doctor came soon after midnight. He would not disturb Guido; he looked at him a long time and listened to his breathing, and nodded with evident satisfaction.

"You may begin to hope now," he said quietly to Lamberti, not even whispering, for he knew how deep such sleep was sure to be. "He may not wake before to-morrow afternoon. Do not be anxious. I will come early in the morning."

"Very well," answered Lamberti. "By the bye, a near relation of his has died suddenly while he has been delirious. Shall I tell him if he wakes quite conscious?"

"If it will give him great satisfaction to know of his relative's death, tell him of it by all means," answered the doctor, his quiet eye twinkling a little, for he had often heard of the Princess Anatolie, and knew that she was dead.

"I do not think the news will cause him pain," said Lamberti, with perfect gravity.

The doctor gave the nurse a few directions and went away, evidently convinced that Guido was out of all immediate danger. Then Lamberti rested at last, for the nun slept in the daytime and was fresh for the night's watching. He stretched himself upon Guido's long chair in the drawing-room, leaving the door open, and one light burning, so that the nurse could call him at once. He had earned his rest, and as he shut his eyes his only wish was that he could have let Cecilia know of the change before he went to sleep. A moment later he was sitting beside her on the bench in the Villa Madama, by the fountain, telling her that Guido was safe at last.

When he awoke the sun had risen an hour.

CHAPTER XXVII

"I am like Dante," said Guido to Lamberti, when he was recovering. "I have been in Hell, and now I am in Purgatory. But I shall not reach the earthly Paradise at the top, much less the Heaven beyond."

He smiled sadly and looked at his friend.

"Who knows?" Lamberti asked, by way of answer.

"Beatrice will not lead me further."

Guido closed his eyes, and wondered why he had come back to life, out of so much suffering, only to be tormented again in the same way, perhaps when the end really came. His memories of his serious illness were vague and indistinct, but they were all horrible. He only recalled the beginning very clearly, how he had glanced through the newspaper article and had dropped it in sudden and overwhelming despair; and then, how he had roused himself and had felt in the drawer for his revolver; not finding it, he had lost consciousness just as he realised that even that means of escape from life had been taken from him. He remembered having felt as if something broke in his brain, though he knew that he was not dying.

After that, fragments of his ravings came back to him with the still vivid recollection of awful pain, of monstrous darkness, of lurid lights, of hideous beings glaring and gnashing their jagged teeth at him, and of a continual discordant noise of voices that had run all through his delirium like the crying out and moaning of many creatures in agony. It was no wonder that he compared what he remembered of his sufferings to hell itself.

And now that he was alive, of what use was life to him? His honour was cleared, indeed, for Lamberti had taken care of that. Lamberti had burned the papers before his eyes after telling him how Princess Anatolie had died, and had read him the paragraph which Baron Goldbirn had caused to be inserted in the Figaro. The Princess was dead, and Monsieur Leroy would probably never trouble any one again. When he had squandered what she had left him, he would probably get a living as a medium in Vienna. Guido knew the secret of the tie that bound him to the Princess, but was quite sure that the proud old woman had never let him guess it himself, in spite of her doting affection for him. Those of her family who knew it would not tell him, of all people, and if Monsieur Leroy ever begged money of Guido he would not present himself as an unfortunate cousin.

Guido foresaw no difficulties in the future, but he anticipated no happiness, and his life stretched before him, colourless, blank, and idle.

Since his delirium had ceased, he had not once spoken of Cecilia, and Lamberti began to fear that he would not allude to her for a long time. That did not make it easier to tell him the story he must hear, and the time had come when he must hear it, come what might, lest he should ever think that he had been intentionally kept in ignorance of the truth. Lamberti was glad when he spoke of Cecilia as a Beatrice who would never appear to lead him further, and knew at once that the opportunity must not be lost.

It was the hardest moment in Lamberti's life. It had been far easier to hide what he felt, so long as he had not guessed that Cecilia loved him, than it was to speak out now; it had cost him much less to be steadfast in his silence with her while Guido's illness lasted. To make Guido understand all, it would be necessary to tell all from the beginning, even to explaining that what he had taken for mutual aversion at first, had been an attraction so irresistible that it had frightened Cecilia and had made Lamberti compare it with a possession of the devil and a haunting spirit.

The two men were sitting on the brick steps of the miniature Roman theatre close to the oak which is still called Tasso's, a few yards from the new road that leads over the Janiculum through what was once the Villa Corsini. It was shady there, and Rome lay at their feet in the still afternoon. The waiting carriage was out of sight, and there was no sound but the rustling of leaves stirred by the summer breeze. It was nearly the middle of August.

"They are still in Rome," Lamberti said, after a moment's pause, during which he had decided to speak at last.

"Are they?" asked Guido, coldly.

"Yes. Neither the Countess nor her daughter would go away till you were well."

"I am well now."

He was painfully thin and his eyes were hollow. The doctor had ordered mountain air and he was going to stay with one of his relatives in the Austrian Tyrol as soon as he could bear the journey without too much fatigue.

"They wish to see you," Lamberti said, glancing sideways at his face.

"I cannot refuse, but I would rather not see them. They ought to understand that, I think."

He was offended by what seemed very like an intrusion on the privacy of a suffering that was still keen. Why could they not leave him alone?

"They would not have gone away in any case till you recovered," Lamberti answered, "but the Contessina would not have the bad taste to wish for a meeting just now, unless there were a reason which you do not know, and which I must explain to you, cost what it may."

Guido looked at Lamberti in surprise and then laughed a little scornfully.

"Is she going to be married?" he asked.

"Perhaps."

"Already!"

His tone was sad, and pitying, and slightly contemptuous. His lips closed after the single word and he drew his eyelids together, as he looked steadily out over the deep city towards the hills to eastward.

"Then it was true that she cared for another man," he said, in a low voice.

"Yes. It was quite true."

"She wrote me in that letter that he did not know it."

"That was true also."

"And that he was not in the least in love with her."

"She thought so."

"But she was mistaken, you mean to say. He loved her, but did not show it."

"Precisely. He loved her, but he was careful not to show it because he understood that her mother and the Princess wished to marry her to you, and because he happened to know that you were in earnest."

"That was decent of him, at all events," Guido said wearily. "Some men would have behaved differently."

"I daresay," Lamberti answered.

"Is he a man I know?"

"Yes. You know him very well."

"And now she has asked you to tell me his name. I suppose that is why you begin this conversation. You are trying to break it gently to me." He smiled contemptuously.

"Yes!"

The word was spoken as if it cost an effort. Lamberti held his stout stick with both hands over his crossed knee and leaned back, so that it bent a little with the strain.

"My dear fellow," said Guido, with a little impatience, "it seems to me that you need not take so much trouble to spare my feelings! If you do not tell me who the man is, some one else will."

"No one else can," Lamberti answered, with emphasis.

"Why not? I would rather speak of her with you, if I must speak of her at all, of course. But some obliging person is sure to tell me, or write to me about it, as soon as the engagement is announced. 'My dear d'Este, do you remember that girl you were engaged to last spring?' And so on. Remember her!"

"There is no engagement," Lamberti said. "No one will write to you about it, and no one knows who the man is, except the Contessina and the man himself."

"And you," corrected Guido. "You may as well keep the secret, so far as I am concerned. I have no curiosity about it. There will be time enough to tell me when the engagement is announced."

"I do not think that there can be any engagement until you know."

"Oh, this is absurd! The Contessina was frank. She did not love me, she told me so, and we agreed that our engagement should end. What possible claim have I to know whom she wishes to marry now?"

"You have the strongest claim that any man can have, though not on her. The man is your friend."

"Nonsense!" exclaimed Guido, becoming impatient. "A dozen men I like might be called friends of mine, I suppose, but you know very well that you are the only intimate friend I have."

"Yes, I know."

"Well? I can hardly fancy that you mean yourself, can I?"

Lamberti did not move, but as Guido looked at him for an answer, he saw that he could not speak just then, and that he was clenching his teeth. Guido stared at him a moment and then started.

"Lamberti!" he cried sharply.

Lamberti slowly turned his head and gazed into Guido's eyes without speaking. Then they both looked out at the distant hills in silence for a long time.

"The Contessina was very loyal to you, Guido," Lamberti said at last, in a low tone. "She could not tell you that it was I, and I did not know it."

Again there was a silence for a time.

"When did you know it?" Guido asked slowly.

"After she had been to see you. It was my fault, then."

"What was your fault?"

"When we went downstairs, I thought I should never see her again, and I never meant to. How could I know what she felt? She never betrayed herself by a glance or a tone of her voice. I loved her with all my heart, and when you had both told me that everything was quite over between you, I wanted her to know that I did. Was that disloyal to you, since you had definitely given up the hope of marrying her, and since I did not expect to see her again for years and thought she was quite indifferent?"

"No," Guido answered, after a moment's thought. "But you should have told me at once."

"When I came upstairs the Countess was still there, and you were quite worn out. I put you to bed, meaning to tell you that same evening, after you had rested. When I came back you had brain fever, and did not know me. So I have had to wait until to-day."

"And you have seen each other constantly while I have been ill, of course," said Guido, with some bitterness. "It was natural, I suppose."

"Since that day when we spoke on the staircase we have only been alone together once, for a moment. I asked her then if I should tell her mother, and she said 'Not yet.' Excepting that, we have never exchanged a word that you and her mother might not have heard, nor a glance that you might not have seen. We both knew that we were waiting for you to get well, and we have waited."

Guido looked at him with a sort of wonder.

"That was like you," he said quietly.

"You understand, now," Lamberti continued. "You and I met her on the same day at your aunt's, and when I saw her, I felt as if I had always known her and loved her. No one can explain such things. Then by a strange coincidence we dreamt the same dream, on the same night."

"Was it she whom you met in the Forum, and who ran away from you?" asked Guido, in astonishment.

"Yes. That is the reason why we always avoided each other, and why I would not go to their house till you almost forced me to. We had never spoken alone together till the garden party. It was then that we found out that our dreams were alike, and after that I kept away from her more than ever, but I dreamt of her every night."

"So that was your secret, that afternoon!"

"Yes. We had dreamt of each other and we had met in the Forum in the place we had dreamt of, and she ran away without speaking to me. That was the whole secret. She was afraid of me, and I loved her, and was beginning to know it. I thought there was something wrong with my head and went to see a doctor. He talked to me about telepathy, but seemed inclined to consider that it might possibly be a mere train of coincidences. I think I have told you everything."

For a long time they sat side by side in silence, each thinking his own thoughts.

"Is there anything you do not understand?" Lamberti asked at last.

"No," Guido answered thoughtfully. "I understand it all. It was rather a shock at first, but I am glad you have told me. Perhaps I do not quite understand why she wishes to see me."

"We both wish to be sure that you bear us no ill-will. I am sure she does, and I know that I do."

There was a pause again.

"Do you think I am that kind of friend?" Guido asked, with a little sadness. "After what you have done, too?"

"I am afraid my mere existence has broken up your life, after all," Lamberti answered.

"You must not think that. Please do not, my friend. There is only one thing that could hurt me now that it is all over."

"What is that?"

"I am not afraid that it will happen. You are not the kind of man to break her heart."

"No," Lamberti answered very quietly. "I am not."

"It was only a dream for me, after all," Guido said, after a little while. "You have the reality. She used to talk of three great questions, and I remember them now as if I heard her asking them: 'What can I know? What is it my duty to do? What may I hope?' Those were the three."

"And the answers?"

"Nothing, nothing, nothing. Those are my answers. Unless—"

He stopped.

"Unless—what?" Lamberti asked.

Guido smiled a little.

"Unless there is really something beyond it all, something essentially true, something absolute by nature."

Lamberti had never known his friend to admit such a possibility even under a condition.

"At all events," Guido added, "our friendship is true and absolute. Shall we go home? I feel a little tired."

Lamberti helped him to the carriage and drew the light cover over his knees before getting in himself. Then they drove down towards the city, by the long and beautiful drive, past the Acqua Paola and San Pietro in Montorio.

"You must go and see her this evening," Guido said gently, as they came near the Palazzo Farnese. "Will you tell her something from me? Tell her, please, that it would be a little hard for me to talk with her now, but that she must not think I am not glad that she is going to marry my best friend."

"Thank you. I will say that." Lamberti's voice was less steady than Guido's.

"And tell her that I will write to her from the Tyrol."

"Yes."

It was over. The two men knew that their faithful friendship was unshaken still, and that they should meet on the morrow and trust each other more than ever. But on this evening it was better that each should go his own way, the one to his solitude and his thoughts, the other to the happiest hour of his life.

CHAPTER XXVIII

On the following afternoon Lamberti waited for Cecilia at the Villa Madama, and she came not long after him, with Petersen. He had been to the Palazzo Massimo in the evening, and a glance and a sign had explained to her that all was well. Then they had sat together awhile, talking in a low tone, while the Countess read the newspaper. When Lamberti had given Guido's brave message, they had looked earnestly at each other, and had agreed to tell her mother the truth at once, and to meet on the morrow at the villa, which was Cecilia's own house, after all. For they felt that they must be really alone together, to say the only words that really mattered.

The head gardener had admitted Lamberti to the close garden, by the outer steps, but had not let him into the house, as he had received no orders. When Cecilia came, he accompanied her with the keys and opened wide the doors of the great hall. Cecilia and Lamberti did not look at each other while they waited, and when the man was gone away Cecilia told Petersen to sit down in the court of honour on the other side of the little palace. Petersen went meekly away and left the two to themselves.

They walked very slowly along the path towards the fountain, and past it, to the parapet at the other end, where they had talked long ago. But as they passed the bench, they glanced at it quietly, and saw that it was still in its place. Cecilia had not been at the villa since the afternoon before Guido fell ill, and Lamberti had never come there since the garden party in May.

They stood still before the low wall and looked across the shoulder of the hill. Saving commonplace words at meeting, they had not spoken yet. Cecilia broke the silence at last, looking straight before her, her lids low, her face quiet, almost as if she were in a dream.

"Have we done all that we could do, all that we ought to do for him?" she asked. "Are you sure?"

"We can do nothing more," Lamberti answered gravely.

"Tell me again what he said. I want the very words."

"He said, 'Tell her that it would be a little hard for me to talk with her now, but that she must not think I am not glad that she is going to marry my best friend.' He said those words, and he said he would write to you from the Tyrol. He leaves to-morrow night."

"He has been very generous," Cecilia said softly.

"Yes. He will be your best friend, as he is mine."

She knew that it was true.

"We have done what we can," Lamberti continued presently. "He has given all he has, and we have given him what we could. The rest is ours."

He took her hand and drew her gently, turning back towards the fountain.

"It was like this in the dream," she said, scarcely breathing the words as she walked beside him.

They stood still before the falling water, quite alone and out of sight of every one, in the softening light, and suddenly the girl's heart beat hard, and the man's face grew pale, and they were facing each other, hands in hands, look in look, thought in thought, soul in soul; and they remembered that day when each had learned the other's secret in the shadowy staircase of the palace, and each dreamt again of a meeting long ago in the House of the Vestals; but only the girl knew what she had felt of mingled joy and regret when she had sat alone at night weeping on the steps of the Temple.

There was no veil between them now, as their eyes drew them closer together by slow and delicious degrees. It was the first time, though every instant was full of memories, all ending where this was to begin. Their lips had never met, yet the thrill of life meeting life and the blinding delight of each in the other were long familiar, as from ages, while fresh and untasted still as the bloom on a flower at dawn.

Then, when they had kissed once, they sat down in the old place, wondering what words would come, and whether they should ever need words at all after that. And somehow, Cecilia thought of her three questions, and they all were answered as youth answers them, in one way and with one word; and the answer seemed so full of meaning, and of faith and hope and charity, that the questions need never be asked again, nor any others like them, to the end of her life; nor did she believe that she could ever trouble her brain again about Thus spake Zarathushthra, and the Man who had killed God, and the overcoming of Pity, and the Eternal Return, and all those terrible and wonderful things that live in Nietzsche's mazy web, waiting to torment and devour the poor human moth that tries to fly upward.

But as for Kant's Categorical Imperative, in order to act in such a manner that the reasons for her actions might be considered a universal law, it was only necessary to realise how very much she loved the man she had chosen, and how very much he loved her; for how indeed could it then be possible not to live so as to deserve to be happy?

She had thought of these things during the night and had fallen asleep very happy in realising the perfect simplicity of all science, philosophy, and transcendental reasoning, and vaguely wondering why every one could not solve the problems of the universe as she had.

"Is it all quite true?" she asked now, with a little fluttering wonder. "Shall I wake and hear the door shutting, and be alone, and frightened as I used to be?"

Lamberti smiled.

"I should have waked already," he said, "when we were standing there by the fountain. I always did when I dreamt of you."

"So did I. Do you think we really met in our dreams?" She blushed faintly.

"Do you know that you have not told me once to-day that you care for me, ever so little?" he asked.

"I have told you much more than that, a thousand times over, in a thousand ways."

"I wonder whether we really met!"

F. Marion Crawford – A Short Biography

Francis Marion Crawford was born in Bagni di Lucca, Italy on 2nd August, 1854, the only son of the American sculptor Thomas Crawford and Louisa Cutler Ward. His aunt was Julia Ward Howe, the American poet, most famous for the words to 'The Battle Hymn of the Republic'.

After his father's death in 1857, his mother remarried to Luther Terry, with whom she had Crawford's half-sister, Margaret Ward Terry.

Crawford's education began at St Paul's School, Concord, New Hampshire and then went on to Cambridge University, the University of Heidelberg and finally the University of Rome.

In 1879, Crawford went to India to study the ancient language of Sanskrit and to edit Allahabad, The Indian Herald.

Returning to America in February 1881, he enrolled at Harvard University for a year to continue his studies in Sanskrit. Crawford had no real career path at this time although for two years he contributed to various periodicals, mainly The Critic.

Early in 1882, Crawford established a close, lifelong friendship with Isabella Stewart Gardner, a noted and eccentric heiress from Boston who over the years built up a large and eclectic collection of art.

Crawford lived most of his time in Boston with his Aunt Julia and Uncle Sam. The family were concerned by his lack of ambition, prospects in general, and his financial ones in particular.

His mother had hoped he might train in Boston for a career as an operatic baritone based on his private renditions of Schubert lieder. With that in mind it was, in January 1882, that George Henschel, the conductor of the Boston Symphony Orchestra, was called in to assess young Crawford's talents. Henschel was direct and to the point. Crawford would 'never be able to sing in perfect tune'. His Uncle Sam, knowing that Crawford was keen on literary pursuits, proposed that his years in India might be good source material to write about. Crawford agreed. He set to work. Uncle Sam also set about developing contacts with a number of New York publishers.

Events moved very quickly. By December of that year Crawford had completed his first novel, 'Mr Isaacs', based on modern Anglo-Indian life flavoured with a touch of Oriental mystery. It was an immediate success. Crawford set about writing a second novel and the result was 'Dr Claudius' in 1883.

In October 1884 he married Elizabeth Berdan, the daughter of the Civil War Union General Hiram Berdan. The marriage would produce two sons; Harold and Bertram, and two daughters; Eleanor and Clara.

Crawford, buoyed by his excellent start, now decided to return to Italy and to live there permanently.
The couple initially went to Sorrento and lived at the historic Hotel Cocumella during 1885 before moving permanently to Sant' Agnello, where the purchase of the Villa Renzi would now be rededicated as Villa Crawford.

As a writer Crawford had more than his fair share of detractors but, perhaps due to the physical distance between author and these detractors, they did not distract from his prolific output.

Each year seemed to bring a new F. Marion Crawford novel. His popularity was evident although some works, such as 1896's offering 'Adam Johnstone's Son', was described by his left-wing English contemporary, George Gissing, as "rubbish". Over half of his novels are set in Italy. He also wrote three long historical studies of Italy and was nearing completion on a history of Rome in the Middle Ages when he died.

His 'Saracinesca' series are considered his best works. The third in the series, 'Don Orsino' (1892) was told against the background of a real estate bubble and is especially effective. The volume immediately after was 'Corleone' (1897), and the first major treatment of the Mafia in literature.

Crawford himself was fondest of 'Khaled: A Tale of Arabia' (1891), a story of a genie who becomes human. 'A Cigarette-Maker's Romance' (1890) was dramatized, and had considerable popularity on the stage as well as in its novel form.

Towards the end of the 1890's Crawford ventured down another path with his writing. He began his historical works. 'Ave Roma Immortalis' was published in 1898, followed by 'Rulers of the South' (1900), and 'Gleanings from Venetian History' (1905). Most were re-titled with longer more explanatory titles for the American market. Within them all his careful and precise knowledge of the local Italian history together with his literary talents combined to great effect.

Whilst on an American Lecture tour in the winter of 1897-1898 Crawford was researching and gathering technical information for his historical work 'Marietta' (published 1901), that describes glass-making in late medieval Venice. Whilst visiting a glass-smelting plant in Colorado he suffered a severe lung injury when he inhaled toxic gasses. This would eventually contribute to his death a decade or so later.

Crawford's commercial popularity and appeal at the time was such that in 1901, the American Macmillan firm began a deluxe uniform edition of his novels as his works came up for re-printing. In 1904 the P. F. Collier Company in New York was authorized to publish a 25-volume edition (which was later expanded to 32 volumes).

In 1902 he wrote a stage play 'Francesca da Rimini', that was produced in Paris by his friend and legendary actress Sarah Bernhardt.

Towards the end of his life Hollywood had begun to realise that his works were a valuable source of stories and ideas and several were turned into movies and continued to be so for decades after his death.

Crawford also had a gift for pulling off excellent short stories. Several, such as 'The Upper Berth' (1886), 'For the Blood Is the Life' (1905, a vampiress tale), 'The Dead Smile' (1899), and 'The Screaming Skull' (1908), are among the most anthologized classics of the horror genre. After his death several collected volumes were published from various sources.

After most of his fictional works had been published, most had the view that he was a gifted narrator; and his books of fiction, were full of historic vitality and energy as well as dramatic characterization. He was widely popular among readers to whom literature was more for escapism than a confrontation with reality or pages of subjective analysis. In 'The Novel: What It Is' (1893), Crawford was both resolute and disarming in defending his literary approach, self-conceived as a combination of romanticism and realism, defining the art form in terms of its marketplace and audience. The novel, he wrote, is "a marketable commodity" and "intellectual artistic luxury" that "must amuse, indeed, but should amuse reasonably, from an intellectual point of view .... Its intention is to amuse and please, and certainly not to teach and preach; but in order to amuse well it must be a finely-balanced creation ...."

Francis Marion Crawford died at Sorrento on Good Friday 1909 at Villa Crawford of a heart attack.

F. Marion Crawford – A Concise Bibliography

Novels

Mr. Isaacs: A Tale of Modern India (1882)
Dr. Claudius (1883)
To Leeward (1884)
A Roman Singer (1884)
An American Politician (1884)
Zoroaster (1885)
A Tale of a Lonely Parish (1886)
Saracinesca (1887)
Marzio's Crucifix (1887)
Paul Patoff (1887)
With the Immortals (1888)
Greifenstein (1889)
Sant' Ilario (1889); sequel to Saracinesca
A Cigarette-Maker's Romance (1890)
Khaled: A Tale of Arabia (1891)
The Witch of Prague (1891)
The Three Fates (1892)
Don Orsino (1892); sequel to Sant' Ilario
The Children of the King (1893)
Pietro Ghisleri (1893)
Marion Darche (1893)
Katharine Lauderdale (1894)
The Upper Berth (1894); with "By the Waters of Paradise"
Love in Idleness (1894)
The Ralstons (1894); sequel to Katharine Lauderdale
Casa Braccio (1895); related to Katharine Lauderdale and The Ralstons.
Adam Johnstone's Son (1896)

Taquisara (1896)
A Rose of Yesterday (1897)
Corleone (1897)
Via Crucis (1899)
In the Palace of the King (1900)
Marietta (1901)
Cecilia (1902)
Man Overboard! (1903)
The Heart of Rome (1903)
Whosoever Shall Offend (1904)
Soprano (1905); U.S. title: Fair Margaret.
A Lady of Rome (1906)
Arethusa (1907)
The Little City of Hope (1907)
The Primadonna (1908); sequel to Soprano/Fair Margaret
The Diva's Ruby (1908); sequel to The Primadonna
The White Sister (1909)
Stradella (1909)
The Undesirable Governess (1910)
Wandering Ghosts; British title: Uncanny Tales.

Non-fiction

Our Silver (1881)
The Novel: What It Is (1893)
Constantinople (1895)
Bar Harbor (1896)
Ave Roma Immortalis (1898)
Rulers of the South (1900; 1905 in the U.S. as Southern Italy and Sicily and The Rulers of the South)
Gleanings from Venetian History (1905; in the U.S. as Salvae Venetia and in 1909 as Venice; the People and the Place)

Drama

In the Palace of the King (1900) with Lorrimer Stoddard.
Francesca da Rimini (1902) The piece was adapted into an opera by Franco Leoni in 1904.
Evelyn Hastings (1902) Unpublished typescript discovered in 2008.
The White Sister (1909) with Walter C. Hackett.

Filmography

A Cigarette-Maker's Romance, directed by Frank Wilson (UK, 1913, based on the novella)
The White Sister, directed by Fred E. Wright [it] (1915, based on the novel)
In the Palace of the King [it], directed by Fred E. Wright [it] (1915, based on the novel)
Whosoever Shall Offend, directed by Arrigo Bocchi (UK, 1919, based on the novel)
Il cuore di Roma, directed by Edoardo Bencivenga (Italy, 1919, based on the novel)
A Cigarette-Maker's Romance, directed by Tom Watts (UK, 1920, based on the novella)
Saracinesca [it], directed by Gaston Ravel (Italy, 1921, based on the novel)

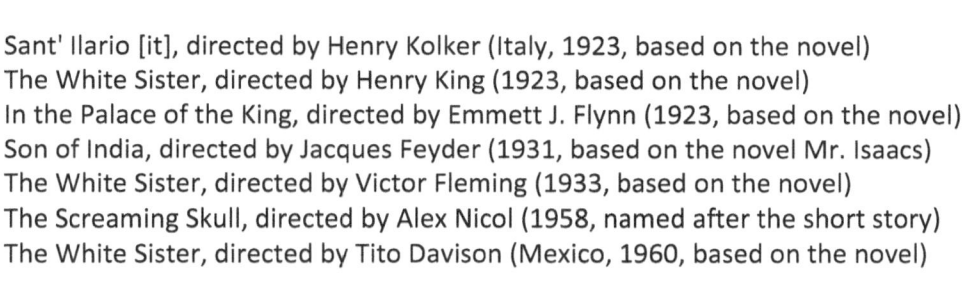

Sant' Ilario [it], directed by Henry Kolker (Italy, 1923, based on the novel)

The White Sister, directed by Henry King (1923, based on the novel)

In the Palace of the King, directed by Emmett J. Flynn (1923, based on the novel)

Son of India, directed by Jacques Feyder (1931, based on the novel Mr. Isaacs)

The White Sister, directed by Victor Fleming (1933, based on the novel)

The Screaming Skull, directed by Alex Nicol (1958, named after the short story)

The White Sister, directed by Tito Davison (Mexico, 1960, based on the novel)